The Witch Who Courted Death

Maria Lewis

piatkus

PIATKUS

First published in Great Britain in 2018 by Piatkus

1 3 5 7 9 10 8 6 4 2

A CIP catalogue record for this book
is available from the British Library.

TPB ISBN 978-0-349-42129-2

Typeset in Sabon by Hewer Text UK Ltd, Edinburgh
Printed and bound in Great Britain by Clays Ltd, Elcograf S.p.A.

Papers used by Piatkus are from well-managed forests
and other responsible sources.

Piatkus
An imprint of
Little, Brown Book Group
Carmelite House
50 Victoria Embankment
London EC4Y 0DZ

An Hachette UK Company
www.hachette.co.uk

www.littlebrown.co.uk

Chapter 1

Corvossier von Klitzing could tell the woman had been dead for some time . . . and not just because her ghost was floating in front of them. Her long, tattered dress was dragging along the ground and leaving a trail through the inches of thick dust that decorated the abandoned mansion. Droplets of blood fell from the gash across her neck, landing on the floor with a soft *splosh* before they disappeared seconds later, leaving no trace they ever existed. Her form was hovering somewhere between the physical and spectral realm, meaning that although anyone could see her, they could also see right *through* her. She watched her brother Barastin walk cautiously around the dead woman, moving slowly so as not to alarm her or cause any immediate reaction. The ghost could see them both, yet in that moment she was engrossed in something else entirely: a locket. She was holding it in her hands, cradling it, and the long golden chain snaked through her fingers. It dangled in mid-air, just like she was, swaying gently in the breeze that seemed to never stop coursing through the house.

'The locket is real,' Corvossier whispered, her brother nodding in agreement.

'Which is significant,' he replied.

They had found her like this when they first entered the home at the request of the new owners: a young, yuppie couple from Berlin. They told Corvossier and Barastin they'd wondered why they had been able to secure the ten-bedroom country estate for little more than the price of an apartment in the city. They'd soon found out, with the ghost making herself apparent within hours of the pair moving in with their newborn. The case had been assigned to them after the local Askari, the supernatural employees in the area, had failed to expel the unwelcome resident.

Barastin had scoffed when the couple had told them about the purification ceremony attempted with grandfather white sage. It was naïve bordering on stupid, with one of the Askari now laying in hospital with a broken arm and deep lacerations running down the length of her body. Corvossier and Barastin both knew it could have been a lot worse.

The material of her brother's jacket brushed against Corvossier's shoulder as he concluded his circling and came to a stop next to her. Standing there side-by-side, they watched the ghost for a little longer, assessing their options.

'I think we talk to her,' Corvossier said, casting her sibling a sideways glance.

'I agree,' he replied. 'At the very least to find out where she got that necklace. It's a stunning piece.'

She rolled her eyes, unable to help the smirk that crept into the corner of her lips.

'Barry,' she groaned.

'What? You know I have a weakness for one-of-a-kind antiques.'

Grabbing his hand, she interlinked her fingers in his to indicate that she was done with his joking around. He gave her a gentle squeeze and together they stepped forward, closer to the ghost.

'My dear,' Barastin called. 'May we ask your name?'

Of course, they already knew it. But as a general rule it was always best to navigate life as politely as possible, especially when dealing with the dead. The ghost looked up, blinking for a moment before glancing around the room with surprise. She registered their presence for the first time, somewhat snapping out of her daze.

'My name is Claire,' she said, in heavily accented English. 'Claire Northwood.'

'Do you know why you're here, Mrs Northwood?' he asked.

Corvossier watched the woman's expression darken and knew immediately her brother had made a mistake.

'*Mrs* Northwood,' she spat, shifting around so that she was facing them directly. 'Nobody has called me that in a long time.'

'We can call you whatever you like,' Corvossier added. 'Is there a title you would prefer?'

'I shouldn't even wear my ring anymore,' the ghost continued, stretching out her long, spindly fingers in front of her. A huge piece of jewellery sat on her engagement finger, the stone rising from the delicate band like a tumour.

Corvossier had carefully researched Claire Northwood before their arrival and her husband, Marque Northwood. They had been a high society couple back in the eighties, known for the exuberant parties held right there at the mansion they were standing in. They'd had a daughter named Eliza, who died after falling down the main staircase as a toddler. Neighbours said the death drove Claire mad and one day – when she just disappeared – there were very few who were surprised by it. There was a search, of course, a heavily publicised reward that was put out, and a teary-eyed husband begging in the press for his 'beloved wife' to come home. She didn't. Eventually there were unsubstantiated reports of Claire being seen in Paris and London. Meanwhile, a much younger and prettier Mrs Northwood moved in.

'He gave her a ruby as well, you know?' the ghost continued. 'Horribly gaudy thing. I had a good laugh watching him try to dig me up and find what he had forgotten. The earth had reclaimed it by then . . . my ruby. Thankfully I have this one with me.'

'You killed him,' Corvossier said. 'And the new wife, just three months after they returned from their honeymoon.'

'Well, I had to, didn't I? Couldn't let him get away with slashing my throat and leaving me to rot under the garden bed. And *her*—'

'They got what they deserved,' Corvossier interjected, understanding the clean-cut ideas about justice ghosts such as Claire Northwood had. 'They died in this house, but they moved forward. Only your ghost remains.'

Barastin nodded. 'What is left for you here, my dear?'

'What is left?' she asked, her chin tilting upwards as she looked to the ceiling and considered the question. 'What *is* left?'

'She's drifting off again,' her brother whispered.

'Good, let her. If we can encourage her to move on willingly that means we don't have to use force.'

'Since when are you opposed to a little force?'

4

'Since this is our eighth job in one week. Plus, she's strong enough to hold spectral form and effect the physicality of objects around her.'

'And she has killed before.'

'Right. We know she doesn't mind spilling blood and frankly? It's a Friday. I don't want the workout.'

Corvossier watched her brother's smile grow wider and he shrugged, his way of saying he agreed with her. Among the two of them, she was the more powerful. It had been established years ago without neither of them saying it that, when it came to matters of importance, Corvossier called the shots.

She turned her attention back to Claire Northwood only to find she had gone. The ghost who had been hovering in front of them had completely disappeared. Barastin look startled by this information, his head snapping around the room as he searched for any sign of her.

'Did she do it?' he asked. 'Did she ascend?'

'No, we would have felt it.'

Their hands still linked, the pair took careful steps forward as they inched around the room. There was a drop in temperature, a significant one, and Corvossier watched her breath form small steam clouds in the air in front of her. The hairs on the back of her neck stood up and goosebumps rose to the surface of her skin like braille. She brushed a strand of her long, white hair out of her face as it moved in the breeze. All light from the room disappeared, although it wasn't any later than early evening.

'I guess we're using force,' Barastin murmured, his grip tightening around Corvossier's hand as they pushed themselves up against each other, back-to-back. There was a scrape of something sharp against wood, like fingernails scratching, and Corvossier braced herself for what was to come. An ear-splitting shriek broke the room and she flung herself and her brother down to the ground as a table flew towards them. Pressed to the floor, she felt the air whoosh over her head as the furniture narrowly missed them. Glancing up to the corner where the object had previously been, Corvossier sprung to her feet and sprinted in that direction. She ignored the sounds of the table crashing into splinters behind her, focusing all of her intent and *will* at the source of the object's movement.

Claire Northwood suddenly reappeared, and Corvossier watched her blinking with shock as she caught sight of her own ghostly body. The surprise was replaced with fury in an instant as she noticed the person who was barrelling towards her. Screeching to a stop just in front of the ghost, Corvossier held up her hands as if trying to press shut an invisible door. She felt Barastin at her back, shuffling around to the side so he would have another angle. The ghost lashed out, attempting to strike wildly with her fist before bouncing backwards. She was blocked, unable to move forwards past Corvossier or through her like she could any other normal human. She tried to turn back, disappearing through the wall behind her, but Barastin was there, mimicking Corvossier's pose exactly. With a frustrated scream, she pounded and pounded against the force keeping her locked in place. The chain of the locket – not restricted to the prism – swung out like a whip, slashing across Corvossier's face. She flinched, but allowed no more reaction than that.

'LET ME OUT!'

'No,' Corvossier growled.

'LET ME OUT NOW, WITCH!'

'I am not a witch and neither is my brother. But you should fear us, ghost.'

'We walk between,' Barastin replied, the words coming out amid pants as he fought to hold the barrier. 'And we can command ghosts like you back to where you belong.'

'I BELONG HERE! IN *MY* HOUSE!'

'This is not your house anymore, Claire Northwood,' Corvossier replied. 'You are dead and you need to go where the dead go. We can do it for you or you can make that call.'

'It's your choice,' her brother added, indicating the direction with his eyes as the ghost looked between them with a horrified expression.

'YOU CANNOT MAKE ME!'

Corvossier heard Barastin's annoyed sigh and smirked.

'Why do they *always* say that?' he huffed.

Maintaining eye contact with him, she asked if he was ready with little more than a tilt of her head. He nodded and together they unleashed the extent of their shared ability.

The ghost screamed, thrashing wildly as she gradually began to dissolve in front of their very eyes. Like sand being blown away by the wind, her form disintegrated, one grain at a time, until she was no longer standing before them. Carefully, Corvossier lowered her hands and so did her brother. They walked forward, Barastin puffing with exertion while nothing more than a single bead of sweat formed on her forehead. Corvossier could feel the woman pulsing away from the house, her presence less and less with every passing minute.

'One of us should follow her,' Barastin said in a way that she knew meant he expected her to do it.

'Whatever,' she replied, closing her eyes and sinking into blackness almost instantly. The room was no longer there as Corvossier let her mind cloud over, the force of the ghost pulling her in the direction she needed to go. Suddenly she was there, next to Claire Northwood, who was hanging suspended in an endless vastness.

'YOU!'

'Me,' Corvossier answered, wishing the woman would stop shouting. 'I know this is all very disorientating first time round, but is there any need to keep the volume at that decibel?'

The ghost spluttered, as if trying to organise a proper reply that just wouldn't formulate on her lips. Swallowing her response, she peered back at Corvossier in sullen silence.

'There, that's better. Now where are you off to?'

'*Where* did you send me?'

'Away from the physical plane, Claire. You do not belong there and you cannot go back.'

'You're a medium, aren't you? I've heard about what your kind can do.'

'Thankfully for you there's not very many of us, otherwise we would have moved you on a long time ago.'

'Why do I have to leave? It was my home.'

'"Was" being the optimal word,' she replied, falling quiet as she let her senses extend beyond where they were.

'What are you doing?'

'Finding a direction.'

'For who?'

'You, of course. There's someone waiting for you.'

'For me?'

'Eliza, your daughter. You remember her, don't you?'

'Eliza . . .'

'She has been without her mother for so long; she misses you.'

'I . . . I want to see her, to hold her. Can I do that?'

Corvossier nodded, allowing herself to slowly let go of the moment. It would work two ways: her hold on Claire lessening and Eliza's hold strengthening. She could already see the ghost being pulled backwards, growing smaller and smaller in front of her. In fact, Claire had already forgotten about Corvossier and her brother, as well as how they had put her there. She was whispering her daughter's name instead, answering questions to sentences that Corvossier could not hear. The vision of the woman grew foggy, with a haze moving between them until it formed something like a wall. She was blocked from viewing anything further, with Corvossier knowing that this was as far as she could follow. Like a release deep inside her heart, she let go and felt herself drop back into her body. Her eyelids fluttered open and she squinted as she adjusted to the light of the room around her.

Barastin was crouched down, picking up the locket that had fallen to the floor as they thrust Claire Northwood from the house.

'Ah, that was quick,' he said, straightening up. 'I thought that would take longer.'

'Her daughter was waiting.'

'Not the husband, thankfully. That could have ended bad.'

'No, he had moved long ago. Couldn't you feel it when she spoke of him?'

'Maybe,' her brother mused. 'Or maybe it was the two shots of espresso I had on the way here, who can tell?'

Corvossier laughed in spite of herself, looking around the space to see if there was anything they needed to take with them. She hoped the couple weren't particularly attached to that table, which was now little more than bonfire fodder.

Touching a hand to her cheek where the locket had slashed her, she looked at the few droplets of blood on her fingertips with interest. It was a tiny cut, one that would heal in a few days, and until then she could cover it with make-up. She followed Barastin through the entranceway and out of the house, inhaling the freshness as they stepped outside. The air inside the mansion had been stale and felt that way when you breathed it in. It was the residue of the woman left behind; her memories and hopes and despairs and agonies. It made the place barely tolerable for an everyday person and Corvossier wondered just how many internal warning bells the couple had ignored when they'd decided to sign the paperwork. There was a light rain falling and the icy cold splashes of water were refreshing as they landed on her cheeks, trickling down her face and her neck.

'Well? How did it go?' barked Collette Blight, from under the protection of an umbrella that was as wide as she was.

Barastin beamed, practically sauntering in her direction as he threw out his arms. 'Who ya gonna call?'

'I hate it when you say that,' Corvossier muttered as she ducked down under the shelter Collette was providing.

'I like it when I say that,' he replied, accepting the bottle of Ribena the woman held out for him. 'Besides, we all know what they call us: the Twisted Twins, the Spook Siblings, the Death Duo: you're Casper and I'm Creeper. When was the last time someone actually used your real name in our community, sis?'

'Two hours ago, when Collette let us out of the car.'

'That's right,' the woman said, nodding confirmation.

Barastin scoffed, downing the last of the sugary drink and scrunching up the plastic bottle. 'You know you don't count, darling. You *truly* know us.'

'Fortunately for me.' She smiled. 'You never did answer my question though.'

'She's gone,' Corvossier replied. 'We sent her on her way.'

'She put up much of a fight?'

'Some,' she agreed. 'She was stronger than your average residential ghost.'

'It was the house,' Barastin added. 'Because she was murdered here, her daughter died here, and she killed here, she was knotted to the place. The house gave her power: as soon as we prodded her away from it, nature took its course.'

'How sure are you?' Collette asked, her spiky head of neon-red hair turning to Corvossier for confirmation. 'Because the Askari who were here before us thought she was gone the first time round too, the rumours of a haunting just residual bad mojo.'

'I followed her,' Corvossier replied. 'Guided her through the lobby and made sure she was pulled.'

'Very well then.' The lady beamed, her chins wobbling with an enthusiastic smile and a small jig of excitement. 'What a way to end the week!'

'There's one last thing . . .'

Corvossier held out her hand, palm extended, towards her brother. He just looked at it for a moment, her fingers gesturing for him to give it up. With a huff, he dug the necklace out of his pocket and dropped it into her hand. She raised an eyebrow, asking him without needing to verbalise it whether that was so hard. Collette was about to slip on gloves when Corvossier stopped her.

'There's nothing tied to the locket,' the medium said. 'She just took a shine to it.'

'Is it any wonder?' Collette asked, wrapping it carefully in a beautifully embroidered handkerchief. 'Poor thing has to watch a young couple with a baby girl move in to the very house where that same thing was stripped away from her.'

'I know what you're going to say,' Barastin whined. '*The husband did it.*'

Corvossier shrugged. 'Because he did. Honestly, that twosome are lucky we got to them as soon as we did.'

'It's *always* the husband,' Collette echoed.

'You two need to cool it with the true crime documentaries,' he said. 'And can we go? I'm bored and the city has so many more prospects than Zehlendorf on a Friday night.'

'Yes, let's.'

Collette beckoned for them to follow her, the woman shuffling ahead at a pace that always fascinated Corvossier given her diminutive height. Barely four foot eleven, both she and her brother had towered over their primary carer by the time they hit thirteen. That difference had only extended over the years, with Corvossier and Barastin sharing many things including their six foot three stature. That was par for the course among his gender and her twin had no trouble navigating the world with his fine frame. Corvossier, although graceful, always managed to stick out like a sore thumb. With hair and skin so pale she looked almost otherworldly, she had a hard enough time as it was passing for regular among the humans of Berlin, let alone factoring her height into the equation. Together with Collette, the three of them looked comical in their contrasting physicality. A black sedan was waiting down the driveway, with a young man jumping out of it enthusiastically as they approached.

'Casper and Creeper, hello, how was the . . . uh, haunting?' he stammered. Barastin crossed his hands over his chest, looking the fellow up and down with disdain.

'Heel,' Collette urged, swatting him as she walked by. 'This is Mike Higgens; he's my new intern.'

'What bog did they drag him from?'

'Barastin, don't be rude. Mike will be here for the usual stay of six months, before moving on to his first official Askari posting. There's a lot he can learn from us, if you're nice.'

'Nice? I'm delightful, aren't I, sis?'

'Eh,' Corvossier said. 'Depends on the day, frankly. Mike, is it?'

'Yes, ma'am,' he answered, accepting her outstretched hand and shaking it. She noted the tattoo that the gesture exposed on his wrist, which resembled a line with three circles around the tip. It was an old alchemist symbol for wood – the foundation on which something great can be built – and was meant to identify all Askari.

'It's lovely to meet you. My brother is somewhat hostile towards anyone newer and cuter than he is.'

He responded to her comment with a deep blush, his skin changing colour subtly but enough that it pleased her. Letting go of his hand, she made her way towards her usual position in the backseat – left side – while Barastin took the right. The car smelled of cleaning products and she slid slightly on the leather of the seats as she got into the vehicle. Corvossier watched Collette speak to the newbie outside of the vehicle for several moments, most of what they were saying blocked to her ears but she was still able to get the gist.

'She's berating him for calling us Casper and Creeper,' Barastin remarked.

She frowned. 'I don't think he knew our real names.'

'Like it matters at this point. I'd much rather be Marilyn Monroe than Norma Jean.'

She turned to face him, watching with amazement as his fingers flew furiously over the keypad on his phone.

'Truly, I have never seen anyone text faster than you can.'

'You should see my swiping speed.' He smiled, giving her a cheeky wink. 'Left, left, right, left, zoom in on his abs, right, left again.'

'You're shameless.'

Collette dropped into the passenger seat with a contented sigh and Mike hopped behind the wheel, starting the car and slowly pulling away from the no-longer-haunted mansion.

'Does that mean you'll join me tonight?' Barastin asked, continuing the conversation as if they hadn't just gained two additional sets of ears.

'You planning on heading out?' Collette chirped up.

'Barastin is,' Corvossier replied. 'I'm doing my best to get out of it.'

'You should go, have a night of festivities and celebration: that last job paid very well. You two have both earned it after this week.'

'Yeah, what is that about?' her brother asked, looking up from his phone screen for a few seconds. 'It was steady there for a while and then, all of a sudden, boom! Ghosts galore!'

'And next week is looking busy too,' Collette confirmed, checking their schedule on her tablet. She had all of their appointments and potential jobs carefully organised on a calendar that was so meticulously annotated, Corvossier had tried to check it once and nearly had an emotional break-down. 'The Askari want us to take a look at a cemetery out in Munich on Wednesday, so I'll have to make some travel arrangements. You should take this moment to let your hair down, Corvossier: we might not get an evening off for a while.'

'Where do you go out in this city?' Mike asked.

'Phases, usually,' Corvossier answered. She caught his confused expression looking back at her from the rear-view mirror. 'It's the supernatural hotspot here, owned by a rogue werewolf pack.'

'You go to a nightclub run by werewolves? *Rogue* were-wolves? That sounds incredibly dangerous.'

'On the contrary,' Barastin replied, 'it's the safest place in Berlin. No one's gonna start trouble under their roof.'

'Plus a lot of your kind hang out there,' she added.

'My kind?'

'The officials, supernatural government types, you name it. There's usually more Treize in that club than any other species on a weeknight.'

'People frequent there too,' Collette noted. 'Unaware, of course.'

'I hope there's some Treize men there tonight,' Barastin muttered, just loud enough so only Corvossier could hear him.

'Where are you from, Mike?' she asked, not missing the way his eyes glanced down at the GPS he had guiding him on the forty-minute drive back to Berlin.

'Canada originally, although everyone here keeps mistaking my accent for American. I just go along with it.'

'Is this your first time in Germany?'

'Yes, I only arrived this morning. Picked up the car from the airport and headed straight to collect Collette and yourselves. It's a good-looking city.'

'Wait until you see where we live,' she said with a smirk.

He didn't have to wait long; in fact, none of them did. It was surprisingly smooth sailing into the heart of Berlin, despite their expectations of peak hour traffic. Fortunately everyone was heading home and out of the city, giving their party a clear run right into the centre of Berlin's busiest shopping district. Corvossier watched with amusement as Collette instructed the newbie to park under what look like a cartoon tower, Mike insisting that he didn't think they could stop there.

'You can, son, now right up to that blue barrier. That's it.'

She reached into her bag, pressing the button that raised the entrance to the car park and his mouth opened with surprise as a previously hidden door rolled back.

'I thought that was a solid concrete wall,' he whispered.

'That's the point, of course. Now go on, drive through.'

He did so, the car creeping forward as the door peeled back down behind them. Fluorescent lights flicked on, triggered by their movement through the garage. The space was larger than anyone could guess from the outside, with dozens of vehicles parked throughout the football field-sized interior.

Rolling into an empty spot, their quartet left the car and headed towards the elevators on the opposite side. Footsteps echoed in their wake, the only sound accompanying them besides Mike's occasional breathy exclamations.

'Wow,' he said, for about the eighth time in a row once they got into the lift and Collette hit one of several floor options.

'Wow is right,' Corvossier murmured. She tried to sound understanding, but it had been a long time since she was amazed by the place. She had grown up here, after all. The doors pinged open and Collette stepped out, gesturing for Mike to follow her.

'There are three levels all up,' Collette said, cutting through a maze of desks that were occupied with people rushing around the office. 'Not including the car park, of course. The Praetorian Guard occupy the second level, with Custodians and Askari sharing this one. Corvossier and Barastin live on the third.'

'You *live* here?'

'That we do.' She smiled, trailing after them.

'It's called the Bierpinsel,' Barastin added. 'This whole building was built back in the seventies, hence the retro, pop art vibe.'

Collette took them up a spiral staircase that led to the next floor. 'Thankfully for us, the restaurant and nightclub that used to be here went bankrupt. In fact, no business has been able to make it work. The Treize bought the building when it went back up for sale in two thousand and six, and it has been somewhat of a base of operations ever since. The majority of Germany's supernatural bureaucracy is run out of the offices you see before you.'

It spread out below them like the roots of a tree, desks neatly lined up and spaced out every few metres. There were stacks of paper teetering on the edge of falling over on one woman's desk, while a series of weapons were spread on another as they were carefully catalogued by a man with small, brown horns.

Corvossier knew most of the people there by name; after all, she saw them every day. The world that she was a part of – the one that humans didn't know existed – was run by thirteen immortal supernatural beings known as the Treize. Although they were the bosses, it was the people like those inside the Bierpinsel that made the whole thing work: the Askari, first point of call for local other-worldly activities and the paper-pushers; the Praetorian Guard, the warriors gifted with immortality and sent out to battle the more testing side of the paranormal; and Collette's corner, the Custodians, those who looked after creatures who had no one else. Werewolves had their packs, witches had their covens, but there were countless others who were left to wander alone. That made them vulnerable and, in many cases, prey.

Corvossier and Barastin were a prime example of that, with their birth parents abandoning them when they were little more than toddlers. Twins with unusual grey eyes and an ability to communicate with the dead, it was fair to say Corvossier had never blamed them for giving their offspring up. Her brother had, though, harbouring nothing but resentment towards them. Their gifts were unique and some of the last vestiges of what the once powerful sub-species of mediums could do. Now, there were hardly any left. The Treize valued them enough to make sure they lived somewhere where they could be put to the most use. There was a low, breathy whistle and Corvossier jerked her head upwards in the direction of the sound. Barastin was waiting at the top of the stairs with an annoyed expression on his face and she jogged up the remaining levels to meet him. She hesitated when she saw the vast chunk of man moving towards her with a beaming smile.

'Casper! Creeper! How are my favourite spooks?' he asked, through a thick Scottish accent.

'Fine,' she managed to squeeze out before she was pulled into an enormous hug. 'How are you, Heath?'

'Aye, you know. Slaughtered a den of ghouls this morning, can't complain.'

She watched with amusement as he planted a kiss on either side of Barastin's cheeks, knowing full well that her brother had a crush on him.

'Creeper, you miss me?' he teased.

'Only in the very literal sense.'

'What are you doing here?' Corvossier asked, watching as Collette and Mike moved on without them. No one exactly knew how old Heath was, although there were guesses. It was no secret he had been a Pictish warrior back in the day, which put him past a thousand years or so. Sometimes he came alone and other times he was accompanied by the ghosts of people he could not see. Often it was a woman, with long red hair that flowed in an invisible breeze. She clutched a babe to her breast, neither making a sound nor uttering a word – it was like they were checking in – whereas sometimes you could have a conversation with the others, particularly a grizzled woman in her sixties who went by the name Scáthach and always wanted to know about European politics.

Corvossier or Barastin had never asked Heath about his dead: it seemed rather redundant. Anyone who had been alive that long had lost people, many of them. Yet the fact he was in town was significant: although he had a penchant for trouble, he was high up among the Praetorian Guard and one of their most prized assets.

'I'm en route to Romania,' Heath said, answering her initial question. 'Thought I'd stop in and check up on various posts as I made my way back. You know, make them nervous, sweaty, twitchy.'

'Your favourite activities.'

'You two heading up?'

'Uh huh, Collette is giving the new guy the tour.'

'I'll come along; I want to see if I can talk her into having dinner with me.'

Corvossier suspected that was the real reason he was in town: their designated Custodian. Although she was now well into her fifties, and Heath looked little more than a day over thirty, the pair had dated once back in the late seventies. It hadn't worked out, but that was no surprise given he would never age and she would continue to. Corvossier often wondered if that's what had driven a wedge between their romantic relationship, but not their friendship.

One night when they had gotten drunk on schnapps and binged *Forensic Files*, Collette had let it slip to Corvossier that she was the party who had broken up with him after a solid three-year relationship. She'd gone on to say it was 'the best sex of my life' before descending into a series of hiccups that heralded the end of the evening. Regardless, the pair had stayed close friends over the decades. No matter what supernatural war was being waged, Heath Darkiro always managed to pop by Berlin a few times a year to visit Collette.

'Are you sure you don't want to come out with us tonight?' Barastin asked, innocently. 'We're going to Phases.'

'Who isn't?' Heath shrugged. 'It's a Friday night in Berlin, every Loch Ness, Big Foot and Yowie within a hundred mile radius will be there.'

Corvossier laughed, earning a scowl from one of the Praetorian Guard soldiers she passed as they walked through the room. He was standing around a map of the city with three others, all with small swords holstered at their waists and guns strapped to their sides. She straightened her expression, trying to appear more serious as they headed up the final staircase to their living quarters. There was a large, timber desk with a rolling cork board behind it that Collette liked to co-ordinate from, often coming and going from the first level to this one, depending on what the day was like.

She was showing Mike her filing system, where she documented every single case they had taken over the years and invoices that were paid or pending. From hauntings to exorcisms, she had the details written down along with phone numbers, addresses and photographs. Collette had been the one constant in their lives since they were children, and, as Barastin and Corvossier had gotten older, their abilities becoming more defined and clear-cut, she had taken to managing their work with the same care she had poured into raising them.

Heath immediately headed to Collette's desk and took a seat – *her* seat – in a move that Corvossier knew would piss the Custodian off in a matter of seconds. Leaving them to it, she followed Barastin in the direction of their bedrooms, nodding when he asked her to be ready 'in an hour'. Truthfully, she only needed twenty minutes but her brother had much higher standards of beauty than she did.

In the fading light of the spring sky, the city looked beautiful out of the expansive windows that wrapped around the length of the building. The whole Bierpinsel was somewhat of a hexagon shape, giving anyone inside it a full three hundred and sixty degree view of Berlin as they were walking around it. The highway stretched out into the distance from the window Corvossier was looking out of in that moment, her footsteps following her down the curving hallway. As she moved, the view was replaced by a sprawling shopping precinct and the tiny, buzzing bodies of people as they entered it.

Closing the door to her bedroom, she paused just long enough to hear Collette screeching Heath's name with frustration, followed by the unmistakable sound of one of her slaps as it made contact.

Chapter 2

The music pulsed through Phases like a heartbeat, everyone in the club dancing and talking and moving to the rhythm. Almost immediately after they passed the werewolf guarding the door, Barastin was splitting off and heading deep into the crowd. He was meeting someone, a guy he'd flashed Corvossier a photo of on their way in. He was attractive, as they always were, because her brother was a good-looking man. He had cheekbones that any catalogue model would envy and rusty, auburn hair that he dyed over their natural white. He was also a snappy dresser, thankfully something he had been able to teach her over the years.

She pulled at the sleeves of her velvet dress, watching her brother melt into the throng of people. Collette had ordered Mike to go with them, something that annoyed Barastin and pleased Corvossier. A Friday night was her least favourite in the club, everyone too rowdy and the music too loud for proper conversation. She usually found a clear space at the bar and settled in for some people watching while her brother worked the room. At least tonight she wouldn't be alone.

Cutting through the mob as they reacted to The Kills song, which came blaring through the sound system, Corvossier felt a pang of relief as she saw a spot that wasn't packed. Heading towards the furthest corner, she nodded and mumbled hellos to the faces she recognised of regular punters and even some from the Bierpinsel who had the night off. She didn't properly relax until she was comfortably positioned on a stool, Mike taking the one next to her. A bartender asked their order – a Midori cocktail for her and a Sternburg for him – and within a few minutes they were both sipping their drinks. Corvossier's eyes ran over the crowd, zeroing in when she spotted an elemental among their midst. No one else seemed to notice as the guy walked by, not even the group of dancing girls who were batting a trail of smoke out of their faces, looking around to find out who the asshole lighting up in the club was. What they didn't realise was that the grey, snaking mist was coming from the man himself.

'What's so fascinating?' Mike asked her.

'Smokey,' she replied, jerking her head in the direction of the man whose jeans somehow managed to stay around his hips despite four heavy chains dangling from his pockets.

'It's too smokey in here?'

'No.' She laughed. 'The guy. He's a half-breed elemental. His mother was a fire crafter or his father was, I always forget which. Anyway, he can shift form into—'

'Let me guess, smoke?'

'Yeah. Whenever he gets a few martinis under his belt he always turns a bit hazy. I haven't seen him in ages though.'

'You two friends?'

'No, he and my brother dated for two seconds. Actually, the last time I saw him was at our twenty-ninth birthday party last year. He jumped out of the cake.'

'Better that than him being a candle.'

'I guess. He dropped off the face of the earth for a while, heard he got offered a job with the Askari in Japan.'

'Guess that didn't work out.'

She wasn't surprised: Smokey was a flake and she had never seen it getting serious between him and Barastin. Speaking of, she sat up a little straighter to catch sight of where her brother might be. Sure enough, he was the centre of attention, with a whole table she doubted he knew before that evening enthralled with whatever story he was telling. He was smiling, his hands arching wildly as he demonstrated his point.

'You look beautiful,' Mike said, the compliment drawing her gaze back to present company.

'Oh, uh, thank you.'

'I've never seen someone wear sapphire blue quite like you.'

She hid a smile as she took a sip of her cocktail, unsure whether the new intern was just being nice or actively hitting on her. To be frank, she always found it hard to tell, and he was much younger than her; he couldn't have been more than nineteen or twenty. Still, he knew how to compliment a woman and that was a start. Barastin had taught her how to compliment herself, with Corvossier sticking to largely jewel tones on his orders: emerald greens, topaz, ruby reds, amethyst hues and blackish blues. They were her colours of choice with such an unusual complexion and she leaned heavily towards them. The other thing was feel: she tended to only wear clothes that she enjoyed the sensation of as they brushed against her skin. She basically never wore pants, preferring long, flowing dresses and skirts that moved like water.

'Casper.'

She looked up, catching the eye of a woman as she strolled past the bar.

'Yu,' she replied, offering a small wave.

'Is that—' Mike began.

'Uh huh.'

'I heard about her,' Mike muttered. 'Gave up centuries of service with the Praetorian Guard for a werewolf. It's a wild story.'

'I think it's romantic.'

Across the room, Yu had come to a stop and was whispering something in the ears of a tiny but fierce girl now watching the door. She was the werewolf Mike spoke about: Dolly, one of the members of the rogue pack that ran the club, aptly titled the Rogues.

Corvossier had never heard anything like that before – someone giving up their sacred duty with the Guard for love, of all things. It had caused a stir at the time when it all first went down, but now it was old news. She glanced at her wristwatch, wondering how much longer Collette and Heath would be at dinner. Truthfully, she just wasn't feeling it. Adjusting one of the many rings she wore stacked on top of each other on her fingers, she downed the last of her drink. Getting up from the bar, she gestured for Mike to remain sitting.

'Stay,' she ordered. 'It's your first day on the job, may as well end it with a good time.'

'You're leaving? Already?'

'My bed and a book are calling.'

'I can walk you, you don't have to go alone.'

'No, Mike, honestly it's fine. There's a U-Bahn station right under the Bierpinsel, practically drops me off at my doorstep.'

'Are you sure?'

'Very. Just let my brother know I've left.'

'Will do, of course.'

She gently squeezed his shoulder in a comforting gesture as she passed by, slipping back out the way she came. The bouncer was a werewolf but he looked just like anyone else for majority of the month and, most importantly, to the regular customers. He nodded as she stepped outside and began walking down the alley that led back to the main street.

It was early, but punters were already beginning to form a line down the length of the wall as they queued to get in to Phases. It was towards the end of May and there were still a few weeks left of spring, but Corvossier could feel summer tugging at the hem. The nights were warm and the days were getting longer, with the promise of lazy picnics in the park and long bike rides whispered on the wind. She was a winter person and thrived in the cold, but for some reason she always liked this time of year best. There was something about the promise it held and the attitudes of people. Everyone in the city seemed to be in a good mood as she passed them by, clusters of people laughing in restaurants and others stumbling home drunk with their arms linked together.

It was almost enough to distract her from the creeping sense of unease she felt inching up her spine. She slowed her footsteps, coming to a gradual stop as she stood there on the busy street. There were people all around her, dozens of them. A U-Bahn rattled by, followed by a family on bicycles ringing their bells enthusiastically and shouting directions to one another. And yet, she couldn't shake the feeling that she was unsafe. Slipping a handheld mirror from her purse, she flicked it open and pretended to be reapplying her lipstick as she took a look behind her. Nothing. There was no one strange or unusual following her, nothing that seemed out of the ordinary, and hardly a ghost in sight. In fact, the ones that she could see were not long for this earth. The pull towards the other side was strengthening on them, as not only could no one else see them but they were not affecting anything around them. She watched one – an older man – trail behind a woman as she waited tables in a café. He didn't even notice Corvossier as she passed by, a sign that his spectral form was on the way out.

She hadn't taken a jacket with her, deciding it was too warm when she left the Bierpinsel. Yet looking up at the Fernsehturm as it blinked down at her, she shivered slightly. Her blood was chilled and she had no explanation for it. Picking up her pace, she walked to the nearest U-Bahn station quickly. Her plan had been to walk all the way home, enjoy the evening by herself, but she was a woman who listened to her instincts and her instincts were telling her to stay where people were. She picked the busiest carriage, the one that was so packed she would have to stand for the duration of the ride. She didn't mind though and her eyes ran over the faces of everyone around her. They all looked human, but so did many supernatural creatures ... so did she. Corvossier went back and forth in her mind about whether she was imagining things or if there actually was a threat. And if so, what kind? What could anyone possibly want from her, a medium? If someone was trying to reach the dead, all they had to do was ask.

She grasped for her phone, unlocking it and quickly typing out a text message to Collette. The woman had no special abilities to speak of; she had simply been born into a family of Custodians and remained one herself. Unlike the Praetorian Guard, who were gifted with immortality, the Custodians had an option: they could choose to live endlessly or have the regular, human duration. Like her parents before her, Collette had chosen for just the one life. She hoped the six foot six Scotsman was still there with her guardian, as she didn't have Heath's number and the only way she could think of getting in touch was through Collette. She tapped out the message, keeping it brief: 'On the U-Bahn home, I have a bad feeling'.

She hesitated sending it for a moment, not wanting to ruin Collette's night over nothing. Then again, she didn't like the alternative either. Hitting send, she felt the smallest tingle of satisfaction as the phone made a *beep* indicating the message had been sent and delivered. Collette's reply was almost immediate.

'Where's the intern?'

'I left him at Phases with Barastin.'

'What station are you at?'

'Passing U Heinrich-Heine-Straße now.'

'Heath and I will meet you at the home station. Stay on the train until then.'

'OK.'

She thought about replying with something else, but as the minutes ticked by she realised there was little else to say. Looking up at the digital display, she saw there were only three more stops until U-Bhf Schönleinstraße where she would be back right under the Bierpinsel. The comfort of home would only be a quick elevator ride away. A crackle ran through the speakers on the tram, an announcer coming on to say that they would be running no further than the next stop: U Kottbusser Tor. There was a disgruntled murmur through the carriage, her fellow customers annoyed about the change of plans.

'What happened?' one of them asked her girlfriend, frustrated.

'Someone jumped on the tracks,' another person replied. 'My pal is stuck on the other side . . . said they saw the whole thing.'

'That's horrible.'

Corvossier fidgeted, annoyed at the change of plans. As the tram pulled to a stop at their new destination, she pulled out her phone again to text Collette her latest location. She barely had one word typed when she was jostled from the side, some- one smashing into the crowd several people away and the movement rippling down the line. She stumbled, her phone slipping from her grip and falling between the gap in the plat- form. She wanted to stop, but she knew reaching down would be stupid, and the masses were pushing her forward. Corvossier winced as she heard the unmistakable sound of plastic and glass crunching. Her phone was broker than Nicolas Cage and there was no getting it back now. She let the tide of people carry her forward, out on to the platform and down the stairs that led to street level.

'Now what?' she whispered to herself, looking around for an idea. This part of Berlin wasn't as busy as the centre where she'd come from, with her fellow passengers heading away from her as they walked to their next destinations or looked for a cab. Corvossier was left standing there alone on the side of a street at night, a position she very much didn't want to be in. Glancing to the left and right, she started crossing the road in the direction of a convenience store, which was still open. At the most she could buy a burner phone and call Collette, and, if not, she hoped the shopkeeper would let her borrow the landline. There was a grey cat dozing on the step that led up into the shop and she bent down, smiling for a moment as she scratched under its chin.

'There she is, finally!'

Corvossier looked up, relief trickling through her every pore as she saw Mike and Barastin walking quickly towards her.

'Thank God,' Mike exclaimed. 'We were so worried!'

'You were?' she asked, leaving the cat as she stood up to her full height. 'Did Collette call you?'

'Sure,' Mike replied, nodding. 'We left the club straight away. Come on.'

He took her by the elbow, steering them forward and down the street. Barastin looked peeved and she cast him a backwards glance.

'I'm sorry,' she said. 'I didn't mean for you guys to come.'

'Really? You weren't *at all* peeved that I left you alone to go off and have a good time?'

'Of course not, that's how it always operates.'

'Try and sound less bitter.'

'Barry, I was with Mike. I just wanted to head home: you knew I didn't want to go out tonight in the first place.'

'Down here,' Mike instructed, with Corvossier slipping out of his grasp so she could walk next to her brother.

'Please don't be mad at me.'

He sighed, rolling his eyes. 'How can I be mad at you? It's not your fault you got sick.'

'What?'

'Collette asked Mike and me to come and get you, cos we were closer – told us you'd called her, said you felt dizzy. So we did.'

'Barastin, I never called Collette. I texted her and said I had a bad feeling. Heath and her were going to come and meet me at U-Bhf Schönleinstraße. You and Mike weren't even supposed to know.'

'Huh? But Mike said . . .'

Barastin's sentence faded away as he came to a halt. He grabbed Corvossier's hand beside him and she followed the path of his horrified stare. The back of Mike's head was bobbing ahead of them, but it disappeared as two robed figures stepped in front. What she had assumed in her peripheral vision were the dark walls of the alleyway he had taken them down actually turned out to be living, breathing things. Spinning towards the exit, she found that obstructed by the same individuals. All around them, Barastin and Corvossier were surrounded by human-shaped beings hidden under cloaks so black they seemed to block out every element of light around them. They were closing in, their ranks tightening with each inched step forwards.

'Who are you?' Barastin asked, not a trace of fear in his voice. He was steady and sure of himself, something that Corvossier definitely was not. The fear and sense of dread she had felt curdling away in her stomach earlier flared to life as she pivoted, trying to look for a way out. She saw a flash of something, silver, that glinted briefly in the limited light.

'What do you want from us?'

With their backs pressed against each other in their instinctual defensive positions, Corvossier wondered if she had enough time to call for help. She extended her senses, reaching out to whoever of the ghost variety was nearby. Hell, she'd even take a sprit if there was one in the vicinity.

'Be quick,' one of them whispered, the voice of a man. 'Give them no opportunity to use their powers.'

Corvossier's breath was already coming out in short, quick puffs and it increased as she began to panic. There was the sound of blades scraping and suddenly she was thrown forwards, shoved by her brother as he dove on top of her. He shrieked, Corvossier flinching at the pain she could hear coming from her own twin's mouth as if she could feel it herself. The robes descended on them, a flurry of slashes and blades and knives and wet flesh being hacked as the screams continued and continued. Someone flew backwards and another was kicked as her brother fought above her. The focus was on him and he'd done exactly what she had attempted to do: call ghosts to them. But he hadn't been fast enough and the ones that arrived were struggling to take physical form. She could barely breathe from her position flat on the ground and in the commotion, she crawled forwards on her hands and knees. These were people, she realised, feeling the kinks of legs and feet as she wriggled over them. She broke out the other side, the alley clear ahead of her and the street beyond that. A car passed by and she felt hope blaze up inside of her: their escape was *so* close and no one had seemed to notice that she wasn't laying under Barastin anymore.

Twisting around, she stumbled to her feet and ignored the strange sensation of sticky blood that seemed to cover every inch of her. She let the anger and fear consume her, powering her, and she screamed without words for the undead to join her. Running towards the sea of black backs, the hood of one of her attackers slid away and she was finally able to view their face. It was a woman, but there was little else that was recognisably human about her. All of the parts were there – mouth, eyes, nose, chin – but it didn't seem right. Her eyes were entirely black, with no white, and blood splatters decorated her cheeks like confetti. The lady swarmed on her, grabbing those nearby and directing them towards Corvossier with a battle cry. She targeted the ghosts that had gathered at her side, pointing towards where she wanted them to go with her outstretched hand.

There was a slice through the air and then suddenly it was gone. Corvossier had barely seen the blade that cut through her like she was soft ice cream. She watched with horror as blood spurted from the wound, her adrenaline pumping and the pain so sharp she couldn't register everything at once. Clutching the flesh where her hand had once been, she dropped to the ground with a cry. Her brother was there and she reached out for him.

'BARASTIN!' she called, her heart swelling as his outstretched hand sought her out.

'Go,' he choked, his fingers shaking. 'Go, Casper. Run.'

'I—'

'RUN!'

Another blade dropped and his next word was cut short, his cries dying off in a silence more horrifying than when the night air was filled with them. She could only see a glimpse of him through the crowd, a silver flash here, a streak of red there, and the ever-present swish of the black robes. She felt lashes against her shoulders and she screamed, over and over again, attempting to crawl backwards until she found herself pressed up against the wall. The lady whose face she had first seen darted towards her, with Corvossier long having lost her ability to hold the ghosts in the alley. She was defenceless and terrified as she clutched her throbbing arm to her chest and squinted her eyes shut. *Please, let it be quick*, she thought. *Let me join him.* She prepared herself for the sound of metal sinking into her flesh, the blade finding bone, but instead there was a strangled cry and a gagging sound. Her eyes flew open and she gasped, digesting the sight in front of her with shock.

'Brother?'

Her voice did not sound like her own as she watched the translucent, bluish grey figure in front of her. She would recognise him anywhere, her lifelong companion. His body looked fragmented, like a jigsaw puzzle that had been assembled but you could still see the outline of where the pieces were supposed to fit. Parts of Barastin were swimming in and out of view as he attempted to solidify, barricading their attackers with his presence. They could not get past him and to her, despite their efforts. Yet Corvossier could not compose herself: if he was standing in front of her in ghost form, it meant only one thing.

'Run, my sister,' he pleaded.

With the words that he spoke, she knew for certain he was dead: the truth coursed through her veins like a drug doing its job.

'*Please*,' he begged. 'RUN!'

Corvossier urged her feet to move, her knees knocking together as she willed her body up off the wall and away from the carnage. Whether it was the blood loss or the shock, she couldn't tell, but the alley swam as she dashed for its opening and the cars she could see driving by. They were behind her, she knew it, and she didn't know how long her brother could hold them. They wanted her, all of her, and in pieces. Just like Barastin. Her breaths were sobs and both cut out altogether as a huge, immovable mass stepped in front of her path. She cried out, trying to run past it as it gripped her tightly and held her there. It shook her and she looked up, her neck arching backwards as her feet finally gave out. Heath caught her, cradling her to him as she watched his face look back into the alley behind her. She knew what he saw: her brother. But not as he was: as he died.

'We have to help him,' she moaned, barely able to get the words out of her mouth. Her lips were going numb. 'Heath! We have to—'

Her pulled her upwards and away, carrying her like she was little more than a baby as he ran. There was a car waiting nearby with the doors open and he threw her into the backseat, his body following a moment later.

'DRIVE!' he shouted, urging the person behind the wheel forward with a frantic gesture. Corvossier pulled away from him, her remaining hand bloody as she pressed it against the window and attempted to get a look. Their attackers were still running after them, the wind whipping their hoods back so their faces were all exposed. Yet she was focused on the man standing at the centre of them, glowing ever-so-slightly. The ghostly figure of her brother was obscured as they ran around and in front of him, pursuing the car as it accelerated out of their reach. She whined, unable to help the pitiful noise that escaped her as they drove further and further away until she couldn't see them anymore. Soon, the black was creeping in at the corner of her eyes. She could feel Heath pulling at her, shouting about a tourniquet or pressure, but it seemed distant somehow. She let herself be taken there and slipped willingly away from the pain and the agony and the sorrow.

'Just tell me.'

'We couldn't save it, without the rest of the limb—'

'How bad?'

'Below the elbow, transradial amputation. We did what we could.'

'Aye, I *know* that. How long until she's back?'

'We want to bring her out slowly, she'll be in quite a lot of pain.'

'Mmmm.'

'I'm sorry, about Coll—'

'Let me know when she's awake.'

The words seemed to float off in Corvossier's mind, as if she dreamed them. She couldn't hold on to their content or their context; it was just a jumble as she was dragged back under. It was comfortable though, where she was: quiet and dark and peaceful. She wanted to stay there, but it wasn't possible. There was something tugging at her, a pain down her right side that she couldn't escape and a pain in her heart that was twenty times worse.

Eventually, when she did open her eyes, she was met with a blinding white light. It took her some time to realise it wasn't actually a light at all, but the ceiling. She focused in on that because it seemed safe to stay laying there and count the tiny specks of dirt on the pristine surface above her. But then she grew thirsty, her mouth feeling dry and parched as she attempted to speak. Lifting her body up slightly, she took stock of the space around her. It was a hospital room, certainly, with the beeping of machines filling her eardrums and the hygienic smell almost nauseating. There was a small couch beside her bed and, on it, the form of Heath Darkiro stretched out in a such a way as to make him spill over every surface. He stirred and she watched him slowly return to the land of the living. Looking around to gain his bearings, she could tell he was surprised to see her awake.

'Casper.'

'Water,' she croaked. 'Please.'

He nodded, not wasting a second as he strolled over to a small table where there was a jug and collection of glasses. She closed her eyes, enjoying the sound of the liquid gradually filling up to the rim of the container.

'I'm going to hold it to your lips, so you don't have to move.'

She nodded, her mouth touching the cool edge of the glass. Opening her eyes, she took a small sip. It hurt her throat to swallow, but she did so anyway and returned for another sip, this one larger, more of a gulp.

Sitting back, she let out a contented sigh as Heath fussed around her and adjusted her pillows so she could stay upright without much effort. Happy with the job, he walked backwards until he dropped down on to the couch.

'Do you know where you are?' he asked, his tone quiet.

'A Treize hospital somewhere,' she replied, glancing around the room again and inspecting its features more closely. 'I think there's one in Wedding.'

'Do you remember what happened?'

She didn't need to close her eyes for the memories to come flooding back. They were like fragments being dropped into her brain, just needing a trigger word to reassemble. *Do you remember what happened?* Her brother's screams, the blood, the blades, her shouts, the faces she didn't recognise . . .

'Casper?'

'I remember,' she whispered, her eyes shifting their focus from Heath's face to the person standing behind him. He was watching her almost as intensely, his expression a reflection of her own features. Heath seemed completely unaware that Barastin's ghost was at his back, but if he'd known she wasn't sure whether he would have been bothered by it or not.

'Did you see him?' she asked. 'Barry's ghost, in the alley?'

He nodded. 'I saw him. He's a large part of the reason you're alive.'

So her brother could be seen, but he was choosing not to be in that moment. She watched him watch her, a sad smile creeping over his face. Corvossier flicked her gaze back to Heath, giving him her full attention.

'I think it's my fault,' she said. 'I was panicking, trying to call ghosts to me, and I accidentally called him.'

'It's not your fault,' Heath scoffed. 'When you're in danger, you reach for your natural defences. In my case, that's a physical weapon. In yours, a spiritual one. You calling him saved your life when nothing else could.'

'Where's Collette? If she doesn't know about Barastin already, I have to be the one to tell her.'

'She . . .' Heath's face crumpled, the ancient warrior dropping his head into his hands for a moment.

39

'No,' she breathed, anaylsing every detail of his reaction.

'When she got your texts, I went to pay at the restaurant and she went outside to get a ride. We would have been apart for less than a minute, maybe two, tops. That's all it took.'

'For them to what?'

'Take her. They were watching us the whole time and had a contingency plan in case either of you attempted to contact someone for help.'

'Is she alive?'

He shook his head, not quite able to vocalise a definitive 'no'.

Corvossier heard a strangled sound escape from her own throat and she closed her eyes, needing to block out the room around her.

'There was a van waiting. They threw her in it and drove off. A lady smoking out the front saw the whole thing and shouted, but by the time I got there they were nearly at the corner. I managed to throw a lad off his scooter and follow, but I lost them between U Kottbusser Tor and Bohnengold. I found the van near one of the U-Bahn stations. It was empty except for . . .'

'Just tell me.'

'Blood. More than a human can afford to lose. They stabbed her and threw her in front of an oncoming train. We're still waiting for a comprehensive autopsy but—'

'What did they need her for?' Corvossier asked, tears streaking down her cheeks. 'It was clear they wanted us, but Collette never did anything to *anyone*.'

'You could never underestimate her. She was resourceful

and quick-witted: she could have thrown a spanner in the works of whatever their plan was. It was the best offensive strategy, to take her off the board.'

'Oh Jesus,' she sobbed, her hand reaching up to cover her face.

'Remember, I was not supposed to be there. Taking Collette could have been as much to keep me busy as it was to get rid of her.'

'She didn't deserve this, Barastin didn't deserve this,' she cried. 'Who did this, Heath? Who could do such a thing?'

'They're saying it's witches.'

She sniffed, composing herself as she looked hard at his expression. Barastin's was just as disbelieving behind him.

'You don't believe that,' she said.

'No.'

'It wasn't witches.'

'I know.'

'There were men there too, I saw them.'

'So did I.'

'Then who's that coming from?'

'The Treize. That's the official line.'

'The *official* line?' she scoffed. 'That's ludicrous! Witches are just like anyone else. They're not goodies or *baddies*: they're just people. They barely interact with the rest of the paranormal community.'

'Now you know why.'

'It's not witches. I've been around witches. Collette knew witches. They hang out at Phases; witches do not have the physical effect on me like these creatures did.'

'Explain.'

'I could feel them, I could sense that something was wrong. Like intuition, but worse. I was worried I was just overreacting, but—'

'Like spirits? Or powerful ghosts?'

'No.'

'You told me that if a ghost is strong enough it can take physical form, move things around them.'

'Not like this,' she explained. 'They can't shadow as human. And these did.'

'Have you got faces? Rough ages? Did you hear a name?'

She stretched her mind back, her memories snagging on the face of the one woman she could easily recall. The others weren't as clear, but each second seemed to sharpen the picture. Yes, she could remember their faces. She would never forget them for the rest of her days.

'Why are the Treize saying it's witches?' she asked, her voice firm. 'I want an answer.'

'I don't have one. At least not yet.'

'Or not here? This is one of their hospitals, after all.'

'Aye, but I shorted their power circuit before I came in.' He shrugged, nonchalant. 'No one's listening to us while they're running on back-up generators.'

She blinked, her head taking a moment to catch up to what he had said. A laugh burst out of her mouth and she tried to catch it with her hand, but flinched. Glancing down, she felt her heartbeat stutter as she viewed what had once been her right limb. Where her pale, slender wrists had been and her fingers adorned with her favourite gemstones like rose quartz and turquoise, there was now a bundle of tightly wrapped bandages. She wiggled the fingers on her left hand, just checking with herself she still had function even though she could see that it was there. Her eyes were as wide as they could go, the blood moving through her veins slowly like clogged pipes. She held her arm up to her face, examining it more closely as it throbbed under the layers of padding.

'How did I not notice this immediately?' she managed to say, after several long moments.

'You're on more painkillers than Michael Jackson, for starters.'

'Heath—'

'Do you remember it?'

'Yes, I remember the blade and the pain but . . . I saw the blood, I just thought it was all mixed with Barastin's.'

She looked at the ghost of her brother, who gave the smallest nod to confirm that she was at least partially right.

'They couldn't recover your hand, so they were forced to amputate below the elbow. You were in surgery for two hours.'

'Couldn't?'

'It was taken. Along with your brother's body.'

'*His corpse?*'

'I didn't know how to tell you.'

'How would you? There's no guidebook for this.'

'The Paranormal Practioner said your arm will take some time getting used to—'

'*You think?*'

'—but there are prosthetic limbs they can fit you with, even bionic ones, which are state of the art.'

'Heath.'

'I know.'

'They took Collette, they took my brother, they took my hand.'

He sat up straighter on the couch, adjusting his posture so that he was at attention. They just stared at each other for a while and she realised this was the longest conversation they'd ever had.

'What are you going to do?' he asked.

'What do you mean?'

'Don't fuck with me, I can see it in your eyes.'

She smirked, the muscles feeling strange as her facial expression didn't reflect what she was feeling inside.

'I'm just a contractor for the Treize,' Corvossier said. 'But you work for the Praetorian Guard, *for all eternity*. What's to stop you from telling them anything I say?'

'A debt,' he replied. 'I owe it to Collette to find the people who killed her and make them pay. If the situation was reversed, you know as well as I do that she'd never stop until she had justice.'

'Her form of justice would have been prison, locking them up, throwing them in Vankila. Your form of justice involves a lot of blood, torture, and probably heads on spikes.'

'I'm not hearing a problem.'

'It's not witches. If you know that and I know that, the Treize know that as well. So what are they hiding, Heath? Why are they diverting blame?'

'Who says they're hiding anything?'

She gave him a withering look. It was enough to crack him just slightly, his own stupid question answered with a shrug.

'You want answers,' he stated.

'To start with, yes: I want answers. And then I want revenge.'

44

There was silence as he got to his feet, pacing around the room and thinking about what she had said. He cast her a sideways glance, considering Corvossier with a calculating stare.

'I *dinna ken*,' he muttered, running a hand through his blond beard. 'What do ya want from me? What can I do?'

'Wait until I have a target to point you at,' she said, voice stern. 'And stay out of my way in the meantime.'

With his hands in his pockets, he leaned against the wall and looked at her as she sat in the hospital bed. Barastin was still there, inching closer towards Corvossier in a way that gave her comfort when she desperately needed it.

'They're waiting until you're awake to interview you. Tape an official statement.'

'Better get it over with, then.'

Pushing himself up off the wall, he strolled towards the door and stepped out into the hall. Closing it behind him to give her some privacy, she tracked his footsteps as far as she could until they died off.

Glancing to the side, she took a shuddered gulp of air as she looked into Barastin's eyes. She had never wondered if a ghost could cry before, but she thought she saw tears welling as he looked back at her. He extended his hand and Corvossier reached out hers, her fingers moving through the air as if he wasn't there at all. She had never been alone before and as she cradled her wounded arm to her chest, smelling the salt as it dripped down her face, she took solace in the fact that her brother was still there with her in whatever form he could manage.

ONE YEAR LATER

Chapter 3

She could feel the small child's eyes on her, fixated on the one part that didn't fit within his limited worldview. Children were always the worst, not having the learned social skills and cues to pretend the lady in front of them wasn't missing a hand. In contrast, she almost preferred their reactions sometimes: at least they were honest. The breathy 'oh my gosh, I literally didn't even notice at all' sentiments always rang false in her mind. But this little boy's fascination was true, and Corvossier cast a downwards glance at him as she waited at the counter to pay for her groceries.

He looked up, realising that he had been caught staring, and gasped when his eyes peered into hers. She knew what he saw: an otherworldly grey that seemed to swirl inside her iris. Regular people didn't have those eyes, but regular people also couldn't walk between the worlds of the dead and the living. His lip trembled and for a second, she thought he might cry.

'How did you lose your hand?' he asked, mustering the courage. Corvossier sensed the clerk serving her stiffen behind the counter and she smiled, crouching down so she was at the same height as the child.

'Do you really want to know?'

He nodded enthusiastically, his head of curls bouncing up and down with the gesture and his big, brown eyes wide with anticipation.

'A shark bit it off.'

'A *shark*?'

'Uh huh.'

'A big one?'

'The biggest.'

'How did you get away?'

'I punched it, right in the nose.'

'Wow!'

'Like this.' She mimicked a punching gesture and his face lit up with a smile.

'Wooooow.'

'NATE! What are you doing? Stop bothering that woman.'

Corvossier straightened up, handing over the notes she owed for her food as the bags were lifted on to the counter.

'Ma! She punched a shark in the nose! Like this!'

'That's, uh, very nice. Now come on.'

The kid skipped away, punching the air as he did so and landing blows on imaginary sharks.

Corvossier smiled, slipping the straps of several bags up her arm and to the bend of her elbow.

'Do you need a—'

'Hand?' she asked, the clerk blushing furiously. She grabbed the remaining bags and headed out the store, choking down the bubble of laughter she felt rising in her stomach.

'Oh, you're feeling *mean* today,' Barastin scoffed, maintaining pace alongside her. It was a busy Wednesday afternoon and the streets were packed with tourists, locals running errands and those just wanting to shop. Her brother moved through them seamlessly or, rather, they moved through him.

'Don't even try to make me feel guilty,' she remarked, not bothering to care if people thought it was strange that she was speaking to herself. She'd given up worrying about what people thought a long time ago.

'Who, me? The Queen of Mean? Never! Lean into it, darling; gnash those teeth. It's amusing to watch.'

'Anything to appease my audience.'

She weaved her way through the crowd, her eyes running over the faces in a move that was instinct now. Corvossier had grown uncomfortable being surrounded by this many people and she tried to avoid it if she could. But she had let her supplies run down, with her fridge empty of anything edible and her cupboards bare. She could feel power prickling under her skin, as if sensing that she was defensive and may need to unsheathe her claws if necessary.

Taking one of the ramps up to the Bierpinsel, she jogged the last few metres until she was at the security checkpoint. She wore her entry pass on a lanyard around her neck, and she swayed it in front of the reader, listening for the electronic beep. Elevator doors parted to reveal a woman from the Praetorian Guard waiting inside the lift, who tensed as Corvossier dashed inside, not relaxing until they were sealed shut in the metallic prism.

Gulping down the panic she had felt spreading through her insides, she let the mechanical movements soothe her as they headed upwards. There were two regular guards in the

51

elevator now when there used to be none. It was either Paddy, an annoyingly chatty man, or this woman, East. She preferred her because she never spoke, never once made a comment or threw Corvossier a sideways glance. She just let her ride in silence. Getting out with some reluctance, she ignored the looks and whispered comments as she stormed through the office. Taking the stairs two at a time, she could feel the eyes burning into the back of her skull as people tracked her movements. Usually once she made it to the third floor, that's when she would feel contentment. But not today: today there was someone leaning against the kitchen bench, flicking a lighter on and off repeatedly as he waited. Glancing up, the man stopped the motion when he caught sight of her. In a pair of cuffed, denim jeans and scuffed black boots, Corvossier's eyes moved up his body slowly as she drank him in. There was a tight, white shirt tucked into his pants, with a leather jacket thrown over the top and an unlit cigarette dangling from his lips. He looked like he had been regurgitated from the fifties.

'Who are you?' she snapped.

'Kentucker Daniels,' he replied. 'Your new Custodian.'

'New?'

'Well, since you chased the last four off it was inevitable they'd deliver a replacement.'

'And that's you?'

'That's me.'

She smirked, dumping the groceries next to where he was leaning. He didn't move, didn't offer to help her as she unpacked the food and ferried ingredients to the fridge. His eyes ran over her right arm, where the long sleeves of her dress covered the limb difference from view. The kid at the store had caught sight of it as she handed her purchases to the clerk, the smooth white skin capturing his attention before it went back to being hidden under the dark purple fabric. This guy didn't linger on it, his attention returning to flicking his lighter on and off rather quickly.

'What did you do?' she asked.

'Excuse me?'

'*Do*. You must have pissed someone off to get this job.'

'There's a long list.' He shrugged. 'I assume they just picked an indiscretion that fit.'

'Huh. You American?'

'Born and bred.'

'In the thirties, per chance?'

'That's right.'

'So you're one of the immortals.'

She had registered the small, metallic object that hung around his neck from the second she walked in, an Egyptian ankh glinting under the light. The Treize, back when it had been founded, was supposed to represent all cultures, all supernatural species, all walks of life coming together: everything from their naming to their symbolism was intended to be a reflection of that.

She looked him up and down. 'They haven't given me one of those in a while.'

'Probably cos you tormented my predecessor with the ghost of their mother.'

'Immortal Custodians have more dead,' she admitted, knowing from that comment alone that he'd studied her file. 'It's really just like giving me more ammunition.'

'Want me to start searching for his loved ones?' Barastin offered, walking around the Custodian with newfound interest.

She shook her head slightly, telling him *not yet*. She'd see if she could break him the usual way first. Filling up the kettle, she hit the switch and waited patiently as the water boiled. One thing she never let herself run low on was tea and she pulled open her cupboard dedicated specifically to it. Ignoring her brother's comment of 'eeeeew' when she selected green, she dumped the teabag in her cup and slowly inhaled the relaxing scent as the water mixed with the ingredients. She left it to steep for a few minutes, walking over to one of the three enormous couches that sat in the lounge and taking a seat.

'Are you going to offer me one?' Kentucker asked.

'No.'

'Well.'

Tucking her feet under her, she looked up at the clock on the wall. 'You have approximately five minutes to leave.'

'What happens after the five minutes?'

'I get mad. Right now I'm only moderately annoyed.'

He picked up her cup of tea from the counter and placed it down at the foot of the couch where she was sitting. She noted the tattoos along his forearms and the words etched across his knuckles: dirt on one hand, dust on the other. With a nod, he walked slowly from the room with a sauntering gait that bugged her. Pausing at the top of the stairs, he threw a look back in her direction.

'Be seeing you.'

The sound of his feet hitting metal as he jogged back down to the levels occupied by the Praetorian Guard, Askari and Custodians brought her only a small amount of satisfaction.

'He's hot,' Barastin noted, jumping on to the couch. 'We haven't had a hot one recently.'

'He's a greaser.'

'I know, I felt like he was going to break into "Summer Nights" at any moment.'

'Ha!' She smiled, taking a sip of her tea. 'You'd like that.'

'With all those hip thrusts in the choreography? You'd like that too.'

Barastin's smile froze on his face. 'He could be a problem.'

'I know.'

'Your plan was to leave tomorrow—'

'It still is.'

'Then you're going to need him out of the way.'

She didn't disagree with her brother. She knew that he was right. Taking a long gulp of liquid, she closed her eyes and let herself slide away, working as fast as she could past the lobby and through the thousands of ghosts lingering there, flashes of their lives and memories flying behind her eyes like a viewfinder on ecstasy.

She zeroed in on something specific, sensing that her brother had come along for the ride with her. There was a boy, dressed in swimming trunks and playing on rocks alongside the shore of a lake. She drank in the details, from the tousled hair to his protruding belly button. The kid couldn't have been more than thirteen. Her eyes snapped open, the memory disappearing just as quickly as it had surfaced. She adjusted to the familiar view of her living quarters once again.

'That was his little brother,' she told Barastin.

'Great, now you're gonna feel bad about it.' He sighed. 'The kid drowned in nineteen forty-six; he's not me, okay? Let's get this over with already.'

'Fine,' she snapped, watching as Barastin's form contorted and twitched and twisted until the person in front of her no longer looked like her twin, but the child they had seen only seconds earlier.

'The hair needs to be darker,' Corvossier noted, the shade adjusting slightly at her order. 'That's better, go get 'em.'

'With pleasure.' Barastin grinned, vanishing in an instant. The first few times he had done this it had startled her, but over the past year she had grown used to it. She had also mostly trained her reactions to remain neutral when Barastin made comments to her in company. No one else knew he was with her and she preferred it that way. His abilities in life had extended into death, giving her brother powers and control most ghosts could never muster. He could take physical form if he wanted and he could choose whether or not to be seen. He could navigate the realm of the dead with immunity, hanging in one while keeping an eye and ear in the other. He could also be in places that she couldn't, learning information that was never intended for Corvossier's consumption.

There was a loud yelp from downstairs, followed by a manly scream and then the distinct sound of someone taking a dive. She smiled, satisfied that Baratsin had done the job, and got to her feet. The heels of her boots clicking along the concrete floor echoed after her as she walked the winding hallway towards her brother's room. Balancing her cup of tea in the nook of her arm, she unlocked the door with one of the keys dangling around her neck. She'd left it the way it had been lived in at first, unable to step over the threshold for months. Her grief was too raw and the one time she had attempted to, she had been overcome with the smell of his cologne. His 'signature scent', as he'd called it, had been Jean Paul Gaultier, with the blue bottles shaped in the form of a man like tiny tombstones dotting the room.

Unsurprisingly it was her brother who had been able to coax her back inside and, eventually, talked her through the clear-out. She had turned it into a combination of an office and spare bedroom, keeping many of his furnishings but removing some of the more personal items. Collette's prized desk now sat in there, right in front of a view of the city that looked like it should have been on a Berlin postcard. An entire wall was taken up by an enormous Hilma af Klint print, one of Barastin's favourite artists and a medium as well. Slipping her fingers underneath it until she found the latch, Corvossier squeezed it and stood back as the artwork rolled away.

Taking another sip of tea, she let the warm fluid trickle down her throat as she viewed more than twelve months of hard work. On one side of the wall were the faces of the people that had stayed with Corvossier since that night, their facial features intricately sketched out by a woman Barastin had suggested. There were ten people present at the execution, three more who had been involved in the abduction and murder of Collette, and Mike Higgens, who had led them into the trap.

She had all of their faces on the board, eight from her own mind and two her brother had helped describe when her recollection wasn't as crisp. Next to them were known movements before and after the murders: where they had been, names they had used, who had seen them. There was a map of Germany, which charted their path out of the country, and to Norway, where they had lost the trail. The culprits already had a two-week head start by the time Corvossier began trying to find them. The trail was chilling when they'd started and now it was all but ice cold.

The question of 'WHY?' was circled, with several more detailed ones written on cards below. 'Why Casper and Creeper?' That was something Heath had asked her when she was recovering in the hospital: 'Why you two?'

Her own questions were up there as well: 'Where is his body?'; 'Why had they taken it?'; and 'What have they done with my hand?' On the one-year anniversary, she had added something else she had been thinking about almost constantly: 'What were they?' Because the Treize's insistence they were witches was not only wrong, it was damaging. Every species of supernatural in Berlin was on edge, the witches who would frequent Phases having scattered and local occult bookshops having to go underground. She and Barastin had alphabetised witnesses and catalogued addresses in a way that would have satisfied Collette's intricate micromanagement skills. There were several photographs of Mike Higgens up there as well, from his staff shots to stills of CCTV footage they had obtained and dead addresses, all of them with lines through them to indicate they were leads that had been chased up unsuccessfully. But to stay ahead of them, Mike Higgens had to get lucky every time. Barastin and Corvossier only had to get lucky once.

'Well,' Barastin said with a huff, reappearing by her side, 'he won't be coming back.'

'What happened?'

'Waited at the bottom of the stairs as he descended the second flight, then regurgitated water.'

'That was dark, Barry.'

'Oh, I'm sorry, was I supposed to be the friendly ghost today? Or the one who made sure an obstacle was permanently out of the way?'

She made a groaning sound, knowing he was right but still not entirely happy with the method they had deployed.

'Anyway,' her brother continued, 'he was shooketh, obvi, and took a stumble. Couldn't be certain whether he hit his head and passed out *or* if it was the surprise of it all.'

'Is someone attending to him?'

'Yeah, there are Custodians fawning all over his unconscious form. You know how much they love a cause.'

'I do,' she replied, the words fading away as she ran her finger over the latest edition to their wall of enquiry. It was a piece of cardboard with an address: the current residence of Mike Higgens. The day she had attained it, she had written it down in black ink so she could physically look at it rather than just repeating it over and over in her mind. Her hand had been shaking at the time, the words slightly wobbly now as she looked at them. *The harder you work, the luckier you get*, she thought. And Corvossier had worked very, very hard to make sure Mike Higgens' luck would eventually run out. She had a ticket booked on Ryanair for a trip to Latvia the following day, where just a short drive from the airport, outside of a town called Riga, was a house currently leased by Valdis Ušakovs. It was one of several aliases the Askari intern had used over the past fourteen months, picking up and dropping names consistently. It made him hard to track through conventional means, but Corvossier did not use conventional means.

It had been a full week before she'd been allowed to leave hospital after the attack and, outside of interviews with the local Askari about what happened, she'd had nothing else to do. There had been no one to visit her. Everyone who would have come by, was dead. So she'd decided to join them. Closing her eyes and slipping away to the place she and her brother had decided to call the lobby when they were children, the place where the dead waited until they were 'checked in', Corvossier had begun hunting. Barastin's form on this plane was more solid, with she and her brother able to physically interact like they had been able to do when he was alive. She had linked her remaining hand in his and started walking through the endless, black, desolate expanse as it had stretched out in front of them. Neither had stated exactly what they were walking towards, but the first stop had been trying to find any ghost attached to Mike Higgens like a cobweb that extended through the world of the living and into the realm of the dead.

She had spent days doing that, not sleeping, barely eating as she'd lain in her bed: physically there but mentally somewhere else entirely. Although he was young, Mike's parents had died in a car accident three years earlier. There was nothing unnatural or unusual about their death, nothing out of the ordinary, which was a pain in the ass because it meant they had transitioned long ago. And where they had gone was somewhere no ghost or medium could follow safely without losing themselves. So she and Barastin had searched for someone else, anyone else, who might have been attached to him in life and were still attached to him in death. There had been nothing.

However, the longer Corvossier had spent in the lobby, the more she'd become aware of a growing audience. When she had been finally cleared to leave hospital, she had retreated to her living quarters with the beginning of an idea. Locking herself away for months, she spent more time among the dead than she did the living as she'd worked out a way to utilise the ghosts that were drawn to the power of herself and Barastin.

The dead were everywhere, usually moving unnoticed through the world as they followed the people that had mattered to them, lingering in the places that had been important. Mostly, they were bored as they waited for something to change, something that would allow them to leave. Corvossier could be that something, but first ... they needed to do her a little favour. To the ghosts that had gathered, she'd told them who she was looking for and why, offering a reward to anyone who could come back with information or – even better – a current location. The news had spread quickly throughout the dead community, the whispers trickling out with a hushed kind of amazement. There weren't that many mediums left and the opportunity to have one in your debt was a rare thing.

Weeks went by, followed by months, but eventually it had started to work. As Mike Higgens went about his life, trying hard to remain unnoticed by anyone who could rat him out to the Treize or Praetorian Guard looking for him, he was completely unaware of who else was watching. People he couldn't perceive had found him as he'd passed through a port in Italy, hired a car in Scotland, caught a plane to Mexico and kept moving, always moving. As the information was passed on to Corvossier, she sought to corroborate it via any source she could; a first-person witness was best, but CCTV footage or second-hand documents were a close second. Gradually she had been able to form an idea of who Mike Higgens was, where he had come from, where he'd fled to after Berlin, and eventually where he would end up. It was a race, and Mike may have had a head start, but in less than twenty-four hours she would be pulling up alongside him.

'Valdis Ušakovs,' Barastin said, staring at the piece of card that contained Mike's address.

Glancing back over his shoulder, he gave her a stare that said *finally* without saying it. She smiled, feeling much the same way. He'd used a lot of names, but weirdly Mike Higgens had been his real one. He really was from Canada and really had been an Askari in training: somewhere along that journey he had been intercepted by the people who ended her brother and Collette's lives. Now there was a small chance she might find out why. Pulling the painting back down and moving all the clasps to their rightful place, she went over to Barastin's closet and pulled out the bag she had ready to go. In it was a fake passport and ID, cash, a change of clothes, a burner phone, basic supplies and a gun. She pulled out the Glock 19 and the ammunition she had for it.

'You're not going to be able to get that on a plane with you,' Barastin said.

'I know.' She sighed, annoyed. 'I'm still trying to organise one on the ground.'

It had taken a lot of practice for her to become competent with a gun: she had never even fired one until she went to Yu for lessons. Even in her limited circle, she had heard stories about the former soldier's proficiency with firearms. Teaching someone to shoot who had never done so before was one thing, but teaching someone to shoot when they had one hand ... well, it had been a steep learning curve for both of them. Corvossier had tried using a prosthetic limb at first; in fact, she'd tried several different options. There was a support group she had been advised to join – the Cyborg Sisters – and although she'd been reluctant, it had actually been endlessly helpful. The women there hadn't made her feel like a failure for not taking to her artificial hand like it was the easiest thing in the world.

'I couldn't stand it at first either,' Mia, the leader of the group, had told her at the time. 'Then I painted nails on it and I felt much better.'

'Really?'

'No. Truth is, it's different for everyone: I have four that I really like and switch between, depending on what I'm doing.'

'Four?'

'Uh huh, that's just the arms: I alternate between half a dozen hands. But Valentina doesn't use them at all, do you, hon?'

'Nope. I have enough dexterity in my right hand; I just use my left for balance or carrying objects.'

'I've only ever seen her wear an artificial arm at parties. It's pretty cool; it lights up.'

'The LED lights distract people from asking annoying questions,' Valentina had added. 'The rest of the time I don't care and it doesn't hinder me if I don't let it.'

Corvossier had learned quickly there was very little that hindered any of the Cyborg Sisters. Valentina was a Paralympian, holding the world record for two hundred metres freestyle and with more medals than she could melt down. She was a congenital amputee, meaning she had been born with a limb difference, and also somehow managed to juggle her sporting career with an interior design business. Mia was a high school teacher who had lost her arm in a motorbike accident when she was in her late teens. She was the one who had actually suggested Corvossier take up shooting because she might find it therapeutic, and taught her how to steady the weight of her left arm to aim, by balancing with the right. It was a similar technique to the one she used for archery, which was Mia's favourite hobby and something she'd even had a specific prosthetic designed for. Then there was the engineering student, Vinessa, mum of five, Ellen, and runway model, Letitia.

Corvossier had a long-standing coffee date the Cyborg Sisters once a month – it was the only social activity she participated in – and she realised with annoyance that she would miss it tomorrow.

'Sorry, girls, just had to take a quick trip to Latvia for a vengeance mission,' she imagined herself saying. 'How was everyone's weekend?'

She smirked, removing the gun from the bag and locking it in a safe inside the wardrobe. It was fine. She didn't need the weapon; she had others. And she had herself. She felt a sense of anticipation and hope that she hadn't felt in months as she slipped out of Barastin's bedroom and locked the door for good measure. It was an unnecessary step, really: no one wanted to go up into what had been the twins living quarters if they could avoid it. Even if they did, they stayed away from her brother's room like it was diseased. It had been the

smartest choice for choosing a base of operations and she
didn't feel bad about exploiting the discomfort of others. In
fact, she kind of relished in it.

'What now?' Barastin asked as she strolled to her room.

'My flight's at six a.m.,' she said, noting the time as she
glanced down at her watch. 'That's a chunk of space to fill.'

'It's barely five p.m. You're not going to be thinking about
anything else until then, are you?'

'Would you? If the situation was switched?'

'Not for a second,' he agreed. 'I wouldn't be able to sleep a
wink.'

'So I don't sleep then.'

Rolling her neck with discomfort as she came to a stop in
front of her closet, she looked at the racks of clothes hanging
there. She let the fabric of a satin top run over her arm, watching as the honey topaz colour shifted to almost bronze under
the reflection of the light. Closing her eyes, she allowed the
different textures of her wardrobe guide her towards what she
wanted to wear. Finally settling on cashmere, she lifted the
garment off the hanger and laid it down on the bed. Corvossier
had a lot of work to do that night, but at least she could feel
good while doing it.

'I just think the teardrop earrings would have been nicer, that's
all.'

'The Tiger's eye pendant matches the outfit,' Corvossier
hissed, trying to keep the movement of her lips minimal as she
snapped at her brother.

'Oh sure, it matches. It's matchy matchy: that's my point.
The earrings would have provided a contrasting colour.'

She sighed, rolling her eyes as he kept up his ongoing commentary on what was and wasn't wrong with her ensemble.

Nodding at Zillia, the Italian woman who headed up the Rogues and kept Phases ticking most of the time, Corvossier let herself sink into the crowd despite how uncomfortable it made her. Tomorrow this would be a protective mechanism, it would be how she blended among the crowd, and she needed to ignore the itch along her skin that she felt as her instincts told her to get to an isolated, clear space. She overlooked them, swallowed them down as much as she could, for as long as she could. Standing in the horde of bodies dancing around her, she closed her eyes and swayed to the pulse of the music in an attempt to relax herself. Of course, she had the benefit of her brother – always her brother – keeping watch and signalling danger as soon as he saw it. They had never openly discussed why he was still there, with her. They both knew. In life they had been tied to each other and in death it was the same. He wasn't ready to leave her yet and she wasn't ready to be left.

'Casper.'

Her eyes flew open, gaze focusing on Yu cutting through the masses towards her. The woman jerked her head, indicating for Corvossier to follow her to the bar.

She headed towards her usual spot, which was empty: not that it was ever occupied. In the time following the attack, rumours had spread and circulated about what had actually gone down. People were afraid of her and she found that useful for the most part: it meant they left her alone and it meant her preferred seat at Phases always stayed vacant, just in case she would show up. Settling in, she ordered her usual and didn't react when Yu slid it to her across the bar along with a piece of paper.

'He'll be in a red cab,' Yu muttered, the words hardly loud enough for anyone to hear. But Corvossier heard them perfectly, her eyes running over the number plate she was supposed to look for: TX 7616. She handed the note back to Yu, with the money for her drink resting on top. In one swift gesture the woman slipped the cash into the register and held the note in front of a chef's blowtorch, which she had been using to prepare a flaming cocktail. Corvossier watched the piece of paper disintegrate almost instantly, just a small piece of ash floating to the floor as Yu warned the customer to wait until the flames had died down before he consumed the drink. She rarely ever worked behind the bar, with Corvossier somewhat curious to see whether her temperament could handle it. Taking a swig from a bottle of beer she had tucked away, Yu headed back in her direction as she waited for the next person to serve.

'What's this I hear about you throwing a Custodian down the stairs?' she asked.

'Me?' Corvossier blinked, ignoring the snort of laughter that Barastin made beside her. There was a shared look between them as she took a sip of her drink, watching Yu carefully from the other side of her glass.

'I heard he tripped,' she muttered, earning a sly smile from the former soldier.

'It's funny, the things you hear. Like how the Custodian they gave you before that claimed the ghost of her ex-husband warned her if she stayed in Germany she'd suffer a horrible fate.'

'Very funny,' Corvossier noted.

'Or the guy who said he kept waking up to find the spirits of his dead pets waiting at the end of his bed each night.'

'That's ridiculous,' she remarked. 'There was only one dead pet.'

Yu choked on a sip of her beer, grinning as she wiped away the fluid from her mouth. A customer held up her hand, signalling to get the woman's attention.

'You packed?' she asked, telling the lady she'd be one moment.

'Yes.'

'All the items we discussed?'

'Yes.'

'Good. My man on the ground is Ivan. He can be trusted but the less anyone knows the better. That goes for me too.'

'I get it. And Yu?'

'Yeah?'

'Thank you.'

Yu paused mid-step, looking back at Corvossier on her way towards the woman waving a note in her hand impatiently.

'I liked your brother,' she said, before turning away.

'She liked me?' Barastin scoffed, after a long silence had passed. 'I died not knowing that.'

Corvossier liked watching the people at Phases, how they laughed and danced and drank and enjoyed their lives in a way that seemed untouched by tragedy. She knew that was unlikely: everyone experienced something horrible at some point. But in her mind, she imagined they had perfect little lives as they swirled about in that club. And she couldn't have felt more removed from it, a deep pang in her chest puncturing her ability to breathe as she thought about never being able to join these people. There were just some things you could not come back from, and the death of Collette and Barastin was that for her. With a shuddered gulp of air, she drained the rest of her drink and slipped from the stool.

She nodded a farewell to Yu, tucking her coat over her shoulders as she stepped out into the night. It was a pleasant evening, with open skies stretching above them and a chill on the air that made it seem like Berlin to her. They walked in silence for most of the journey and it was comfortable: she never felt the need to fill in the gaps with mindless chatter when she was with Barastin.

Instead of walking straight home to the Bierpinsel, she took a slight detour towards a part of the city less occupied by tourists and more heavily populated by locals. The pungent scent of marijuana was the first clue she was close, with the smell becoming an all-out aroma by the time she turned a corner and made her way towards a small crowd of people. They were smoking and chatting near a shop front, with loud industrial Goth music pumping through the neighbourhood. One of them looked up as she approached, the woman's face illuminated by a pink glow that came from a neon sign above her head that read '1984'.

'He's inside,' she said, maintaining Corvossier's stare as smoke slowly escaped her lips. Her hair was wrapped up in tight victory rolls that sat on either side of her head, not only matching her mod aesthetic but perfectly hiding the set of horns Corvossier knew were underneath. She muttered her thanks, stepping into the venue, which was a cramped attempt at resurrecting an arcade hall popular in America during the mid-eighties.

There was a kitsch quality to this place that meant it was always packed full of people enamoured with the charm of a decade long since past. What the odd human customer didn't know was that most of the regulars to 1984 remembered arcade halls very well and looked exactly the same age as they did back when Space Invaders first hit the scene. For whatever reason, this bar had been popular with the immortal clientele for as long as Corvossier could remember. One entire wall was dedicated to playing movies from the eighties, with a dozen people perched on couches in front of it and enthralled by a scene from *The Thing* where an ill-fated man attempted to perform CPR.

'Oh, I love this bit,' Barastin said excitedly, a chorus of moans coming from the audience as the chest turned into huge teeth, severing the man's limbs.

Corvossier ignored him, her eyes searching for the David Hasselhoff pinball machine towards the back of the space and past the kitchen. A man was playing it with gusto, yanking back the lever and slapping the buttons on the side with enthusiasm as he tried to make the small, silver balls do what he wanted. He had an afro so huge you could barely see the machine on the other side, a bright green comb wedged into the front of his hair. Silently, Corvossier leaned against the machine as she watched the final moments play out, Barastin sandwiching the man on the other side.

'Hello, Hogan,' she said.

'You mediums scare the shit out of me,' he replied, his eyes in their natural state as he focused on the game. Anyone paying attention would have reacted strongly to the rectangular pupils sitting inside a purple iris, but the goblin was too far hunched over the glass for anyone except Corvossier to see.

'Why's that?'

'You always just show up.'

She opened her mouth to say that's kind of what people did, medium or not, but she hesitated. 'You've met one before?'

'One what? Argh, damn it.'

'A medium.'

He nodded, taking a sip of his soft drink before resuming the game. 'You know the packs have their own, right? Not like you and Creeper, but still scary.'

'How so?' she asked, unable to help her curiosity. It was rare she got to speak about her gifts and even rarer that she met someone else with them.

'Well, into every generation only one is born and their names are always Buffy.'

'Here we go,' Barastin mumbled.

'But seriously, the gift gets passed down through the pack and that's how they stay in touch with the spirits of yesteryear. If they go off pack land, the ability lessens: it's strengthened or weakened by geography. There's a werewolf pack in Delhi whose tribal elder told me once that I was being followed by the ghost of an old woman.'

'Did you know who he was talking about?'

'My grandmother. She was murdered.'

'I remember hearing about that,' Barastin told her, the goblin completely unaware of their other conversation. 'A banshee foretold her death a month before it happened. She ignored the warning.'

'Huh.'

She was thoughtful for a moment, watching as Hogan's ball spun over a jet of lights and towards a likeness of the car from *Knight Rider*.

'What were you doing anywhere near a werewolf pack?'

'Goblins are affected by the lunar cycle too,' he muttered. 'Gotta stick together.'

She glanced over his shoulder, nervous about discussing so much openly.

'Please,' he scoffed. 'You know what day of the week it is?'

'Uh . . .'

'Geez. And I thought I had to get out more.'

'Wednesday.'

'Bingo. There's not a single human allowed in here on the even-numbered days, you know that.'

'Why not just ban them altogether?'

He rubbed his fingers against each other, showing her his answer without saying it: money. Goblins loved money.

'C'mon, I've got your stuff.'

He stepped away from the pinball machine, it now having sufficiently eaten the coins he loved so much. She followed him to the bathrooms at the rear of 1984, with Hogan waiting until the coast was clear before opening the door to the staff toilet, which had an 'out of order' sign hanging crooked from the handle. Once inside, they were plunged into darkness, both crammed into the tiny space before he pushed back the phantom wall. Behind it were stairs leading to a horrendously messy room, with a plethora of screens – all of them on – providing the only source of light. Well, that and a lava lamp the size of a toddler, but she didn't count that as sufficient illumination. Hogan dropped into his chair, rolling along

the surface of the ground and to a trio of monitors that sprung
to life when he began typing.

'Your boy hasn't popped up anywhere for the last thirteen
days. I'm still not convinced that last photo was him.' A Tribe
Called Quest were bragging about never having a cavity out of
his speakers and he increased the volume.

'It was him,' Barastin whispered, referring to the grainy shot
that appeared on one of the screens and had been pulled from an
airport security camera. *It was him*, Corvossier silently agreed.
They'd had two ghosts confirm it in the meantime, once Hogan
had shown her the image, and one of the dead was planted at his
house, keeping her eyes on him at all times. If he tried to run,
Corvossier and Barastin would be alerted within seconds.

'What about the accounts?' she asked, scanning the finan-
cial records Hogan brought up over his shoulder.

'All quiet. And they're mostly empty too, which tells me he's
down to using cash and *only* cash out of necessity.'

Corvossier nodded, handing him a vinyl wallet with a fake
pearl buckle.

'Do I just help myself?' he asked, taking it from her.

'All the money I owe you is in there. Thought that would
look slightly less suspicious than if I was stopped and discovered with an envelope full of Euros.'

'No one in this city is brave enough to stop you,' he mumbled,
pulling out the money and counting it while she stood there.
'Or fool enough.'

'How's the other thing going?'

He sighed, looking up at her with consideration. 'It's prov-
ing harder than I thought.'

Barastin snickered. 'He wants more money.'

'I want more money,' Hogan said.

She crossed her arms, letting her frustration show. The goblin held her stare for a few seconds, before relinquishing with raised hands in surrender.

'What I mean is, I need a favour as well.'

'What kind of favour?'

'My cousin Rowdie has a thing for you.'

'No.'

'He's a nice guy, honest.'

'No.'

'I heard you date men?'

'Men, yes. Goblins named Rowdie, no.'

'What if it was a *female* goblin?'

'Would you like to see your dead grandmother again?'

'Fine! Yeesh, point made. But I still need a favour: Rowdie needs a job.'

'Do I look like I'm hiring?'

'I'd hire him, but you shouldn't mix family and business. You reckon you could see if there's anything going at Phases?'

Barastin smiled. 'He's literally throwing his cousin to the wolves.'

'He can tend bar and he'll work whatever hours they toss at him. It would really sweeten the pot, Casper.'

'No more money,' she said, 'but I can get his résumé in front of the Rogues.'

Hogan's mouth twisted as he thought about it, before finally agreeing.

'Deal,' he said, holding out his hand. She took a moment to run through everything in her mind once more, quickly, before reaching out and shaking. A bargain with a goblin was not something to be taken lightly and most supernaturals tended to avoid doing business with them for that very reason. Their price was high and if you didn't pay up, you wouldn't like what they took in return. Hogan's long fingernails tickled the skin of her hand, his eyes twinkling with the pleasure of a freshly made deal.

'I should have progress for you within a day,' he noted, leaning back in his chair and tapping the laptop folded up on his desk. 'This baby is mostly set up and ready to go, with the final checks running on the program now but I'm confident it will work.'

'But?' she asked, sensing an issue.

'Buuut ... I'm still trying to figure out a way into Treize systems. Everything is sectioned off, you see? The Praetorian Guard prefer paper and keep meticulous physical records—'

'I don't need access to the Praetorian Guard.'

'I know. The Custodians are half and half, with only a split of their records digitised while the Askari are all databases, all the time, but that means they have boosted security as well.'

'You said you could do it.'

'I can, Casper.' He grinned, his teeth and their sharp points distracting her. 'And I will. I just want you to know how hard it is. So hard, that it has never been successfully done before.'

'Nonsense,' Barastin replied. 'There's a goblin doing thirty years for hacking at Vankila right now.'

'I think that's what he meant by *successfully*,' she said, before realising too late that she'd spoken to Barastin out loud. Thankfully, Hogan hadn't noticed as he slipped a retainer from a plastic case and adjusted it in his mouth. He opened and closed his jaw, until he seemed satisfied.

'How do I look?' he asked, straightening up and grinning so that Corvossier could inspect his smile.

'Contacts.'

'Crap, yeah, I almost forgot. Thanks.'

'You got some place to be?'

'A date,' he answered, blinking as he added the other contact. 'With a *human* girl.'

'Ew, why?' Barastin muttered.

Corvossier had nothing to say, wondering what possible hope Hogan could have for a lasting relationship with a civilian woman. She knew he was a romantic and had tried – and failed – dating within the Berlin supernatural pool. As she followed him back up to the main floor of the arcade, she didn't think a human was likely to improve his streak: they were just messy by nature. She was about to push off towards the exit when he called out to her.

'Hey, any last minute words of advice?'

She arched an eyebrow, shocked he would even consider asking her. 'If she was dead, then yeah.'

Hogan's shoulders deflated and he batted a hand at her. 'You're no fun.'

'That's what they say,' she muttered to herself, turning and navigating her way through the hall of gamers until she was outside, alone, in the night once again.

Corvossier didn't need an alarm clock: they were loud and noisy. Besides, she had her brother. He whispered in her ear, repeatedly, until she stirred to consciousness. His face was hovering above her own and she squinted, waiting until he fully came into view.

'Believe me,' he said, 'I don't want to see this either.'

'Go,' she whispered, shooing him away with a hand. He vanished from the room instantly, leaving her to carefully extricate herself from the bed. Standing there in just a silk slip, she stretched her arms above her head as she took a moment longer to wake herself up. Her feet connected with a discarded glass she had left by her bedside, only the tiniest drop of gin remaining. She'd needed it to get to sleep, she had reasoned, but the alcohol had helped little. Corvossier had dozed for little more than an hour before she'd woken up, panting and suffering from the early signs of what she'd recognised to be a panic attack. It was a symptom of Post Traumatic Stress Disorder, or at least that's what the Paranormal Practioner had told her when she'd experienced her first one back in the hospital in the days after her brother was killed. There was little she could do to fight them, instead having to embrace the rising swell of panic and fear she felt within herself and the racking sobs that accompanied it. She'd had to endure, her brother whispering soothing words to her, until eventually, like all things, it passed.

More gin and sheer exhaustion had helped her fall into an uneasy few hours of dozing after that, *The Staircase* playing in the background for comfort. Barastin always insisted that her obsession with true crime documentaries didn't help her sleeping issues, but she had been drawn to them long before the murders and would remain so long after. She couldn't explain it, yet there was something weirdly cathartic about watching her fears play out on screen. Grabbing her dressing gown hanging off the back of the door, she wrapped it around herself as she saw the beginning of sunrise forming outside her bedroom window, just the faintest hint that dawn was coming.

Her bare feet padded down the hallway towards the bathroom, where she took a quick shower. Grabbing the bag she had prepared and getting into a change of clothes as quickly as she could, she took a little more time tucking her hair into a brunette wig with dark, black roots. Adjusting it so it sat square, she left her face bare of make-up and added a pair of thick-framed glasses. She attached a cosmetic prosthesis: an arm that was the most realistic-looking one she had, but otherwise had no function or movement. She threw on a pair of gloves to help the concealment. Between her height, her arm, and how she looked, Corvossier as herself stood out. Her best chance at moving safely outside of Berlin required her to blend.

'You barely look like yourself,' Barastin said, appearing behind her.

'That's the whole point.'

'The flannel shirt, the jeans, the overcoat, the muted palette . . . it's very "Canadian winter".'

'You've never even been to Canada.'

'I've seen how their dead dress.'

Quickly brushing her teeth, she double-checked everything for a final time then stepped out of the bathroom. She left her phone switched off and in her handbag, which she tucked out of sight in a cupboard in her brother's room. She followed Barastin's lead to what had previously been used as a spare bedroom for Collette or visitors if they were required to stay. Inside it was a wardrobe – same as all the other rooms – except this one had a door that opened to a maintenance stairwell. It wasn't on the original building plans and no one had known it existed: not until Barastin died and his ghost form was able to explore parts of the Bierpinsel without restriction.

Corvossier had done one trial run and established that she needed to take it slow down the stairs, which were old and rusted. There were spider webs everywhere, but spiders had never bothered her the way they did some. Shutting the wardrobe door behind her and then the stairwell door, she switched on a flashlight and descended gradually. Her brother also helpfully brightened himself, providing extra illumination. It was slow going, as the stairwell took three levels and then continued down the length of the main tower, running parallel to the elevator. It took her right to the U-Bahn station directly underneath, with Barastin ducking outside to check the coast was clear. When he returned with a nod, she unlocked the door from the inside and gave it a shove. Using the full weight of her body to shut it behind her, she crept along the track for two metres before quickly jogging up stairs built for maintenance workers and ducking under the barrier.

She had timed it perfectly, arriving on the platform to catch her ride with less than a minute to spare. She walked on to the train just like any other customer, settling in to a seat for several stops until she switched and jumped on a train bound for the airport. Her brother was uncharacteristically silent beside her. While he was usually the one keeping up a conversational commentary, he was stoic on their ride and remained so as she navigated her way through the airport. She appreciated it, assuming his silence was largely because he didn't want to increase her nervousness. Yet Corvossier made it through security without a hitch and then on to the plane just as easily. Airports were busy places by nature and among the chaos, she was just another number: no one cared about her. And that's what she had been counting on. As the plane left the runway and she gripped her armrest, she let herself be pulled towards something she did care about: answers.

Chapter 4

The air felt different in Riga. Corvossier couldn't explain it any other way than that, or maybe it was just that *she* felt different in Riga. She was closer to her goal, closer to it than she ever had been before. When she landed, she took a moment watching happy families reunited and couples kiss affectionately. Her eyes observed the businessmen scuttling by, easily identifiable by their suits and small, compact suitcases that dragged behind them on wheels. Barastin was scanning everything around her, appearing and reappearing constantly as he made sure there was no unexpected threat. Having taken just an overnight bag with the bare minimum supplies, Corvossier was able to skip the baggage pickup altogether. She strolled straight out of the airport and to the taxi rank, her eyes searching the line of red cars until she spotted the number plate she was after. Walking towards it purposefully, she slid into the backseat and set her bag down beside her without another word.

'Hello,' the man said. 'Nice to see *Yu*.'

'Good morning,' she replied, meeting his stare in the rear-view mirror.

'I'm Ivan. You'll find what you need under the seat in front. Now where can I take you?'

'Towards the highway,' she said, crouching down to retrieve the package. 'I can direct you from there.'

'As you wish.'

The car rolled forward, with Corvossier grasping the handle of a case and laying it down next to her.

'I couldn't get a Glock, but that there is the Witness Elite 9MM. It's a better gun in my opinion, practically no recoil.'

'Thank you,' she whispered, not wasting any time as she loaded the weapon. 'This will be perfect.'

Shifting her eyes back to the road, she spent the next hour directing Ivan as they neared closer to the target. The town didn't have a name; she guessed that's maybe why Mike Higgens had chosen it. It was little more than a market centre and a tapestry of streets, with just one school and a kindergarten. There were a few properties wider out, where the trees were thicker and the homes were spaced further and further apart. It was on one of these streets that Ivan began to slow down, pulling up behind a battered electronics van. They both sat there in silence for a beat, Corvossier running her eyes over the suburban setting outside of the car. She was just one person and she didn't have many allies, so when she'd realised that at some point she'd have to travel to find Mike Higgens, Corvossier had been initially overcome with fear.

Since the attack, things had changed in Berlin. Not only had security at the Bierpinsel stepped up, but everyone was on guard. She'd had her own detail for six months, until her lack of going anywhere or doing anything meant they were largely unused. Yet wherever Corvossier went in Berlin, people tended to notice, and that meant she was safe in a way she hadn't been before. Outside of her home city, she didn't have that same protection. Even more, she didn't know where her attackers were or what methods they had used to find her previously. She'd started learning basic techniques like switching up your appearance and disguising parts of it, pretending to travel in a group rather than by yourself so the numbers would be thrown if someone was looking for a solo traveller, and using cash. Heath had helped her access the Berlin black market and there she bought passports for four different women, setting up credit cards and other identity documents in those names. It would have been easier for her to work contacts within the supernatural community, but she was a known entity there: she used human forgers as another safeguard. But it was Yu who had hooked her up with Ivan, the former Praetorian Guard soldier realising she was up to something when Corvossier had began trying to question her about ways you could get your hands on weapons in different countries during one of their afternoon sessions at her shooting range.

Yu had answered Corvossier's carefully phrased hypotheticals as best she could, with Barastin suggesting she'd be the perfect person to ask, given she no longer worked for the Treize but still had centuries worth of knowledge. A few weeks passed between Corvossier's initial feeling out of the topic, before Yu had made a comment to her one night at Phases when she had gone there in the hope of trying to cheer herself up. She'd taken a seat next to her, a Janelle Monáe song blaring through the club, and muttered casually that if she was given a date, time and location, she could arrange essentially anything from a shotgun to a rocket launcher so long as a) Corvossier had cash and b) accepted Yu's ten per cent commission on top. The old warrior had slipped away then, leaving Corvossier open-mouthed and shocked at the offer.

'She could go to Vankila for that,' Barastin had whispered to his sister at the time.

'So could I.'

'Yeah, but she trusts you.'

Corvossier had filed that information away. None of her contacts overlapped: the humans who provided her with documents didn't know about the supernatural world, Heath was always moving in and out of the country, the ghosts could only communicate with her, and Yu had no idea who Hogan was. The goblin rarely stepped foot outside of the lattice-like network of streets his people ran, which was partially why she'd chosen him. All together, each party was sealed off from the other. It wasn't exactly bulletproof, but it was a solid mechanism to prevent the Jenga tower tumbling with the movement of one brick. Corvossier had personally chased leads in New Zealand and Turkey first, which had acted as solid practice runs despite none of them panning out. Yu had done as she promised, insisting she organise not only a weapon but a driver who would take the medium where she needed to go. These people never knew Corvossier's real name or her true, intended purpose, and she doubted the names she was given were their real ones either. Yet it had been an effective system so far, with the first two drivers Yu had set up being quiet, efficient women who'd handed off the weapon and got her to the locations. She hadn't been able to tell whether they were supernaturals or just long-term contacts of Yu who knew the business.

Regardless, their effectiveness had built up a sense of dependence for Corvossier: she knew the moment she slid into the back of a car, that person would do the job. Not asking questions was one of the integral elements. Looking at Ivan from the backseat, she sensed he was just like the others – steady and professional – which was exactly what she needed. She asked him if the doors to the car were locked and he said they were, demonstrating by wiggling the handle of the driver's side.

'Good,' she answered. 'Watch my body.'

'Watch your—'

She didn't hear the rest of what he said, closing her eyes and letting herself sink away as quickly as possible. She knew what he'd see, as she'd watched Barastin do exactly the same thing countless times over the years. Her body would go still as the grey of her eyes spread, like milk in a cup of tea, clouding over the rest of her iris. Physically she would be there, sitting upright in the car but very still, barely breathing. Yet the rest of her was somewhere else: navigating the spectral realm, wherever she chose to go.

Her body retained a weightlessness when she entered there. Gravity shouldn't have existed in a place that wasn't *physically* real, yet it operated in much the same way thanks to the memory of the ghosts. The lobby could shift and evolve depending on the dead: what they recalled, what they remembered, what they wanted, unintentionally creating the environment around them. Corvossier and her brother were among the few mediums who could bend it to their will, but they rarely did. It was easier to navigate the lobby as it appeared. It was the same place she would slip to when making sure a ghost was leaving the way they should be. And on the days she missed Barastin the most, when his ghost wasn't enough, it's where she would hang out with him.

He appeared next to her as she arrived at the lobby, the two not wasting time as they walked through the shapeless dark. As they moved, however, a structure began to materialise around them. Soon they were strolling through the back door of an ordinary, slightly rundown home. The house was quiet inside, with all the lights and appliances switched off. Corvossier glanced at the red digits of an alarm clock on the kitchen counter, the time clicking just past 9.31 a.m. She was right on schedule, with the ghost of a woman – her face framed by a hijab – ushering them forward.

The bedroom door was shut, the lady walking right through the wood and to the other side. Barastin could command more physical control and twisted the handle, watching as it slowly swung back to reveal Mike Higgens, fast asleep in his bed. Her eyes darted to the ground, where light glinted along the length of several pieces of string that zigzagged across the floor. The ends were attached to tiny bells, with the idea being that anyone who approached his bed would trip at least one of them and alert Mike to their presence.

'What's the alarm code?' Corvossier asked the ghost.

'Zero-six-zero-seven-eight-nine,' she answered. 'And there's motion detectors in the lounge.'

'I can disable them,' Barastin answered. 'You right with the door?'

'I can pick a lock. What about in here?'

'There's a loaded gun under his pillow,' the ghost said, pointing at the exact spot.

She nodded. 'If he wakes before I get here, let me know immediately.'

'Yes, of course.'

'I'll meet you at the woods,' Barastin said, Corvossier gripping his hand slightly before she let herself fall back to her body.

She came to in the backseat of the car, exactly where she had been, her chest pulling slightly on the seat belt. Straightening up, she unclipped the buckle and threw a backpack over her shoulders. Slipping a hip holster from one of the front pockets, she clipped it around her body and tucked the gun neatly into it. The fabric of her flannel shirt fell perfectly, disguising it from view. Ivan started the car without being told, unlocking the door mechanism so she could step out on to the street.

'Come back in two hours,' she told him. 'Same spot.'

'Will do,' he muttered, driving off as she walked towards the tree line at the end of the road. The huge trunks grew close together, blocking out the light as she stepped into the small portion of woods that separated one line of houses from the other. Pine needles snapped under her feet as she moved, Barastin's glow soon visible to her on the other side as she neared a fence that ran along the back of someone's home. That person had left for work two hours ago; a ghost had monitored their exit, and the latch to their backyard was easy to release given her significant height. Hearing the metallic click, she pushed her way inside and shut the gate behind her, moving along the perimeter until she neared several hedges that divided one property from the next. Looking for the lightest patch of growth, she pushed her way through and climbed a knee-length fence on the other side. Barastin was waiting for her, his form darting through the back door and into the house.

Setting her backpack down on the ground, she extracted the titanium tools she needed to pick the lock: the tension wrench first, followed by a rake with several ridges that meant she could lift multiple pins simultaneously inside the lock mechanic. She'd had to practise at home first, for hours, with most of the techniques taught online designed for people with two functioning hands. After many attempts she had learned she could do it just as effectively if the rake was positioned in her teeth and the other tool in her left hand.

She listened carefully, the sound of a metallic click telling her the lock had been released, and her gloved fingers twisted around the knob to be sure. The door pushed back, with a beeping immediately coming from the alarm system at the wall. She marched to it and hit the code, the display flashing green for a second to indicate that it was disabled. Standing there, she remained perfectly still for a moment as she took deep breaths, listening to the house and centring herself at the same time. Her pulse was racing and her heart was pounding beneath her breast, but this would only work if she remained calm.

'The motion detector is now a motion defector,' Barastin joked, pointing at a series of wires that jutted from a device in the corner of the room. She smiled at him, not really feeling it as she stepped back outside to grab her equipment.

'Weapons,' the female ghost said, when Corvossier returned. She followed the woman through the house, collecting two pistols and one shotgun from where they had been stashed by Mike for security. She packed them away, adding their ammunition to her bag as well. Moving slowly, she laid the items she needed out on the kitchen bench and slipped a facemask over her mouth and cable ties into her pocket. Taking a floral hand towel and what looked like a traveller's

size bottle of Dior perfume, Corvossier made her way towards
the bedroom. The ghost was hovering inside, her form floating up and down as if she was bouncing on the balls of her
feet with excitement. Mike was still asleep, his mouth open
and deep snoring sounds rolling from it. She tiptoed her way
to his side, careful not to trip a single piece of string or jingle
a lone bell. Internally, she was so happy to see him after all
these months of searching that she wanted to cry. She could
physically reach out and touch him if she wanted to. And
boy, did Corvossier want to.

'Five, four, three,' her brother said, counting her down.
'Two, one.'

She pumped the contents of the perfume bottle liberally on
the hand towel until it was soaked, holding her own breath
out of habit. She dived on Mike's sleeping body, holding the
chloroformed material over his mouth and nose with her
hand, while immobilising the rest of him by pressing the
weight and length of her body over the top of his. He went to
jerk awake, but your first instinct when you do that is to take
a gulp of air – and his gulp was full of chemicals designed to
knock him out. She felt his limbs relax quickly underneath
her, waiting probably longer than she needed to before
moving off him.

'Atta girl,' Barastin said proudly, clapping his hands together.
'Now let's get him to the bathroom.'

It took some manoeuvring, but between her and Barastin
they got Mike Higgens' unconscious body into one of the steel
chairs she had dragged in from the kitchen. She took extra
time to make sure he was secure, first with cable ties connecting his hands and ankles to each other, then duct tape around

his thighs, midsection and forearms. Barastin tried to tell her that was overkill, but she thought it was just enough kill. Corvossier was not taking chances.

Content that he wouldn't be going anywhere, she took the Beretta from under his pillow and located the extra rounds for it as well. Placing them in her backpack, she moved around the house pulling the blinds shut and locking the back door. The siblings used the chair to drag Mike to the bathroom, positioning it over a drain built into the white, tiled floor. Peeling off the facemask, she dumped it, the towel, and chloroform into a paper bag in the kitchen sink before returning to their subject. It was time to wake him up.

'Let's move it,' Barastin said.

Corvossier glanced at the ghost of the woman who had witnessed the whole thing. She nodded, indicating that she would stay with the medium's body while she followed her brother. Letting go, she internally released the tethers that held her, leaving the bathroom and the unconscious Mike Higgens behind. It was true that only the dead could find a sense of direction in this place. Well, the dead and a skilled medium. She found Mike sitting on a chair in exactly the same position he was in the physical realm: head drooping down on to his chest, neck bent over. Barastin slapped him awake, delivering another blow when he didn't stir fast enough.

'W-what . . . where . . .? Oh my God.'

'Remember me?' her brother asked. 'Of course we only knew each other for a day before you had me slaughtered, but I assume that probably makes me pretty memorable in someone's mind.'

'You're ... you're dead! I saw you die! I saw the pieces! Wait, am I dead?'

He shifted on the chair, realising that he wasn't restrained. He processed Corvossier and then their surroundings, confusion drowning him inside and out.

'*Am I dead?*'

'Not yet,' she answered. 'You're unconscious, technically.'

'Then how are you—'

'This is where you go, Mike,' Barastin cut in. 'You can find lots of interesting people here; those in a coma, those trapped forever unable to pass through, and you, now.'

'This is purgatory?'

'Yeesh,' Barastin scoffed. 'He's Catholic?'

Corvossier shrugged. 'Like it matters.'

'No, Mike. This isn't purgatory. This is the lobby. You wait here until you're called somewhere. Sometimes you're not and you just end up waiting for a room allocation, forever.'

'Forever?' he gasped.

'All eternity,' Corvossier answered. 'If you're lucky, a medium might help push you along. If they're feeling nice: but I'm not feeling particularly nice. Are you, brother?'

'I was never the nice one,' he replied. 'And especially since I'm dead, I don't have much incentive for seeing you go either way, frankly.'

'You're just going to leave me here? You can't!'

Barastin smiled, a gesture that showed all of his teeth and somehow managed to keep his eyes entirely cold.

'Do you remember what happened to me? Did you stay for that part? Did my blood splash up on to the sole of your shoe as you listened to me get hacked to pieces?'

'I . . .'

'Look at me,' he said. 'This is the only place where I'm whole. Back in her world, I'm a ghost held together by sheer will. And I could leave if I wanted to, release myself and surrender to the pull. But there are things I want to do, Mike: to you specifically. Now my sister is sans a hand because of your robed pals. She's gonna let me do what I want and I can assure you, I will do what *I* want for a *very* long time. That duration is reliant on the answers you give.'

'Please—'

'You can scream all you want, in here it makes no difference. But out there you're silent, understand?'

He nodded his head frantically, stiffening when Barastin slipped a finger under his chin to hold it still. Corvossier let herself pull back, the scene fading slowly as she gave in to the anchor of her body. Mike saw her leaving and shouted, screamed, begged for her to stay. Barastin remained with him, grinning as she left the pair of them alone in the dark.

She felt her feet under her and the return of gravity as her eyelids flung open. It didn't take long for Mike to snap back to consciousness in the real world as well, his eyes wild as soon as he saw her. He attempted to thrash around in the chair and pull against his restraints. Mike was done up tight and despite his desperation, he must have known he wasn't moving from the bathroom. Sweat was pouring from every possible inch of his body as she lifted the wig from her head and let it drop to the ground. Her white hair fell free and trailed behind her like a ghostly curtain. She knew it unsettled people for the same reason her eyes did and in that specific moment, it gave her power.

'Hello *Mike*,' she purred, leaning low so their eyes were level. She sniffed, curling up her nose in disgust.

'He pissed himself,' Barastin said.

'Ergh.'

Stepping back until she was shoulder to shoulder with her brother, she assessed the man in front of them. He had lost a dramatic amount of weight, looking like there wasn't enough skin to stretch over his skeleton. He'd shaved his head, losing the curls he'd had when she'd known him. Barastin began moving around Mike and it was a strange thing to watch: someone treading water while unbeknownst to them a shark was circling the entire time. His screams were muffled through the duct tape and she held up a finger to her lips as a reminder.

'Remember what we discussed?' she asked him, his head nodding up and down enthusiastically.

'He won't scream,' her brother said. 'He knows what happens if he screams, don't you?'

Mike froze, his eyes wide with horror. They were fixed on Barastin and remained so as Corvossier inched forward and ripped the tape from his mouth.

'Do anything we don't like, make a noise we don't want or answer a question too slowly, and I'll be waiting for you on the other side,' Barastin said.

'I understand,' he whispered, the words barely more than breathy panic.

'Don't look at him,' Corvossier snapped. 'Look at me.'

She pulled back the sleeve of her shirt, exposing the cosmetic prosthesis where her arm used to be. Carefully, she pulled it free so the white skin of her right side was clearly visible. Mike whimpered as she held it closer to him, making sure he *really* looked at her.

'You know what we want to know,' Barastin said.

'Who are the people in the robes?' Corvossier asked.

He gulped, a droplet of sweat streaking down the side of his face.

'T-they call themselves Oct, *the* Oct.'

'Never trust anyone who gives themselves their own nick-name,' her brother scoffed.

Corvossier ignored him. 'How many of them are there?'

'There are ten of them, there has to be ten.'

'And what are you?

'On . . . on the bench.'

'What?' Barastin spat.

'I am!' Mike cried. 'There's four of us, myself and the three who took Collette. We do jobs for them and tasks in the hope that if one of them is unable to complete the transformation, we would take their place.'

'Ten of them and four Igors,' Corvossier repeated.

'Only two now,' Mike corrected. 'There were four, but two were killed.'

'By the Oct?'

'No.' He laughed. 'By the other *one*: Hans Guilford. Who do you think I'm on the run from? The Treize are the least of my problems.'

'Hang on,' Corvossier said. 'The other one like you . . . he's killing you off? Why?'

'If there's less people on the bench, you're the one who will get called up,' Barastin offered. 'It improves your odds.'

Mike nodded. 'And the Oct don't care. He killed Cici and

Irish, but it doesn't matter to them. So long as there's someone to do the jobs they need them to do, when they need them done, well . . .'

'It was your job to package us up and lead us to them,' Corvossier said.

He gulped, nodding. 'Yes.'

'And you knew what would happen?'

'Yes.'

'Why do it? What do they offer?'

He opened his mouth to respond, but stopped himself. He pressed his lips shut, sealing the line of his mouth.

Reaching for the gun at her hip, she pulled it free and swung it above her head so that it whipped his face.

He yelped, clearly surprised at her outburst as blood sprung from a cut above his eyebrow.

Corvossier inched forwards, pressing her finger hard into the edge of the laceration so that Mike bit his lip in order to prevent himself crying out in pain.

'What. Do. They. Offer?'

'They're evolving, becoming more than human.'

'Are they even human to begin with?'

'Yes,' he puffed, his breathing growing erratic as she pushed down on the cut again. 'They were Askari!'

'What?' Barastin snapped. 'What do you mean?'

'That's how they all met. I don't know their real names, but two of them were Askari and that's how they discovered it: a way to be more than human. To change.'

Corvossier glanced at her brother and he shook his head. 'I've never heard anything about this.'

'Why would you?' Mike laughed. 'Nobody knows.'

'Change into what?' she asked.

'More,' he chuckled. 'Just *more*.'

'Knock him out,' her brother said.

'No, wai—'

His protests were cut short, Corvossier using the metal of the gun to render him unconscious, her left arm flying in a blur of motion as Mike's lights went out. Barastin didn't leave her side, the two siblings standing there in the bathroom as they worked through their thoughts.

'You didn't know they were Askari?' she asked.

'How would I know? I didn't see any of their tattoos. Did you?'

'No. And they didn't move like Askari.'

'Which means what?' Barastin questioned.

'Like *people*, like everyday regular people.'

'There are some supernatural Askari, but the majority are humans who intersect with our world and want to work their way up.'

'The Treize must know,' she said, leaning on the basin. 'They must know something; why else would they push this witch line so hard?'

'Because it's easy?' Barastin offered. 'They've never considered witches a real threat to their power: they stepped in centuries too late to stop the humans' persecution of them, and they have no witches higher up. You remember Bamberg, when we were kids?'

'How could I forget?' she murmured, her mind dragging her back there against her will. She and Barastin had both just turned fourteen, with Collette taking them on a week-long vacation to Luxembourg to celebrate. They had driven, with their Custodian stopping at small towns along the way, to really make an adventure of it. One of those towns had been Bamberg, a picturesque place that sat near the convergence of two rivers: the Regnitz and the Main.

It had been spring, with water bubbling through the centre of town and under arched bridges where medieval-looking buildings perched precariously near the edge. Within the first five minutes of their arrival, Barastin and Corvossier had both known something was wrong. In old, heritage-listed towns like Bamberg, there were bound to be ghosts: there were ghosts everywhere in her country. But the place had been drowning in them, the figures of mostly women and young children immediately drawn to the twins as they sensed their power. Collette had been strolling ahead of them, happily chatting about a popular bakery she'd heard about, while unbeknownst to her a procession had formed behind Barastin and Corvossier as they walked.

It turned out Bamberg had been the site for one of largest witch trials in Germany in the sixteen hundreds, with Corvossier estimating over a thousand people had been executed, judging by the sheer number of ghosts. It had been overwhelming for both her and her brother, especially since there had been no one to teach them about their abilities growing up. They'd had to learn everything for themselves, mostly by trial and error. They'd been young and adventurous, just pushing boundaries until they found where the limits of their capabilities were and sometimes that was terrifying. The only perk had been that they had each other. Whenever things got too scary or they became afraid of losing themselves in the realm of the dead, there had been someone watching the other one's back.

They'd had to leave Bamberg quickly; it had been too much for either of them to handle. Barastin was practically hyperventilating by the time they got back to the car, Collette not understanding the sheer panic as Corvossier urged her to drive onwards. Not everyone who died became a ghost and not everyone who was murdered became one either; just like not everyone who had been killed at Bamberg had been a witch. Some had been; most had not.

What they all had in common, however, was mass displacement. They had been trapped, wandering the streets of the same town they had been killed in for centuries, watching it change around them while they never changed themselves. In the hospital when Heath had first said the Treize were claiming witches killed her brother and Collette, she had made it crystal clear she didn't agree. From the moment the words were out of his mouth, she knew they were wrong. She'd never told him why, but the witches she and Barastin encountered in Bamberg were a big part of that.

'Bring him back,' she told her brother, her mind half in her memories and half in the present. 'We have more questions.'

Barastin dipped away momentarily, returning just as Mike threw his head back with a gulp of air, his eyes twitching with the pain as he returned to the room.

'Where's my brother's body?' she asked. 'Where's my hand?'

'They . . . they took them.'

'I know that, but where?'

'They needed them. They were ingredients.'

'I . . . ingredients? For what?!'

'To transform! They have to kill specific targets, that's how they move on to the next step: there are rituals, processes, things that have to be performed. It can't be rushed or it won't work.'

'And they haven't evolved yet?'

'No, it takes years if they do it right. And they haven't got everything they need.'

'How is this funded?' Barastin scoffed. 'How has this stayed under the radar for so long?'

'There are no bodies if they're successful, no witnesses, no survivors . . . usually. The targets are different, and the hunting grounds: you wouldn't even know what to look for.'

'What about Collette?' Barastin growled. 'Why kill her?'

'Because they asked us to,' Mike replied, blood dribbling over his lips. 'I swear . . . I *swear* that's all I know.'

His eyes had taken a crazed quality and Corvossier wondered how much more they would be able to get out of him. They had hurt him in both the physical and spiritual worlds: the human mind could only take so much. Mike was panting, his eyes darting from Corvossier to Barastin and back again with a desperate hopefulness. He thought they were going to leave him there, she realised. She watched what life was left drain from his face as she cocked her weapon and aimed it square at his head. His eyebrows shot up, the words 'no, no, no' flowing from his lips in a stream.

'YOU'RE NOT THE ONLY ONE!'

She hesitated. 'What?'

'Th-there was another, another survivor.'

'He's lying,' Barastin muttered.

'I'm not! There was another, strong like you.'

'Who?' Corvossier pushed, not wanting to waste anymore time.

'A witch, from Australia. Her name was Kala Tully.'

'*Was?* If she survived, then why are you using past tense?'

'Because she disappeared, okay? That's all I know! They tried to get her and she fought them and escaped, like you did. She was never seen again and they spent months trying to find her. She just vanished.'

'She was smart,' Barastin whispered.

'When was this?' Corvossier snapped.

'Six months before the Berlin attack.'

Her finger twitched towards the trigger, the slightest hesitation dancing through her mind. She dealt with the dead all the time, but delivering them to this state ... that was different. She took a breath, feeling pain and anguish coil up inside of her. *You're not the only one.* That meant others had been through what she had. Worse, others had suffered the same fate as her brother. Barastin was waiting for her to deliver Mike to him and if there's one thing she never did, it was let her brother down.

She squeezed the trigger, using her right arm to steady herself as she fired one bullet directly at her target. He was too close and the blood sprayed back on her face. She closed her eyes, shutting herself off from the sight for just a moment. There was immediate silence: complete and utter silence. Opening her eyes, Mike's tied-up body hung limp with his brains splattered over the bathroom wall. Barastin disappeared and she knew what he was doing: tracking Mike's journey.

'Well,' the female ghost said, their mostly silent witness. 'He's dead.'

Tucking her gun back into the holster, she felt something close to satisfaction, although she wouldn't exactly describe it as that. There was pain as well. She waited until Barastin returned, giving her nod to indicate Mike had truly gone.

'What now?' she asked him, feeling somewhat like a helpless child. 'Do we get rid of the body?'

'I think not,' her brother answered, looking thoughtful. 'We leave it for someone else to find, specifically this other "assistant" who was on his tail. It will give him a rough idea of what's coming.'

'Send a message?'

'In a manner of speaking. We don't know how else to find this Hans Guilford; now we have the perfect draw card.'

Corvossier stooped down to grab the wig, leaving the bathroom and tucking her hair back under the disguise. She readjusted her glasses and attached her arm, not saying a word as she packed up all of her things left in the kitchen. She took off her clothes, placing them in the paper bag with the towel and chloroform, before changing into fresh ones.

Resetting the alarm, she walked out of the back door with Barastin and the female ghost alongside her. Corvossier's legs felt unsteady as her body tried to adjust to everything that had just happened. Her brother hung back, talking quietly to the other ghost about keeping an eye on the house. Throwing her gloves into the paper bag as well, she crouched next to a tree and created a small mound among the brush. Pulling out a lighter, she was careful as she poured accelerant over the bag and set it alight. Standing back, she stared as the flames took hold. It was a small fire, growing steadily as the heat consumed the bag and its contents. She stood by and watched for a long while, until it had burned itself out and there was nothing remaining but a smouldering pile of ash. Kicking several damp leaves over the top, she marched from the woods and pulled the hood of her coat up over her head.

Ivan was waiting in the cab, two houses down from where he had dropped her off. Silently she got in the back, the wheels moving forward before she had even finished closing the door. It didn't occur to her that she was supposed to say anything, with the surrounds flying by the window outside as Corvossier thought carefully about what to do with Hans Guilford.

'You have blood on you.'

She stirred, casting her eyes forward towards the driver. Ivan hadn't taken his eyes off the road; in fact, she was certain he had barely looked at her.

'Excuse me?'

'Blood. You have it on you.'

'Where?' she asked, certain she had been careful enough and it wasn't on her clothing.

'I don't know, but I can smell it.'

Pulling a handheld mirror from her bag, she inspected her reflection. Several splatters of Mike's blood dotted her cheek, like grim freckles. She scrubbed herself clean with a make-up wipe, double-checking her neck and hands once more.

'You got it,' he informed her.

'You can ... are you a werewolf?'

'Nope.'

His response stumped her, Corvossier's brain working over-time to think of any other kind of supernatural whose sense of smell was as keenly focused as a lycanthrope. Ghouls were practically blind, with slits for noses and relying almost entirely on hunting their prey via scent and sound. Yet ghouls couldn't pass for human, not even close, and they didn't have the intelligence either. She examined the man's appearance from behind, the thick grey sideburns that crept down his face and the tufts of hair that seemed to grow away from his scalp in a horizontal fashion. There was something distinctly wild about him, something she couldn't place.

'You're a shifter.'

'Correct.'

'What kind?' she asked, wondering what species were native to the area.

'Lynx,' Ivan answered. 'My ancestors have lived in these parts for nearly a millennia.'

'The Latvian lynx,' Corvossier murmured, liking the way it sounded. A light rain began falling, the noise as it connected with the exterior of the car soothing. Barastin had arrived beside her just in time for the alliteration, keeping himself visible only to her.

'Ivan, if you don't mind me asking, what is it you do for a living?'

'This,' he said. 'Errands for people who are willing to pay.'

'Illegal errands?'

'Almost exclusively, yes.'

'And your family, what do they do?'

'A bit of this,' he answered. 'A bit of that.'

'Uh oh, what are you thinking?' Barastin asked.

'And you're local? You live and work locally?'

'Yes, we do.'

'I may have another job for you, if you want it. It will require more than one of you, however.'

Ivan swivelled around in his seat, glancing at her for a second before turning back to the road.

'Alright. Guess we better talk.'

He indicated off the main road, taking several side streets before pulling into the car park of what looked like a community hall.

'Let me go in first,' he said, dashing from the vehicle and through the rain.

'Follow him,' Corvossier ordered her brother, Barastin vanishing for a stretch of minutes that felt painfully long to her. When he came back, she exhaled.

'His brother-in-law, a cousin and someone I think is just a family friend are sitting at a table right now deciding whether to meet you or not.'

'Is it safe?'

'I don't know how to tell you this but, well, it's a bingo hall.'

'What?'

'Yeah, smells like old people in there: old people and shifters. Plus, they all look like lumberjacks.'

'*Is it safe?*' she repeated, urging him to stay on point.

'If you don't call bingo, sure.'

When Ivan returned, he was carrying an umbrella. He held it out for her as she followed him inside, her shoes wet as she walked through the puddles. Barastin's description was not inaccurate: she found herself looking at a sea of grey, blue and bald heads sitting at long, plastic-folding tables in unforgiving fluorescent light. There was a woman standing at the front of the hall, calling out numbers over a microphone as she pulled the wooden balls from the cage, one by one. She was wearing an intense knitted sweater that Corvossier thought depicted a demented rendering of a cat, only to realise it was actually a lynx.

'Young and keen, it's number fifteen,' the woman said in a deep monotone, her eyes tracking Corvossier in a way that made her nervous.

Ivan brought her to a table separate from the others in the hall, which was occupied by three men and scattered with bingo sheets, glasses of beer and ashtrays. She took the seat one of the gents offered her, politely declining the question of whether she would like a drink as there seemed to be only one type of beverage on offer. Corvossier hated beer and she didn't enjoy the thought of alcohol coursing through her system in that moment either. Each of the men looked like slightly different versions of Ivan, all of them short and gruff, with scratchy looking stubble and – in the case of one of them – an impressive beard.

'What can we do for you, Miss . . .'

'Mrs,' she corrected. 'Mrs Tori D'Cruz.'

'Mrs D'Cruz, right,' the man said, smiling. 'I'm Ivan. To my left is Ivan, next to you is Ivan and I believe you've already met Ivan.'

'I have, yes.'

'We hear you might have a job?'

'I'm expecting someone to show up at this address in the coming days,' she muttered, sliding a piece of paper across the table with the address written on it.

'The cops?' one of them asked.

'Very much no,' she replied. 'A man called Hans Guilford.'

'Is he dangerous?'

'Yes. But he's also not expecting to find what he'll discover there.'

'A body,' Ivan, her driver, stated.

'Yes,' she answered, seeing no reason to lie since he had already smelled the blood on her. 'Hans is going to that address to kill the man who was living there.'

'Bait,' Ivan number two snickered. 'You want us to watch the house?'

'I want you to take him at the house. I already have someone who can alert you to his presence, so all you would need to do is be nearby.'

'If someone is already inside the house, why do you need us?'

'That person is a ghost. They cannot take physical form. They're strong enough to be seen by you, speak to you, but that's it.'

'A *gho—*'

That Ivan was shut up by her driver, with a swift kick under the table.

'I need utmost discretion,' she said. 'And I'm willing to pay for it.'

'You want us to punctate this person?'

'No.' Corvossier smiled, amused by the language. 'I would like you to retain them until I'm able to be there in person. That should be no more than twelve hours.'

'Alright. With the materials and the manpower, how does this sound?'

One of them wrote a figure down with a bright red marker designed for circling digits and showed it to her.

'Haggle,' Barastin said. 'They won't respect you if you don't.'

'Make it five,' she said, holding up her hand as the man opened his mouth to object. 'And I can throw in four clean weapons, with ammunition.'

'Shit, girl, what was in that house?'

'Just a corpse now. Do we have a deal?'

They glanced at each other, silently having a discussion with their eyes. They came to a resolution, turning back to her with a head jerk of approval.

'Done.'

'You can reach me on this number,' Corvossier said, writing down the digits for her burner phone. 'Now if you'll excuse me, I have a flight to catch.'

They muttered their shared goodbyes, three Ivans remaining behind and one taking her back to the car. As they drove, she offloaded the weapons she had promised as part of the arrangement. She packed the Witness Elite back into its case, sliding it under the seat and placing the others into a canvas bag Ivan provided. When they pulled into the public drop-off area, the lynx shifter told her he would be in touch. She thanked him, silently hoping it would be soon.

As she followed the throng of people heading to the departures, Corvossier wasn't sure what Hans would know. At the very least, interrogating him could corroborate some of what Mike had said, and, at the most, she had the opportunity to learn more.

Her flight was delayed by an hour, but it made little difference to her mood. When she touched back down in Berlin, it was relieving and frustrating to be home again. She thought she would have been coming back with all the answers she wanted, not more questions. And yet . . . Taking a fragmented route, she switched her clothing once more and ditched the wig in a public bathroom. She felt immediately better to be dressed as herself as she walked into the Berlin City Library, her eyes scanning the desks until she found a free computer.

Sliding into the empty seat, she brought up a search engine and typed the name 'Kala Tully'. There was very little, but she hoped adding 'Australia' would improve things. The results were a lot of unrelated pages, including an accountancy firm that seemed to be based in Sydney, but when she clicked into it she couldn't find any mention of the witch who had bested the Oct. She felt the presence of her brother at her back as she continued digging, checking the other sites and then social media for any trace of this woman. There was a crackle across the loudspeaker telling those inside the library that it would be closing in twenty minutes. Grabbing her things, she took the long way out: weaving through the stacks and the desks and trolleys of books.

'He's gone,' Barastin said, relief crisp in his voice. 'I can't believe Mike's really gone. And *we* did it.'

'I know,' she replied, feeling like there was more he had to say.

'Thank you,' he added, her skin prickling with the sensation of him attempting to touch her. She stopped walking so she could turn to him and examine his face. The pain there was raw and difficult for her to look at, but she forced herself to.

'I would do anything for you,' she said.

'And I you.'

She smiled, continuing her path to the exit.

'What now?' he asked.

'Now—' she sighed '—if we want the rest of them, I need to find this witch.'

Chapter 5

No one cared where Corvossier had been: no one even paid attention as she strolled back in to the Bierpinsel late that evening, the building its usual hum of activity. Phones rang and people called back and forth to each other as she walked through the maze of Askari and Custodian desks. She felt different about it now, knowing the people under those robes in the alley had once been just like them. The Praetorian Guard's floor was almost entirely empty save for two women running through fight drills in the training area. She knew she would be left alone and she welcomed it, closing the door to the living quarters behind her and seizing the solace. She reorganised her emergency bag, switching out her alternate forms of identification and adding the leftover cash back to where she had taken it from. She double-checked the stairwell for signs of disturbance – nothing – then moved everything else back in place exactly the way it was. Switching on her normal phone, she left it on the coffee table in the lounge while she took a long, cleansing shower.

There was something soothing about standing in front of the mirror, naked, and taking her time to brush through the knots in her long, wet hair as it fell past her waist. When he was alive, Barastin had been pushing for her to 'switch it up' and get a messy bob. The reality was Corvossier didn't know who she was without her hair, which she knew sounded silly, but it comforted her: the sensation of it brushing against her back or wrapping around her arms like a vine. It was a chilly night and she switched on several heaters as she walked back to her bedroom, pulling on a pair of woolly pyjamas in deep red.

Snatching up her dirty laundry, she occupied herself with a meaningless task as she threw in her clothes from that day as well and turned on the washing machine. She caught herself standing there, listening to the sound of water as it filled the inside, her mind back in Riga.

A sob wracked her body, seemingly from nowhere, and she couldn't bring herself to stop it. The whooshing of clothes being cleaned covered the noise for the most part as she let herself feel everything for just a moment. It had been a long while since she had let herself cry like this, sinking to the ground as the emotions fought for dominance inside her body. At first there was grief, always just simmering below the surface, but mixed among it this time was relief. She had killed Mike Higgens and it brought her *pleasure*. That scared her more than she cared to admit.

She yanked her prosthesis from her arm, throwing it across the room as she rested her head in her hand. Corvossier stayed like that for a long while, her cries finally settling down but her body shuddering again every few seconds with the after-shock. Sniffing, she brushed back her hair and leaned against the vibrating washing machine. Barastin was watching her from across the bathroom, his body crouched in an almost-identical position to hers. She met his stare, not wanting to think how she must look to him.

'Get back on your feet,' he told her, voice soft with understanding, 'and pour yourself a drink.'

'Yes, brother.'

He reached towards her, allowing himself to physically manifest in a way few ghosts could. His spectral hand dragged her upright, Corvossier stumbling for a second until she found her bearings. In the kitchen, she squeezed some juice from the last of the limes in the fridge and made herself a Gin Gimlet. She sipped it slowly, carrying the glass with her as she walked around the empty apartment.

Both siblings had an extensive library, with almost an entire wall dedicated to books in their private quarters, most of them for pleasure. Their former Custodian, on the other hand, had a collection that would make most librarians weep. Besides what was in the spare room, the hallways around the building on their floor were lined with shelves that ran at hip height. They were reference books mostly, things that Collette had either collected or found useful in her day to day. From tomes on werewolf coming-of-age rituals to the history of the Treize, there was almost anything one could want and *still* Corvossier knew this was just a limited view of what was documented about their world.

'Do we have anything on witches?' she asked, her fingers skimming the spines as she looked for the right title.

'Not on my shelves and definitely not on yours.'

'I meant in Collette's collection.'

'Oh, probably, yes.'

'Would she have organised these by author, title or subject?'

'By author, looks like.' Barastin sighed. 'Given she was the only one who really used these, she would have likely known who had written about what.'

Corvossier began properly scanning the shelves, shuffling along the wall as she made her way down the line of the books, pulling volumes and inspecting their contents. When the Eagles started playing in the background, she knew Barastin had taken care of the music like he usually did. Whatever band came out of the speakers, that was usually a good indication of her brother's mood. That night it was the opening chords of *Witchy Woman* and she smiled. Of the thousands of books they owned between the three of them, the pile that Corvossier assembled looked rather pitiful. She glanced at the five volumes beside her, draining the rest of her drink and feeling like the last thing she wanted to do in the world was read them. As if her body agreed with her, Corvossier's stomach emitted a deep growl. She couldn't remember the last time she'd eaten: maybe a muesli bar on the plane that morning? Her nerves were shot and they'd suppressed her appetite most of the day.

Within twenty minutes she was dressed, throwing on an enormous, thick trench coat that had once been Barastin's over a velvet dress. It was freezing outside, with Corvossier layering thick socks under her boots for extra protection. She stopped in at an enormous Bavarian hall on her way, the place so large she was anonymous among the nightly crowd of hundreds. She sat at the corner of a wooden bench by herself and quietly ate a meal of sausages and sauerkraut. The roar of people laughing, talking and drinking around her provided a soothing kind of white noise. When she was done, she took a wide loop around the city streets so that she ended up at 1984 just before they were about to close for the night. The woman who was always there – hair stiff and horns hidden – paused as she went to lift one of the benches inside. Any regular person would have torn the muscles in their back trying to move the stone structure, but she appeared unbothered as she watched Corvossier approach.

'We're about to shut.'

'I'll just be a moment,' Corvossier replied.

'Alright. You know where he is.'

'Thanks, Ginger.'

The woman looked surprised that Corvossier knew her name, her drawn eyebrows arching together with shock. Sure enough, Hogan was spending time with the Hoff, smashing levers and shouting in frustration as he competed to get the game's highest score. The fact that the only person he was competing with was himself didn't seem to matter much to the goblin, with his name proudly displayed next to the top seven figures.

'Casper,' he barked, groaning as the pinball slipped through his clutches.

'Hogan. Is it ready?'

'Yup, let's go. I'm not gonna get there tonight.'

Annoyed, he pushed himself away from the machine and headed towards his usual haunt. He grabbed a USB from his computer, handing it to her.

'You need to insert this into an Askari terminal at the Bierpinsel,' he said. 'Not a Custodian or Praetorian Guard soldier . . . an Askari.'

'Because they have different systems.'

'That's right.'

'Look at you go, IT girl,' Barastin said, Corvossier clicking her tongue at him so she could concentrate on what Hogan was saying.

'You'll need to open the file saved on here and run a program called Sesame. It's the only thing on the USB, so you can't confuse it with anything else.'

'How long will that take?'

'Two minutes at the most. A window will pop up telling you when it's completed.'

'Are you sure you can do this?' Barastin continued. 'You don't even have Instagram.'

'Take the USB out, then open this baby up,' Hogan said, flipping open the laptop he had constructed just for her. She watched him navigate his way around the desktop, clicking an icon that read 'Open'.

'I've arranged it to look like just any other laptop: it functions like one as well and has all your usual programs. When you click on this though, and hit the "run diagnostics" button in the drop-down box, what you see now will cease to exist. You'll have a mirror of the Askari computer.'

'How does that work exactly?'

'It's some back-end software I developed and I don't need to get into it unless you'll pretend to be suitably impressed, but basically you can move about and access everything an Askari would be able to access at that terminal: databases, archive files, you name it.'

'Can I enter information?'

'Yeah, but why would you need to? The aim is to remain unseen for as long as possible, ideally forever. Or until they improve their security systems.'

'And this won't show up on the original person's computer? They won't be watching me move their mouse without agency?'

'Nope.' He grinned. 'That's the beauty of it: it's one portal. Only thing you need is an internet connection, this laptop, and you'll have access anywhere. Well, maybe not remote parts of Australia. I hear their internet's shit.'

His comment surprised her, tugging on her thoughts about Kala Tully. She watched him pack up the laptop with one hand, fishing a fork into a pot of noodles with the other.

'What do you know about witches?' she asked out the blue, causing Hogan to choke on a mouthful.

'Witches? As in, the people who did that to you?' he said, gesturing to her arm.

'Sure.'

'I'm eighty-two and I've never met one, which tells you plenty right there.'

'How so?'

'There aren't that many. And the ones that there are, they're specific about where they live: it's either big cities or places with magical significance.'

She nodded. 'I understand that. Safety in numbers, especially when you have a history of being persecuted.'

'Right. I mean, it's the same with werewolves: they like to stay close to their territories and the ones that don't – rogue wolves – they're the exception, not the norm.'

'Have you ever heard of a male witch?'

'No,' he said, shaking his head. 'It's passed down through the female line, so males can carry the witchcraft gene but it's not active. Like haemochromatosis.'

'What's that?'

'A blood disease humans get: too much iron. You know, when I was a kid the Treize thought witches could only be born on the thirteenth of each month.'

'What?'

'You have to understand, this was before they had any idea about what made one person a selkie and one person a sprite, or one person a demon and another a banshee. They suspected it was genetics, but they didn't have the tools to prove it yet. And they had trouble explaining how a daughter born into a seemingly normal family – non-witch mother, non-witch father – could end up being a witch.'

'That's their own fault,' Corvossier muttered. 'You show people it's dangerous to be who they are and then lend them little support when humans start burning them at the stake? It's no wonder they're secretive about saying, "oh hey, I'm a sister of the night".'

'None of them say they're a sister of the night.' He smirked, Corvossier taking the laptop from him. 'And hey, Rowdie has an interview at Phases next week. Thanks for that.'

'Thanks for this,' she said, gesturing to the USB.

'You paid for it.'

She nodded, taking the stairs up out of his basement den while he remained down there by himself. Ginger was waiting at the entry to let her out, locking the door behind her as she stepped outside.

'I can't believe he's eighty-two and looks like that.' Barastin sighed. 'Meanwhile, I'm here, gorgeous and dead.'

'Goblins don't live forever,' she replied. 'Hogan will join you one day.'

'They live long enough. You know, Collette reckons their

lifespan is about three hundred years on average. She said she knew one who managed books for the Treize, who was at least three hundred and twenty.'

'What's your point?'

'Most of them don't even avoid UV rays. It's unfair.'

She smiled, her brother dancing ahead of her and checking around a corner before she turned it. The Bierpinsel was in sight now, only a dim glow coming from the windows at the middle of the tower above her. Corvossier's thumb ran over the USB in her hand, her mind repeating the instructions Hogan had given her. The question she had been asking herself since Mike had first told her about the witch was how on earth was she going to find this Kala Tully? The only confirmation she had the woman was even still alive was the Oct hadn't given up looking for her. She and this witch, wherever she was, shared a unique and horrible bond. They had both escaped fates no innocent being deserved. Glancing over at her brother as she walked up the ramp towards the entrance elevator, Corvossier wondered if the witch had fared a little better than they had in the fight. Yet now she had a resource to find out: the only other thing she needed was an opportunity to put it in play.

The night security guard was Paddy, who chatted to her insistently about a football match between two teams she didn't care about as she rode to the first floor. It was past 1 a.m. by that point and Corvossier's eyes ran over the row of Askari desks as the elevator doors pinged open. Paddy bid her farewell and she mumbled a response, not entirely sure what she said. She was working up the courage to make her move, watching the five heads that were crouched over their keyboards and working by lamplight. There was one furthest away from the others, his name something like Tande, she couldn't quite remember. She skirted her way along the perimeter, liking the placement of his desk and how close it was to the spiral staircase that led up to the Praetorian Guard's floor.

'Draw their attention,' she told Barastin, her lips barely moving as she said the words. 'Draw them away.'

He needed to take only one glance at her intended path before understanding perfectly. Her brother disappeared in a flash, Corvossier not looking towards the sound of a computer crashing to the ground, along with a collection of other items she guessed had all just been swept off a desk in one big effort. Her mouth twitched into a smile: Barastin never did anything in halves. She watched the male Askari leap to his feet, muttering something to one of his colleagues across the room before they rushed towards the commotion. Seamlessly she slid the USB into the port at his machine and took his seat all in one movement, her index finger tapping on the mouse until Sesame was up and running. She watched the staff crowding around the desk, the distinct smell of burning plastic rising from whatever had hit the ground with such force. Their heads were swivelling about, trying to find the source of what had caused an entire workstation to self-destruct. Corvossier's eyes darted back to the progress bar as it ticked to the thirty-six per cent mark.

'Hurry up,' she muttered, tapping her foot impatiently.

'Was that too much or not enough?' Barastin asked, appearing sprawled across the desk next to her like a life model.

'I'll let you know,' Corvossier whispered, watching as it loaded to fifty-two per cent.

'How's it going over there?'

She threw him an annoyed look. 'It's going.'

'Are we there yet? Huh? Are we there yeeeet?'

She felt heat rising in her cheeks, her eyes gaze flicking between the desk debris across the floor and the loading program: eighty-four, eighty-nine, ninety-five, ninety-six.

'Come on, come on,' she urged, her fingers hovering over the USB so she could yank it free the moment Sesame was completed.

'Ding ding ding!' Barastin shrieked, Corvossier feeling relief as she went to get to her feet. 'Wait.'

Her brother held up his hand to stop her, Corvossier remaining frozen where she was: hunched behind the monitor and shielded from view. There was another bang and a cry from one of the Asakri as they reacted to whatever Barastin had done now. He re-formed at her side, a bashful expression on his face.

'I had to,' he said. 'One of them was turning to look this way.'

'Can I move?'

'Yes, yes, go.'

She shot to her feet, not looking behind her as she dashed to the staircase and ascended it in a manner that was quick, but not too quick so that it was suspicious. She trusted Barastin to have her back, sensing that he was following behind her. There were more bodies on the Praetorian Guard level than below, but none of them even glanced her way as they went about their nightly duties. It was as if Corvossier was a ghost herself, something that was actually beneficial in the moment. Sealing the door to her private quarters, she wished there was a lock and felt a sense of annoyance at the security guidelines that insisted there never be one.

'It's for your own safety,' one of the soldiers had told her, when they'd done a sweep of the apartment after the attack to double and triple check for any potential weaknesses. 'We need to be able to get to you quickly if we have to.'

It was only because she'd been able to keep them out of Barastin's room that they hadn't found her investigation board. That's where she headed now, knowing that if her sanctuary was intruded upon, the line was always his doorway. She slid a chair under the knob for good measure, pulling up the painting to reveal all of their hard work at a glance.

Grabbing the laptop, she opened the icon Hogan had created, clicked 'run diagnostics', and waited for the program to whir into gear. As the seconds ticked by, she found herself drawn to the faces on the board. Grabbing a pen, she put a black cross through Mike Higgens picture. She badly sketched three more blank faces on cards, writing the name Hans Guilford under one, and Cici and Irish under the others. The last two were crossed out immediately according to Mike's testimony, but she put them on the board anyway along with Hans. There were question marks next to all of their names. As she settled into the chair at Collette's desk and wrapped the familiar smell of the woman around her, she vowed to resolve those question marks as she pulled the laptop towards her.

Chapter 6

Having grown up in Berlin, Corvossier knew the city streets intimately. She'd spent time exploring them with Collette as a child and then Barastin as a teen. They'd let the ghosts found along the way lead them to new places and avenues they would have never discovered otherwise. It was how she had found one of her favourite spots, Oslo Kaffebar, after she'd wandered through Planschbecken am Nordbahnhof following the ghost of a little girl.

It was only when she crossed over on to the street and the child remained where she was, that she realised the girl could not follow: she had died in that park and remained there. The smell of coffee beans brewing had drawn her across the path, and, given it had been the middle of summer, she had sat on a bench out the front of the café and drank her cappuccino as she watched the ghost dance and play by herself. Her name had been Jacinna and she wasn't there anymore, Corvossier had seen to that. But that hadn't stopped her coming to the café, where she now knew everyone by name and had a 'usual' order. She liked it best towards the back, past the rows of light wooden tables and one couch, to where there was a mustard-yellow seat positioned neatly between an overflowing collection of vinyl. Some nights, once the café had closed to the public, the staff would have their own kind of impromptu party and spin records until the small hours of the morning.

At 10 a.m., the work crowd had thinned out and the lunch influx was still a way off. It was the perfect opening for her to sit down, bleary-eyed, after a night of trawling through Askari records. She'd had only a few hours sleep, waking up with her face pressed into the keyboard shortly after 9 a.m. But Corvossier had spent a long time waiting for the kind of access she now had: she wasn't sure how long that window would remain open, so she wanted to make the most of it. With a steaming hot cappuccino next to her in a mug that more closely resembled a soup bowl, Corvossier rubbed her eyes as she opened up the laptop again.

So far, everything Mike had told her had been true. Cici and Irish turned out to be Cici Kulogvish and Irish Barber, the former based in Russia and the latter in Costa Rica. Hans Guilford had been transferred from Algeria to Iceland, all of them working Askari just like he had said: right up until the point of the Berlin attack. Whatever they'd done with the Oct prior, it had been low-key enough that they were able to maintain their cover and therefore access to the Treize systems and resources. Corvossier and Barastin weren't exactly under the radar, however, and after that job was only semi-successful, the four lackeys had gone to ground. Well, three of them had; Hans had begun the hunt.

Cici had been thrown from a bridge in Launceston, Tasmania, off the coast of Australia. Her death had come to the attention of local Askari only after a homicide investigation was commenced by human police. Before that, she had been put on leave from her Askari posting in Moscow for erratic behaviour. Irish was found mangled in a car wreck in Alaska. It was treated as accidental in reports filed by the State Troopers and the Askari had labelled it the same way. Clearly the people at the bottom didn't know what the people at the top did. Mike's whereabouts were listed as unknown, along with Hans. Mike had said the Oct were former Askari too, which meant they were in there, somewhere: she just had to find them.

Her starting point was Mike, Cici, Irish and Hans: in their records there must have been something that made them likely candidates. If you were still in the organisation, it wouldn't be that difficult to decide who to attempt to recruit by analysing psychological profiles, examining skillsets, seeing who harbours a particularly unhealthy obsession with the occult and who's hungry for power. It was likely there had been failed attempts: Askari who had given them a hard pass and ended up dead. It was just as likely she'd find a consistent name, someone who crossed paths with a few or each of them at some point, with their face belonging to one of the Oct pinned to her board. She hadn't been able to find them yet, but Corvossier was meticulous. She had relevant information documented in spreadsheets and folders of screenshots saved just in case she lost access.

She'd searched for the phrase 'the Oct' twenty different ways, trying different spelling and different languages, but nothing had surfaced in their records. To the Askari, they didn't exist. Just like Kala Tully . . . almost. Her cursor hovered over the file that held the witch's name. The picture was blurred in black and white, meaning that Corvossier couldn't even see what the woman looked like. She also couldn't gain entry to the file, a red warning box sitting at the top of the right hand corner telling her that permission was limited to on-site offices in Transylvania, Hatherleigh and Roodepoort. She knew the first was Treize headquarters in Romania and a quick Google search told her the other locations were based in the UK and South Africa respectively. Although the limited access meant she couldn't learn anything, it also told her a lot: Kala Tully was a real person. Kala Tully existed. Kala Tully's information was not for all eyes.

'Did you try just her last name?' Barastin asked, sitting nearby.

She threw him a look, not even dignifying his question with a response. She thought her glare communicated 'of course' clearly enough. That search had been blank too, not even the existence of a redacted Tully file able to tell her anything.

'I could look,' he offered.

Corvossier turned to him, her snarky response from earlier replaced with a thoughtful stare.

'If she has dead, I can find them and hope they're still trailing behind her.'

Corvossier nodded slightly, indicating that she agreed with his suggestion. Her brother hesitated.

'I might be gone for a while,' he said. 'This could take time; you know how witches are difficult.'

Her back stiffened at the thought of being alone, of being without Barastin for an unpredictable period of time. She didn't like it, but she also didn't have much choice. At the end of the day, she could utilise the ghost network for her other needs and safety while he was gone. They needed to find Kala Tully. They needed to know what she did and learn how she had escaped the Oct. It might be the only hope Corvossier and Barstin had. She reached her hand to her neck, where a small, silver letter 'b' was hanging off of a chain. Corvossier was someone who liked a lot of jewellery: she had six piercings in each ear, a myriad of rings and bracelets on every day, and didn't feel comfortable if she wasn't wearing at least one pendant. And she never took off her 'b' necklace: her brother had given it to her on their twenty-first birthdays and she had given him one with a 'c'. Barastin smiled, not needing to say anything else to understand how she felt. He disappeared in an instant, something she was used to but felt jarring in that moment.

Blinking back tears, Corvossier wished she hadn't been in a public café, surrounded by people, so she could have said something to him. But when she thought about what she would say, well, her mind came up blank. Slapping the laptop shut, she tried to keep herself busy by digesting everything held inside the pages of *A History of Witchcraft*. She slipped the dustcover of a tawdry romance over the top, hoping the artwork of a shirtless man with breasts larger than the heroine laying down on a bale of hay would be enough to prevent any curious glimpse at what she was reading. Frustratingly it was the only book in Collette's collection that covered the desired topic: there were thousands of books in their home, but just *one* on witches. She had tried to find relevant paragraphs in other volumes she'd pulled from the shelves, but that had proven fruitless.

'*What A Farmer Wants, A Farmer Will Have?*'

She glanced up, her shoulders tensing at the unwelcome company until she realised it was one of the waiters.

'Hot.' He nodded appreciatively, before moving on to clear the table next to her.

She smiled, averting her eyes and concentrating hard on the book in the hope he would go away. Eventually he did. The book had been little more than a recital of what human historical accounts said about witches, with a huge chunk of the page space being taken up by a verbatim reprinting of *Malleus Maleficarum* which, frankly, she felt was cheating on the word count.

The hammer of witches, she thought, noting the translated title sounded just as sinister as the original. She did find it interesting, however, that suspected werewolves were frequently persecuted alongside witches. In fact, there was a whole section dedicated to enlightening the reader on how to spot a werewolf – often redheads, apparently – and how to execute them. It intrigued Corvossier, as although werewolves were much more embedded in the supernatural community than witches were, they were notorious for their fraught relationship with the Treize and any official representing them. If they were tortured and executed by the humans alongside their supernatural counterparts, she had a better understanding of where their disdain for authority figures might come from.

Her phone buzzed, Corvossier confused for a moment as she looked at the device on the table next to her, which was perfectly still. Yet the vibration continued and she realised with a start it was actually coming from inside her jacket pocket, where she kept the burner. Glancing at the number, she knew that if a call was coming through it was only from one source: the lynxes in Latvia. Gathering her things in a rush, she practically sprinted from the café and across the road to the park, where she found a spot free of any people.

'Hello?' she answered, breathless.

'Mrs D'Cruz?'

'Yes, it's me, Ivan.'

'Great,' he said. The voice she recognised as belonging to her driver sounded relieved when she addressed him.

'Do you have him? I can be there in—'

'About that . . . do you want the good news first or the bad news?'

Her skin pricked with anticipation, noting the pressing silence in the background on Ivan's end.

'Good news.'

'The good news is we have him.'

'Oh thank God,' she breathed.

'The bad news is he's dead.'

'He's . . . *what*?'

'Yeah, your ghost friend got to us quickly, when he was still on approach. We were in the house minutes before he entered and he had no idea we were there for the most part. But the body you left had started to smell by then, even for a human. He was on his guard and when we attacked, he saw he was outnumbered.'

'Were you in lynx form?'

'Two were, two weren't. We thought that was best in case Hans had a weapon with him, which he did, as that would make it harder for him to use it on us.'

'And?'

'He didn't use it on us.'

It took a moment for his words to sink in, Corvossier finally registering the meaning. Without consciously intending to, she slipped away right there in the park until she was standing in the lobby.

'I wondered when you'd get here,' the female ghost said, rushing forward.

'How long ago did it happen?'

'Twenty minutes.'

'Twenty minutes!'

'I know, I told them to call you straight away but they snapped my head off and called me a poltergeist.'

'A polter – for fuck's sake, let me touch you.'

She remained still, Corvossier touching her fingertips to the woman's temple. They could physically interact here, on this plane, and she could tell just by the way the ghost's body stiffened that she had forgotten what it was like to be touched. Images flashed in front of her eyes, like a deck of cards being shuffled. The woman's real life mixed with her afterlife: moments of a child sprinting forwards with open arms, a husband embracing, an older woman crying, a tiny hand curling around an index finger. That morning was jumbled among it, with Corvossier focusing in on the hallway of the home she recognised. She watched the scene play out, Hans' hollowed eyes wide as he reacted to the presence of four lynx shifters and a ghost. Two of their number were non-verbal, springing into action and racing towards him in the limited space while the others crouched low, moving with their knuckles dragging along the ground.

He backed further into the bathroom, screaming something she couldn't process, his feet treading over dried blood. Hans shifted the gun from being aimed at them to aimed at his own head, the image cutting out as he pulled the trigger. Two men had died in that space, in mostly the same way, within a few days. Someone was going to have to cleanse that bathroom with more than holy water.

'He thought they were Praetorian Guard,' Corvossier said, lowering her hand. 'He didn't want to be taken alive.'

'You'll get nothing from me,' the ghost muttered. 'That's what he said.'

'They weren't soldiers for the Treize, but either way he was right.'

'How so?'

'We won't get anything from him.'

She turned around, searching the darkness behind them. There was fog encroaching on the horizon, slowly rolling closer as Corvossier took a step towards it. She needed to look, at the very least. A periphery search hadn't yielded the results she wanted and deep down, she knew he was gone. He'd died with purpose, intent, and at his own hand: it was unlikely Hans Guilford was a ghost. She hesitated, looking back at the woman who watched her.

'Hiralda. That was your name, wasn't it?'

'Y-yes,' she stammered, surprise painting her features.

'I'm sorry I didn't know that until now.'

'That's alright. It was an honour to help out, in any way.'

Corvossier smiled, sadness tinging the gesture. Hiralda had died far too soon and with no one else from her family dead to lead her away, she was truly alone.

'Someone will come,' she said. 'Not for a while, but someone will come.'

'I hope it's in a very, very long time.'

Corvossier backed away, her view of Hiralda obscured by the fog as it moved between them, the woman's form growing less visible with each passing moment. Eventually she was entombed in a wall of white, it almost blinding in contrast to where she had been standing.

'Hans Guilford,' she said, making one final effort as she begun to feel the limbs of her body sitting on the park bench. The words fell flat, sounding hollow as she spoke them. *He's gone*, she thought, annoyed at the injustice of some finding finality so quickly while others were left with an indefinite existence.

'Hello? Hello? I don't think she's there.'

The tin-sounding voice shook Corvossier back to her present setting: the park, the secluded spot, and Ivan's voice coming from the phone she had dropped on the ground. Bending down to pick it up, she cleared her throat as she went to answer him.

'I'm here, sorry.'

'Not a time to put us on hold, love.'

'I didn't mean to; I dropped the phone. My apologies.'

'I was asking what do we do now? This was our stuff up, so we're happy to get rid of both the bodies for no extra charge.'

'Both of them?'

'Eh, why not? It's just as easy to dispose of two as it is one.'

'I don't know if that's true, but sure. Go ahead. Hiralda is likely to stick around, in case you need anything.'

'Hiralda?'

'The ghost.'

'Right. She's handy. Listen, half the payment came through—'

'The rest will be transferred to you now.'

'Great. Well, sorry it didn't work out the way you wanted.'

'That's okay.'

'Be seeing you.'

'I hope not.'

There was a weight on her chest as she hung up the phone and Corvossier knew exactly what it was. There was a shining, gold string of truth that led from Hans Guilford directly to the Oct. Sure, in her mind she knew it wouldn't be simple, but she hadn't expected an enormous pair of scissors to cut that string, limp strands falling unconnected to the floor.

Corvossier felt aimless over the next few days, unsure of herself and aching with the loss of her brother. *He's not lost,* she reminded herself. He was busy, searching for the witch she needed to help her put everything together. Each piece of information she had didn't quite make sense and leads she chased up felt pointless. She found herself not sleeping as she poured through file after file in the Askari database, sometimes imagining connections where there were none. The whole endeavour seemed completely void of hope to her. When she'd gone a full forty-eight hours without leaving the Bierpinsel, she decided it was time to hurl herself from the premises for better or worse. She hoped Phases would prove more useful, especially given the average age of punters was in the hundreds. The older someone was, the more likely they had encountered a witch at some point. And if Hogan had never met one, well, she needed to be speaking to people over eighty-two. Yu, in particular, was her primary target.

'They're suspicious of other people,' she told Corvossier, pulling up a stool next to her at the bar when it was her break. 'The witches that come here are different because they're younger, haven't been out in the world long enough yet to be distrustful. I suspect that's changed now, after what happened to you and Barastin.'

'I've barely seen a witch here since.'

'With good reason: they trust the Treize about as much as they trust the Catholic Church.'

'If you were trying to make contact with a witch, how would you do it?'

'Without knowing them previously?'

Corvossier nodded.

'With an introduction from an associate, but besides that . . . with caution. They're protective of themselves and protective of those they let in: after the witch hunts they really locked their shit down.'

'How do you mean?'

'You said it was hard to find literature on witches.'

'Yes, incredibly hard.'

'Because they don't let outsiders close. They don't let them into their covens, they don't let them know the extent of what they can and can't do. They let people underestimate and forget about them. It's a defence mechanism that has worked very well in recent centuries. The downside is you never really know what you're up against.'

Her words stayed with Corvossier, the medium thinking about how different that was to the werewolves who – after persecution in the middle ages – made sure the rest of the supernatural world didn't underestimate them. They were loud about it, ensuring others knew how ferocious they could be and what a threat they were. That too was a defence mechanism, although a very different kind. Yu stayed with her longer than she had to, with a smaller crowd and markedly different vibe in Phases that night. The house DJ was playing an LCD Soundsystem track that suited the mood of the room perfectly, lyrics about knowing when something was nothing swirling around her. Yu's comments gave her an inkling of an idea, Corvossier waiting until daylight to execute it.

Yu had said that living witches didn't like to talk to outsiders. They kept to themselves, not sharing their secrets or their stories with any being outside of a coven. Dead witches, on the other hand, were different. There weren't as many of them lingering around Berlin as Corvossier would have liked, but she knew where to look. She didn't have the time to venture further out of the city to places like Fulda and Trier where the witch trials had occurred. She also didn't want to without Barastin by her side. Corvossier did feel safe strolling through a Berlin graveyard during the day; however, families frequently used them as makeshift parks and kids played among the gravestones so she wasn't alone. In the most secluded corner of the cemetery, where vines had sprouted from the earth and were threatening to take the marks of the dead hostage inch by inch, Corvossier found the bluish grey of three ghosts sitting together in the grass. In actual fact, only two of them were ghosts by definition; the third one, an apple-cheeked woman in her mid forties, was a spirit.

'Casper!' one of them exclaimed. 'It's so good to see you!'

'You too, Marta. Happy Thursday, Geneva . . . Beatrice.'

The spirit nodded at her, the other two witches grinning with contentment as she sat down to join them.

'We haven't seen you in a few months,' Geneva said. 'Is everything okay?'

Corvossier opened her mouth to say *of course* but stopped herself, closing her lips into a hard line. These women weren't exactly friends of hers, acquaintances at best, but she valued them enough not to lie.

'Things have been ... hard,' she replied, watching her phrasing.

'That's being alive though, isn't it?' Marta chirped. It had been a good thirty years since either of these witches had been breathing, but that didn't mean she wasn't right.

'I guess so.' Corvossier shrugged. 'I keep wondering if all the easy years are behind me and if I should just be grateful for having them at all, not agonising over right now or tomorrow.'

'You talk to the dead too much,' Geneva noted. 'Have you tried saying this to the living?'

Marta made a move to gently whack her friend on the shoulder, her hand moving right through her.

'I meant a therapist!'

'You still visit Bamberg?' Beatrice, the spirit, questioned.

She nodded. 'Once a year.' Corvossier had been doing it since she was sixteen, when she and Barastin were more adept at controlling their powers. They'd return to the town that had terrified them and position themselves near the foot of one of the seven hills that made up Bamberg's borders. There they would wait, seeing ghosts one by one and moving on as many as they could until whichever twins' legs gave out first. Usually it was Barastin, but for the first year Corvossier had gone alone – her brother accompanying her in ghost form – and she stayed until well past dusk. Previously it had been Collette's job to escort them away, but without her she had found it challenging to know when was enough. It had been over fifteen years, but there were still so many more ghosts to go.

Marta frowned as she watched her. 'What is weighing on you, Casper?'

'I need to find a witch named Kala Tully.'

'Oh dear.'

'She's from Australia and she escaped a great evil known as the Oct. That's all I know, but I *badly* need to find her.'

Geneva and Marta shared a glance, the emotion exchanged between them bordering on pity. Beatrice just watched her, silent but unflinching as she sat alongside a gravestone.

'Honey,' Geneva started, 'I'm sure you mean well, but we just can't.'

'Not in life and not in death,' Marta added. 'Our loyalty can only be to our fellow sisters. We might all be from separate times and separate countries, but ultimately we're part of one, big coven. Forever.'

'That's what I thought,' Corvossier breathed, trying to keep the disappointment out of her voice. 'I'm sorry for asking.'

She stayed for a while longer, speaking to the witches about the sixties and seventies, times they both fondly recalled in great detail. Beatrice excused herself abruptly, as spirits often did, and Corvossier took solace in the fact she wasn't alone as she sat there, plucking weeds from the ground.

A buzzing woke her and she sat up, frowning as she tried to reconcile the sound she was hearing. She reached for her phone, letting out a frustrated grunt as she realised – again – that it wasn't *that* phone. She didn't recognise the number and Corvossier hesitated before she hit the button, her heart pounding as she held the phone to her ear with some suspicion. She didn't say a word, just listened carefully as music blared down the line.

'No, you hang up. *No, you* hang up! Are we playing this game?'

'Heath?' she shrieked. There was no mistaking that accent anywhere.

'Aye, of course it's bloody me. Who else would be calling ya at – what is it – three in the morning there?'

'Where are you?' Corvossier asked, straining to hear him over the ruckus in the background.

'In Texas.'

'What are you doing in Texas?'

'Trying to duck questions like these. Do you want the message or not?'

'What message?'

'I got called in by the old crones, which hasn't happened in over a century.'

'Heath, what are you talking about?'

'They said I was to pass on a message to you.'

'Who did?'

'Three. Old. Crones. Have you gone from Death to deaf over the past few months?'

'How—'

'They told *me* to tell you, that what you're looking for is in Boscastle. Sorry, not what: who.'

Corvossier ceased to breathe for moment, her entire being freezing as her brain processed the words Heath barked through the phone at her.

'Boscastle,' she murmured.

'They threatened me too, just to make sure you and only you knew this information. Now I don't know what it pertains to or what you're up to, but I'm assuming they're talking about the place and not the brand of pies.'

She'd fallen asleep with the laptop next to her and in that instance she was grateful as it meant it was close by. She typed the name into a search engine as the Scotsman spoke.

'In Cornwall,' she said, eyes scanning the information. 'Population of only a few hundred people.'

'Tiny town. Off the grid.'

Somewhere no one would think to look for an Australian witch, she thought.

'When were you told this?'

'Yesterday? Today? Could be a few days ago, it all blurs into one.'

'Why didn't you tell me this sooner?' she exclaimed.

'I've had more important things to do.'

'Like what?!'

There was a cough on his end, the line going crackly for a moment before his voice was clear again.

'Like, uh, attend a thirtieth birthday party.'

'*What?*'

'In Austin.'

'Heath!'

'Argh, come on, it's a werewolf party! You've clearly never been to a werewolf party. And this werewolf? He likes to party.'

She groaned, her shoulder keeping the phone to her ear as she already began looking up flights on the computer.

'I'm not just here to get blootered,' he continued.

She rolled her eyes in the darkness. 'No, just to bloviate.'

'Although getting blootered is a top three reason,' Heath pressed on, either ignoring her comment or not hearing it. 'One of my oldest mates has been based here for a decade, and, frankly, the way people are dropping at the moment? You gotta appreciate the ones left.'

'This friend is human?' she muttered, only half paying attention.

'Nah, Praetorian Guard, like me. I'm running several raids while I'm over here.'

There was a series of cheers and Heath's voice joined the fray.

'I gotta go, they're bringing out the cake and something's gonna jump out of it.'

'Oh God.'

'Keep the burner though, I'll check in again in a few months.'

There was an unceremonious click as she hung up the phone, Corvossier wondering for a moment if he'd actually used a landline. If there was anywhere landlines still existed, she supposed it would be Texas. Sitting in the sudden silence of her bedroom, she ran her hand down the length of her arm, cupping her limb and feeling the familiar skin there. It had been unusual at first: she'd found herself reaching for things and then cringing with the realisation. But now, its absence was part of her; it made Corvossier who she was.

Something else that made her who she was? Purpose and drive. Now that she knew where she was supposed to be looking for the witch named Kala Tully, she wouldn't be able to sleep. Grabbing a dressing gown and wrapping it tightly around her for warmth, she balanced her laptop in her left hand and walked to Barastin's bedroom using only the glow from the screen for guidance. Already she started reciting the things she needed to do in her head: secure flights under one of her names, book others with a different pseudonym, switch airports, choose which arms she would take, work out several disguises and where she could change into them at different points of the journey, how much cash she would need and where she could get a vehicle. She had to be painstakingly careful to make sure no one followed her to Cornwall otherwise this whole thing could be over before it even began.

Chapter 7

She had only been in the country for six hours, but Corvossier's overwhelming takeaway about Cornwall was that it was green: very green. Everywhere she looked, she was met by the colour. From green fields that stretched over gradual hills to green bushes bookmarking winding country lanes, she was almost overcome. It made her feel clean, somehow. It scrubbed her of the grime and greyness of a big city: not that she had ever considered Berlin those things before. It was her *favourite* place in the world, but in contrast to Cornwall she felt exposed. And in many ways, she was. She'd spent the past twenty-four hours completely alone, not even risking speaking to strangers due to a fear of then being noticed by someone.

Her first stretch was a flight to Charles de Gaulle Airport in Paris as Jessica Smith, a perfectly ordinary name for a perfectly ordinary woman dressed in a mousey brown wig and clothes that didn't stand out. Once there, she never left the building. She waited as long as she could in a nearby bathroom – managing a few hours – before switching into a black wig and corporate attire. She'd made sure to take only carry-on luggage to avoid the bag switcheroo, even swapping over shoulder straps for the hidden rolling wheels so the bag would appear different. This woman – Clara, she named her – headed to a café inside the airport. As the hours ticked over from mid-morning to evening, Clara had walked on to a flight to London. Once there and through security, she headed to another loo and donned her final 'look' complete with shredded denim skirt, punk rock band tee, fake lip piercing and bright green wig. That girl – Elvira – had left Heathrow Airport and hopped on the train, heading to Hanwell where she stayed at a hotel over night. A more everyday-looking lady had checked out, stopping at a nearby house to buy a secondhand car with cash. When she was finally on the road and beginning her four-hour journey to Boscastle, Corvossier was safely able to ditch the disguise and relax into herself.

It wasn't a perfect ruse, but it was all she had and without Barastin to watch her six, she wasn't taking risks. Her brother's absence had Corvossier looking over her shoulder more frequently than she ever had before, taking winding routes and ducking into stores as she waited to see if she was being followed. She wasn't, but the paranoia only began to ease once she was driving, Cornwall cleansing her palate unlike anything else.

She found it comical the first time she had to slow down behind a tractor, having never had that experience before. The roads leading to Boscastle were so narrow she kept dropping to a crawl when another car approached, worried there wouldn't be enough room for them both on the road. There was, of course, but that didn't stop her edging a foot off the accelerator every time. When she mounted the final hill that led to the town and the route opened up on the other side, Corvossier was smirking. Passing an old pub called the

Cobweb Inn, she could tell just by glancing at it that it was definitely haunted. The main road stretched out over another steep hill in the distance and away from the centre of town, while branching off it were several smaller roads where the bitumen shifted to gravel. They looked like something only locals would use, so she switched on her indicator and pulled into a sizable tourist car park. Turning off the ignition and grabbing her bags, it felt good to move her body after so long sitting in the vehicle.

'Hey!' a woman with blonde dreadlocks called to her from out the back of a van that was stacked with mattresses and had Fat Freddy's Drop rocking from the speakers. There were a handful of people clustered around, smoking weed so pungent that Corvossier resisted the urge to crinkle her nose. She smiled at the girl, but kept walking: she wasn't here to make friends and get high in the car park.

She strolled by caravan after caravan, with hire cars wedged between those with shiny stickers plastered to the windscreen telling you what company they were from. She played a game as she walked, called Hertz, Hertz, Euro. Boscastle itself was pretty in the afternoon sun, with families out on day trips lining up for lunch at fish and chip vendors and ice cream stores. There was a small creek that ran alongside her as she walked, opening up wider and wider in the distance as it raced towards the sea. It was low tide, so fishing vessels rested on a bed of pebbles and shallow water. She wanted to explore this place and find what she was after: but first, she needed to be patient.

There weren't enough buildings for her to get lost, so instead she pivoted on the spot until she found what she was looking for. The Wellington was easily the biggest place in town and she wandered towards it, momentarily comforted by the warm interior. The red carpets and the dark wooden furniture felt homely as she cut a path through the empty bar: it was too early for proper drinking and the place had more of a dinner vibe than lunchtime. Oil paintings in antique frames hung along the walls, depicting everything from landscapes to old, white men in fancy clothing. There was a chalkboard telling her about Cheap Tuesday and also trivia on Wednesday nights: the winning team walked away with one hundred dollars' worth of seafood. *I wouldn't mind that*, she thought as her tummy growled accordingly. Craning her head up a staircase, she caught sight of a more formal dining area and a hallway stretching on.

'Be with you dreckly,' a woman called as she pottered behind the bar.

'Not a worry,' Corvossier replied, taking a look at the menu as she waited.

'Sorry about that, what can I do you for?'

'I have accommodation booked here for the next few weeks.'

'Oh! Excellent, ah, let me just check the books ... yes, Georgia Wall?'

'That's correct,' she replied, handing over the credit card, passport and driver's licence she all had under the name Georgia Wall.

'And we've got you staying with us for three weeks?'

'Uh huh.'

'That's a nice long chunk; do you have family in the area?'

'No, I've never been to Cornwall before. I wanted to take some time to explore it properly.'

143

'Sounds wonderful! It's a beautiful part of the world we have here. Are you going to pop over and visit Tintagel?'

'Tintagel?'

'Oh, you absolutely *must*. You know, they say it's where King Arthur had his castle back in the day.'

'Really?' Corvossier smiled. 'And that's near here?'

'Not much more than a wee drive. Here's your room key, number fourteen, which is up on the third floor. We have breakfast in the dining room from eight a.m. to eleven a.m. daily, which is included in your price of stay, and I've also tucked some local tourist guide brochures in there as well so you can take a look.'

'That's lovely, thank you so much.'

'Not a problem at all, my dear. My name is Mary and I'm here most days. My sons and daughter-in-law handle the bar during evenings, so if you need anything just let them know.'

'Actually, is it too early to order food?'

'Not if you come eat it here in the bar.'

'Wonderful, could I get the mussels as a main please and an apple cider?'

'Excellent choice. If you pop back down here in about twenty minutes, we'll have that ready for you.'

Corvossier thanked her, slipping away up two flights of stairs and down a hallway that creaked under her feet as she searched for her room. It took a few goes of jiggling the key before she could get inside, but there was someone waiting for her when she finally made it through the door. The ghost of a man in his late fifties or sixties and dressed in fishing overalls was lingering near the bed with an expectant expression.

'She left me waiting here,' he said. 'I waited and waited.'

'Who did?' Corvossier sighed, throwing her bag down and flopping on to the bed ungracefully.

'My Sarah . . . she was supposed to wait for me.'

'Your wife?' she asked, closing her eyes as she tried to listen to the ghost's story.

'No, my wife was Cassandra. Sarah was my life.'

'Christ,' she groaned, rubbing her face. 'Your mistress, right?'

'She was my *lover*. I've been waiting for seventy years . . .'

Half sitting up, her eyes ran over the man who was wringing his hands together nervously. She couldn't see any noticeable cause of death, but she could see right through him. Grabbing a pillow, she tossed it in his direction and watched as it sailed through his midsection.

'Hey!'

'Oh shush,' she snapped. 'You didn't feel it.'

'But—'

'You're dead, okay? Do you know that? You were waiting up here horny and alone for a woman that never showed up and probably had a heart attack or something. You're *dead*. By now Sarah is dead too; Cassandra as well. You're the only one left. Now if you wouldn't mind, I have things to do and I would like the privacy to do them.'

'I'm . . . dead?'

She reached out with her senses, feeling his grip on this plane loosen just by speaking the words of truth. He'd be gone in a matter of minutes, she guessed, but with a display of mental concentration she gave him that extra push until eventually he dissipated in front of her.

'Peace and quiet,' she said, enjoying the words as she said them to herself. 'That's all I wanted.'

She felt momentarily guilty about moving the ghost on so cold-heartedly, but she was *not* in the mood. She detached the hand she was wearing, which she found obtrusive more than helpful most of the time. It was designed for cosmetic purposes, not practical ones, and she had needed it to disguise who she was while travelling. Now that she had made it to Boscastle, there was little point in being uncomfortable: she could wear long shirts with gaping sleeves that would mostly keep it out of sight of the villagers. And if the witch saw it, that could work in her favour: her unique physical appearance meant the woman might know who she was on sight. If she wasn't actively trying to disguise it, and wasn't actively trying to antagonise anyone, then it would imply Corvossier came in peace, metaphorical white flag waving. The one thing said over and over again, was how carefully she needed to tread when it came to entering a threatened witch's territory. Her plan was relatively simple: show up in Boscastle, make herself visible and seemingly passive, hope the witch came to her. Taking a moment to freshen up, she unpacked a few things and grabbed a light jacket before heading downstairs for lunch.

'Ah, perfect timing,' Mary said when she caught sight of her.

'I might take a table outside, if that's alright.'

'Why not? It's a glorious day for it.'

She wasn't wrong: it was stunning for early August, with the breeze still chilly but the sun out and packing a little bit of heat to go along with it. Taking a spot at a set of wooden table and chairs under a bright green umbrella, Corvossier breathed in the salty smell of her plate of mussels when they arrived. She ate slowly, taking in the surroundings as she carefully plucked the meat from the shells. She loved seafood, it was probably her favourite thing, but she so rarely had the occasion to eat it when it was this close to the source. Breaking the roll of bread that had been served with it, she dipped it in the remaining sauce and slowly chewed as she watched people milling about. From the inside, her room was quaint and homely with a view of the river out her window through delicate lace curtains. But viewing it from the outside, The Wellington looked more like a mini-castle with grey bricks and foreboding parapets along the roof, which added to the medieval vibe.

Downing the last of her cider, she decided to go for a stroll along the length of the river that cut through the middle of the town. She wandered down the only other road that led in or out of Boscastle, with the local church and a cluster of homes higher up on the hill, out of the way of seasonal flooding. The other buildings followed the water, with a knot of shops and a hostel soon transitioning to quaint cottages that had names like Tulip Gate and Bridgson Lodge as she walked closer to the ocean. The high cliffs on either side of the town gave way to a small crack that exposed the Celtic Sea on the other side. Carefully she negotiated the steep, rocky climb to where tourists were snapping photos and pointing out in the direction of Ireland. A sharp wind hit her as Corvossier crossed the threshold of where she had been sheltered from the elements, the gust whipping her hair off her scalp and attempting to snatch it away.

Even in Cornwall, her fair skin needed a layer of sunscreen protection and she had used most of it covering her face and chest. She watched with amusement as the flowing sleeves of her dress fluttered in the wind, the material looking like colourful streamers. With a fleeting look at the rocky crag of an island just offshore, she turned away from the horizon and began scaling her way back down to the path. Seagulls squawked as they flew overhead, the smell of sea salt and fish rich in the air as she wandered along the river. Dogs barked happily down below and she followed their path as they splashed along the edge of the water, chasing small fish she couldn't see. They were a pair of golden Labradors, not the smartest of dogs, but their joy was almost infectious. They sprinted past a little girl sitting on the concrete embankment, throwing stones into the water and watching them skip along the surface. She was singing a song to herself that Corvossier couldn't quite hear, but the thing that drew her in was the unusual company she kept: two ghosts sat on either side of her, smiling as they listened to her.

The child had no idea, of course, but that didn't stop the draw Corvossier felt towards her. She was on the opposite side of the river and she crossed an arching footbridge to get near. As she walked closer to the girl, one of the ghosts looked up and made direct eye contact with her. She seemed astonished that Corvossier stared back and she whispered something to her male companion. When he looked up, she had a better idea of who these people were: the girl looked like them and they looked like her. They were her parents; it was unmistakable.

'What are you looking at?'

Corvossier raised an eyebrow, surprised the girl was talking to her.

'Yeah, you,' she said, pointing a finger straight at her. 'What are you looking at?'

'I, uh . . .'

'Did you see a crab?' She jumped up quickly off the edge, backing up so that she was next to Corvossier. 'Cos I've been trying to catch one for ages, but they're never big enough.'

'Big enough for what?'

'To eat, what do you think?'

'You like crabmeat?'

'I *love* it. But the crabs here are so tiny.'

The ghosts hadn't moved from their position, the man and woman watching Corvossier and the girl interact with interest.

'I'm Sprinkle,' she said, thrusting a hand forward.

'Sprinkle.' Corvossier smiled. 'That's a cool name.'

'I'm pretty cool. What's your name? And how come you're so tall? I've never seen a girl so tall!'

She laughed, crouching down to level the playing field. 'My name is a bit of a mouthful: it's Corvossier von Klitzing.'

'Whoa, you sound like an *Indiana Jones* villain!'

'Thank you? I think.'

'That's your real name? Your full name?'

'Uh huh, although most people just call me Casper.'

'Like the ghost.'

'Exactly,' she replied, meeting the eyes of the dead who were watching. Something close to recognition crossed their features. So they had heard of her.

'You wanna skip stones with me?'

'I'd love to,' she replied, taking a seat next to where Sprinkle gestured on the hard ground. 'I don't know how to though; you'll have to teach me.'

'It takes practice, but you can learn. Now put out both your hands.'

Corvossier did as she was told, extending her left hand and then shaking free the sleeve of her right to reveal her arm.

'Oh! You don't have a hand!'

'No I don't.' She smiled, trying to stifle a laugh at the girl's reaction.

'Where did it go?'

'It got cut off in an accident.'

'Ouch! Did it hurt?'

She nodded. 'Very much.'

The kid's eyes were wide as she looked at it, her fingers inching forward with interest.

'Can I . . . can I touch it?'

'You want to touch it? Most children are frightened.'

'Yeah, but I'm cool, remember?'

'My mistake,' she said, nodding solemnly. 'You can go ahead and touch it.'

Her fingers reached out, tentatively at first, as if testing to see whether it hurt or not. When Corvossier didn't shriek or jerk away in pain, she properly inspected the skin and the muscle there. Her fingers were inquisitive, much like her mind, and Sprinkle's face looked up at hers for a reaction.

'Will it grow back?' she asked, in an adorable Cornish accent. 'Like a lizard's tail?'

'You have lizards here?'

Sprinkle shook her head. 'What I mean is will it stay like this, forever?'

'Yup, although sometimes I wear fake arms when I feel like

it. My friend even has one just for archery, do you know what that is?'

'Shooting arrows.'

'Exactly. There's a type of arm she can wear that has something like a small hook at the end, perfect for holding the bow.'

'And she still hits the target?'

'Every time.'

'That's *awesome*,' she replied, a smile breaking out so large it seemed to swallow up half her face. Her intelligent eyes didn't seem to miss a thing and they moved to inspect the rest of Corvossier, her fingers moving to her other hand where she examined the rings there.

'You have nice jewellery,' she noted. 'Pretty bracelets.'

'Thank you, I like your necklace.'

Sprinkle's hands shot to her neck, where a small crystal hung on a piece of cord. It was an unusual item for a kid, seeming better suited for a teen from the nineties.

'Where are you from?' she pressed. 'I haven't seen you before and I'm here all the time.'

'All the time?'

'*Allll* the time. I'm homeschooled, so I never get to leave Boscastle.'

'I was homeschooled too, back in Berlin, which is in Germany. That's where I'm from.'

'Did you hate it too? There's no one to play with. It sucks.'

'Well, I had my brother so I could always play with him.'

'Does he have a weird name like you?'

'He did. Barastin, if you'd believe it.'

'B-Barastin,' she said, testing the word out loud.

'People used to just call him Creeper though. Or Barry.'

'Those aren't very good nicknames.'

'No.' She laughed. 'I guess they're not.'

'I'd call him Bazza.'

Taking a stone from the small pile beside her, Sprinkle threw it towards the water and watched as it skipped perfectly across the surface. She repeated the movement several times, until her little collection of rocks was gone. Her parents hadn't moved since Corvossier arrived, but they muttered to each other back and forth. Unfortunately they were quiet enough that she couldn't hear what they were saying, despite her strained efforts.

'Come on,' the girl ordered, springing back up to her feet. 'If you're new here, I gotta show you something.'

'If you insist,' Corvossier replied, taking the extended hand that Sprinkle held out for her. 'How old are you anyway?'

'I'm eight.'

'When's your birthday?'

'October twenty-eight.'

'Ah, so you're a Scorpio. That explains so much.'

'You're into horoscopes too, just like Opal.'

'Who's Opal?' she asked, letting herself get pulled along towards a two-storey white building.

'My mum. And hey, is that why you speak funny? Cos you're from Germany?'

'I thought my English was very good.'

'It is, but you still speak funny.'

They passed a small herb garden and the kid increased her pace, dragging Corvossier faster towards a wooden door that jingled with chimes as she pushed through it.

'What is this place?' she breathed, ducking under the low hanging handle of a broomstick that was suspended from the roof.

'This is the Museum Of Witchcraft And Magic!' Sprinkle said, triumphantly throwing her hands around the room. 'Founded in nineteen fifty-one, this is the largest collection of occult artefacts in the world.'

A woman looked up from behind the counter, a rope braid dangling in front of her face as she inspected the child with a frown.

'Who have you dragged in here against their will?' she asked, getting to her feet as she assessed the new guest. 'I'm sorry, my daughter is forceful by nature.'

'That's okay,' Corvossier said, letting go of the girl's hand as her eyes focused in on the woman. She couldn't help it: she was immediately struck by her beauty. In a tie-dye halter top, the myriad of markings that adorned her body were exposed, with Corvossier recognising the goddess symbol inked at the centre of her chest. There was also an elaborate tattoo that began at her neck, then went across her collarbone and down to her fingertips. Flowers she didn't recognise sprung from the ink of a vine that wrapped down the length of the woman's arm. It was breathtaking, much like the lady herself.

'This is really a museum of witchcraft?' she said, trying to regain her composure.

'And magic!' Sprinkle added.

'It is, blessed be,' the woman replied, walking around the counter until she was out in the shop front with the two of them. 'We've got exhibits on witches, wicca, freemasonry, ceremonial magic – you name it.'

'And we can show you what to do with a dog's heart and some pins if—'

'*Sprinkle.*'

'Sorry,' the girl mumbled, properly scolded.

Corvossier picked up a mug that had an intricately designed pentagram on it and 'Museum Of Witchcraft And Magic' printed on the other side. She placed it back down at the merchandise station she had plucked it from, noting the key rings, notepads, pens, tea towels and shirts all with the same design and font. Her eyes caught on a snow globe that had a little witch inside, complete with a broomstick and hat. She shook it gently, watching as green glitter swirled around inside the ornament.

'Do people buy this stuff?' she muttered, before realising too late that she had an audience. 'Ah, sorry, I didn't—'

She was cut off by the woman's laughter, which took Corvossier by surprise as she enjoyed the rich, velvety sound of it.

'The snow globes aren't a big seller, no. Weirdly it's the key rings that always do well: something about the fact they look like they're cut out of a tree . . . I've never been able to work it out. But we do have all your needs for the practising witch, whether you're just starting out or more experienced.'

'Oh?'

'Crystals, herbs, animal feathers: whatever you need. Actually, we have a recharge and revitalise ritual coming up under the Sturgeon Moon if you'd like to take part?'

She handed Corvossier a leaflet, depicting an illustration of nude women gesturing towards a sphere in the sky. She couldn't be certain, but the paper smelled distinctly like patchouli.

'Ah, is nudity required?'

'We have no such hang ups about the natural form here,' she said, smiling tight.

'Do you wanna see the museum?' the child pushed. 'It's ten bucks.'

'Sprinkle,' the woman snapped. 'While I appreciate the ambitious energy, we've talked about this: you can't just drag people in off the street.'

'Why not? It works.'

Corvossier glanced between the grown woman and the smaller yet formidable one, who stood there defiant with hands on her hips.

'She has a point,' she said, handing over several notes to relieve the tension from the room. 'And I'm more than happy to buy a ticket.'

'Let me get your change,' the woman said, flashing her a grateful look.

'I take it you're Opal?' she asked, following her to the counter.

'I am. I see you've already met Sprinkle.'

'Fantastic name.'

'You know, you can try and argue with a kid that their given name is more appropriate but sometimes it's better to just *not* fight it.'

Corvossier accepted her change, accidently dropping it as she attempted to do her best not to stare at Opal. Crouching down to the ground to pick up the coins in a fluster, she felt heat rise in her cheeks as Opal skipped back around to help her. With their hands snatching the change up off the floor-boards, Corvossier knew the moment she spotted her limb difference. The woman's hands froze for a second, just as she was reaching for a coin, before quickly picking up pace again as if nothing had happened.

'Sorry about that,' Corvossier apologised, straightening up and slipping the coins back into her purse and taking the ones Opal gave her. 'I'm clumsy sometimes.'

'Is it because you only have one hand?'

'Sprinkle!'

'What? She does!'

Opal snatched the girl in a flash of movement, pulling her back around the counter where she deposited her in front of a textbook.

'Homework! No more time outside, no more lip. What you said to the lady was terribly rude.'

The girl didn't push her luck, clearly knowing the extent of Opal's wrath and wisely choosing to obey. With a sigh and an apologetic smile, she turned back to Corvossier.

'Now it's my turn to apologise.'

'It's fine, honestly.'

'Kids can—'

'Really, don't even mention it,' she stressed, immediately hating the awkward encounter.

'My daughter can be, well, like me: a little too forthright sometimes. But we're all sisters of the same spirit.'

She heard the words clearly, but Corvossier also didn't believe them. *My daughter.* Glancing through one of the huge arched windows, she double-checked the ghosts were still where she had left them. Sure enough, they were sitting and staring at the river as the water flowed by them. They were Sprinkle's parents – she was sure of it – so why the fib? With a small smile, Corvossier headed towards the entrance of the museum and nodded her farewells to the pair of them at the counter.

'Go on through,' Opal gestured. 'Take your time and soak everything in. There's a lot of magic in these walls.'

Magic in these walls, Corvossier scoffed to herself. The woman may be gorgeous, but she doubted the 'spirit sister' would recognise real magic if it booped her in the face with a broomstick. Crystals, funky smells and affirmations wouldn't get you far in the real supernatural world – they'd get you dead.

Heading up a set of narrow, wooden stairs, she came to a stop in front of a huge glass cabinet that appeared to have every piece of witch-themed pop cultural item ever made. From cereal boxes and board games, to advertisements from the 1950s featuring a witch vacuum cleaning, it was like a time capsule made of paper.

She moved past a range of witch dolls that varied from hypersexualised versions drawn for the male gaze to grotesque witch heads with warts, hooked noses and scraggly hair. Continuing on, it shifted to the more historic items with a collection of artefacts preserved and displayed from the local area. There were drawers with neat, small labels that told you what to expect inside: titles like 'Salem' and 'witch dolls' and 'home charms'. Sliding one of them open, she found dozens of small, homemade dolls woven together from found items like twigs and yarn and hay. The deeper she progressed into the museum, the less fun it was and she felt her stomach drop as she walked under a carved, wooden sign that read 'persecution'. *Nothing good can come on the other side of this*, she thought. Sure enough, she was met by a mannequin dressed in a plain robe and wearing a horrific combination of chains and facial shackles.

'Fuck,' she whispered to herself.

'It's not pretty, is it?'

She jerked around to see Opal standing behind her, the woman uncrossing her arms as she sighed sadly and shook her head.

'Pretty is probably the last word I would use to describe this,' she gulped, wondering how long the woman had been observing her. She had been completely oblivious to her presence.

'It was called a Scold's Bridle,' she explained. 'The idea was to prevent the woman from being able to speak or use her tongue.'

'Now why does that sound familiar?'

'It wasn't just used for suspected witches; sometimes they'd make the town gossip wear it or any woman who was particularly sharp-tongued or naggy.'

'Couldn't you just ask the person to politely shush?'

Opal smiled, a gesture that didn't spread to her eyes as she stepped forward and pointed at the mannequin's hands.

'Those are thumbscrews, said to be incredibly painful and used mainly to torture anyone accused of witchcraft once they were imprisoned.'

'It moves pretty quickly from the cheery, pop culture depictions to the reality in here,' she noted.

'Well, we couldn't open with the systemic sexism and abuse of women for centuries,' Opal agreed. 'It's really hard to appeal to people as a tourist attraction that way.'

'I'll bet.'

She moved on to a section called 'witchcraft and healing', which had dozens of glass vials filled with ingredients and annotated notes attached explaining which ailment they would heal. There was 'magical tools' after that, featuring a significant collection of animal skulls and intricately carved items. Corvossier was aware of the fact that Opal was trailing after her, her eyes watching every movement as she walked around the museum. It made her feel uneasy, and not just because she was passing a wall that displayed the nooses used to hang witches in England, although she suspected that added to it. There was a ducking stool and she leaned in to read the description on the wall about it, frowning as she learned it was used to plunge people fastened to the metal chair into a pond or river. She liked the collection of mandrakes and a display of curses that had been found in the local area, including one recovered from an office in the 1940s.

But her favourite thing in the whole building was the Ouija boards: there were nearly thirty of them, all different and of varying quality. From a more traditional-looking one protected behind a glass case, to another that had been purposefully defaced by the owners, they were beautiful in how unique each of them was from the other. There were several well-preserved planchettes mounted on the wall that drew her attention and she wished Barastin was there to see them with her. She couldn't help but wonder what he would think of this place. The whole building smelled vaguely of incense and Corvossier let the promise of fresh air carry her towards the exit, all the while Opal remained a conscientious distance behind her. She had to leave the way she had come in and Sprinkle's excited face popped up from behind the desk with a grin.

'Did you like it?' she chirped.

'It was wonderful,' Corvossier admitted. 'And terrifying. Things can be terrifyingly wonderful, I guess.'

'Often the best things are,' Opal said from behind her. 'Here, you should take this.'

'Oh?'

'It's just a little a charm.' She smiled politely. 'It will bring you good luck and prosperity.'

So would a fortune cookie, Corvossier thought.

'Thank you, thank you so much for the tour.'

'We also do readings here, every second evening if you'd like to book an appointment?'

'I'm okay for now,' she replied, respecting the woman's attempt to upsell her. 'It was nice to meet you both.'

'Are you sure you don't want a tea towel or something?' Sprinkle called. 'Or a magnet?'

'Let the lady leave with grace,' Opal muttered, giving Corvossier that same breathtaking smile.

'Maybe next time,' she replied, throwing the small girl a wink.

Letting the cool breeze slap her in the face as she stepped outdoors, she halted automatically as she came face to face with the ghosts from earlier. She didn't like to push through their forms if she could help it and she awkwardly stepped around them, observing a handmade sign in the garden that said: 'carry lavender to see ghosts'. That was something she definitely didn't need help with.

Walking slowly away from the museum and back towards the river, she cast a glance over her shoulder. The two ghosts stayed still, side by side, watching her leave. They weren't the only ones: Opal's face peered out at her through the window, waving gently. Glancing down at the charm in her hand, which featured a metal pentagram dangling off the bottom along with some cheap beads, Corvossier tried not to give in to the frustration she felt itching at her shoulder blades. She'd come here looking for a fearsome witch, not displaced ghosts and a hippie who wanted to read her horoscope. *It will take time,* she told herself. She hoped time was what she had.

Chapter 8

Corvossier had been attempting to walk back to The Wellington when the rain started, the weather shifting from clear skies to foreboding storm so quickly she thought of it as stereotypically European. She had an umbrella, but the downpour was that heavy it appeared to be splashing out of the very ground beneath her as well. There wasn't much else to do except return to the hotel and dry off, curl up with a documentary and wait until the storm was over.

This is what she pledged to do in her mind, but just as she thought it the weather seemed to worsen. With every step she took, the rain increased both in frequency and force. She had never experienced anything like it and she wondered if this was the start of one of the Boscastle flash floods she'd seen in her online research of the town. Part of her umbrella collapsed, cold water pouring down on her face as she tried to look ahead and pick her way towards the path that led back to shelter. But the harder she tried, the less her efforts seemed to matter.

She hitched the handle of the umbrella under her armpit and used her arm to attempt to hold the protection from the rain up above her. She had her other hand free to try and feel around for a landmark. Yet there was nothing. Her limbs went numb eventually, first her toes inside her soggy boots and then her fingers and her nose. The wind was howling and the rain was relentless. It seemed like she'd spent hours outside and, for all she knew, she had; any concept of time was lost to her. Minutes seemed like months, but she felt a small twinge of hope when she caught sight of an arch. Despite the poor visibility, she made her way towards it greedily, gripping the wooden rail for dear life. It was a bridge, she realised, but not the one she had crossed earlier that afternoon. This bridge was smaller, barely wide enough to fit two people, and way up river away from the museum. Had she really wandered this far? She needed to cross so she could start heading back towards the centre of Boscastle and be on the right side of the body of water.

She took a step on to the bridge and knew immediately she had made a mistake. The surface was damp and unsteady, straining under her feet as she attempted to move across it. She was unwilling to release her grip on the railing, which meant the gusts were strong enough that the wind tore the umbrella away from her and she watched helplessly as it spiralled up into the sky. She yelped as her next step sunk right through the wood and into the river below, her foot plunging into the water while her thigh kept the rest of her stuck in the middle of the bridge. Corvossier tried calling out for help, but her cries barely seemed to make it out of her mouth: it was as if the very wind was stealing her words from her. She attempted to wiggle her way out of the hole, pausing when she felt the rest of the wood around her body weaken as well. It was soggy, not solid the way it should be. Tightening her grip on the railing, the whole thing gave way as it was swept off into the river and she was left hanging to the arch where the bridge had once been. The current grew stronger as more and more water and debris fed into it, her grip beginning to weaken as she tried to clutch desperately.

With a gasp, she felt the wind knocked out of her as she was hit in the stomach by a floating log. Her hand loosened and she rolled with the debris, her head disappearing under the water before she struggled to the surface. The river was like ice and she cried out, fighting to keep the water out of her mouth as the current tugged her downstream. She knew what was at the end of all this: the ocean. Corvossier was a good swimmer – it had been part of her physical therapy with the Cyborg Sisters after the attack – but fully clothed it was a struggle. Her coat and her boots weighed her down and with a kick to the surface, it felt like she was tugged back under by some unseen tree root or rough edged rock. It was exhausting, the continuous fight, but she had never been a quitter. Instinctively she reached towards whatever ghosts were near, letting her vision cloud only slightly as she fought to keep herself in the present. If she clocked out of one reality and poured too much of herself into the other, she would drown.

Corvossier could sense the dead around her, swirling amongst the water but not being carried away by it like she was. These were the ghosts of the drowned, the ghosts of people who many years ago had either perished in this river or in the waters close by it. *Come to me*, she pleaded. *Help me*. She willed them to her, like a magnet with intent, and urged them with everything she had. Cold hands gripped at her, tugging and pulling her higher until she broke the surface.

Water clouded her vision almost entirely, the salt stinging her eyes as she tried to look for the riverbank she could swim towards. Coughing and spluttering a mouthful of water she accidentally swallowed, she hated the burning sensation she felt in her chest, the weakening of her limbs. Her hair seemed to tangle through the water, as if it too wanted her to drown and plunge down into the icy depths. Corvossier was yanked against the current, moving sidewards instead of further down the river like she should have been. The force strengthened and she gave herself over to it, watching the half-submerged head of a man as he dragged her by one arm towards the shallows. There was something – no, someone – at her feet as well and she fought against the instinct to squirm and immediately kick at the slippery sensation that wrapped around her legs. A trio of ghosts were helping her, having heard her cry for the dead and being powerless to resist the call.

Thank you, she thought, over and over again as she felt pebbles beneath her feet. She tried to rush forward, desperate to reach the shore, but her exhausted body wasn't able to react as quickly as she would like. Slipping and stumbling, she practically crawled up on to the riverbank, the ghosts handing her over to faces she recognised: Sprinkle's parents, her *real*, ghost parents.

The woman took Corvossier's hand, guiding her over a concrete ledge and on to solid ground. She collapsed there, laying flat as the rain continued to pour down, splashing off her body and forming pools around her. She couldn't move for a long while, her eyes closed as she gulped in huge amounts of air. Her lips were slick with water when she eventually felt strong enough to sit up, propping an elbow underneath her as she looked back at the raging river. The three ghosts were waiting there for her, only one of them acknowledging her with a miniscule nod as they walked backwards under the surface, their features disappearing an inch at a time until they were gone. She turned to Sprinkle's parents, a question in her mind, but they had both begun to walk away from her.

'Hey,' she croaked. 'Hey!'

They didn't respond, didn't turn around, their backs just moving off into the distance until she couldn't see them anymore. When she got to her feet, her legs feeling wobbly and uneasy, Corvossier took in the town around her. The rain was lighter, but all of Boscastle seemed – ironically – like a ghost town. There wasn't another human in sight, with everyone having dashed inside when the storm started, she guessed. The Wellington was visible on the horizon and she stumbled towards it, parts of her hurting that she didn't know could hurt. When she entered the pub, she caught a glance of herself in the mirror behind the bar: her skin was so grey she looked like a selkie, with the weeds and debris tangled up in her hair adding to the effect.

'Jesus, Mary and Joseph,' a man breathed, coming around the corner carrying a crate of wine. 'What happened to you, love?'

'I got caught in the storm,' she managed to strangle out. With a panic, she slipped a hand in her pocket and felt around to see what was left. Somehow her wallet remained, which wasn't any great gain as it only had a fake ID and a twenty pound note inside: the rest of her cash was in her room. The burner phone was gone and so was her room key, Corvossier having to ask one of Mary's sons for a replacement. The charm she'd been gifted at the Museum Of Witchcraft And Magic was lost to the river as well; she caring little for it as she trudged up the stairs to her room.

It took another long, hot shower before she started to feel okay, not wanting more water on her body at first but knowing it was necessary. There were a few cuts and abrasions along her frame and her dress was torn, but Corvossier didn't mind so much; she was alive and that counted for something. It rained most of the night and the next day, with her shaken enough that she stayed inside The Wellington. Trawling Askari files was safer than venturing outside, she figured, at least until the weather cleared. And for once, it felt like she was finally getting somewhere.

Corvossier had identified the first member of the Oct that she recognised from the night they had killed her brother: Gerald Simpson. His face had been only somewhat configured in her mind, but Barastin had recollected him perfectly and from that they had a sketch that looked fairly close to the staff shot logged in the system. He had been Irish Barber's supervisor once, with Hans Guilford having worked at the same Askari outpost in Costa Rica for a stretch of three months before being transferred on. That was the connection: it was thin and fleeting, but now she had *something*. She began the tedious process of going through Gerald's entire fifty-year career for the Treize, most of the material fairly dry and not helping keep her awake.

She fell asleep in the position she had been researching: neck arched at an uncomfortable angle and the warmth of the laptop on her thighs. What woke her up wasn't daylight, however; it was a searing pain that broke out along her legs. She jerked to consciousness with a yelp, glancing down at her toes as the burning sensation inched its way up her calves and to her knees. She bit into the material of her pillow, the pain nearly causing her to cry out. It felt like she was burning alive, but her skin wasn't reacting to what she was experiencing internally. She rushed to the bathroom, turning on the cold tap and sticking her foot underneath the stream of water. It helped somewhat, but Corvossier was soaked with sweat by that point. She stripped off her clothes, submerging herself in the ice cold bath once it reached capacity. She held her hand in front of her eyes, her vision blurry as what she thought were small flames danced from the edge of each finger tip. She was hallucinating. It was like the worst fever she had ever experienced, coming on so sudden she wondered if she had been bitten by something.

It's Cornwall, she thought. *What the hell could I have been bitten by, a mince pasty?* Corvossier didn't move from the bath until well after sunrise, skipping her complimentary breakfast to remain in the tepid water, which had warmed with the heat of her body. Closing her eyes as she sunk deeper, she searched for her brother in the lobby. She couldn't find him, which frightened Corvossier; her own need for Barastin should have brought him out, wherever he was. But he was nowhere to be found. Eventually she pulled herself from the tub, her limbs shaking slightly but the fever mostly having subsided by then. Her skin looked perfectly fine, its usual shade of porcelain, but it was sensitive to the touch and she flinched as she attempted to dry herself with a towel.

There was a deep sense of discomfort creeping along her spine and these days she never ignored the tingles of a feeling when she got it. Desperately she wanted to leave Boscastle, but she knew that she couldn't. She had to stay until she found Kala Tully. Dressing herself slowly, she wandered from the hotel and in the direction of the cliff top. It was the only place that put the most distance between herself and the town, without her needing to abandon Boscastle altogether.

She stayed curled up against the rocks and watching the sea right until the sun set. Even then, long after her fingers had gone numb and her coat had stopped being adequate protection against the chill, she was reluctant to leave. Just *feeling* the cold was a welcome relief to the spontaneous self-combustion curdling inside her from earlier. Boscastle was quiet at night; heck, it was quiet during the day as well. Yet the streets full of tourists during the daylight hours gave way to a peacefulness she found deeply unnerving. It was a stark contrast to what she was used to in Berlin and it would take some adjusting.

The Wellington was one of the few lively places in town, with a handful of locals from Boscastle and the surrounding areas keeping the energy of the joint alive with their patronage. Having not eaten since the night before, Corvossier was starving as she took a table in the corner by herself and ordered the house special of lamb stew. There was steak on the menu as well and truthfully she wouldn't have minded it, but she couldn't take the discreet glances in her direction as she cut the meat with a knife wedged under her armpit or the overzealous offers of help. There was a band made up of just two older

men – one on the guitar and the other on percussion and vocals – and she ate her stew slowly as she watched them. They worked their way through a collection of covers and even a few Cornish folk songs before the night began to wind down. Mercifully she was left alone, with no one approaching the table of the strange lady who preferred to be by herself. The most she got were a few fleeting smiles and greeting nods, which she knew would lead to someone attempting a conversation with her in the coming nights.

The hotel above was just as quiet, with the wind outside having picked up enough that she could hear it whistling as she walked down the empty corridors. She was tired in her body and soul, craving the sanctuary of the double bed that was waiting in her room. Pocketing her wallet so she could open the door with one hand, she frowned as she stepped into the darkened interior. Her window was wide open, with the lace curtains fluttering wildly in the wind as it whipped its way into the space.

She let the door slam shut behind her as she rushed forward, struggling to yank the frame of the old window down by using her body weight. Eventually she got leverage, almost too much, and she had to slow its descent in case the glass shattered with the sudden force. Cutting off the howl of the night, she let out a relived sigh as the room stilled around her. Brushing the hairs off her face, she looked out the window, down to the river below and froze. One of the ghosts from earlier had returned and was standing there, looking up at her: Sprinkle's real mother.

'It's funny, for one of them I thought you'd have better senses.'

Corvossier stiffened as the voice spoke from behind her, the tone cold and menacing. Spinning around slowly, she couldn't quite see who was there. It was as if the very darkness itself was cloaking this person, hiding them from view, the shadows wrapped around them like a coat.

'One of them?' she asked, not bothering to hide her nervousness.

'Treize, Askari, Praetorian Guard, whatever,' the voice said. 'It matters little to me. What does matter is that you leave. Now.'

'I'm none of those things,' Corvossier replied, shaking her head furiously as she realised the person she was in the room with had to be the witch she was looking for. 'I'm not here on behalf of anyone. I'm here by myself, for myself.'

'Well, now you can leave.'

'No,' she snapped, risking a step forward. 'I'm not leaving until I get what I came for.'

'And what's that, exactly?'

'Your help, Kala Tully.'

There was pointed silence from Corvossier's guest, not a breath or a word audible as she squinted, trying desperately to penetrate the darkness and see their face.

'Be very careful now,' they growled. 'I'll do anything to protect those I love and if that means making sure you don't tell anyone what you *think* you know—'

'I'm not here to tell anyone! Please, just listen to me. The people who came after you, came after me.' She held up her arm to emphasise the point. 'I escaped, but my brother wasn't so lucky. They slaughtered him right in front of me. They took my hand.'

'That's a tragic story, but none of that is my problem. *You* are my problem: you barely look human enough to pass. The longer you're here, the more risk you're putting us under.'

'Us?' Corvossier questioned. 'Kala Tully and who else?'

It was as if just saying the witch's name again helped clear up some of the deception, the shadows softening ever so slightly as Corvossier began to make out a woman's form. She gasped, her mind finally registering *who* it was standing in the shadows and blocking the only exit out of the room. Gone was the tie-dye, the breezy manner, and the warmth from earlier: in its place stood Opal, her body squared against Corvossier in a pair of jeans and plain black T-shirt. Her façade at the museum had been polite, but the longer Corvossier thought on it the more she realised it was just that: a façade. She noticed the woman wore an identical necklace to Sprinkle's, which was looped around her neck like a choker and glinted for a moment as she observed it.

'You stay away from me and my daughter,' Opal hissed, her fingers twitching as her hands hung by her side.

'She's not your daughter though,' Corvossier muttered, uncertain where she found the courage. 'Is she? She's your niece: your sister's child.'

Something flashed over the witch's expression, the darkness in the room growing once again as Opal dashed forward and threw her hands around Corvossier's neck. The woman was tiny compared to her, probably not much more than five foot four to her six foot three, but that made no difference as she tightened her grip on her windpipe, causing Corvossier to choke and struggle for breath. Her first instinct was to lash out, protect herself, and call whatever ghosts she could to her as quickly as possible. But at the same time, she knew she needed to make this woman feel safe, make her believe that she wasn't a threat and presented no danger to her and the kid whatsoever. Reluctantly, she would have to take it.

'How could you possibly know that?' Opal growled.

'I . . . I can see . . . I can see them,' she gasped.

'*Who?*'

'Th . . . their ghosts.'

The witch released her instantly, backing away with shock on her face.

'What did you just say?'

Corvossier dropped to her knees, gasping. Looking up at her assailant, she willed her to believe the truth in what she was saying.

'I'm a medium,' she puffed. 'I can see the dead, communicate with them, control them if necessary.'

'And you can see her? You can see Willa?'

Corvossier nodded. 'She's standing right outside this window.'

Opal raced over there, desperately looking down at the street and the river below for a sign of her sibling.

'You can't see her,' she explained. 'Not unless she wants you to. Besides, she's not here for you. She follows the kid.'

'*Mayra.*'

'Her and a blond man, with wild hair.'

'Alistair,' Opal breathed, still staring out the window at something she couldn't see. She wasn't quite talking to Corvossier: it seemed as if she was talking more to herself.

173

'That was her husband, the whitefella: Alistair and Willa North.'

'How did they die?' she asked, using the nearby desk to help drag herself back up to standing. The witch spun around at that, looking at her with an accusatory glare.

'I thought you would know.'

'Unless there's a sword protruding out of their stomach or their body is riddled with bullets, you usually can't see cause of death on a ghost. They either have to tell you or you find out yourself: it needs to be very obvious.'

'No, I meant that they were killed by the same people who murdered your brother.'

'The Oct?' she asked, noting the interest that washed over Opal's face.

'That's what they're called?'

'That's what I was told.'

'By who?'

'Someone who worked for them, a lackey.'

'Where is that someone now?'

'Dead,' Corvossier replied, 'along with his three associates.'

'Are you sure?'

'One hundred per cent certain. He died via the bullet from my gun.'

She narrowed her eyes at that, as if trying to discern the truth from Corvossier's words alone.

'*You* killed him?'

'Yes.'

'And the other three?'

'No.'

'And you want to kill these . . . Oct, right? Not catch them and throw them in Vankila?'

'I want them dead,' she whispered. 'More than you could ever know.'

The witch laughed, but there was no joy in it. 'Oh, I might.'

She walked around the room, thinking deeply for several long minutes. Corvossier dared not move, sensing how precarious the situation was. All she could do was watch, and wait, and pray to whatever she believed in. Finally, she turned back around and stared so hard at Corvossier it was like she saw right through her.

'You need to leave.'

'Please—'

'I'm letting you go with your life, that's enough of a concession.'

'But you—'

'I don't care about what you're trying to do; I don't care for getting wrapped up in some ghost girl's vendetta. All I care about is keeping my niece safe and alive. To do that, *I* need to be safe and alive.'

'This is—'

'I have given up everything to do that. I'm hiding in a seaside town in Cornwall pretending to fit in here so they'll never find us again. I'm not risking discovery for a vengeance ploy: it gets you nowhere, believe me. So you need to leave, tomorrow morning, and never come back, never say a word, *never* think of Boscastle again.'

She pointed a finger squarely at Corvossier, the digit wavering just slightly from barely contained rage. Unblinking, she held her gaze for an uncomfortable beat. Suddenly, she spun on her heels and stormed from the room. The door slammed shut behind her and Corvossier jumped, letting out a shaky breath.

Panting with fear, she clutched the space around her neck where the witch's grasp had been. Stumbling to the window, she looked down at the ghost of the woman she now knew was Willa, Opal aka Kala Tully's sister.

The lady was gazing up at her sadly and she shook her head, as if disappointed. Even in death, she was beautiful too: like her sibling.

She watched as the witch left The Wellington, her figure shrinking away into the night as she walked with purpose, braids swinging behind her like a tail. The ghost held up a hand as if to say farewell and turned, trailing after her living sister. It was the spectral bluish grey of Willa through the night that showed Corvossier where Opal and her niece lived, in a cottage directly across the river from the museum.

She filed that information away as she walked to the shower, her limbs unsteady from the adrenaline that was still coursing through her veins. She thought the hot water would help as it trickled down her back and spread all over her body. It didn't. When she left the steamy bathroom nearly twenty minutes later, she was still just as shaken. But with a towel wrapped around her and hair dripping on the carpet as she crossed the room, she knew what she had to do. The witch was *wonderfully terrifying*, as she had said. And Corvossier believed she would do anything to protect what was left of her family. What Opal didn't know, however, was that *she* would do anything to avenge what had happened to hers. Wiggling under the covers of the bed, hair damp on the pillow, she didn't expect to sleep much that evening. That was something she knew, deep down in her bones. She also knew that despite Opal's very real and potent threats, she wasn't leaving Boscastle: not tomorrow, not the next day, not the week after that. She would stay in this bloody town until she got her answers, even if it killed her.

Chapter 9

Corvossier was nervous when she woke up, she was nervous as she got dressed, and she was nervous as she ate breakfast. She had tossed and turned in her sleep, dreaming jumbled scenarios where her brother and Opal and Sprinkle mixed together while the Oct continued to pursue all of them. She walked out of The Wellington into a clear, blue-skyed day that she analysed with suspicion. She had to believe what she was doing was the right thing. She had risked a lot to get here and she wasn't going to go away just because a witch scared the crap out of her. Corvossier took her time strolling back in the direction of the building that made her palms sweat, trying to find something in the local shops to distract her. It was to no avail. She stood to the side to let an excited gaggle of Swedish tourists out of the doorway as they left the Museum Of Witchcraft And Magic, gift bags under their arms. Stepping in to the darkened interior, she was met by the piercing brown eyes of Opal almost immediately. The witch blinked, as if not sure what she was seeing, before she narrowed her gaze.

'You must be very dumb to show back up here,' she murmured.

'Or very desperate,' Corvossier answered. 'And what, no "blessed be" for me today?'

Sprinkle dashed around the counter, ducking under Opal's outstretched grip as she tried to stop her niece.

'Opal said she told you to leave,' the girl chirped, coming to a halt right in front of her.

'She did.'

'She's scary, Casper. When she wants to be. You should do what she says.'

'I wish I could,' she replied, sincerely meaning it.

'Opal says you're dangerous.'

'Does she? Your auntie and I have a very different versions of last night then.'

'I don't think you're dangerous. I can tell.'

'It's funny how this situation doesn't at all look like the crystal chart you were supposed to be memorising,' her auntie barked.

'Already finished it,' the kid chirped, darting back around the counter to hold up her exercise book. On the page were sketches of dozens of crystals, complete with names and uses written next to them.

'See, I told you.'

The older witch frowned. 'Geode?'

'To keep your powers and spells grounded.'

'And?'

'Internal healing.'

'Point?'

'Directs and concentrates energy. Useful for helping enhance spells.'

'Good.'

'This is more interesting than crystals,' the kid quipped, casting the witch a sheepish glance. There must have been something she saw in her auntie's face that made her back down, because Sprinkle promptly returned to the work in her exercise book. The ghosts of her parents were there, watching over their daughter as she began pointedly scribbling away.

'Leave,' Opal repeated.

'No.'

Her braids were done up in an elaborate bun on the top of her head and she raised her chin in defiance, as if daring Corvossier to try her. Instead, she placed the correct change for an entry ticket on the counter.

'One for the museum, please.'

Without another word, she wandered up the stairs and into the heart of the building. Although every part of her was screaming to run from the place and as far away from this threat as she could, Corvossier willed herself to stay. She sank her feet into the floorboards like it was wet cement, her eyes seeing but not really digesting the exhibits as she took as much time as she could painstakingly treading her way through the museum. It was somewhat of a hoarder's dream, with treasures and information packed into every corner of every room. There had been tourists milling about when she first entered, but the longer she stayed the emptier the place became. She sensed the witch was right behind her, watching Corvossier as she pretended to peruse. One of the exhibits did actually bring her to a halt, with the medium pausing in front of the ducking stool she had inspected on her first visit.

'It was you,' she murmured, suddenly coming to a realisation. 'You tried to drown me.'

She spun around to face the witch, not doubting that the two of them were purposefully alone in the building. With her arms crossed over her chest as she lurked behind a display of 'witchcraft from around the world', Opal didn't even try to look sorry.

'Unsuccessfully.'

'Then you tried to *burn me alive*?!'

'Please, it was a charring at most.'

'Those . . . those are the ways witches died,' she stammered. 'That's what humans put them through.'

'A little bit of mutual suffering breeds mutual understanding,' Opal replied, voice dry.

Corvossier was simultaneously horrified, shocked and impressed: all three responses fighting for dominance in her mind as moved on to the next exhibit. The witch's footsteps trailed behind her, not giving the medium any room. She faced her, looking down at the woman from her higher vantage point.

'Seems a bit on the nose, doesn't it?'

'What does?'

'A witch,' Corvossier pressed. 'Working at a museum of witchcraft.'

'It's called hiding in plain sight,' she replied. 'Besides, it worked on you.'

She opened her mouth to argue, but swallowed the sentence instead. The witch was right: one mention of a naked moon ritual and she had been scoffing at the prospect of taking the woman seriously. The more she thought about it, the more genius the act was: Opal was playing on people's stereotypes and exploiting their assumptions. The witch clearly took

Corvossier's silence as a sign of victory, a smug smile creeping on to her face.

'I don't know what to call you,' she admitted. 'Kala Tully or Opal—'

'Thomas, Opal Thomas. And only ever call me that.'

'Why? Because it's dangerous to use your old name? Who here would recognise it?'

'I don't take those kind of risks. I don't any risks, if I can help it.'

'And your accents! You're Australian, both of you, and you haven't been here for more than two years at the most. How is it that you can speak with flawless Cornish accents?'

Opal reached up and undid the clasp of the necklace that hung around her neck. Unlooping it, she placed it in her hand.

'Gidday mate,' she said, drily. The stark contrast to her earlier voice caused Corvossier to jump in shock, the witch flashing the first genuine grin since they had met.

'You . . . your accent, it's—'

'That's what we would normally sound like,' the witch said, redoing the necklace. 'I have a knack for charms and spells that are very specific. That's my talent.'

'So you hide your accents, that way you stand out a little less,' Corvossier said, deeply impressed.

'Hey, we're still two Aboriginal women in Cornwall: we stand out. But it helps. Any little thing that makes us noticeable, I have to file back.'

'I understand,' she replied. 'To get here unnoticed I had four outfit changes, four different IDs and a prosthetic hand. In Berlin, I've never had to disguise my uniqueness: I've never had to try to blend in. You get used to living in the world like any supernatural and begin to think that's just how it is.'

'It's a blessing to be able to live how you really are in this life and one that not everyone gets,' Opal said, her voice barely more than a whisper. 'But it does make it a bit more difficult to camouflage among the everyday folk.'

'That's why the kid is homeschooled at the museum. Regular school is too risky; you might draw attention.'

Opal looked surprised at how much Corvossier had put together, her mind snagging on another detail.

'The charm you gave me. It wasn't for good luck and prosperity, was it?'

'A disorientation spell,' Opal admitted, no trace of regret in her tone. 'A near-death experience would be a fairly good motivator for most people.'

'I've been called "Death" since I was thirteen years old,' she snapped. 'I'm not *most* people.'

The two women found themselves at a standoff, neither one willing to give up ground as their conversation moved into more hostile territory. Instead they just stared at each other, in silence, the only reprieve coming from the occasional blink. There was a jingling of bells that indicated someone had entered the store, Opal's name being called out loudly and in a distinctly whingey fashion. The witch looked annoyed, reluctantly backing away and heading to the counter.

Corvossier took the regular route through the rest of the museum, surprised as she found a different lady behind the counter when she went to exit. She barely looked out of her teens, with a black, glossy fringe so long Corvossier struggled to see her eyes underneath it.

'Yeah?' the girl asked, popping a bubble of gum with her snakebite piercings.

'Uh, is Opal still here?'

'She don't work past four, I'm on the late shift. You a girl-friend or something?'

'No, I . . .'

'Don't have a cow, she's just packing up her stuff. She'll be out in two seconds. You don't wanna see the museum again? Lots of cool shite in there.'

'I've seen it, thanks. I'll wait for her out the front.'

'I like your hair,' the woman called as Corvossier stepped back outside.

Opal rolled her eyes the second she saw her lingering there, her possessions shoved into a shoulder bag made of straw. As the medium's gaze ran over the mystical unicorn T-shirt she was wearing with crochet pants, she wondered how she could have ever been so stupid to accept what this woman presented to the world.

'What *now*?' she moaned. 'I already sent Sprinkle home so she wouldn't have to deal with this.'

'I am not going to quit,' Corvossier replied, voice firm. 'And I am not going away. At the very least, let me show you what I have? That way if you still want me to bugger off at the end of it, I will.'

Throwing a hand on her hip, the witch considered her with a frustrated scowl.

'I don't want you in my house.'

'Fine. Come to The Wellington, you clearly already know my room number.'

Opal chuckled. 'I'm not leaving an eight-year-old alone by herself, no matter how well she's protected.'

That last comment intrigued Corvossier, but she let it go. 'Then what? I'm out of solutions here.'

'Come after nine,' she said. 'Sprinkle will be asleep and at least that way I'm on my home turf.'

'Fine.'

The witch began walking away, Corvossier watching her leave before she came to a stop.

'Wait,' she said, turning around. 'You don't know where I live.'

'Yes I do,' Corvossier answered, savouring the small amount of shock followed by anger that skipped over the witch's face. Without another word, she headed off in the opposite direction.

Corvossier had been standing outside the witch's cottage for twenty minutes. There was no reason not to walk right up and knock on the door: she was expected, after all. But she was feeling some kind of way about it. There was a fence that ran around the perimeter and a stone path that cut across a tidy, manicured lawn. There was a flower garden, complete with gnomes smiling at her in the dark, and a windmill spinning slightly from its position staked in the ground. The pair of ghosts were sitting on a bench out the front, which was secured to the ceiling via thick chains. They were swinging on it, the movement causing a subtle creaking sound. To anyone passing by, it would have just looked like the furniture was swaying in the breeze. Only Corvossier could see that it wasn't. There was a tinkling of wind chimes, the noise dainty and sweet: just like the whole exterior of the house.

Opal had made Corvossier reassess appearances and it was because of that, she was nervous about crossing the threshold. Turned out, she didn't have to as the wooden front door creaked open and the witch peered out into the darkness, spotting her.

'Could you be less creepy?'

'No,' she grumbled, 'I don't suppose I could.'

'Get inside,' Opal hissed, Corvossier moving cautiously up the path and not taking her eyes off the garden gnomes. It was something about their enormous, dead smiles that had her convinced at any moment they were going to spring to life and attempt to throttle her. *If only Barastin was here to see this*, she thought, recalling his love of a terrible movie called *Puppetmaster* about murderous dolls and stupid people. The inside of the home was warm, Corvossier shrugging off her jacket and grabbing the shoulder bag that contained her laptop and whatever paper files she risked taking with her from the investigation board at the Bierpinsel. She hung her garment on one of several hooks near the door, with shoes lined up neatly below them. She kept her pair on, in case she had to flee, and followed Opal past a carpeted staircase and into the kitchen. A rustic, wooden dining table took up much of the space there and a small window provided a view of the garden and cottage next door. There was an empty bottle of wine sitting unattended, with a glass almost the size of a fish bowl containing just one more sip's worth. Opal grabbed the stem as she walked past, draining it quickly before heading towards a cupboard that Corvossier thought was filled with plates but – upon opening it – was actually stocked with wine. The witch's eyes ran over the bottles, her eyebrows furrowed as she looked deep in thought.

'I think it's more of a red night, don't you?'

She didn't wait for a reply, slipping a bottle from the shelf and beginning the process of uncorking it. She took a long, deep inhale when she fully opened the bottle, groaning with pleasure.

'Australian wine makes me homesick,' she whispered, pouring the liquid into two large glasses. 'The options in this country are crappy.'

Corvossier accepted the one that was handed to her, looking at it like it was poison. For all she knew, it could be. The ghosts of Opal's sister and her husband had come inside and were silent witnesses at the table with them.

'It's not arsenic,' Opal snorted. 'It's cab sav.'

'I'm sorry, what?'

'Cabernet Sauvignon,' she clarified. 'Kirrihill Tullymore Vineyard two thousand and thirteen, Clare Valley.'

'Forgive me if I'm not completely trusting,' Corvossier said, sarcastic.

'Look, drink it or don't drink it. I myself need wine to get through this and at least this bottle tastes like home.'

She took another big gulp, Corvossier turning to the woman's sister with what she was sure was a sceptical expression on her face. The ghost nodded towards the glass, smiling as if it was okay. Taking a small mouthful, she took a moment to enjoy the rich tastes as they swirled around. It was delicious, but she wasn't about to tell Opal that. Instead, she put down the glass and opened her laptop. Methodically, she began spreading out small piles of information across the table. She stacked some of it under faces of the various members the Oct, while their now dead Askari recruits were clustered underneath, like a macabre family tree.

'If you talk,' Opal said, her voice hardly a whisper as her eyes focused in on the faces Corvossier guessed she recognised, 'I'll listen. I can't promise you more than that.'

'I'll take it,' she agreed, watching as the ghosts both got to their feet and stared at the documents. Taking a hearty sip of wine, she steadied herself and launched into the speech she had practised that afternoon, by herself, in her hotel room.

'Irish Barber, Cici Kulogvish, Hans Guilford and Mike Higgens were all junior, low-ranking members of the Askari,' Corvossier started. 'They were recruited by former and present members of the Askari, a kind of secret society *within* the secret society, if you will. Those people refer to themselves as the Oct and the four names I mentioned at the start ran errands for them, everything from organising a murder to tracking records through the Treize database.'

'And they're dead?' Opal asked, looking up at Corvossier with tears welling in her eyes. 'The four of them?'

'Yes. Two were killed by Hans, who wanted them out of the way so he'd likely be the next one to officially join the Oct. I killed Mike, after interrogation, which is where I got the bulk of this information from. Hans killed himself before I had a chance to get to him, taking whatever answers he had with him.'

'You can't, like, ghost question him or something?'

'I can, hypothetically, within a small window and I was notified of his death too late. He'd gone by the time I searched for him in the lobby.'

'The *what*?'

'Spectral realm ... listen, that's not important. What *is* important is these ten people are the ones who murdered my brother, Barastin. They cut off my hand and attempted to kill me. And they executed my Custodian, Collette.'

'When did these happen? Where?'

'In Berlin, where I live, approximately six months after your attack.'

Opal had been about to take another sip of wine when she paused, glass at her lips.

'I'd be curious to find how it is you know about what happened to me.'

'I don't, not really. I don't have the specifics, mainly because like my attack I'm guessing yours was covered up.'

'Ghouls,' the witch snorted. 'A ghoul attack in suburban Sydney. Never happened before, never happened since, but it sure as hell was a great excuse for the Treize to clear out every nest in the country. For everyone's safety, *of course*.'

'Of course. They said our attack was witches.'

Willa's head snapped towards Corvossier, her living sister mimicking the same gesture as a deep, curdling rage crept over their expressions.

'And you didn't believe it?' Opal asked, the tone pointed.

'No,' she replied. 'I'd met witches. I knew this wasn't witches.'

'Who? What coven?'

'They're not . . . witches you would know.'

'Are you lying to me, Casper?'

'Dead witches,' she said with a sigh. Understanding passed over Opal, the woman leaning back as she rocked in her chair.

'I suppose there's a lot of those, in Europe.'

Corvossier nodded, keeping her eyes trained on the stacks of paper so as not to give anything more away about herself than she already had. A fat, ginger cat waddled its way into the room, wrapping itself around her legs and purring affectionately.

'Is this . . . is this your familiar?'

Opal laughed, it being the first time Corvossier had heard her outright react with happiness.

'My familiar,' she breathed, wiping away a tear from under her eye. 'That's Bunyip. She was a stray, used to hang out around the cottage when we first moved in. It decided we were its new humans. And you know that when a cat decides something, there's very little you can do about it.'

As if knowing she was being talked about, the pet strutted over to the witch and meowed.

'Here's the thing,' Opal began, bending down to scratch Bunyip behind the ears. 'I might have cut us off from the world here intentionally, but I still have some friends. I reached out to a woman from my coven and asked if she had heard of a medium named Corvossier: she didn't. But she did start telling me about another woman, one that she had learned about through the grapevine who it's rumoured can make the dead do her bidding: someone who looks more like a ghost than she does a girl, with eyes grey from crossing over into the spirit world so often.'

'That sounds familiar.'

'She had a lot to say about Casper, which I thought was just something Sprinkle had decided to call you. I mean, she gave herself the name *Sprinkle* so it wasn't entirely out of the realm of possibility.'

'Casper is a nickname, like Death. They used to call my brother Creeper and we were the Spook Siblings or the Death Dealers depending on the day.'

'I think you got that last one from a movie.'

'Whatever,' she said. 'They like alliteration. And I have no control over it either way so . . .'

'Your brother, Creeper, Barastin, you miss him?'

'I do,' Corvossier answered carefully, not wanting to tip her hat to the fact Barastin was still around. Well, usually. 'Every second. He seems . . . very much alive to me, even after a year.'

'I know what you mean,' Opal replied, gesturing at a framed picture sitting on the mantelpiece. In it were the ghosts Corvossier had seen, but they were alive and grinning wildly at Sprinkle who was frozen in a ridiculous pose.

'Your sister,' she whispered, feeling the loss heavy in the room as both of the ghosts looked on as well.

'I lost my sister, my brother-in-law, but the kid . . . she lost her parents. She used to call out to them in her sleep, just after they died, over and over again. It was horrible: I didn't know what to say or how to help her: I only knew how to run.'

'Sometimes it's the only thing you can do.'

Opal and Corvossier shared a significant look, both of them united by the grief of losing their siblings. Except neither of them were really gone. The witch broke the stare first, glancing down at the paperwork in front of them.

'I want to know how you got all this. The specifics.'

'Mike Higgens, as I mentioned. It took months to track him and even longer to lock him down in one location. The details on his colleagues are all in the Askari database.'

'Which you have access to?'

'No, I mean, yes. I'm not supposed to, but a contact—'

'Who?'

'A contact – I'm not giving up their name – built a program that once I installed it directly on an Asakri computer meant I could access a mirror of their system. Here, let me show you.'

Corvossier swung her laptop around to face Opal so she could see as she typed 'Kala Tully' into the database. It came up with the locked, redacted file. She typed another name – her own – and showed her the information that appeared.

'How did you get close enough to an Askari base to upload this?'

'I live above one.'

'Convenient.'

'For this purpose, yeah.'

'Type in Mayra North.'

Corvossier did as ordered, relief crossing the witch's face when the database returned a blank result.

'Try Willa North and Alistair North.'

Both of their files were the same: locked and available from one of only three physical sites.

'What does that mean? Those places?'

'Far as I can tell, it means you need special clearance to view what's in your file and theirs, clearance that's only available at bases in those locations.'

'Hatherleigh's near here.'

'What?'

'It's a few hours' drive, less depending what time you go. It's an airfield. What would be in those files?'

'I don't know,' Corvossier answered truthfully. 'Something they don't want anyone to see or understand.'

'So something valuable, otherwise it wouldn't be locked?'

'Sure. It's your file, do you have any idea what that could be?

'It depends . . . on what we have common.'

'Us? Me and you?' Corvossier wanted to laugh, just from physicality alone they couldn't have been more opposite. But then she understood Opal's point. 'Because we survived.'

'And because we were targets to begin with, which I guess comes down to them.'

She nodded her head at the faces of the Oct, their two dimensional sketches looking up at them from the paper.

'How did you get those composites?' the witch wondered.

'They were drawn from my memory. I suppose you remember them pretty well too.'

'Not as clearly as you,' she said, picking up one of the drawings and sliding it towards her. 'Just this guy.'

'That's Gerald Simpson, he's the only one I've been able to name so far and I think I just got lucky.'

'I don't think we're the lucky type, do you?' Opal asked, a smile teasing her mouth.

'No, I guess not.'

'How did you get the name?'

'The lackeys were supposed to have been recruited from inside the Askari, by other Askari, so I cross-referenced people in the system against the four we already had. It's time-consuming, but that's how I got Mr Simpson over here. He had worked with both Irish and Hans at one point, so tick. But also tick when I saw his face.'

She brought up the file so Opal could see, the witch looking confused.

'Why isn't his locked?'

'My only thought is they don't know he's part of the Oct. He resigned years ago and if they don't know—'

'Then why hide it,' Opal growled. 'That's why they're covering it up: they know at least some of the people responsible for this came from within their own organisation. They fear how they'll look to the rest of the supernatural community if this comes out, it will be embarrassing.'

'It would make people question their government,' Corvossier stated.

They both stared at each other in silence, quiet as the words of the medium's sentence really took effect. The crackle of a fireplace coming from another room was the only true noise: it was such a small, subtle sound when you thought about it. But that's all there was: the echo of burning. Bunyip was crouched with her eyes closed on one of the chairs around the dining table. It was the same one Alistair North was sitting at, the visual looking weird to Corvossier as she watched them both.

'Ingredients,' she whispered, recalling something Mike had said. 'That's what he referred to us as. He said the Oct had to kill specific targets so they could transform or evolve or elevate. It was something like that.'

'Into what?'

'I don't know.'

'That means there's other murders.'

'Definitely, but he didn't seem to know where or when or who they were. Just they had to be killed and it was a process of years. The only other useful piece of information I got was the one survivor: you. He had your name, K—'

'Don't.'

'Sorry. It was your name, not your sister's or your niece's, just you.'

'And you: you survived too.'

Corvossier took a deep breath. 'I guess. Sometimes I wonder how much of me survived. The person I've had to become to hunt them, just because they hunted me . . . I don't know.'

She shook her head, finishing the last of her wine and getting to her feet. She felt the slightest buzz from the alcohol, her cheeks warm to the touch. Corvossier washed out her glass at the sink, looking out the frosted window and into the night. The light outside had faded completely, with darkness wrapping around the town. Rain had started pelting down on the roof in the last few minutes, with droplets splashing against the glass from the force.

As she looked for a towel to dry off the glass, her eyes were drawn to a shelf in the kitchen. At first she thought it had been allocated for alcohol too, given the unusual bottles looked like they contained boutique spirits. Yet there were things she could see inside them that weren't designed for human consumption: one even seemed to preserve the body of a mouse.

'Witch bottles,' Opal said, answering a question Corvossier hadn't yet asked as she joined her at the sink.

'Oh, they're real? There's a bit about them in the museum.'

'Those witch bottles aren't real, just food colouring and harmless herbs to look nice for visitors. These are.'

The witch's fingers swept across the dozens of bottles, symbols that were tattooed down her digits visible with the gesture.

'What do they do, exactly?'

'Depends.' Opal shrugged, pointing to one. 'This was actually an abandonment spell I was going to bury in the garden here when I first came to town. Eventually the previous tenants would have been compelled to leave.'

'What happened to the people who used to live here?' she asked, not sure if she wanted the real answer.

'Originally we were renting a room at a boarding house across the road, but I had my eye on this cottage. It's built on top of sacred stones that were once used in rituals by the druids, giving it added protectional energy.'

'And let me guess, the previous owner got mysteriously sick?'

'Divorced, actually.' She smirked. 'Nothing to do with me at all: got caught rooting the barmaid at the Cobweb Inn and that was that. I had the abandonment spell ready to go, which was a total waste of ingredients.'

'And that one?' Corvossier asked, pointing to a tiny vessel that looked more like a perfume bottle than some of the larger additions.

'Pneumonoultramicroscopicsilicovolcanoconiosis.'

'What?' she spluttered.

'It's the most dangerous spell I know; it creates an accelerated form of lung disease usually caused by fine silica from volcano ash.'

'Fuck.'

'It's defensive magic, which is why I have most of these prepared here in case I need them.'

'You have something protecting the house too, right?'

'Could you sense it? Is that why you were waiting outside?'

'Maybe, I'm not sure. It just didn't feel . . . right. I can't sense most magic, so I don't think it was that.'

'Huh.'

'Why Boscastle?' she blurted, not wanting to ruin the rapport they were building but also having a thousand questions of her own.

'To hide?'

Corvossier nodded, watching as Bunyip stirred and leapt from one seat to the other, avoiding the floor like it was lava.

'There are certain places that hold power, Boscastle is one. If you're paying attention, you can feel it almost the moment you step foot in this town: every inch, every stone, every surface is alive with magic. This place has a well-known history of it and people push it aside, thinking that it's just that: history. But magic doesn't have an expiry date.'

'How does that help you?'

'Selkies have their family pondants, werewolves have packs, arachnia have nests, goblins live in geographical clusters, and it's the same with witches and our covens. We have safety in numbers, strength, and unity. Rogue werewolves have a harder time of it: many don't survive or end their own lives outside of the pack structure. Witches can suffer the same fate and it's true, we are weaker without our sisters.'

'You know a lot about werewolves.'

'Every witch does; they're our siblings. Witches and werewolves were persecuted alongside one another throughout history, while the Treize sat by and watched, stepping in only when they *felt* like it.'

Opal looked as if she dared Corvossier to disagree, but nothing she had said was incorrect.

'My sister and her husband gave up their lives trying to save Sprinkle. All I could do was spend the rest of mine trying to fulfil their dying wish. After we got away, I hid out for a few days, trying to figure out what was happening and where was safe. When my coven got word to me they were calling it a ghoul attack, that's when I knew I had to run from the Treize as well, which meant leaving the coven. So I needed to pick up power where I could find it: a place that was already rich with it.'

'Are there a lot of places like that?' Corvossier asked.

'Thousands, all over the world. Many witches don't even know these places exist until they cross them. I was able to use the power of Boscastle to help Sprinkle and I disappear, to cloak us. The rest was just logistics: new names, new IDs, the accent charms, crafting a backstory that people would believe we'd always been here, just in another part of Cornwall.'

'And the job?'

'The most powerful spot in town is that building: it's a hotbed of magical history. It made sense the place where we'd spend the most amount of time would be the safest, which was at the museum. They only had one full-time staff member previously and six casuals for the weekend, but unfortunately he fell rather ill.'

There was a knowing flash in Opal's eyes and Corvossier knew the witch sitting across from her was the cause of the man's illness.

'The rest was easy: I knew so much about witchcraft anyway, I just needed to learn the stories they told as truth and I had the job.'

'And practise your acting,' she remarked.

'I'm good, right? Like, not Oscar-winning good but I could definitely score a Golden Globe nomination at the very least.'

Corvossier smiled, enjoying the lighter direction the conversation had taken. She didn't want to bring it back to the depressing present and her real purpose there, but it was exactly what she needed to do.

'Does this mean you will help me?'

The witch was clearly thinking about it, Corvossier trying desperately to handle the mounting tension she felt building before Opal gave her an answer.

'I didn't come all this way to expose us,' she said. 'I've worked too hard to keep Sprinkle safe, to keep myself safe, and build these lives for us. They mightn't be the lives we used to have and I might ache for my land and my country, but we're *alive*. Sometimes that has to be enough.'

'So that's a no?'

'You said trying to find them in the system was time-consuming.'

'The Oct? Yeah, extremely.'

'I'll help you with the paperwork side of things and the research. Outside of that, you're on your own.'

What's new? she thought, immediately scolding herself for the negative response. Truthfully, this was more than she had expected from the witch. And she did need the help.

'Do we shake on it?' she asked.

'We pinky swear.'

'Really?'

'No, what are you? Five years old? You get out of my house and come back tomorrow, same time.'

'Alright.' Corvossier nodded, heading towards the door. The cottage had seemed smaller from the outside when she had observed it, but inside it was burrow of tight hallways that led to cosy rooms. Sliding back into her coat, she gave Opal a small wave that doubled as a goodbye to the ghosts standing behind the witch. Without another word, she headed back down the path and towards the lights of The Wellington, feeling not quite as lonely for the first time since her brother had gone.

Chapter 10

They fell into a routine over the coming days. At exactly 9 p.m., Corvossier would show up at the witch's door, laptop and paperwork in hand, and long after Sprinkle had gone to bed. They'd work for as long as they could, usually into the small hours of the morning or until one of them conked out: Opal, more often than Corvossier, given she still had a day job to maintain. It was frustrating, having to share a laptop between them, not to mention the residual hostility left over from their initial interactions. But the wine helped with that: so too did having a purpose.

They worked the names and they worked the database, fastidiously analysing every line in the files of their targets. They had Gerald Simpson so he was the focus, but they couldn't discount the lackeys having crossed paths with *other* members of the Oct at a different point: especially Cici and Mike, given there didn't seem to be a visible connection to Gerald. Had he got to them another way, off paper? Or was it someone else altogether? They couldn't make assumptions and risk missing something crucial. The witch was a lot better at the social media side of things than Corvossier was, finding accounts for Irish and Mike when they had still been alive. She trawled that for information too.

'I'm not expecting a tweet from @TheOct_89 or anything,' she muttered, when she caught Corvossier giving her a strange look. 'They're unlikely to have sent a message like "hey, come kill with us #death #murdersquadgoalz".'

'You could be speaking in a foreign language to me right now, just so you're aware.'

'What I mean is social media is a handy tool for seeing where they've been: a selfie walking the Great Wall tells you they were in China and it tells you when. Why were they there? Who were they with?'

'I think I get what you're saying: it charts their movements.'

'Exactly.' Opal grinned, the gesture still startling to Corvossier. They were barely friends, more like frenemies with a shared aim, but the witch was so attractive she found it hard to stare directly at her in such a close setting: it was like looking at the sun.

She did, however, appreciate how much the witch valued her desire to be organised. They had been two nights into the process when Corvossier had showed up with a bag of highlighters and Post-it notes from the local store, only to find Opal had laid out practically identical supplies on the table as well. The witch began building timelines for the five names they had, which soon became six when Corvossier identified another member of the Oct. She'd been clicking through idly, searching every name that worked in the same office of Gerald Simpson's third posting in the nineties. He'd started out in Tonga, then moved to New Mexico and Switzerland after that: a place that Siegfried McKenzie also worked. The second her face was up on screen, the medium launched to her feet. Her chair fell back and landed on the ground with a clatter, Opal scolding her for the noise that could wake her niece. The witch fell quiet when she saw the look on Corvossier's face, noticing the way her fingers trembled slightly. She got up, standing at the medium's side as she viewed the staff photo taken more than twenty years ago.

The woman staring back at her had a vague smile dancing on her lips and a ghastly shade of peach lipstick that clashed with her complexion. She looked like someone who would tell you everything about their day when all you had done to initiate the conversation was say 'hi'. This lady – the one in the photo – was a far cry from the woman who had worn her black hair pulled back into a tight ponytail and stared at Corvossier with eyes that chilled her to the very core. She selected her out of the pile, adding it to the concrete list.

'You recognise her,' Opal stated.

Corvossier nodded, not quite able to form words just yet as she held up her right arm for emphasis.

'Oh Christ,' she whispered, glancing at the medium's limb difference and gulping. Slowly, without another word, she pulled up a Post-it pad and wrote Siegfried McKenzie's name in capital letters. Peeling it from the block, Opal stuck it on top of Corvossier's sketch of the woman.

'Two down,' she finally managed to say. 'Eight to go.'

It took a while for Corvossier to get her heart back to a reasonable level, with her being mostly useless for the rest of the night. She found herself watching Opal instead, intrigued by the way every few minutes, like clockwork, she would glance towards the faces laid out on the dining table. There were four she kept returning to, looking at them like they made her uneasy, until it got to the point that she positioned objects in front of them. It was subtle – one of the bottles of wine, a pencil case – but she moved things so they were blocked from view. Analysing Siegfried McKenzie's face, Corvossier reached out and flipped the page over. There was no need to give the drawing anymore light.

She had terrible nightmares that evening when she got back to her room or, more specifically, one nightmare, recurring. Corvossier would be walking down that Kreuzberg alleyway in the evening, her hand linked in Barastin's as they walked and walked onwards endlessly. The sense of dread grew in the pit of her stomach because she knew what was coming, she knew who waited in the shadows and what they were willing to do to her and her brother. Except they never attacked: she sensed them there, watching, as Barastin dragged her deeper into the alleyway. He was chatting excitedly about something frivolous, a guy he was meeting or a new nightspot he wanted to try out, completely oblivious to the danger just outside of view. Meanwhile anxiety curdled in her stomach as she tried to staunch the rising panic, wanting desperately to warn him but unable to enunciate a single word. She was mute and powerless. And Barastin just kept walking.

She woke with a start, the sound that pulled her out of the nightmare being the landline next to the bed. Taking a deep breath, she ran her hands over her face as she attempted to compose herself before answering. They had worked until 4 a.m. that morning, and a glance at the clock told her she had slept until just after 3 p.m. She croaked a hello into the receiver, her mind still trying to reconcile the fact she was no longer trapped in that horrible vision.

'The jig is up.'

'Jig?' she asked, surprised to hear Opal's voice down the line.

'Sprinkle knows you've been coming over.'

'Does she know why?'

'No, but the little tyrant is pissed. So I need you over here early tonight.'

'To . . . handle your niece?'

'To have dinner, Casper. An official invitation has been extended and if you don't accept, I'll probably be smothered in my sleep.'

'That would clear up a lot of problems for me.'

'Har-de-har. Are you coming or not?'

'I'm coming.'

'Good. How's an hour?'

'Also good. What should I bring?'

'I've already got ingredients, but you could take care of dessert. Sprinkle likes these little cake things called Angel Slice.'

'Angel Slice, got it.'

'By Mr Kipling.'

'By who?'

'That's the brand.'

'Oh, right. You okay for wine?'

'Nice one,' the witch scoffed, that being her form of farewell as she hung up the phone. With a hint of a smile on her face, Corvossier turned around to say something to her brother before she froze with the realisation: Barastin wasn't there. Her lips were already parted as she had begun to instinctively start speaking to him, as she always did, but there was a void where he should be. It took her a moment to reboot and adjust to his absence, the pang in her chest just something she had to live with until he returned. Corvossier poured herself into fussing over her appearance instead, not being able to decide between a dark violet dress and a sapphire one, before eventually going with the former. When she got to the cottage, her hand had barely reached for the door before it flew open, Sprinkle standing there with her hands on her hips.

'Well.'

'Well,' Corvossier replied, awkwardly.

'I guess you better come in then.'

'You invited me, right?'

'I did, I did,' the kid's tone super serious for an eight-year-old. 'I just want you to know that I feel very left out by the movie nights that have been happening *right* under my nose, all along. Just because I'm a kid, that doesn't mean I like movies?'

'Um . . .' She didn't know quite how to respond, following her into the kitchen where Opal was preparing dinner.

'I told you, kiddo,' the witch said, glancing up. 'They're bad movies: full of violence and swearing and sex.'

'Name one,' she challenged, Corvossier finally catching on to the cover story.

'*Suspiria*,' she blurted, Opal mouthing 'what the fuck?' at her behind Sprinkle's back. 'It's an Italian movie about ballet and witches. It's very old, way older than you.'

The child looked suspicious, her face contorted as she considered whether the medium's answer was up to scratch or not.

'Here,' Corvossier said, shoving the contents of her bag into Sprinkle's arms. 'I bought dessert.'

'Angel Slice!' she shrieked, doing a little victory dance right there on the spot.

'And this is *before* the sugar,' Opal noted.

'What can I do?' Corvossier asked, her eyes running over the preparations.

'Not a thing,' the witch said, casting a quick glance at her arm before her eyes diverted back again. 'You just take a seat.'

'You think I can't help because I have one arm,' she scoffed.

'What? No, I didn't say that. I'm sure you can—'

'It's a limb difference, not the end of the world. How do you think I eat the rest of the time?'

'I . . . uh, I don't know. I guess I didn't really think about it.'

'I can dice,' she said, looking around for the knives. 'I can dice like nobody's business.'

'Alright,' Opal said, laying down several onions and a chopping board. 'Choose your weapon.'

She gestured to a wooden slab where several larger knives were held and Corvossier grabbed the one she was after. She got to work, peeling an onion with one hand and then positioning it with her arm while the other one sliced and diced. She could feel Opal's eyes on her, watching how she did it, but the witch said nothing as she began her own preparations. When she was done, she scraped the onion slices into a large tray where ingredients were being added. Opal silently placed several tomatoes in front of her without comment and Corvossier hid a smirk, cutting them as if it was for salsa. She liked that never once did either of the witches tell her what they were cooking for dinner: they seemed to know and that was enough. There was never even a question of what she might or might not eat: it was said without words that this was their house and if you wanted to be fed, you would eat what was put in front of you. Or you wouldn't.

Eventually Opal took over the final tasks, mixing several ingredients together in the tray before inserting it into the oven for several minutes. She took it out, laid several chicken breasts across the mix, then put it back in. Every ten minutes or so, without the use of a timer, the witch would retrieve the tray and add another layer: first it was the tomato and onion salsa mix, then the rice with chorizo, followed by peas, all the while the chicken was flipped over and the ingredients all stirred together. Covossier watched her freehand chilli flakes and paprika, feeling grateful in the moment for her tolerance of spicy foods. Sprinkle slipped a CD into an old, portable player behind them and began humming along to the music as it rolled through the house.

'Is that Nick Cave and the Bad Seeds?' Corvossier asked, watching as the little girl danced strangely from room to room.

'All witches love Nick Cave,' Opal replied. 'Didn't you know?'

Corvossier threw her an incredulous glance, which elicited a deep laugh from the woman beside her at the sink.

'Your face, good grief. You mob are just clueless, I swear.'

'Clue me in, then. Where does a witch's power come from?'

She snorted. 'Aiming high, with the big questions to start.'

'Well?'

'We don't know. No one knows, really: our magic isn't good or evil, it's neutral. More importantly, it's a power that's loaned to us for the temporary time that we're on this earth.'

Turning off the tap, Opal dried her hands on a tea towel and handed it to Corvossier who did the same. She noticed it was one with the Museum Of Witchcraft And Magic logo printed on it.

'She's a morbid child,' the witch said, leaning against the counter as she watched her niece. 'She was even before everything that happened.'

'I can understand what she sees in this particular discography then.'

'It's really her mum's fault. She used to play *Nocturama* on repeat when Sprinkle was first born, it was the only thing that seemed to quiet her down.'

'I was always more of a *Let Love In* person myself.'

The oven timer in Sprinkle's mind must have gone off, with the subject of their conversation dashing back into the kitchen and hopping up on to the dining table. Opal gestured for Corvossier to take a seat, with the dish set down in front of them a variation of Spanish baked chicken. Herbs were sprinkled on top, along with quarters of lemon to squeeze over the chicken. Sprinkle tucked in, politely serving Corvossier first before filling her own plate. Opal went last and silence hung between the three of them as they ate, just the sounds of clinking forks as accompaniment. It was Sprinkle who broke the silence, with a barrage of questions that were less like a conversation and more an integration of the highest order.

'What's your favourite colour?' she began.

'Green.'

'Why?'

'Because it looks the best on me. What's yours?'

'Yellow. What's your favourite video game?'

'Doom.'

'What's that?'

'Not one you should play for a few more years yet.'

'What was your brother's favourite colour?'

'Anything autumn-toned: brown, bronze, amber.'

'Eh, those are barely colours. Favourite movie?'

'*Cronos*. What's yours?'

'*Indiana Jones and the Temple of Doom*. How many languages can you speak?'

'Three: English, German and French.'

'Oh! Say something in French.'

'*Tu as tellement de questions dans cette si petite tête.*'

'What does that mean?'

'It means "you have so many questions stored up in a head so tiny".'

'Cooool. What was your favourite subject when you were homeschooled?'

'History.'

'Who taught you?'

'Collette, the woman who raised me – my Custodian.'

'Where's she?'

'She's dead.'

'That's enough questions,' Opal said, drawing the back and forth to a close as she began collecting the plates. 'Don't drive Casper to throwing herself back in the river.'

Corvossier smiled at the girl, giving her a shrug when Opal's back was turned. She grabbed the rest of the dishes, happily washing them by hand at the sink while she continued to drink her glass of wine. She glanced at the label, noting that it was

Two Paddocks, which now – thanks to the witch's education – she knew was Sam Neill's Pinot Noir. Behind her there was a triumphant rustling of wrappers, the kid wasting no time as she tore into dessert. Glancing at the clock on the wall, Corvossier was surprised to see it had just ticked past 8 p.m. Sprinkle seemed to be feeling it, slouching at the table and doing her best to hide enormous yawns from her auntie as the two women dried plates. The witch didn't miss much though, soon disappearing with the girl to tuck her into bed. Sprinkle couldn't manage much more than a hazy 'goodnight' before she was carried away. When Opal returned, she examined what was left of the bottle of wine and the two now-empty glasses.

'Shall we finish it off?' she asked, wiggling the bottle in her hand suggestively.

'May as well,' Corvossier replied, holding out her glass as Opal distributed the last of the red equally between them. She followed the witch and the sound of music into the lounge, her bare feet brushing over the thick rugs that seemed to cover every surface. They were all different patterns and styles, overlapping each other throughout the house as they fought to suffocate the floorboards beneath them. The fireplace was generating a fair amount of warmth through the house, Opal curling up in front of it with her back resting against an ugly, green armchair as she watched the flames burn. Corvossier did the same, sitting on the ground, which was surprisingly comfortable due to all the layers of rugs. She realised with a start that what she had thought was a cushion was actually Bunyip, rolled up and fast asleep on the chair.

'Does it get too much, seeing what others can't?' the witch asked, the question surprising the medium as it seemingly came from nowhere.

'Oh, well, I mean . . . it depends. I grew up with it, seeing the dead everywhere was normal for me and it was normal for Barastin too: we had each other to rationalise it, so it never seemed strange or too much to bear. And Collette always made sure we felt valued because of it: the Treize pay us a lot of money to use what we have. As our Custodian, Collette never once called it a curse, it was always "our abilities" or "our gifts".'

'You must miss her.'

'I do, every minute. But at the same time, she was fulfilled. No ghost means she had somewhere to be.'

Opal grabbed a few pillows from the couch, placing them behind her back as she settled in, the glass of wine held between her outstretched legs. It was supposed to be comfortable, and it was, but Corvossier was also thinking about the fact that a witch bottle containing an accelerated course of volcanic lung cancer was only metres away from a Merve Ozaslan picture of a romantic couple that hung on the wall.

'Do you have a grimoire?' she asked, addressing a question she had always wanted to know.

Opal looked surprised as she glanced across at the medium. 'Yes. Although it's kind of an old-fashioned thing to do now.'

'Why's that?'

'Every witch has one main talent, something they excel at. Then there are usually two other cursory ones, like potion making or herbal remedies. They might be fine at those, but their supernatural gift lends itself the most to the first talent so keeping a grimoire when you're naturally good at a thing . . . well, not many witches do it anymore.'

'But in the museum it says it's like a magical cookbook passed down from generation of witch to generation, with each family member adding their own spells or improving pre-existing ones.'

'I'm glad your trips were so educational.'

'They were,' she admitted, taking a large sip of wine. 'I went from knowing very little, to knowing a lot. Now I just have to sift through what is true and what's—'

'Bewitched?'

'Exactly,' she laughed.

Opal nodded, as if satisfied with something in Corvossier's response. 'Yeah, I have a grimoire. My talent is a technical kind of magic. My sister, Willa, had the same kind of raw power I see growing inside of Sprinkle everyday.'

'The talents differ within bloodlines?'

'Oh yeah, it's completely unpredictable. Kind of an evolutionary assist, if you will: our skills as a species have spread out among everyone, so we're all equally able to defend ourselves and use the gifts to our advantage. I'm surprised your dead witch friends didn't explain all this to you.'

'Ah, see they love to talk: about the weather, who's dating who in the supernatural community, what Praetorian Guard soldier did this and what banshee did that. When it comes to the specifics—'

'They're cagey?'

'Just like living witches. I asked them to help me find you, something I would usually never do.'

'I'm sure that went well.'

Corvossier felt a twinge of something that surprised her: it was jealousy. The more Opal explained the traditions of the witches and her people, the more she talked about the details of what defined them as a species and the legacies they passed on, the more jealous she became.

There was no one to tell her and Barastin about their abilities growing up: they had to learn everything for themselves. There wasn't a soul who could teach them or literature they could read; it had been trial and error. Even after Barastin was murdered and Corvossier adjusted to the weird grief of losing him physically but not spiritually, he was always there for her when she needed him: unconditionally. His absence recently had felt like a loss, but it was in that moment she realised how alone they both had been their whole lives. There weren't enough mediums left for a community and the ones that were didn't have anything near the level of ability Barastin and she had. And now, it truly felt like she was one of the last of her kind.

'You look sad,' Opal said, stirring her from dark thoughts.

'Huh?'

'Your face just now. You went quiet and then ... I don't know, just sad.'

'It's not really something I can put into words,' she whispered, taking a deep breath. 'Anyway, what did you do before all this?'

'Before everything went to shit?'

'Yes, then. You were a teacher?'

'What? No, God no.'

'Oh, I just assumed with you teaching Sprinkle and everything.'

'No, that's out of desperation. I was an accountant in Sydney.'

'An accountant? You?'

'Hell, yes, I'm great with numbers. I'm very detail orientated.'

'I've always wanted to go to Sydney,' she said. 'Barastin had this dream of both of us going to Mardi Gras for our thirtieth birthdays. He wanted to make out with a surfer; it was on his bucket list.'

Opal laughed. 'Did you guys do it?'

'No.' She smiled sadly. 'He never made it to thirty; I did.'

'That must have been a crappy birthday.'

'It was,' she agreed. 'I got very drunk and didn't leave my tower.'

'It was me getting drunk that saved Sprinkle's life. Willa and Alistair lived out in the suburbs while I had a place with some friends in the city. I was seeing a girl at the time whose house was near them and we'd gone to a party nearby. We had a fight over something stupid, I can't even remember what it was. We were always snapping at each other over something petty. Anyway, I was too drunk to go home so I crashed at Willa's like I usually did. Sprinkle had a bunk bed set-up so I would always take the bottom and she was on top. That was the night they came.'

'Jesus,' Corvossier breathed, horrified by the witch's story.

'They must have been watching us for weeks, waiting for the perfect moment until we were both under the same roof. Once I heard the commotion and stumbled out of Sprinkle's room half asleep, Alistair was already dead and Willa was holding them off at the stairs, fighting to stop them from getting any further. I was able to wield two charms quickly and immobilise three of them in the robes. If my sister hadn't been injured, I feel like we would have had a fighting chance. As it was, we took half of the pricks down between us before she begged me to run, to get her daughter out of there.'

Corvossier closed her eyes, Barastin's scream coming back to her in an involuntary flash. '*RUN!*' he urged, the memory so painful it felt like a physical stab and yet it so similar to what Opal had endured as well.

'We were born two minutes apart, but she always bossed me around,' the witch continued. 'So I did what she ordered: grabbed Mayra – Sprinkle, you know – who was hiding under the bed. I got us both out of there and ran to the coven. I waited a few days to see if my sister reached out and when she didn't, I knew she was dead. Hearing the ghoul attack line, I couldn't risk staying put if the Treize were in on it—'

'Wait,' Corvossier said, sitting up straighter. 'Go back.'

'What?' Opal asked, confused at the interruption. 'To where?'

'You said Willa and you were born a few minutes apart. You were twins?'

'Identical.'

'Barastin and I were fraternal twins.'

'Casper, we're different species: there's nothing about us that's similar except for the fact we're both from sets of twins.'

'Supernatural sets of twins,' she pressed. 'We don't know what it is that made them seek us out, hunt *us*. What if it's that?'

The witch sipped her wine, staring at the fire as if it would somehow produce the answer she was searching for.

'We look for murdered or missing twins in the database then,' Opal muttered. 'How hard can that be?'

'Hard,' Corvossier emphasised. 'If their files are redacted like yours and your sister's.'

'Yours wasn't though. Neither was Barastin's.'

'Maybe that's because we're too public, we're known. If you locked ours, someone might ask why and that would lead to an uncomfortable situation. You disappeared, your coven knows this even if they don't know where, and who would be looking for you outside of the Treize?'

'No one, probably.'

'So lock it down.'

Corvossier felt like she was right, but she didn't want to get her hopes up. Between the two of them, they had wasted so many hours chasing names through the system that they liked as potential members of the Oct, only for it to turn into a dead end. She wasn't sure how many more disappointments she could take.

'In my version of hell,' Opal said, 'I'd be trapped in my sister's house, reliving that night over and over.'

'In mine,' Corvossier whispered, her voice so low it was barely louder than the sound of the fire, 'I would be stuck there too, down that alleyway in Berlin, covered in my brother's blood and unable to help him.'

She felt a warmth pressing against her hand and looked down to see the witch's nudging her own, her fingers wrapping around Corvossier's long, white digits. She glanced back at the fire, savouring the sensation of being comforted by a living, breathing person who was flesh and blood. They sat like that for a long time, not saying anything else as the fire burned in front of them and they slowly sipped their wine.

Chapter 11

Corvossier von Klitzing was planning on doing something really stupid. In her mind, however, if she approached this stupid thing with a smart plan, maybe it would cancel itself out. She didn't really believe that, but a positive mantra was essential as she started looking at the logistics of *if* and *how* she could break into the Askari base at Hatherleigh. The information she needed was there, so one way or another she was going to get it. It was all a question of if she could pull it off without being caught. From the files she could access, she learned the location was a converted boarding school and since then the Treize had added an additional airfield. The base was situated down a country lane, with the nearest farmhouse about a kilometre away. It was difficult to tell on Google Maps, but to Corvossier the house looked abandoned or at the very least derelict. It gave her a smudge of hope and she lay down on the bed, tucking herself in like she was about to fall asleep.

Instead, she released her consciousness until she was stumbling to find her footing in the lobby. She urged herself forwards, keeping the visual of the house in her mind until it began to form in front of her out of the darkness. *Yes*, she thought. *There are ghosts here.* As if they had sensed she was coming, five of the dead assembled out the front of the residence, one with a chain dragging behind her like an industrial bridal train and the other with a pair of gardening shears protruding from his abdomen. Something bad had happened here, a long time ago, and none of these ghosts wanted to let go of it. She wasn't going to be able to bargain with them, offering to push them away from the earthly plane: they didn't want to leave. Thankfully for her, their anger made them strong.

Her time with the dead was interrupted by the living, with the sound of banging on her hotel door penetrating the prism of the lobby. She rushed her farewells, telling them she would return as she lurched backwards and into the bed. Her head throbbed as she sat up, her fingers gently massaging her skull as she waited for a reprieve in the pain. A headache came on almost immediately, a side effect of her not taking her time entering or leaving the lobby. She had to respect the process and when she rushed it, her body suffered. Stumbling to her feet, she headed towards the door before pausing for a second. Her pulse was still rapid from the plunge and she couldn't shake the adrenaline coursing through her veins. Was this that bad feeling she'd had before? Or a hangover from her spiritual voyage? With the dull thud of her heartbeat beneath her chest, she wrapped her hand around the letter opener that was set up on the room's desk as a display item. *The Oct wouldn't knock,* she thought. That was the only comfort she had, because if it came down to it, a letter opener was going to do jack shit. Wedging the weapon under her armpit, she opened the door with her left hand and stood back, letting it swing open and giving her enough time to grab the blade where she had stored it.

'Opal?'

'Hey, I know you probably have . . . nice negligee.'

'Huh?' Corvossier glanced down at herself, realising she was still dressed in what she had been sleeping in: a black teddy. 'Oh, uh, thanks. Do you wanna come in?'

'Yeah, okay,' the witch replied, stepping over the threshold and closing the door behind her. 'Are you alright?'

'Mmmm.' She nodded, backing up until her legs hit the edge of the bed and she practically dropped on to it.

'Really? Cos you don't seem alright and you look ready to stab someone with that letter opener.'

'I . . .' Corvossier couldn't quite finish her sentence; she was still trying to reckon with her racing heartbeat and the fact the danger she had been reacting to was nothing at all. She tried to focus on the letter opener in her hand, which had made her feel the tiniest bit better in the moment but was stupid in hindsight. She gripped the silver hilt tightly as it rested on her thigh. She could tell the witch was watching her, analysing her every feature as she stood in front of her with her arms crossed. Eventually she took a seat next to her on the bed, her hands reaching and gently prising the letter opener free. She got up and placed it back on the desk, before returning to sit next to her again.

'What happened?' she whispered, her eyes sweeping the room as she took in the details: the open screen sitting on an aerial view of Hatherleigh, the checklist Corvossier had begun to make, the pulled blinds. 'Have you been up since you left my place?'

'Huh? Oh, yeah, I guess.' She shrugged. 'Is it morning?'

She tried to sound nonchalant, looking up at the ceiling with frustration as she told herself to pull it together.

'When you were knocking on the door I thought, shit, it could be them. I don't have my gun or a knife or Barastin and I didn't have enough time to . . .'

'What?'

'Summon anyone or anything. I can do it quickly, but I still need about ten seconds best-case scenario.'

'It's okay,' the witch said, her hand stroking Corvossier's hair in a calming gesture. 'It's day: this isn't usually their preferred hour.'

'How do I know that?' she snapped, wiping a tear from her cheeks as it trickled down. 'I spent fourteen months trying to find out everything I could about them and where did that get me? Here, to you, and then maybe no further if I can't get into Hatherleigh. I got to kill one of their lackeys and that's it, kid, that's all you get.'

'Aren't there more important things than getting revenge?'

'Like what?'

'The outfit you're currently wearing, for one.'

Corvossier laughed, the sensation feeling weird after how raw she was just a second earlier.

'And staying alive,' Opal continued. 'You came here to try and get me to risk everything for your vengeance, but there's something no one told you about my kind.'

'Oh?'

'Witches don't avenge, we *survive*.'

Corvossier sniffed, letting the words sink into her skin.

'It didn't always used to be this way, we were much more open with our powers and how we used them, who we used them on and why. But the Middle Ages taught us lessons we couldn't afford to ignore: the weaker they think we are, the less they care. The smaller we are, the smaller the target. Enduring is more important than a blood vendetta: the legacy of our kind takes priority.'

'Yeah, well, I don't have a legacy. I don't have a kind. There was two of me and now there's one. There's no coven to protect me or give me advice when I need it, there's no power I can hide behind. It's just me.'

Opal folded her hands back into her lap, the two women sitting side by side on the edge of the bed as the bustle of The Wellington could be heard just outside the door. The silence was thick between them: there was too much pain, too much baggage that both of them had brought to the surface. Finally, it was the witch who broke the drought.

'I didn't come here for this,' she said, it almost sounding like an apology. 'I came because today's my day off from the museum. We were going to Tintagel and wanted to see if you would like to come with us.'

'We?'

'Okay, Sprinkle insisted I invite you. But I didn't mind either.'

She smiled. 'Mayra is such a beautiful name, but Sprinkle's pretty cool too.'

'The first means the wind and the second means she looked at a piece of fairy bread and was like "that'll do".' The witch laughed. 'The Norths: Willa, Alistair and Mayra. My sister took her husband's name when she married. It always kind of pissed me off, actually.'

Opal got to her feet, her movements seeming heavier to Corvossier than when the witch had first walked in.

223

'Be at the cottage in half an hour if you want to come,' she murmured. 'If not, I'll tell Sprinkle you weren't feeling well.'

Opal walked slowly from the room, the door clicking shut quietly behind her. It felt like Corvossier stayed glued in position for a while, but eventually she was able to muster the energy to get up and walk to the bathroom. She looked at the large bags under her eyes, her fingers prodding at them as if that would make them go away. She knew from experience it wouldn't. Washing her face and brushing her teeth as she analysed her reflection in the mirror, Corvossier thought seriously about curling up and just going straight back to bed. She glanced at the clock and realised with a start that it was already 10.30 a.m.: it had felt early to her, pre-7 a.m. early. Spitting out the toothpaste, she wandered around her room as she thought about whether to join the witches or not, the seconds ticking by.

Finally deciding, she dressed at rapid speed and dashed from The Wellington as quickly as she could. On her walk, she pulled out the replacement phone she'd bought after her original burner had been lost to the river. She had an emergency number for Heath in there, along with Yu, Hogan, Ivan and anyone else who could be of use to her. None of the digits were saved with a name, Corvossier deciding at one point that it was safer that way. But she knew which was the Pict's from memory and dialled it as she made her way to the cottage, worrying she'd left it too late to catch a ride to Tintagel.

'What?' a voice grunted, picking up on the second ring.

'Heath, it's Casper.'

'I repeat: what?'

'Well, you're grumpy. Last time we spoke you were about to have cake.'

There was a groan of recollection that came down the line. 'Aye, it was good cake.'

'I need something from you.'

'It's time?' he asked, seeming excited at the prospect of battle.

'No, not yet. I haven't found them yet.'

'*Them* sounds solid,' Heath noted. '*Them* sounds like a target you can point me at.'

'Soon,' she promised. 'But first, this thing that I need . . . do you have schematics for the Hatherleigh outpost?'

There was a loaded silence on his end, one that bordered on dangerous.

'Hea—'

'What do you need that for?'

'That's none of your business. You said you'd be willing to help however you could, remember? Back at the hospital that's what *you* said to me.'

'Aye, I remember what I bloody said. I stand by it.'

'So get this for me then.'

'Is anyone going to be in jeopardy? Is the security of the base at th—'

'They LIED, Heath! The people you work for, they lied repeatedly so no one would look too closely at who killed Collette and my brother. You know that much, but do you understand the extent of it? How deep into this are you?'

'Don't throw that back on me,' he growled. 'I'm not the Treize.'

'No, you just work for them. Doing whatever they ask, no questions.'

'I always have questions.'

'Get. Me. The. Schematics,' she urged. 'I can give you an email address that's safe, send them, I'm not hurting or haunting anyone. The wider security of the base won't be comprised, no matter how morally comprised you lot already are.'

There was quiet on his end as Corvossier crossed the footbridge near the Museum Of Witchcraft And Magic, watching as the witch reversed her car out of the cottage's driveway. She stopped in the middle of the road so they wouldn't miss her, the kid seeing Corvossier first and pointing excitedly from her position in the passenger's seat. She waved, enjoying Opal's expression of surprise for a moment.

'Give me the address then,' Heath said, his voice barking down the phone.

She gave it to him, hanging up without saying goodbye as Sprinkle opened the passenger door, scrambling out and into the backseat with a bounce in her step.

'Opal said you weren't feeling well,' she chirped, buckling up her seatbelt as Corvossier folded into the car.

'I wasn't,' she replied, flashing a look at the witch. 'But I thought Tintagel might make me feel better.'

'Oh, it *so* will! It's where King Arthur lived!'

'Allegedly,' Opal corrected, taking them down one of the two roads that led out of town.

'Allegedly,' the kid muttered. 'But it's so cool! There are all these steps and a cave with a secret entrance through the water and a rickety bridge.'

'I haven't had a great experience with bridges lately,' Corvossier remarked, drily.

'Don't worry, we'll make sure you don't drown,' Opal answered, shifting the car into fourth gear as the road opened up.

She watched her manoeuvre the stick shift with envy, recalling the time Collette nearly had a mental breakdown teaching her and Barastin how to drive a manual car on the back streets of Berlin. An automatic was just easier now, but she missed the satisfaction of being in control the way she was when driving a manual. Besides, she always thought no automated function could change gears better than she could. It was a short drive of just ten minutes, but one that needed to be handled carefully as the road dropped to one lane at times and they had to wait to give way to oncoming traffic. They only got stuck behind one tractor, which Corvossier knew was actually good going given her experience driving into Cornwall. The spaced out cottages and country manors on the side of the road began to get closer and closer together, with the green scenery being replaced by quaint bed and breakfast establishments.

'Why don't you have a robot arm?' Sprinkle asked, completely out of the blue as they drove on.

'Strewth.' Opal sighed, long having given up apologising for her niece's line of questioning.

'They can be very expensive if you don't have insurance,' Corvossier started to explain. 'Although the Treize would take care of the expenses, it's more that—'

'You'll turn into the Terminator?'

'Not exactly.' She laughed. 'A friend back in Berlin has the coolest arm ever. She's a transradial amputee, like me, but she was born that way so learned very early on how to use a bionic arm and what she could and couldn't do with it.'

'Like what?'

'Like tying shoe laces, that's a big one.'

'How *do* you tie laces?' Opal glanced away from the road to look down at Corvossier's feet, noting her footwear.

'I don't. I have one pair of joggers that are free of laces, but everything else I wear are either boots that I slide on or boots with a zipper down the side. It just makes things easier.'

'What's your robot friend's name?' Sprinkle asked.

'Vinessa. And she's an engineering student. She wants to come up with the prototype for the best bionic arm in the world using myoelectrics, where you can control the muscles and the prosthetic entirely via brainwaves.'

'Is that possible?' Opal wondered aloud.

'They're already kind of doing it,' Corvossier said.

'You never answered the question,' the witch pressed. 'About a robotic arm.'

'Huh.' She smirked, 'Funny that.'

They passed a slab of stone with the words 'Tintagel' engraved into them, the cars in front slowing as the traffic increased. The footfall outside of the vehicle got busier too, with clusters of tourists and small families pushing prams navigating their way along the footpaths. Opal pulled into a car park off the main road, gently guiding the vehicle into a spot vacated by the same group of stoners who had greeted Corvossier on the first day she arrived in Boscastle. Hanging out the window, the girl who had spoken to her recognised her sitting in the passenger seat and threw up the peace sign by way of greeting.

'You know them?' the witch asked, surprised.

She smiled. 'Not in the slightest.'

'Come on,' Sprinkle huffed, practically diving out of the car before it had even stopped moving. 'We go the rest of the way on foot.'

Opal and Corvossier trailed behind her; it was easy to track her movements as Sprinkle had her hair done up in two Leia buns at the top of her head, each one adorned with blue bobbles. Taking in the sights as she walked, her eyes poured over cafés, pubs, Celtic souvenir shops, an ice creamery and, seemingly every few metres, a place that sold homemade fudge. They passed a shop called The Cat's Whiskers and she nudged Opal, jerking her head at the sign.

'Maybe there's something for Bunyip in there.'

'Stop,' she scoffed, rolling her eyes.

Signs made sure there was no confusion as to which way the castle was, with a line of people spilling out from a side road and inside a shop where tickets were sold. Sprinkle skipped right past them and began making her way down a steep road. They followed her, all three of them skirting to the side as two jeeps charged up the hill loaded to the brim with people. Corvossier watched them drive by with interest.

'For those who don't wanna leg it,' Opal explained.

'I take it that's not your style?'

'The air's nice,' she replied. 'Besides, a lot of people bring their dogs here. Sprinkle likes to pat as many as she can on the way down.'

In a moment of perfect timing, an English bulldog as wide as it was long waddled past them making a series of grunts and puffs as it attempted to keep up with its owner. The girl let out an excited shriek of glee, dropping down to pet it and holding out the back of her hand like a seasoned dog-patting pro.

'Would you get her a dog?' Corvossier asked.

'Maybe, if I could teach it to attack on command. That could come in handy, a good guard dog.'

'I think she's more into the kind of dog that borders on piglet.'

At the bottom of the hill, the road widened up to reveal the beautiful bluish green of the ocean. It was sheltered on three sides by jagged cliffs, with long cracks at the base creating the caves Sprinkle had told her about. The water was calm, gently colliding with the rocks below rather than crashing into them like she imagined they would during a storm.

Looking up, on both sides she could see ancient ruins and an antlike trail of people trekking their way to the top of the cliffs to inspect them more closely. There were ghosts too, following behind the humans on the path but also standing on rocky ledges that jutted out at dangerous angles. They were everywhere, roughly two dozen according to her rushed count, their unearthly death glow dotting the scenery like strange markers. Opal gestured for her to join a line of people as they moved along a wooden bridge, a small hut waiting at the end as attendants checked tickets.

'We didn't get tickets, did we?' she asked, leaning down to whisper the question in the witch's ear. Opal just gave her a sly smile, pulling out three tickets from her pocket that were clearly old and tattered. The cardboard was weathered at the edges and the timestamp was from several months earlier. The witch's fingers ran over them, moving gently down the length. Like nothing at all was out of place, she handed them to the clerk who blinked at the tickets, nodded, and let them through. As they began a slow climb up a never-ending series of stone steps, Corvossier took larger strides to catch up.

'Was that magic? Did you just use magic on that guy?'

'A small visibility spell,' Opal replied. 'Tiny, really: like a glamour to make him see what he was expecting to be there.'

'And you didn't need to, like, call the corners or anything?'

The witch frowned, pausing mid-step to turn around and examine Corvossier's face. 'You really think the way this whole thing works is a bunch of us get together and play light as a feather?'

'Can you levitate?'

'Oh my God.'

'Can you?'

'No, bloody hell. And no one rides anything either: not brooms, not vacuum cleaners, not our familiars.'

They made it to the top of the incline, passing through a stone archway and to the other side where the ghost of a child was playing a game of hopscotch with herself. The wind was intense at that height, whipping Corvossier's white strands around in the breeze. She pulled it back with a hair tie she had looped around her elbow, looking at Opal's own hair begrudgingly as it was tucked neatly under an orange patterned headscarf. There were small stone mounds everywhere, the only remnants of the building that had once sat on top of the cliff and looked out at the ocean stretching before it. Paths led further along the hill and Corvossier wandered down one to join Opal who was looking off in the direction the wind was coming from.

'Boscastle is that way,' the witch said, pointing. 'St Ives is the opposite direction.'

'We're *right* above Merlin's Cave.' Sprinkle grinned, pointing at the grass below her feet.

'This view is astonishing,' Corvossier breathed, truly blown away by it. Everywhere she turned, there was something to look at.

'There would have been huge towers going up and up,' the girl theorised, her hands arching in loops created by her imagination.

'You know, I live in a tower.'

'You do?' she asked, fixing Corvossier with a serious stare that said 'don't play with me'.

'I do, for real. It's called the Bierpinsel. It's not old like this, it went up thirty years ago and it's painted in a whole rainbow of colours.'

'That. Is. Awesome.'

'Go on,' Opal said, ushering off Sprinkle. 'Do your thing, be careful, come get us if you need us, blah blah, you know the drill.'

The girl didn't need to be told twice, dashing off in pursuit of other children that were playing nearby. Opal and Corvossier took a seat on a grassy hill, where they could watch her from a safe distance and still take in everything around them.

'She loves it here because people are excited about magic,' Opal said. 'The museum has that too, but you get a lot of people coming by to make fun of it. She misses that about home: people used to take it seriously.'

'Will she be a strong witch?' Corvossier asked. 'Like you, like her mum?'

'I don't know; her magic is still developing but I think she has a gift that leans towards the environmental.'

'Oh?'

'She's good with fire. I know that sounds like a fucked thing for someone's legal guardian to say, but I caught her once playing with the fireplace and the way the flames moved . . . it was like she was testing out how much she could control them.'

'Is that common?'

'There are witches good with water and air and earth, all of the elements. There are those who have dreams that predict the future in a way, if they know how to interpret them, and there are the witches who are gifted healers. In my coven, there was a quiet, unassuming lady who could manipulate people's emotions: only on a small scale, but that was long thought to be a talent that died out. My mother had a mind for potions and my two aunties were each unusually capable at dealing with other species of the paranormal.'

'Dealing with?'

'I wouldn't say controlling exactly, but Auntie Maggie could draw ghouls to her like flies in summer.'

'Yuck.' She grimaced. 'Have you ever seen a ghoul?'

'Gross, slimy things with grey skin, no eyes, slits for noses and one serious under bite.'

'Amen.'

'Still, very useful skill in a crisis: she lived in cities for that exact reason.'

'Ghouls love a sewer system,' she replied. 'It's no wonder the Treize didn't try to pin Willa and Alistair's death on Auntie Maggie.'

'She lives in Melbourne; we were in Sydney. It would have been a bit of a stretch to make it work on the timeline, even for them.'

The witch gazed out at the sea, focusing her gaze on the tiny white crests of waves that attempted to form and collapsed into foam on the ocean's surface.

'You're going to break into Hatherleigh, aren't you?' she asked, expressionless. 'You're going to search their records.'

'There's no point in lying to you, so yes: I am.'

'You're going to get yourself killed. Or worse, lead them back to us.'

'How?' she scoffed. 'No one knows I'm here, no one knows you're here, no one knows we have even met each other. If I go down, it's a completely self-contained explosion.'

'That doesn't make it any less terrible,' Opal muttered, something hitched in her voice. Corvossier looked sideways at her, surprised for a moment. She might be crazy, but it almost seemed like the witch was concerned for her.

'I can't take anything off-site,' she shared. 'I won't be stealing anything so there's no absence to notice. I just need a window of a few hours to take a look inside, see what other supernatural twins have been hidden from the system and check what's in your file along with Willa and Alistair's.'

Something nagged at Corvossier: not something that was there, but rather something that wasn't. Willa North. Alistair North. She hadn't seen their ghosts in ... she strained her mind back, trying to think of the last time she saw their spectral forms. It had been days. They were gone, but she didn't think they had moved on. This felt different, purposeful.

'What is it?' Opal asked, the witch's eyes examining Corvossier's closely.

'I don't know,' she admitted. 'Something I just thought of, something I need to look at.'

'Can I help?'

'No,' she said, regretting the quickness of her reply as she saw the witch flinch. 'I have to do it on my own.'

'Then we should go,' Opal replied, the warmth in her tone from earlier almost entirely absent.

'Sure, give me a minute.'

She got to her feet, wandering away from the witch and Sprinkle. She walked slowly, following a human-made path across the cliff top and towards the ghost of a large man who was sitting on the ground, legs crossed and palms facing the sky as if in meditation. Corvossier was alone, with no one near her whatsoever. She could sense Opal watching her, but she didn't look back. She pretended to be inspecting a plaque next to the ghost, reading the words but not really digesting them as she watched him instead. Corvossier reached out her senses, feeling his form and the restrictions of his powers. He had drowned off the coast, she realised with some surprise. He had gone down in a ship with dozens of others and been tied to this place ever since.

'I see you, strange woman,' the man said. His eyes were shut, but as she had been feeling him out he had been sensing her too. 'Are you here to take me away?'

'Do you want to be taken?' she asked.

He opened one eye, peering at her. 'I did not imagine that death would come in a form like you, so I suppose this is much better than what I had foreseen for myself.'

'You've been dead for a long time; it won't take much for me to give you a little nudge.'

'Will it hurt?'

'No. Go back to closing your eyes, as you were, and let yourself feel the tug skywards. Give in to it. Float away with the river.'

'Will you stay until I go?'

'If you like.'

He didn't say anything else, just remained as he was. And she stayed, watching him for another fifteen minutes until he left just like she promised he would. When it was done, she strolled back down the path. Opal was leaning against the archway, watching her carefully as she negotiated the uneven trail and passed several other ghosts. None of them were as ripe as the man had been, needing more time to come to terms. She could have forced them to leave of course, but they weren't hurting anyone. It was just as kind to leave them as they were.

As soon as she made it to her, the witch turned her back and began heading down the endless stairs that had taken them up there. Sprinkle was already halfway down, following behind a group of kids her own age and their father who had two beagles with him. Corvossier opened her mouth to speak several times and stopped herself, before finally deciding against silence and blurting out the first thing that came to mind.

'Are the talents completely random?'

Opal paused, stepping to the side so an older couple could pass them on their trek to the top.

'And who teaches you how to use them?' she continued, when they had moved on. 'Especially if every witch in your coven has a power that's unique to them.'

She didn't think Opal was going to reply at first and just as she was coming to terms with that, the witch spoke up.

'No matter what your skillset is, the basic function of using it is the same: persistence, patience, power. The three Ps. It's a lot of stuff that people think of as New Age bullshit but it works: mindfulness, being in tune with your sisters, knowing your limits and when to push them, respecting your gifts.'

A woman and her dog were climbing the stairs towards them, the drooling boxer shifting to a Siamese cat as Corvossier blinked. She stumbled to a stop as she stared at the animal, which trotted past her like nothing was out of the ordinary. The owner too didn't react at all, the pair moving past them and towards the ruins as Corvossier gripped the railing in shock. She caught a glimpse of Opal out of the corner of her eye, the witch watching her with an amused smirk.

'Is perception the fourth P?' she managed to croak, realising what she had just seen was intended for her and *only* her.

'Come on.' Opal gestured, guiding her by the elbow as they returned to moving down the endless sets of stairs. 'The talents are random and the way we can use them differs, but they come from *somewhere*. Witches believe they're loaned to us for a specific time and when we die, the gift moves on to find a new witch.'

'Like a supernatural hand-me-down,' the medium muttered. 'Reuse, recycle, reincarnation.'

'I guess. The talent stays the same, but some witches are better at manifesting it than others and that's where you get a variation in powers. Two women might both have weather-based skills, but one can only control the tide while the other can summon gigantic waves or floods.'

'Huh,' she said, the sound seemingly insignificant as a response to the influx of information, yet Corvossier was unable to form anything more appropriate. What use was a dead witch with a knack for technical spells, as she called them? What use was Barastin and Corvossier? Her foot nearly slipped through a gap in one of the wooden steps that dropped to a rock surface and she gripped the handrail at the last moment, saving her momentum. She needed to concentrate on the present if she was going to avoid tumbling down Tintagel cliffs and to her untimely death. There was a relief that came with finally hitting the wooden bridge that led back to the steep road and the main part of town. Sprinkle was waiting for them on the other end as Corvossier and Opal took their time strolling across.

'Alistair wasn't a witch,' her company muttered. 'Obviously, but he was Askari. He met Willa when he was assigned to monitor the covens in New South Wales and that was that.'

'What was her talent?'

'Energy, I guess you could say. I mean, that's the easiest way I can describe it. One time we got into such a huge fight when we were teenagers that she blew out every circuit in the house.'

'An expensive talent, I imagine. Barastin just used to give me the silent treatment.'

'Oh no, we were both fire signs, Willa and I. It was all heat all the time, which would be kind of funny if Sprinkle ends up being the firebug. Man, it was such a stupid fight too: she didn't like my new tattoo.'

'How many do you have?' Corvossier asked, only able to see the small, intricate markings inked on Opal's fingers given the rest of her was covered beneath the layering of a sweater and leather jacket. There were dots and black rings, which she didn't understand the significance of, but she did recognise others; triangles positioned in a way so that they represented the elements, the moon cycles, a zodiac symbol and a tiny pentagram so small it looked a star if you didn't inspect it close enough.

'I lost count. I tried to talk Willa into getting little bolts down her left arm once, but she was dead set against it.'

Corvossier watched the lazy smile on Opal's face as she thought about her sister.

'Was Alistair still working as an Askari when they died?' she asked.

'Yeah.' Opal nodded, looking at her with interest. 'Why?'

'They might have found you guys that way. Askari have all the ground information, all the files, that's how they're selecting their recruits: why not also their victims, through those channels? We should double-check if anyone on our list spent time in his New South Wales base.'

There was a pause for a heavy moment as the witch processed Corvossier's information.

'Sprinkle, you can run ahead. We'll meet you at the fudge shop.'

'Which one?'

'Grandma somethings.'

''Kay, can I get a treat?'

'One thing, you pick, and when we get there I'll get it.'

'Later alligator!' she exclaimed, skipping off.

They watched her back growing smaller and smaller, Opal deciding only then was it safe to talk.

'What happened to the witches they accused of attacking you?' she asked.

'Even though my official statement to them made it clear I didn't agree with that assessment, I heard there was a coven in Munich that was interrogated. A few of their members were thrown in Vankila—'

'The prison in Scotland.'

'Yes, but that's all the progress that was made. Someone started putting out rumours that it had nothing to do with our abilities, that the witches wanted our bones because we were albino and they hold magical properties.'

'Oh come on,' Opal snorted. 'Other supernaturals believed that?'

'There's no witches to dispute it. And the way our kind gossip in Berlin, well, I wouldn't be surprised if people started expecting me to burst into flames every time I stepped into sunlight.'

'You are very pale.'

'My nickname is Casper; what do people expect?'

Opal attempted to smile, but couldn't quite manage it. 'My brother-in-law had no abilities, you know, nothing that made him special outside of who he was. Yet he still put everything on the line. So did Willa: all of Stanmore lost power that night. I got away with my niece because she fought with everything she had.'

'I know,' she said, sensing the witch had something else to say.

'I'll come with you, to Hatherleigh. I think a part of me has to.'

Corvossier suppressed a smile: she was glad for the company, but the stakes were raised just ever-so-slightly. She had to survive now: no way could Opal get caught. They let their conversation go quiet as they reached the top of the road where all the tourists were milling about buying tickets, both of them puffing slightly from the incline as they let discussions of death and murder fly away on the breeze.

Chapter 12

They lingered in town for longer than was necessary, Sprinkle enjoying herself as she poked fun at 'occult' items for sale in the tourist shops. She didn't have the guts to say it, but Corvossier thought a pearly coloured crystal ball with a pewter base was actually pretty cool. If she had been alone, she might have bought it. In the company of two actual witches, however, she didn't want to risk the mocking she would have to endure on the ride home.

After eating chocolate orange fudge until she proclaimed that she was 'going to puke', the kid found a wooden sword that was supposed to be a replica of Excalibur itself. Opal caved and bought it for her, with the tiny witch proceeding to brandish it down the footpath that led to the car and then through the cottage once they made it back to Boscastle. It had been a long day and no one could be bothered to cook, so they picked up takeaway fish and chips instead. Thankfully, Opal had all the wine they needed in her well-stocked cupboard and once she put Sprinkle to bed they worked their way through a bottle of shiraz and then another 'cab sav' as Corvossier was getting used to calling it.

When the minute hands ticked over from midnight, she was well and truly past the giggly stage of drunk and heading into flushed cheeks territory. It was alright though, because Opal seemed to hold her booze better than Corvossier did and she was relying on the witch for superior judgement at that point as they sprawled in front of the fire. She put it down to their internal worries about what they were attempting to do, both of the supernatural women needing the booze to push them past the theoretical stage to the actual planning of it. The blueprints Heath had sent were printed out, along with something else he'd attached completely unprompted: the security timetable. On it were the documented patrol times of two Praetorian Guard soldiers who were permanently stationed at the base and took a walk around the perimeter every three hours. That was their window, they decided: they needed to get in and get out, unseen, within three hours. There was also a line in Heath's email; in fact, it was the only text at all: it read 'the guards are first-year rookies on their debut assignments out of training camp'.

The days at Hatherleigh were the busiest and so too early evening: the outpost went into a form of shutdown after 9 p.m., when flights weren't able to resume again until 8 a.m. due to residential restrictions.

'Skeleton staff on night duties,' Opal said, placing her wine glass down to re-examine their notes. 'If we aim for, say, the tail end of the two a.m. patrol that might be our best opportunity.'

'I agree.'

'I think we should go soon. Like, this week.'

'What about tomorrow night?'

Opal tilted her head, thoughtful. 'The protections on the house will hold: we'd be gone for a total of five, maybe six hours. If I put Sprinkle under a sleep charm, she'll wake up in the morning and never know I was gone.'

'Tomorrow night then,' Corvossier said. 'Do you have a camera on your phone?'

'Of course.'

'Good, bring that with you. We can't leave with physical copies of anything, but we can take photos. Get as much as we think we need, then get out.'

They both had their backs leaning against the couch, plans and laptop and paperwork spread out across the floor in front of them. The only light in the house came from the fire, which was dangerously low to burning out altogether.

'It's okay,' Opal said, noticing Corvossier's stare. 'Most of the other cottages don't even bother with a fire this time of year. It's too warm for them, but it's still bloody freezing for us.'

'You haven't gotten used to the climate at all?' She smiled.

'No! When we first moved in, the stone floors were so cold that I could feel them through two pairs of socks and slippers. I had to buy rugs and throw them everywhere just to try and keep some of the heat in.'

'I did wonder about that.'

'Look, even though we've been inside this whole time my nose is still freezing and my fingertips are ice.'

'Maybe you just have bad circulation,' she suggested, leaning forward. 'But I know an old German trick for a cold nose.'

She blew out a stream of warm breath on to Opal's face, directing it squarely at her nose as she cupped it with her hands.

'How's that?' she asked, hovering close to see if it looked noticeably warmer.

'My fingers are still popsicles,' the witch replied, pressing them to Corvossier's neck.

She jumped at first, surprised by the cold shock of them. But the longer Opal held them there, the more she grew used to them and the more they warmed under her skin. The witch's brown eyes watched Corvossier, holding her in a way that felt hypnotic and almost completely out of her control. They were too close, she should have shuffled back to her spot, but she didn't want to. It felt as if there was something spreading through her bloodstream, something dangerous. Corvossier wasn't sure exactly when she had decreased her breathing, but she felt too frightened to take a gasp of air in case it shattered the small amount of space they were sharing together.

There was a loud *clink* that broke them apart, both women jumping back at the sound. They turned to find that Bunyip had knocked over one of the empty wine bottles in her quest to leap on to the armchair and find the optimum position for dozing.

'I should get working on the sleeping charms,' the witch said, using the moment as an excuse to get to her feet. 'And I found another two, by the way.'

She made a few quick keystrokes on the laptop, before sliding it over to Corvossier as she headed to the kitchen.

'That's the first person I can track it back to,' Opal called, watching as the medium focused on the image of a nondescript man who looked more like a librarian than a murderer.

'Harrison Taper,' Corvossier said, reading his name and tasting how it felt on her lips.

'He dropped off the grid in the early two thousands, along with her: Carthy Diego. They both worked out of one of the London outposts.'

'They were there,' Corvossier confirmed. 'In Berlin.'

The witch looked annoyed. 'That's what I was afraid of.'

'How so?'

'Once I saw her picture, I remembered her more clearly. The night they attacked, I thought I hurt her beyond what a regular human could come back from. I was sure of it.'

'She was there the night they murdered Barastin, Opal. I swear it.'

'I believe you.'

Moving away, Corvossier collected their assortment of glasses and bottles and took them to the sink as the witch began chopping and crushing various dry materials into a bowl at rapid speed. She recognised a few of them, like rosemary, lavender and thyme. Others were completely foreign to her or things that she thought had no right to be in a 'sleeping charm', like pepper. Opal grabbed a piece of parchment from a stack in the cupboard and wrote a series of words as she spoke them at the same time, her fingers trailing the length of the page as if she was sealing their power with a touch. Pouring the ingredients into the middle, she spread them out along the parchment and began it rolling up carefully with one end tight and the other opening to a larger space like a novelty joint. Snapping off some thread, she wrapped it up and down the length until she was happy and held the object up for inspection.

'One down,' she said. 'Twelve to go.'

'You're making thirteen?'

'Better to be safe than sorry.'

'I do not disagree with you.'

She packed up all of their materials, Opal telling her to leave them at the cottage for safekeeping.

'It's better than your room at The Wellington,' Opal remarked, her attention only half on Corvossier as she continued working.

Corvossier left the witch and their plans at the house, walking the short distance back to her hotel through the night with a strange cocktail of anticipation and fear mingling together in her stomach. Her mind was split too, half of it on what they were up to it and the other half noting how already things just seemed a little emptier every step she took inside the hotel and away from the Australian witches. She shook her head slightly, as if trying to dislodge sticky fairy floss from the corners of her mind. It was no use. Unlocking the door to her room and stepping inside the darkened space, it was as if all her doubts came flooding back in a heartbeat. Barastin's absence, the Oct, the Hatherleigh mission, the murders, Carthy Diego being seemingly impervious to harm . . . Corvossier felt overwhelmed and breathless. She curled up in the window seat, resting her chin on her knees and folding her legs up close to her chest. She breathed in the scent of Opal that was seemingly stuck to her clothing like cigarette smoke and watched a sleeping Boscastle out the window.

They took Corvossier's car because logically it was the safest bet: she'd paid for it in cash, under a fake ID, and it couldn't be traced to either of them. The trip was quiet as Corvossier drove them in the direction Opal advised. Cornish roads were dead at that time of morning, and pitch-black. There were no streetlights, only the occasional lamp as they passed through a town, so she spent most of the journey with the headlights on high beam.

'Are we close?' she asked, looking out the window for any kind of sign.

'Outside of Hatherleigh,' the witch replied. 'Turn left here.'

'Where?'

'On the A386. A few hundred metres up ahead you'll be turning right down a country lane. You'll need to slow down; it's not marked so it's hard to see.'

'There's no one behind me so I can drop to a crawl,' Corvossier muttered, squinting as she looked for the turn. The witch leaned forward, guiding her with a pointed finger. She felt gravel under the tyres as she navigated down the thin road, hedges taller than the car blocking their view on either side. Eventually they came to a dead end, where an enormous, abandoned farmhouse was sitting. There was a stable attached to the side of the building and a shed in disrepair, with Corvossier pulling up alongside the latter.

'Is this the place?' Opal asked as they got out of the car. 'It gives me a bad vibe.'

'That's because there was a murder here,' Corvossier replied, watching as the figure of a ghost moved past the window inside the house. There was another, an elderly man, who was wandering the grounds with a mallet protruding from his skull.

'How do you . . . oh, you can see them?'

She nodded.

'*These* are the ghosts you said would help us?'

'And they will,' Corvossier affirmed, offering a small wave to the woman dragging the chain and the gardening shear guy as she called them to her.

'Will they hurt us? *Can they?*'

Corvossier didn't answer. The witch stepped directly into her path, her frame short enough that she was able to duck beneath her. With a finger under her chin, she lifted her head upwards and took Corvossier's face in her hands. Opal's eyes seemed to burn into her soul as she watched her warily. She knew what the witch would be seeing: the grey of her iris would bleed into the whites of her eyes as she let her full abilities take effect. It was a terrifying sight for someone to look at, her entire eyeball no longer resembling that of a human but instead looking like a grey, swirling storm. Eventually it would settle as her pulse returned to normal and the ghosts did what she asked. When she wasn't in danger, Corvossier could do it without even raising her heart rate.

'Can you see me?' Opal whispered.

'Yes, I can see you. I can see everything exactly the same as I usually would.'

'Then what's happening to your eyes?'

'I'm seeing something else at the same time.'

'Huh.'

'It's how I see between worlds,' she said, eyes scanning the four assembled ghosts: the fifth was staying with the car. 'And they're ready. Scope ahead for us please, light the path.'

Three of them moved off further along the route they would need to take, the fourth waiting to guide them from their point of origin.

'My turn,' Opal mumbled. 'Your hand?'

Corvossier reached out for the witch, Opal pressing something between their two palms before interlocking their fingers together. The woman's free hand hung loose, her fingers twitching slightly as she began whispering furiously under her breath. Corvossier couldn't make out the words or determine whether they were English, but she jumped as if she had received an electric shock as something surged through her. It passed just as quickly, her hackles still raised from the sudden surprise of it all. It was like the tingle of magic she could sometimes sense from other witches, but more potent, more purposeful. Her eyes must have been wide as she stared at Opal, the witch's smile mildly amused.

'Wha . . . did you just turn us invisible?'

'Yes, with my magic cloak, Casper.'

'Don't tease me, that felt—'

'It was a visibility charm, not an invisibility one. That's impossible . . . I think.'

'What did it do?'

'It's not that dissimilar to what I did with the Tintagel tickets and the dog, except it will last on the people at the base for four hours. Essentially when they look at us, they won't perceive us: they'll see what they're expecting to see. Works on camera systems too, since the juice is all in perception.'

'I don't feel any different, should I feel different?'

'No, but we should go if we want to be in position after the patrol.'

'Right,' she murmured, still amazed. 'Let's move.'

The ghost led them towards one of the neighbouring fields, Opal not able to see it clearly but the way illuminated for Corvossier so she could guide the both of them. There was a wooden fence ahead, which she negotiated carefully before reaching a hand back to help Opal.

They walked across an old paddock that – like the rest of the property – had stopped being taken care of a long time ago. The ground was uneven and difficult to stroll across, with both of the women having to slow down so they didn't roll an ankle or trip into an unseen thorn bush. The ghost that walked with them came to a stop when they reached one of her family members, that ghost continuing with them towards the next one who was barely more than a glowing mark on the hill.

Even without their assistance, it became quite clear where they were going. As the paddock started to arch downwards, the Hatherleigh base and airfield swam into view. Truthfully it looked like no more than a well-lit basketball court with a large expanse of concrete illuminated by spotlights. There was a small hangar and several other nondescript buildings positioned around it, along with windsocks hanging limp in the breeze as if disappointed by the lack of a strong gust.

There had never been an attack on Hatherleigh, never even a major incident from what Opal and Corvossier were able to deduce from the database. So although it was a major operational location, it was also in the middle of Cornish nowhere. The easiest way to get in and get out without drawing attention to themselves was on foot. The farmhouse was enough distance away that it required a bit of a hike, yet it was also unguarded and forgotten about. It was outside of the security perimeter, which they had now officially crossed over. The women came to a stop when they neared the edge of where the darkness ended and the illuminated airfield truly began.

'We're going to that building there,' Corvossier told the ghost, pointing at a structure that sat apart from the others. Checking her watch, she glanced up just as two figures strolled around the building's corner and proceeded on a direct path to the rest of the complex. When they were far enough away, they moved again.

'The layout's just like a school,' Opal whispered as they inched around the runway and towards the desired target.

'It was, once.'

'I hated school.'

They fell silent as they drew up alongside the old, brick building, which couldn't have fitted more than four or so rooms. There was a flickering light coming from inside and Corvossier peeked through a window, smiling as she saw a male Askari dozing at his desk. His neck was hanging at an angle that would make him uncomfortable in the morning, with a steady trickle of drool running from his mouth to his shoulder. There was a large candle burning nearby, providing the only illumination inside the cluttered room. She jerked her head at the final ghost, who moved directly through the wall until she saw him on the other side. He disappeared from view, returning a few seconds later and held up one finger, indicating just one occupant inside: sleeping beauty.

'He's fast asleep,' Opal murmured, slipping the charm from inside her jacket. 'Way to make our job easier.'

Corvossier headed to the door, pulling her lock-picking kit from her pocket and inserting the tension wrench between her teeth. Before she placed it inside, she paused and reached for the doorknob. Gently she twisted it and pushed the door open, shaking her head with disgust, as it swung open, unlocked.

The witch passed by her into the house, lighting the charm at the tip and waving it around like a sage stick. She started where the Askari was, before moving room to room. She left it lit in the hallway, the smoke tendrils reaching out and curling up into the air.

'I made it extra strong,' she whispered. 'So it would send up to five people into REM.'

'It won't put him into a coma or anything will it?' Corvossier asked. 'And should I hold my breath?'

'No.' Opal smirked. 'Why do you think I got a hair from each of us? We're immune.'

'Clever, specific witch,' she murmured, looking impressed.

They stepped into the room with the Askari, Opal wheeling him out of the way while Corvossier shut – and *locked* – the main door behind them. There were two ghosts with her and she told one to stay, guarding the exterior of the building. With a wide loop of her finger, she indicated the other should go on the perimeter and warn them if there was anyone unexpected heading their way. There were multiple screens in the room, with one that lay dormant clearly used to monitor incoming and outgoing flights. Corvossier scanned the list as the witch typed, navigating her way to where they needed to go. They were fortunate both of them had had time to familiarise themselves with what an Askari database looked like and how to use it, otherwise they could have been wasting precious minutes.

'Your timer is on, right?' Opal asked, not looking at her.

'Set for two and a half hours.'

'We want to be well out of here and back at the farmhouse before the patrol even gets close to looping around.'

'I'm with you,' she answered. 'And hey, there's ten flights scheduled tomorrow and they're all to the Middle East or Central Asia.'

'What's your point?'

'Nowhere tropical, that's all. We could've hitched a ride for vacation. There goes that pipedream.'

'I'd want to go somewhere with snow for vacation. Oh, this is good: I just searched for witches in Australia and they only have a list of names, no one is broken down into covens.'

The medium frowned. 'Why is that good?'

'Because it means they don't know who belongs in which,' she replied, bringing up her sister's folder.

'Are you sure you—'

But it was too late, Willa North's records appearing on the screen along with the crime scene photos in full, horrific colour.

'Opal,' Corvossier said, covering her mouth. 'Don't look at this.'

'You saw worse,' she replied. 'You had this happen to you. I need to see it: I need to know.'

At the top of Willa's file was a white marker that read 'deceased' when the cursor hovered over it. Opal continued clicking through to her own folder, sighing slightly when she viewed just the few lines of information they had on her which included 'whereabouts: unknown'.

'Anything that leaps out as to why they'd hide this?' Corvossier asked, snapping pictures of every screen Opal went to just in case. They'd talked about it before: Corvossier would document everything and the witch would navigate the keyboard as she was quicker.

'No. Wait, my file has a family link to Willa.'

'I see it,' she breathed, watching her click through. 'It regis-ters siblings.'

'It registers *twins*,' the witch exclaimed. 'Breaking them down into gender categories. This is what we're after.'

'It doesn't separate fraternal or identical though.'

'Who cares? This is a list of targets, maybe the same list the Oct are working from.'

'There's hundreds of names there,' Corvossier said. 'I'm not goblin-levels of good when it comes to crunching numbers. What about those white dots, what does that mean?'

'Dead,' Opal answered. 'Deceased. Dust. Doneski. Are you getting all of this?'

'Every page,' she confirmed, knowing that the sand in their very small hourglass was running faster than they could track. 'Prioritise the ones that have the lock icon first, then we can do the others.'

It was mind-numbing work and it felt like the minutes moved five times slower than they actually were. If time was truly dragging, Corvossier wouldn't have minded so long as it dragged in the real world as well and not just in her head. Sadly, that wasn't the way this thing worked. Opal clicked into a file, checked the cause of death, then if it wasn't anything particularly brutal and the body itself wasn't missing, she moved on.

'We can't afford to skip one,' the witch muttered, mostly to herself. 'We don't know if this is like a murder Noah's Ark: there's nothing to say they need just *one* set of everything.'

The witch was correct, but Corvossier couldn't help the itch she guessed they both felt as the seconds escaped them. She kept checking over her shoulder to see if everything was fine with their lookouts, the ghost giving a tilt of the head each time to indicate yes. When they neared the final names on the list, they had to rush through them, the medium giving her a 'yah' each time it was safe to click away from a page. Glancing at her watch, she realised there was one minute left until their deadline was up. It was like Opal already sensed it, opening the final folder just as Corvossier snapped its picture. She closed the windows in a flurry of clicks, making sure the screen was how they had found it. Both of the ghosts were there now and she asked them to switch, the man heading out to double-check their rear while the woman stayed.

They hustled to the door, with Opal quickly rolling the Askari back into place and adjusting the office to her liking. Corvossier grabbed the sleep charm on the way, which had burned down to half its size now. She took a big gulp of the Cornish morning air as she landed on the grass, with Opal stepping out beside her. Gentle splashes of rain landed on her cheeks, the witch shuffling closer as Corvossier followed the ghost and her chain as it wiggled through the grass like a snake. They set a sturdy pace as they mounted the hill that led back up to the paddock, quiet as they moved, only the sound of their breath keeping them company as they puffed towards their ride. Small clouds of steam formed as Corvossier exhaled and she blew out another, watching her breath dance into unusual shapes. The rain was getting heavier, increasing from a light drizzle to a steady downpour.

Corvossier spun around in a slow circle, taking in the setting as she did so. The airfield was clear and the buildings surround-ing it: they were far enough in the distance now that she thought they'd be nearing the fence. The light was beginning to show on the skyline, but it wasn't enough to illuminate everything. Behind Opal was a spot darker than everywhere else, the hedge fence that lined the road, and to the left of that she could see something bright and otherworldly. The three remaining ghosts were waiting for them, the other pair walking side by side behind them.

She pointed Opal in a straight line to where they needed to go, which wasn't more than a few hundred metres ahead of them. They walked a little quicker, Corvossier linking her arm in the witch's so they were both steady over the uneven footing of the field.

Sure enough, the fence seemed to loom out of the dimness right at them and they climbed it together, hopping back down on the other side and landing on the familiar gravel. At a steady jog, they rounded the tattered remains of the shed and headed towards the car, which was still left in exactly the same spot. The old man with the mallet was lingering by and he was joined by a woman missing a huge portion of her midsection. They were watching Corvossier with a forlorn expression as she pulled her keys from her pocket, their sad eyes tracing her every movement.

'Thank you,' she said, unlocking the car and diving in. 'When you want to, come find me. There are other places to be than here.'

'We quite like it here, dear,' one of the ladies said, speaking up in a croaky voice. 'But we don't get many visitors.'

She leaned across and unlocked the passenger side for Opal, whose gaze was flicking between her and the dead space Corvossier had just been speaking to.

'I'll visit; you have my word. My brother too.'

Starting the car, she had it going and in reverse practically before the witch had time to fasten her seatbelt. Pulling to a stop, she went to drive forward and back down the country lane now that she was in position when she hesitated. The ghosts had moved directly in front of the vehicle. She tightened her grip on the steering wheel, revving the engine just enough to let them know they needed to move. With no more time to waste, she drove through their translucent forms – right *through* them – because she was out of options.

'What just happened there?' Opal asked, looking back at the farmhouse as it faded from view.

'Nothing,' she replied. 'I'll come back when I can but . . . nothing.'

She didn't start to feel a sense of relief until they were on the main road, turning right and heading in the direction of Boscastle. There were other cars driving now, only a handful, but it made her feel comforted somewhat as they started the trek back to town.

'Did we . . .' Opal paused, trying to find the right words. 'Did we just pull that off?'

Corvossier met her incredulous look, her one hand gripping the wheel. Both women broke into a giddy smile, the medium laughing as Opal slicked her wet hair back off her face.

'Holy shit,' she breathed. 'I'm intoxicated. I feel like I just ran a marathon!'

'Ew, don't ruin this for me,' Corvossier teased.

They were both drenched, but there were items in the back-seat the medium kept for emergencies, including a hoodie. Opal leaned over to grab it, peeling off her T-shirt, which was plastered to her body. The witch stripped down to just her bra in the passenger seat, Corvossier doing her best to keep her eyes on the road. Desperately she tried to find the black bitumen interesting and not sneak a sideways glance at Opal's toned, brown stomach and her black bra. Shrugging into the enormous jumper, the witch let out a contented sigh and began fiddling around with the two CDs Corvossier had picked up when she stopped at a gas station on her drive into Cornwall. Like weighing invisible scales in her hands, she ended up going with The Cranberries over INXS as she slid the disk into the player.

'Not a lot of options,' Opal said, adjusting the volume so they had some background music.

'I was a teen of the nineties, what do you want from me?'

'Nada.' She laughed, reaching into Corvossier's coat and grabbing her phone from the pocket. It was inside a zip lock bag to protect it from the elements.

'Do you think we missed anything?' the medium asked.

'Oh, definitely. I just wish we had more time.'

'I know,' she yawned. 'But we were gifted with what we got. It won't all be there, anyway.'

'What do you mean?'

'The Askari track ghoul nests and their locations; they don't track individual ghouls. They're considered a different class of supernatural: they don't really have sole personalities and are of lower intelligence.'

'Like vampires,' the witch offered.

'Exactly, the feral cats of the paranormal world.'

'So it would have been a lot easier for the Oct to take out two ghouls or two vampires, and no one would really notice.'

'Vampires are endangered, so they might. The harder thing would be trying to work out which ones were twins cos they all pretty much look the same.'

'This is a nightmare,' Opal groaned, rubbing her forehead with her hands.

Corvossier didn't disagree, but she had been living in a nightmare for a long time. She hadn't run or removed herself from it, she hadn't tried to start over and build a new life: she had embedded herself in it instead. She had lived and breathed a single purpose, regardless of what it had cost her. Corvossier realised with a start that she had been down so long, it had started to look like up to her. She glanced over at Opal, who had her eyes closed as she rested her head against the window.

There was the honk of a horn from the car behind her and she sped up slightly, having dropped down way below the speed limit as she got caught up in introspection. By the time they were on the home stretch and taking the winding road back down to Boscastle, the digital clock on the car was ticking past 8 a.m. The town had emerged from slumber, with it still too early for the tourists to be flitting about but just late enough that school kids were walking towards buses, their backpacks bouncing on their shoulders.

Corvossier had to wait for a line of them to pass in front of the thin road that led to the cottages Opal and Sprinkle lived along, with her car slowly crawling forward once they had moved. Pulling in to the witch's driveway, she positioned the vehicle slightly up on the lawn so that it sat next to her ride. Opal was fast asleep in the passenger's seat, her chest rising and falling gently as she breathed through her mouth. Corvossier reached across, shaking her shoulder as softly as she could. The woman jerked forward with a start, her eyes flying open and her hands instinctively reaching into her pocket.

'Hey, it's just me,' the medium said, leaning forward so that she was well and truly within her line of vision.

'Are we . . .'

'We're home. Well, you're home.'

'Ah.'

She settled back in the seat, inhaling deeply. 'I should go check on her.'

Corvossier nodded, craving the sanctuary of her own bed. She'd backed up a night of tossing and turning from nightmares with a sleepless one full of stolen documents and adrenaline. She was exhausted. And yet, she didn't want to leave. She wanted to say something to Opal, but she didn't know what to say or even how to say it. So she said nothing, leaning back and biting her tongue.

'You should leave your car here,' the witch said. 'Save you having to move it back to the public car park.'

'Thanks,' she replied, grabbing the handle and hopping out of the vehicle. It was going to be a beautiful day, with the rain having given way to clear skies and crisp sunshine strong enough that Corvossier already had to squint.

'Morning, Opal!' a portly man called, hobbling past the cottage.

'Morning, Mr Robertson. Lovely day, isn't it?'

'Glorious, just glorious.'

They watched him go, with Corvossier making a move to leave herself. Opal too headed up the stone footpath to the house, the sound of a door opening and closing behind her.

The medium felt eyes on her back, but she didn't want to turn around and see if the witch was watching her leave out the window. Part of her wanted to glance, but another part kept her head forward as she lifted off the knit cap from her head and shook her hair free. Stepping into The Wellington, she took breakfast in the dining room with the other guests and made polite chit chat with Mary as best she could. Back in her room, she rolled on to the top of the mattress. Corvossier had been running on little sleep, only a sense of urgency keeping her going. Until now. She didn't even have the energy to pull the curtains shut or kick off her shoes, she just concentrated on the sensation of her mind slipping away as she drifted off to sleep.

Chapter 13

When Corvossier stirred, it was hours later, and she was unclear as to why she was awake when she could still see sunlight outside her window. Heck, it wasn't even midday yet. She flinched as she pulled herself up from the bed, her damp clothes having dried underneath her. She rubbed her stiff neck muscles, trying to loosen them as she adjusted to the familiar layout of her room. She had been dreaming, she knew that much, but she was struggling to retain the details of what it was about. She had been left with more of a feeling and just one, specific recollection: Barastin. His face was still in her mind as he spoke to her, calm and urgent as they walked through the dark lobby together. What he had actually said was a mystery, even though she could remember his tone and the way he looked as he gestured to her. Closing her eyes again, she tried to block everything else out as she dropped her head into her hand.

'Keep going,' he had said. 'I'm coming, but I'm working on something that can help.'

That's it: that was the only sentence she could shake loose from the mush of her mind. The rest of it slipped away like dreams so often do. Even more frustrating was the fact she couldn't discern whether it was actually Barastin visiting her or a scenario her subconscious had conjured up because she desperately wanted to see him. The landline buzzed beside her bed, Corvossier wanting to hurl it out the window as it rang and rang. She was about to leave it off the hook when she thought better of it, answering with a bark instead.

'Yeah?'

'Casper. I've called three times already, where were you?'

'Asleep,' she told the witch. 'Momentarily. Why are you awake?'

'I'm working, obviously, and running purely off the line of coffee beans I snorted on my way into the building.'

'Is that a joke?'

'Sometimes I do that. And listen, as much as the idea of anyone else enjoying sleep right now makes me personally offended, I need you to get down here.'

'To the museum?'

'Yeah, ASAP.'

'Are you okay?'

'I'm fine, just . . . get here.'

'I'll be there in five,' she said, hanging up and changing out of her wet clothes immediately. She didn't want to sprint to the museum and draw unnecessary attention, but she practically flew from The Wellington, walking as fast as she could move the significant length of her legs.

She expected the building to be busy, it just *always* seemed busy, but it appeared she had caught the Museum Of Witchcraft And Magic on a rare quiet day. Opal's head snapped up the second Corvossier rushed through the door, the witch looking both excited and relieved to see her. Knowing she could elicit that sort of response from not just anyone, but that specific someone made the medium feel a flutter she didn't want to examine too closely in the moment. Yet she could acknowledge it was there.

'CASPER!'

She jumped, spinning around to see Sprinkle appear from behind a rack of umbrellas, a mischievous grin on her face.

'Whoa,' she breathed, her heart taking a moment to settle.

'See!' the kid shouted at her auntie, triumphant. 'I told you I could scare her!'

She popped one of the umbrellas open, a white pentagram standing out against the purple background as she spun it like a victory flag.

'You were right,' Opal agreed. 'So not only do you get this five-pound note as promised, you get to watch the front counter for fifteen minutes.'

'What?! Really, I do?!'

'A promise is a promise. Now get over here.'

Sprinkle was a blur of motion as she snatched the money from Opal's outstretched hand and darted around the counter, springing up behind the barrier with a gleam in her eyes. She looked ready for any customer – tourist or literal bridge troll – that came through the door.

'Call out if you need anything, Casper and I are gonna be back in the exhibit. Near the Ouija boards.'

'Yes, ma'am!'

'Ma'am.' Opal frowned, clearly not liking the way that sounded. She gestured for Corvossier to follow her, the two women walking the opposite way through the museum by entering at the exit. It was the quickest route to what the witch wanted: privacy.

'It's dead today, so you should feel right at home,' Opal joked, coming to a stop and pulling out a notepad she had been scribbling in.

'I've got a house dress on already.' She smiled. 'Have you been going through what we got?'

'I had to,' she moaned, looking exhausted. 'At least if the place was busy, time would fly and I wouldn't feel so wrecked. Soon as I realised it was a snooze, I needed something to do. Desperately.'

'What did you find?'

The witch unfolded a large piece of paper she had in her pocket, spreading it out over the width of an old table that was supposed to have been used to conduct séances once. It was a timeline, just like the ones she had been building piece by piece as she attempted to track the movements of the compromised Askari and the Oct they'd become. This one wasn't quite as detailed, Corvossier realised as her eyes poured over it, with the span of time confined to a few years. There was a Le Tigre song playing gently over the sound system in the museum, the melody feeling like a grotesque companion for what lay in front of her.

'It's . . . it's everyone they've killed,' she whispered, glancing at Opal. The witch's grim expression was enough of a confirmation.

'I have male and female elementals from America, fraternal twins. One sibling had been living in San Diego and the other in a Wisconsin city called Eau Claire. They were murdered seven hours apart, implying that the female was taken out first in California and then the male: both in their homes. Both of their bodies were found, but limbs were gone.'

'What?'

'Parts, they're taking parts . . . keep up. Then there's these twins in the Philippines, shifters, some assembly required. Identical arachnia twins followed in Ghana, but one of the brothers was never recovered.'

'I can't breathe,' she whispered, stumbling into a chair that was nearby.

'There's goblins that went missing in Chile and were marked as deceased, but a body was never found for either of them. I marked it down as the Oct too.'

Corvossier frowned. 'They can't be trying for one of everything, right? How many supernatural species are there? Across all countries and cultures? That would take years.'

'It *has* taken years,' Opal said, exasperated. 'We don't know definitively who was first or who we've missed, this is all guesswork. The first one *I think* is the selkies in Scotland, then the goblins in Chile three months later. There's a gap – we have to assume ghouls or vampires fit in there – and that rounds out the first twelve months. Kicking off the next year was Willa and I in Australia, then the elementals in America, and finally your brother and you in Berlin. The arachnia are spread out over the next few months.'

'Demons follow.' Corvossier nodded, her eyes moving on to the next annotation on the witch's timeline. 'The demons in Jerusalem. The shifters in the Philippines, then that's it: we're up to date.'

'Not quite.'

Opal handed Corvossier her phone, where just hours earlier the medium had snapped an image of the screen they were looking at. Neither of them had analysed the specifics at the time, just grabbed the information from locked files and then worked their way through the unlocked ones.

'What's this?' she murmured, scanning the details. 'Two werewolf brothers in Uzbekistan, twins, one body taken but victim presumed dead due to amount of blood found at the scene. Parts removed from the other . . . oh my God, Opal.'

'I know. It was logged literally *an hour* before we broke in.'

'This is them, they were there! You know what this means?'

'That they've been busy.'

'No, that we *know* where they are! For the first time in years! From everything we've looked at, what do we know? They stay mobile and they stay quiet until they strike a target. This makes them hard to track but here we have a location! How long does it take to get to Uzbekistan?'

'No.'

'The city of Kokand, where is that exactly . . . shit, not close.'

'No.'

'Yes!' she hissed, consumed with the idea as it began to form in her head. 'At Hatherleigh we saw their flight schedule for the next day. I can stow away on one to Tashkent or Angren, depending on how soon I can get back there and if I haven't missed them already.'

'And then what, Casper? Take on all ten of them by yourself? They nearly killed you last time and you weren't alone then.'

'How long will another visibility spell last? I can track them unseen at the very least, find them while the trail is hot—'

'Listen to yourself, this isn't a plan! You're reacting and panicking because you're so desperate to find these people.'

'So are you!' she pleaded, gripping the witch's arms. 'Come with me! We're stronger together and with your magic—'

'We'd still be killed. And do I just leave my niece behind, unprotected and without anyone? Think about what you're asking. Then there's that other thing.'

'What other thing?'

'Look at the list of victims for a moment, will you? There are no other witches. It was Willa and myself, then that's it: they haven't gone after others.'

'That we know of.'

'You saw the same crime scene photos I did: Willa was missing her entire right arm in a wound almost identical to yours, as well as a foot. Alistair's body was ... mangled, but he seemed intact.'

'They never found Barastin's body,' Corvossier whispered. 'And they never recovered my hand.'

'There are whole bodies missing, pieces gone at every crime scene. Casper, I think they're trying to perform a blood ritual.'

She blinked, her brain hearing and registering the words but not truly understanding their meaning.

'What do you know about it?'

'Not much, only stories about witches who tried to conduct them and suffered horrible fates: powers going wrong, transformations ending horrifically, the ritual backfiring.'

'Transforming? How so?'

'Depends on the ritual. For witches, that's something you never want to participate in: remember what I told you about our magic being redistributed when we die?'

'Uh huh, you don't know where it comes from and who, or what, gives it to you.'

269

'That's why my Auntie Maggie said blood rituals never succeed for witches: it's greedy and wherever our magic is dispensed from, well, that place or thing doesn't appreciate those trying to take more than what they deserve.'

'Everything in balance,' she mused. 'But the Oct are Askari, so they're human. Any transformation would be considered an improvement in power ... to evolve, that's what Mike was saying.'

'Into what, though? I don't know and neither do you, which is why you can't run towards something you don't know how to fight.'

'At least I'm trying to fight. It's better than staying here, hiding out from psychos.'

'Psychos can't kill what they can't find.'

Opal kneeled down in front of where Corvossier was sitting so the medium could see the seriousness in her eyes.

'To them,' the witch said, 'we're both unfinished business.'

Her heart pounded beneath her chest and she felt her arm throb in a way it never had before, as if Opal's very words reminded her of what had been taken. She felt the pores of her skin prick up and she quickly wiped a hand across her forehead, noting the sudden sweat there. *Unfinished business*, she thought. She stood, trying to put some distance between them.

'They're there, in Kokand right now. While we're here, so far away from being able to stop them or understand what they're doing.'

'You could leave this morning and still not make it there in time.'

'Or I might get answers.'

'Or you might get killed!' Opal shouted, her voice raised to a level Corvossier hadn't heard since the witch first threatened her at The Wellington. She was inches from the medium's face, tears welling in her eyes and her cheeks flushed with emotion. Corvossier went to take an unsteady step backwards, but Opal reached out and grabbed her by the waist as she bumped into the table.

'Then at least I'd be somewhere I recognised,' Corvossier whispered, hating the way her voice trembled.

'Don't go,' Opal replied, a hand cupping her face as she attempted to console her. 'Stay here, where it's safe, Casper.'

Her eyes were flying around the room until Opal used both of her hands to hold her head still, focusing Corvossier's gaze entirely on her. She nodded slightly, her body not quite working the way she wanted it to. She was distracted again, but this time not by fear: this time by Opal's lips. The witch closed the distance between them, pressing her mouth to Corvossier's. Her kiss was fire and heat, Opal's passion feeling like an exposed spark and dangerously out of control. She was surprised at first, having not expected it, but it wasn't long before she responded in kind. The witch was clearly sick of telling her not to go: instead she was showing her. Corvossier towered over her by several inches, but it didn't seem to matter as their arms locked around each other, finding a tiny piece of solace. It took everything the medium had to pull back, breathless and immediately missing the sensation of Opal's lips against hers *the second* they were apart. But she had to.

'Hate me if you want, but I hope you understand,' she whispered.

She ran a thumb along the witch's jawline, tracing the lines there and needing to memorise them for what was ahead. Corvossier leaned down and planted a kiss on her forehead, wishing this wasn't so hard, before walking away from her and out of the museum. She wanted to think it was the sudden change in temperature as she left the building that was the cause for her watering eyes, but the excuse all but evaporated as tears rolled down her cheeks. Wrapping her fingers around the key to her car and squeezing it as tightly as she could, internally she told her brain to pull it together. *It's not your brain that's the issue*, she thought angrily, increasing her pace to a slow jog.

'WAIT!'

Opal was running towards her, Corvossier's heart light for a moment as she dared herself to hope the witch would come with her.

Instead, Opal planted a hand on either side of the medium's face and closed her eyes with concentration. If Corvossier thought the shock she had experienced before at Hatherleigh was something, she wasn't braced for this as she felt her knees buckle like an invisible weight was being pressed to her scalp. Opal, again, was muttering: her eyes flying open and staring with fierce concentration at Corvossier as she spoke the final words. Snapping out of it a few seconds later, she released her and backtracked, the witch's footsteps inching away from her.

'Good luck,' she murmured, as if she couldn't quite believe what she had done.

'I thought you said we're not lucky people?'

'We're not. But I need you to prove me wrong.'

With a nod, Corvossier hoped the look on her face told Opal she would be back. Wasting no time, she sprinted the final metres to her car. Her suspscions that the witch had done a new visibility spell, an even stronger one, were confirmed when Opal's neighbour didn't seem to register her at all as she darted by. There was no time to waste stopping at The Wellington: she'd have to make the trip with what she had on her back. Thankfully, Corvossier believed in being prepared and she had two different emergency backpacks stashed in the spare tyre compartment of the car: one full of batteries, first aid supplies, wet weather gear, snacks, tampons and blankets. The other was a mix of back-up identity documents and basic clothing with two wig options to choose from and a few accessories like glasses, a spare prosthesis and lipstick. She checked the weather estimates on her phone as she drove out of Boscastle, feeling fortunate that it would be twenty degrees in Kokand as it meant she could take less.

It was barely after lunch and she risked the speed, watching as she crept past the legal limit and then kept going. The ghosts were surprised to see her, only one being able to assemble in time for her arrival as she screeched into the same spot she had parked in earlier near the farmhouse.

'Don't worry about it,' she panted, jogging to the boot and throwing things into a backpack. 'I don't need you guys right now, but I'll draw you out if I'm back.'

She shook her head, feeling the need to clarify. '*When* I'm back.'

A rolled ankle wasn't going to help the situation, so she negotiated the downhill distance to the Hatherleigh outpost carefully. There were two planes on the runway, both being loaded by Askari and what she guessed were Praetorian Guard soldiers. Her care factor had crept all the way to zero as she took a deep breath, marching down the tarmac and watching them closely to see if they responded to her presence at all. Nothing: not even a cursory glance. She wanted to jump in the air and whoop with the elation she felt, but for obvious reasons she didn't. Regardless of the effectiveness of Opal's spell, she took a wide berth around the beings, listening to pockets of their conversation in order to work out which plane was going where. The first was heading to Kabul, which she'd take if she had to, but when she learned the second was bound for Angren she climbed on.

Luck be my lady tonight, she thought, squirelling down to the back of where all manner of materials had been loaded and finding what she thought would be the safest possible spot for landing and take-off.

There were two seats on her level, like those used by flight attendants: both of them built into the wall and facing the opposite way to whatever direction the plane would be flying. She liked the idea of the harness straps she saw hanging loose from the chairs, but couldn't risk taking one of the seats in case they were occupied by someone guarding the cargo. Either way, it wouldn't be as comfortable as the cabin above her, but stowaways could not be choosers. It was another half an hour before the lower level she was hiding in was sealed off and a further twenty minutes before the aircraft began to move, Corvossier's nerves inching up higher and higher as she listened to the murmur of the engine. Everything seemed to vibrate around her, the medium making a mad dash to the unattended seats once she knew they'd remain empty. With her back flat against the wall and the buckles pulled tight, her teeth rattled in her skull. It was very different to riding economy, but as long as it got her on the ground and closer to her goal, she could live with it. Exactly how long the flight would be, she had no idea: the Treize had their own rules, their own airports, their own schedules. There wasn't a guide for this and shivering alone in the darkness, Corvossier wrapped one blanket around her followed by another. The descent would wake her and until then, she had to try and get sleep where she could.

Closing her eyes, her body was tired but her mind was busy as she thought about what she needed to do on the ground. She'd have to get a car, stealing someone else's the only way she could feasibly think of managing it. She needed clothes that meant she could blend, in case the visibility spell wore off sooner than she needed it to: it was too dangerous to be seen as herself among both the supernatural community and the local one. The dead would be her biggest allies and she knew she would need them every step of the way. Of course, she'd left her most valuable ally back in Boscastle. Naturally, her brain went there: the kiss, the way Opal had touched her, the sensation of her soft breath so close to her own lips. She felt exposed in the darkness as her mind hit the replay button, the smallest smile playing on her face.

'You look far too happy for someone in your situation.'

The voice sliced through her thoughts like a knife, Corvossier slapping a hand to her mouth to avoid shrieking out loud. That didn't stop the suppressed cry that managed to escape her throat as she stared at the form floating in front of her.

'Fuck!'

'Afternoon, sister,' Barastin said, looking absolutely delighted about the fact he had frightened her.

'My heart,' she croaked, placing a hand over her chest. 'I didn't even sense you.'

'You were sensing something: you had an expression on your face like the cat who ate the canary.'

'What are you, Collette now? Throwing old adages at me.'

'Hang on, where are we this moment?'

'Where were *you*, brother?' she asked. 'You've been AWOL for ages.'

'I told you it would take me a while. And I've been checking in every now and again, keeping an eye.'

'I thought I imagined all that.'

'You know better.' He smiled. 'And you got safely to Boscastle all on your own.'

'So where have you been?'

'I think *you* should explain where we are first, because I have the vaguest memory of joining the mile-high club coming back to me.'

She smiled, the grin faltering the longer she looked at her brother and fought the impulse to try and physically hug him. 'Barastin, I have a lot to catch you up on.'

Chapter 14

It took a solid few hours for Corvossier to bring her brother up to speed, once he got over the fact they were flying to 'Central freakin' Asia'. Barastin listened, his eyes glazing over somewhat as she talked and talked and talked. When she was done, he was quiet for a long while: thoughtful, almost. Corvossier watched him run a hand over the sharp angles of his chin, something he always did when he was nervous. She knew exactly why that was.

'I'm going to leave you,' he said, holding up a hand to stop her when she opened her mouth to protest. 'Not like before, just an hour before we land, if I can work out whenever that is ... At the very least I can give you a clear route. I have some friends who can help.'

'Friends?' she questioned, noting the sparkle in his eye.

'*Dear* friends. Care to join me?'

He extended his hand as a symbol rather than an actual gesture, Corvossier nodding as she attached herself to him in spirit and let Barastin's purpose carry her to the lobby. She had missed doing this together and she had wanted it so badly, she slipped easily between the realms until she was standing along-side him. And they were not alone. A small crowd had assembled and they were clearly waiting for her, the cluster turning to face the siblings.

'You see,' Barastin began, 'I started to look for the witch through the dead, which was taking longer than I had initially expected. But word got out and soon, what and who I was looking for began to spread. You may recognise some of them, Ramona and Ray for one.'

'They . . . the elementals?' she muttered, recognising them from the shots in the database. 'The elemental twins from America?'

'Hello,' one said. 'Pleasure to . . . ah, make your acquaintance, I guess.'

He nodded. 'Zane and Taj, too. They're from Ghana, but I suppose you probably already know that.'

'Arachnia.'

They nodded with confirmation, raising a hand by way of greeting.

'Who would have thought? I always wanted to meet giant fucking spider people in life, but at least I got to in death.'

'They're with you?'

'All of them. It was like Pokémon: I had to collect them all. And once I found one set, we started working together to find the others, all wandering the lobby and completely lost.'

'How strong are they?' she asked. 'As strong as you?'

'We're strong!'

'And tough!'

The voices belonged to the youngest among them – a set of two teenage boys – who pointed excitedly as she appeared.

'I told you she was tall,' one said, stepping forward so he was right in front of her. 'I'm Farhod, this is Akmal.'

'Hello, there,' she said, looking around the faces of all those gathered.

There were sixteen people all up, not including Barastin, ranging every age and skin colour and body type: these supernaturals would have had very little in common during their lives. But in death, they were united. She felt her mouth pop open in shock as two faces pushed through the group, faces she recognised: Alistair and Willa North. *So this is where they had gone*, she thought. They had heard and responded to the call of her brother. And now they were standing in front of her, chins raised and expressions determined.

'I . . . I don't know what to say to you,' she admitted, figuring honesty was the best policy. 'I'm sorry about what happened, about what you suffered.'

'We have all suffered,' Willa replied, her voice a few octaves higher than Opal's. She wasn't sure why that surprised her, but it did.

'What matters is what comes next,' Alistair said, his hand gripping his wife's shoulder. Willa reached up and interlaced her fingers with his.

'And people thought I was too consumed with vengeance.' Corvossier smirked. 'Now you've finally found our perfect audience, Barry.'

'You're damn right I did. Everyone here can take physical form, but the length is going to vary and I didn't want to risk it too early. I thought it would be easier if you came to us.'

'Too early for what?' she asked.

'To fight,' Willa said, her face serious.

'I don't have anything for you to fight,' Corvossier admitted. 'I'm trying to find them right now, figure out a way to face them where I'll have the advantage. I don't know how far off that solution could be.'

'We're patient,' said a woman so short Corvossier thought she might have been a child, but she corrected her estimate when she saw the deep lines on her face and the age behind her eyes. 'We'll be waiting and watching.'

'Alright.' She nodded. 'I'm just one woman and there's ten of them. I will need you, all of you.'

'Yeah, yeah,' Barastin said, undercutting her serious moment. 'They know what they signed up for.'

'Thank you,' she whispered, addressing all of them.

'No, thank you,' Alistair answered, 'for giving us this opportunity.'

She caught her brother's eye and he made a gesture with his head, meaning that it was time for her to go. She raised a hand in farewell and let herself be pulled back to her worldly body. Opening her eyes, she blinked for a few moments as it took her a beat to readjust to the setting. Straightening up slowly as the rest of the cargo hold came into view, she let her hair fall around her face like a pearly curtain. She didn't need to see him to know her brother had returned with her a few minutes later, Corvossier's senses not taking long to readjust to being in tune with his ghostly presence.

'I still need to find them,' she said. 'The Oct.'

'I know.'

'Picking up a trail now in Kokand is my only hope.'

'Then we still have some. And that's all we need.'

'You've explained to them what happens if we kill the Oct?'

'I know, I've told them.'

'That will be it, once they take form and fight, they won't be able to visit anymore.'

'Corvossier, *they know*,' he said patiently. 'I've explained everything in detail, all of it, nothing is being left to chance.'

'Okay. Okay. Okay.'

'You'll have to loan the weaker among them some of your power if they're all to be present physically.'

'Mmmm,' was her only response, her mind working through the complications.

'You should try and relax.'

'Relax?'

'Fine, let's work out what to do on the ground.' He sighed, sitting next down next to her and crossing his legs beneath him. He looked patient, as if he was willing to listen to whatever crazy idea she threw at him next. Barastin didn't have to wait long.

The city was plagued with a sandstorm that prevented Corvossier from seeing more than a few feet in front of her as dawn broke over Kokand. The call to morning prayer echoed out from speakers, the sound somewhat garbled through the roar of the wind as it whipped around her. Everything was orange: from the sky, to the sand and dust as it mixed together and coated whatever was standing in its way.

The plane had landed some hours ago, with the medium having to grip on to the seat harnesses for dear life as they hit the tarmac. It was the middle of the night there and they began unloading almost right away, giving her the opportunity to slip from inside. She nearly fell to her knees and kissed the ground she was so grateful to not be cooped up anymore, but there wasn't a minute to waste on hysterics.

Barastin had her walk to a nearby village, telling her that was the best bet for finding a car to boost. She did as he ordered, stopping momentarily to acquire the clothing she needed off the washing line that hung at the rear of someone's farm. The theft added to Corvossier's growing guilt as she drove away from a grocer car park a short time later in a banged-up van. It was a manual, so for the first few kilometres of the drive she had to take her hand off the steering to shift gears as quickly as she could. It didn't need to be perfect; it just had to get her to Kokand. Of course, she had no idea exactly where she was driving, but Barastin rode shotgun and the twins Farhod and Akmal in the backseat provided all the answers as they directed her through the dark, hilly countryside at night. The petrol tank was nearly on empty when they hit the outskirts of Kokand and the sandstorm began in earnest.

Farhod assured her that was okay though, as it would be enough to get them to the apartment building where they had been killed. It wasn't. The van died a full block away, with the trio of the dead having to guide Corvossier through the weather as she tried to shield her eyes and use the protection of the clothing she had wrapped around her body and head. When they made it, she needed to take a second to catch her breath inside the corridor of the building. The walls and stairs were made of concrete, the cold material never so welcomed by her as it was in that moment. The lights were dim there and the one above flickered a few times before turning off completely.

'Great,' she whispered, preparing to head up the first flight.

'No,' Akmal said. 'It's down. In the basement of the parking garage.'

The ghost boy looked sad as he pointed in the direction she needed to head, the grey stairs disappearing into shadow. She didn't like the look of it and neither did Barastin. Without needing to say a word, her brother went first, the werewolf siblings following at the rear, and Corvossier wedged uncomfortably in the middle. Her movements were quiet and it didn't take long before she saw light coming from the other side of a doorway that had been wedged open with a brick. She was about to step through when she heard the footsteps behind her, spinning around just in time to see two men descending the stairwell she had climbed down. Pressing herself flat against the wall, she dived out of their way with less than a second to spare: the visibility spell wouldn't have protected Corvossier from people barrelling headfirst into her. She was about to move again when she heard the rattling of a chain and a guttural, snarling sound. Frozen in place, the medium looked up the stairs as a ghoul on all fours raced towards her.

When it reached the final three steps, it launched itself through the air. The creature's mouth was open and exposed, the rows of razor sharp teeth jutting up from the underbite and paralysing her with fear. At the last moment, the ghoul flew backwards, landing on the stairs in a jumble of limbs. She hadn't noticed the collar around its neck, nor the woman who was holding the other end of the chain as she dragged the creature along after her. Corvossier slapped a hand over her mouth to supress the whimper she felt bubbling up as the ghoul fought to get back to her, closer to where it could sense someone even if its owner couldn't see the same thing. They were blind creatures so the magic would never have worked: it could smell her instead.

'Come on,' the woman grunted, yanking the chain with force. The ghoul struggled through the air again, wanting Corvossier, before it disappeared around the corner. She took a moment, barely able to stand she was shaking so badly. Only Barastin remained with her, gently whispering, 'are you okay?', over and over again.

She nodded, staying silent as she eventually pushed herself off the wall and followed the glow of Farhod and Akmal. They were both hovering near the body of the former, most ghosts unable to help the draw to their previous physical forms. The ghoul couldn't help it either, the sheer amount of blood at the scene sending the creature wild.

'Venus, was it really necessary to bring *that thing* down here?' one of the men questioned as she fought to control it.

'I asked her to,' the other man answered, leaning against what Corvossier thought was a boiler. Dressed in a blue, Adidas tracksuit from head-to-toe and sporting a gold chain, it was clear he was the one in charge.

'Is it just me or does he look like a stereotypical Serbian drug dealer?' Barastin muttered. 'The slicked back, oily hair, the moustache . . .'

'What happened to the local Askari, Iggy?'

'They covered the preliminary scene,' the tracksuit answered. 'Got the details they needed for the paperwork, spoke to the family, and I relieved them a few hours ago.'

'You watched all this?' Venus asked. 'You supervised them?'

'Are you questioning my capabilities?'

'Yes,' she replied, stoic. 'There can't be any loose ends.'

'Why do you think I asked you to bring the ghoul, huh? See if it can pick up their scent at the very least. This whole thing is getting out of hand.'

'No shit,' she mumbled, moving around the crime scene. Corvossier kept the woman in her line of sight, making sure she put enough distance between Venus and her pet.

'Congealed blood pool,' Barastin told her, pointing just as she was about to step into it. She thanked him, finding a safe position where she could observe the Praetorian Guard soldiers unnoticed: because undoubtedly that's what they were. None of them looked similar or as if they would ever know each other in real, everyday life. Venus wasn't dressed that differently from Corvossier, appearing like any other local, Kokand woman. With the exception of Iggy, the other guy looked slightly more businesslike but could blend seamlessly into the city if he needed to. The woman seemed the strongest of them all, with broad shoulders and significant bulk to her, while both males were weedier, thinner. That didn't fool her though: every Praetorian Guard soldier was a weapon, whether they looked like it or not.

'Darius, you've been posted in this area for a while, what do you think?' Iggy's thick necklace jangled as he moved, crouching down to examine the corpse.

'I know the pack these boys are from. They'll be grieving right now, but they'll want answers. These two couldn't have been more than a year or so post their first werewolf transformation.'

'I'm more concerned about the location,' his boss replied. 'This isn't the first time I've seen murders like this.'

'Tansel Kieger was killed over four hundred years ago. All copies of the *The Book Of Species* were burned,' Venus scoffed. 'There's nothing left to salvage.'

'Where's Kieger's body then, hmm? Have you seen it?'

'My commander saw it,' the man called Darius replied, his hands deep in his pockets. 'My commander was there when he was executed. And I believe my commander.'

'I'm your commander now,' Iggy growled.

'Boys,' Venus pleaded, clearly annoyed. 'We don't have time for a sword fight. And Fluffy has something.'

'Fluffy?' Darius questioned, looking at the ghoul with disgust.

'The clean-up crew is twenty minutes away,' Iggy said, looking at his phone.

'Shall we?' she pushed, gesturing behind her. 'They came through the back, probably parked among the rest of the residents' cars.'

'It's what I would do,' Iggy noted. 'Wait down here, find a way to lure them . . .'

Their voices trailed off as the three soldiers walked deeper into the parking garage, Corvossier listening as their footsteps grew softer and softer. When she thought enough distance had been put between them to follow, she started heading in the direction they had taken as she walked around a parked vehicle. Suddenly the car's door opened up and *into her*, knocking Corvossier back slightly as she scrambled to find her footing and make as little noise as possible. Her mouth dropped open as she watched the enormous body emerge from the backseat, throwing the tattered rug he had been hiding under off his shoulders.

'*Heath?*' Barastin breathed, the two siblings watching as the man strolled directly to the body of Akmal. Slipping on a pair of gloves, he lifted up one of the limbs and examined the wounds there. Whatever he saw clearly interested him, with

Corvossier drawn to his process as he fidgeted around the corpse. Following the path of drag marks back to near where the boiler was, he gently touched five scrapes that ran along the length of the metal.

'I tried to hold on,' Farhod whispered. 'That's where I tried to grip before they pulled me away.'

Laying flat on his stomach, Heath directed the beam of a torch under the cylinder, before reaching underneath. Corvossier peered over him, risking getting dangerously close as she watched Heath examine the werewolf claws resting in the palm of his hand. She had never seen them up close, the overhead fluorescent light reflecting against the curve of the talons. Suddenly he spun, his body shifting on the spot as he launched upwards and directly at her. Grabbing her by the throat, Heath had her pinned against the wall and struggling for breath before Corvossier even realised what happened.

'I sense you there, stranger,' he hissed, the words coming out through gritted teeth. 'And I don't like it.'

His eyes were moving wildly, unable to focus on her face: he couldn't see her properly even though he was choking her to death.

'He – hea . . .'

She struggled, attempting to say his name as his eyebrows shifted with confusion. The more he looked at her, the more it was clear that she was beginning to swim into view.

'*Hef . . . it's me! It's Cas—*'

'Casper?'

His fingers loosened their grip around her throat, just slightly but enough that she was able to take a breath. Corvossier's eyes were drawn to the figure of Barastin solidifying behind the Pictish soldier, his hands raised as he attempted to launch himself at the man.

'Barastin, no!' she yelled, reaching to push Heath out of the way but the man not needing her help as he pivoted in a blur. Barastin's blow met with dead air, but he seemed unbothered as he moved protectively in front of her, putting a barrier between Corvossier and Heath.

'Ha!' Heath grinned. 'I knew it! I knew Creeper was still around!'

She didn't respond to his comment, hunching over as she took a moment to gulp huge mouthfuls of air.

'How are ya, lad? How's death?' the Pict continued, seemingly unbothered as he lowered a Bowie knife Corvossier hadn't even seen him pull.

'Keep your distance, Heath. I don't want to hurt you, but I will if you step any closer to my sister.'

'Aw, calm down, ya bawbag, I thought she was a spy! Tell me you wouldn't react like that if someone was lurking over your shoulder?'

'How . . .' she gasped '. . . did you even know I was there? The others had no clue!'

'Amateurs,' he scoffed. 'The lot of them. Imagine getting Iggy *fookin'* Soewkin to clean up your mess. What a laugh.'

'You know them?' Corvossier questioned, finally feeling well enough that she could pull away the headscarf.

'Aye, I trained the lass and worked with Darius once or twice during the Hawaiian sprite attacks. Iggy I know through a reputation of being absolutely *shite*.'

'Not so shite, they're following the Oct right now!' she snapped, realising that every second she remained the harder it would be to catch up to them. She went to brush past Heath, but he grabbed her by the wrist.

'Don't even bother, you're wasting your time.'

'Oh, why's that?'

'They won't find them using a ghoul, those things are unreliable and unspecific in their tracking methods. Bloodhounds, I said, doesn't look as cool but they're damn effective. You know, they can store scents by furrowing—'

'Heath, who are they pursing then?' Corvossier said, cutting him off.

'Ten bucks says *Fluffy* will lead them to the door of the Askari who worked the case earlier. You're better off coming with me.'

'And where are you going?'

'Out of here before the clean-up crew arrives. Just like you, I'm not supposed to be here. I'm not supposed to even know about all this.'

Barastin disappeared momentarily, Heath's eyebrows raising with surprise. He reappeared a few seconds later as they were walking towards the staircase and blocked their path.

'Not that way, there's company coming that way.'

'Handy,' Heath mused, tilting his head. 'Come on, jog to keep up.'

He moved in the direction his colleagues had gone, Corvossier hot on his heels as ordered. They dashed past a row of cars before he came to an abrupt stop, with her colliding into his back. He was staring at a grey van with tinted windows and shrugged nonchalant as he marched to the driver's side.

'Get in,' he ordered, Barastin throwing her an impressed look as Heath jacked the car in a matter of seconds. Unlocking the passenger's side for her, she slid in and did up her seatbelt. The tyres made a low screeching sound as he took off, their heads bumping as he sped up the exit ramp and took a right turn on to the main road. The traffic was essentially non-existent, the day being too young for many people making their morning commute and the storm having cleared out the rest.

'Where are we going?' Barastin asked from the backseat, Corvossier noting with a glance that the twins had gone.

'How about I ask the questions first, huh? And you do the answering.'

'How *about*—'

'Barry,' she snapped, cutting him off. He looked momentarily hurt as he sat there, arms crossed and eyes shooting daggers at his sister.

'Why couldn't I see you?' Heath asked.

'Visibility spell,' Corvossier replied, noting the way he nodded as if that's exactly what he had guessed.

'I thought you were supposed to be in Cornwall.'

'I was, then I heard about this and I came as soon as I could. I knew it was them, it had to be them.'

'And them would be . . .?'

She remained silent, her lips pressing into a hard line.

'Oh, come on!' he whinged, hitting the steering wheel.

'You come on!'

'No, *you*! Wait, no, that's not right . . . hang on, what's your point?'

'What are you doing here, Heath? What were you looking into?'

'The second suspicious death of supernatural twins,' he answered. 'And the incompetent team sent to clean it up.'

She snorted. 'Second? Try seventh, that we know of.'

'You have been diligent, haven't you?'

'Are you here on behalf of the Treize? Because I'll be honest with you, I do not trust them and by association, I can't trust you.'

'I'm here on behalf of myself.'

'And Collette,' Barastin added, earning a scowl from Heath.

'Far as anyone knows, I'm off the grid: I took personal leave.'

'For what?' she scoffed.

'A birthday party that turned into a funeral. They think I'm in Fiji. Who are the Oct, you mentioned them earlier?'

'Where are you going?'

'Ghost girl, you have two hours and fifteen minutes, now talk.'

So she talked, dealing Heath in fully: she had to take the risk and trust him. Her back was against the wall and Corvossier was running out of options. She'd promised to only call on him when she had a known target, but she needed Heath's resources. And soon – probably sooner than she would like – she would need his brute strength. She told him what she knew: Mike Higgens and the three compromised Askari, plus the others who made up the Oct and the names of the ones they knew.

'And how did you get access to the Askari database, exactly?'

'Mind your business.'

He laughed, the sound like a deep siren through the interior of the car. 'Oh, touché! Touché.'

'Who's Tansel Kieger?' she asked.

He didn't reply immediately, but his knuckles were white as they gripped the steering wheel. For the first time she got the smallest glimpse of a tattoo: a greyish blue line that seemed to curve down his forearm. He pulled the sleeve of his shirt back down quickly, making sure it was concealed again. *So it was true*, she thought. The Picts were painted in elaborate tribal tattoos. It was no wonder he always seemed well covered: clearly he didn't want anyone to see it.

'Where could you have possibly heard that name?' he asked.

'From your colleagues who were there before you,' Corvossier muttered, intrigued by his response. 'You couldn't hear them?'

'I could barely breathe in the backseat of that car let alone hear. What did they say, word for word?'

'Iggy said the murders reminded him of Tansel Kieger. He mentioned something about a book of—'

'Species,' Heath finished, his face looking grim.

'I didn't hear them say anything about the Oct,' Barastin chimed in. 'And if our Scottish friend here is dumb enough to think there has been only two incidents—'

'There's probably others unaccounted for,' Corvossier noted. 'Opal thinks maybe vampires or ghouls, something no one would miss. And we haven't found any dead banshees or sprites.'

'Opal's the witch, yeah? The person the Three wanted you to find in Boscastle?'

'The . . . Heath, the Three? Is that who told you the name Boscastle? They told *you* to tell *me* the name Boscastle?'

'Three old crones,' Barastin whispered.

'They tell me things from time to time,' he said, winding

down the window of the van as he pulled out a cigarette and lit it. 'They call me in and ogle me for a bit, touch a bicep here, a forearm there, then let me on my way.'

'Do you need that cancer stick dangling from your lips like a lollipop while you tell me something as important as this?'

'Yes. You try doing something for a few centuries and see how easily you can give it up.'

'Why are the Three interested in the witch?' Barastin questioned. 'She probably wouldn't even believe they're real, just an old legend that no one knows too much about and who live in a tower at Treize headquarters, advising them on matters past, present and future.'

'See no evil, hear no evil, speak no evil,' she said. Corvossier knew the stories just as well as her twin, the Three allegedly the origin of the phrase. She'd also heard they were immortal and blindingly beautiful in some stories, old and frail in others, with a trail of grey hair right down to the floor.

'I didn't say they were interested in the witch,' Heath answered, pointing a finger across the space between them and wiggling it at Corvossier. 'Her.'

'Me?' she squeaked. 'What do I have to do with anything?'

'Maybe nothing, maybe everything.' He shrugged. 'They perceive time differently, question them. The important thing is, they wanted you in Boscastle.'

Corvossier ran a hand through her hair, trying to compose herself. Opal wouldn't know what this would mean, she couldn't comprehend the magnitude of it, how could she? How could Corvossier possibly explain it in a way that would make sense to her? As long as the Treize had existed, so had the Three: she had grown up hearing whispers about the all-seeing, all-knowing women who choose to be confined to a tower for all eternity. For some reason, despite everything they could perceive, Corvossier had registered on their radar. She wasn't sure whether to be elated or terrified by this news, her brother expressing a mixture of both.

'Whoa,' she said, gripping the seatbelt as Heath took a hard turn off the main road and down a dirt one. The tyres seemed as if they wouldn't be able to take much more at that pace, the suspension groaning under the stress the driver was putting it under.

'Are you about to murder me in a paddock?' she asked him, half joking but also not enjoying the reality of the situation she had put herself in. He smirked by way of response, the cigarette jiggling in his mouth with the movement.

'That would be interesting, wouldn't it? Seeing as Creeper here was definitively killed, yet here he is: quite more than ghostly, innit? What would happen to a dead Casper? I don't think that's something I want to find out.'

She opened her mouth to reply, the words flying out of her throat as he brought the van to a sudden stop. Corvossier grunted as her body pulled against the restriction of her seatbelt, yanking her back into place. From a cursory glance, it looked like they were in a mechanical graveyard. There were the skeletons of whole buses, along with a broken-down truck and at least a dozen cars in various states of disrepair. A wing was half submerged in the ground, sticking out like an absurd dorsal fin. There was a house tucked amongst all of that, the windows boarded up and exterior curtains fluttering in the wind.

'Stay here for a moment,' Heath said, unbuckling himself. 'I need to make sure it's safe.'

She watched him move away from the van, stubbing out the cigarette with his toe before walking on. He held his hands out wide, palms extended upwards with a lazy smile on his face.

'My darling, oh me darling,' he called.

The door to the house was kicked open, a woman walking outside towards Heath with an assault weapon aimed squarely at his chest. She wasn't dressed like someone from here, in cargo pants and a grey singlet that exposed the muscles on her arms as she clenched the gun in her hands. Her skin was so dark it looked like the night itself, with hair pulled back into a tight ponytail. There was a scar that ran diagonally across her face from the top of her temple down to her chin, pulling her lip in such a way that it looked like she had a permanent snarl.

'Heaf,' the woman said, that being the only word Corvossier recognised before she began speaking to him in a language she didn't understand. He was replying to her, seemingly unafraid as he moved closer and she refused to lower her weapon.

'What is she saying to him?' she asked her brother, who had reverted to the form only she found visible.

'Afrikaans, I think. I can't tell if it's going well or poorly.'

The woman let out a shriek of laughter, dropping the gun as Heath pulled her into an embrace, sweeping her down into a dip as he kissed her full-bodied on the mouth.

She smiled. 'I think it's going well.' She grabbed her backpack, stepping out of the van as he gestured to her. She watched Heath's eyes scanning the space behind her, searching for her brother, but he didn't mention it out loud.

'Casper, this is Duo.'

'Hello.' She smiled. 'Pleasure to meet you.'

She shook the woman's hand, noting her firm grip.

'Any friend of Heaf's,' Duo replied.

'Duo is going to take you back to Boscastle.'

'Back to—' She couldn't help but glance around, looking at the wrecks around her with a sense of uncertainty. The woman grinned, seemingly enjoying Corvossier's discomfort as Barastin mirrored her concern.

'Hey—' he shrugged '—this has to be better than the cargo hold, right?'

'Calm down, she's the best pilot I've ever met,' Heath scoffed, before turning to Duo. 'When you're back, let me know and I can fix up the expenses. But she has to go now, within the hour.'

Duo nodded. 'I'll do the job. And only charge you double.'

'Such a gentle lady, ye are.'

They pulled each other into another kiss, Corvossier glancing away in a futile attempt to give them a form of privacy they obviously didn't care for. A slap on the shoulder told her the public display of affection was over, Heath strolling past her towards the van.

'You're leaving?' she asked.

'I've got work to do,' he replied. 'And not a word about the things we discussed during the drive, not even to the witch.'

'I'm telling her.'

'You're not.'

'I am.'

'You *are* not, Casper. Do not even mention me until I can get there myself, you can't fathom what kind of danger you're in and could be putting her in as well.'

'Oh really?' She sighed. 'Given the fact I can't flip you the bird with my right hand this instant should tell you how much I fathom.'

His smile faltered, Heath hanging his head as he opened the door to the van.

'Aye, you're right. I'm sorry. What I meant to say is, this runs deep: you know it, I know it. That's why you've kept this small and it's smart, it's safer. So we keep doing it your way.'

'Until I hear from you again?'

'Soon,' he agreed.

'Soon,' Corvossier repeated, holding his stare for a moment. She gave him a swift nod and he tipped an invisible hat, wasting no more time as he got behind the wheel. She watched the van drive away, growing smaller and smaller amongst a landscape she didn't recognise. There were green hills in the distance, looking like unusual mounds juxtaposed against the orange ground. Corvossier turned back to the woman who now had her life in her hands just as Duo pulled down a pair of sunglasses over her eyes. With a sheepish smile, she pointed directly up at the sky: the medium had no choice left but to oblige.

Chapter 15

Removing her clothes in a daze, Corvossier walked naked to the bathroom and began running a bath. She had barely made it up the stairs to her room at The Wellington, she was that bone-tired. But she had scrambled enough energy to get there, get her key in the door, and message Opal to say she was back.

Despite her fatigue, she was delighted to find a small collection of lotions, soaps and even a bath bomb positioned neatly at the sink, which she had never paid any attention to before. Corvossier held the cylinder of dried ingredients to her nose; inhaling the scent of peppermint, lemon and something else she couldn't quite place. When the tub was dangerously full, she watched with satisfaction as the pale green and white bomb fizzed and dissolved into the water. She ran her hands through the liquid, enjoying the colours as they swirled around together before slowing plunging herself into it.

Closing her eyes, Corvossier let herself slide deeper into the water until it was above her head. Holding her breath, she savoured the silence and isolation it brought her, even for a moment. She stayed submerged for as long as she could, until eventually she felt the slight burn in her chest from withholding oxygen and she burst to the surface. Slicking her hair back off her face, she took a gulp of air and settled back against the ceramics. Her white mane broke up the colours of the water, snaking out gradually like tentacles searching for prey. Corvossier stayed in the bath for what well and truly could have been an age. Her fingertips went wrinkly after about half an hour, but she couldn't bring herself to get out even after the water cooled. She traced shapes in the liquid, past her floating breasts and right to the wiggling toes that poked out of the surface like tiny icebergs. Eventually she had to get out: she couldn't soak away her problems, much as she would like to.

Washing off one final time, getting rid of the dust and the dirt, she climbed from the bath and wrapped herself in two enormous, fluffy towels. Her stomach rumbled, as if reminding her it was dinnertime, and she dressed slowly in a low cut, velvet dress with three-quarter sleeves. *Food first*, she thought. *Then sleep, so so much sleep.* The frock fell to midway along her calves and she smoothed out the fabric, enjoying how it felt underneath her hands when the rest of her felt so crappy. She touched the 'b' hanging around her neck, it bringing her some comfort.

'What kind of hellhole doesn't have room service?' Barastin asked, floating along next to her as she left her room.

'The kind that has a perfectly good restaurant one floor down,' she replied, ignoring the strange look an elderly couple gave her as they passed.

At the bar, she ordered the plate of mussels again and a cider to be served with her meal. She searched for a table, her preferred one in the corner having just been vacated. She hovered to the side, waiting as the former patrons cleared space. She didn't care about the discarded glasses and empty jug of beer: she liked this spot. She had her back to the wall, there was no one behind her, she had a clear path to two exits and she could see everyone in the bar, including the band. One of Mary's sons – she couldn't remember if it was Roger or Robert – delivered her plate of mussels and a board of bread, along with her cider, and she smiled politely. They were just as good as the first time she ordered them and once she had a mound of empty shells, she lapped up the rest of the white wine sauce with the bread. It was simple – there was little more in there than shallots, garlic and parsley – but when the mussels were that good you didn't need anything else.

'Is anyone sitting here?'

Corvossier looked up to see Opal standing in front of her, braids out and falling down her shoulders in a breathtaking wave. In a pair of skin-tight jeans that hugged her curves and a top with dozens of intricate straps, she swallowed her mouthful with more force than was necessary as she digested the sight of her. Nodding, she was unable to take her eyes off the witch as she pulled out the chair across from her and sat down, laying her bomber jacket over the arm of the seat. She already had a glass of beer in her hand and looked relieved as she crossed her legs.

'Not wine?' Corvossier asked.

The witch looked down at the beverage, as if surprised to find it there. 'It seemed more like a beer kind of night.'

Corvossier slid the bread tray across the table: she had demolished the mussels, but there were still plenty of carbohydrates left behind.

'Thanks,' Opal said, taking a slice and biting into the crust. 'Where's Sprinkle?'

'Pretending to be asleep, but I know the second I walked out the door she would have sprung out of bed and started playing Zelda.'

'Lil' rebel.'

'She's not used to that kind of freedom, me leaving her alone, especially *home alone*. I think it's a dream come true.'

'She'll be safe, right? She's got protection and—'

'The charms will hold. I've also got this.' She held up a phone, wiggling it slightly. 'She has one too, so if there's any dramas I can be back there in less than a minute if I sprint and two minutes if I walk.'

Opal straightened up, her head tilting towards the band as they began playing a new song.

'You know this one?' Corvossier smiled, leaning back as she watched the witch's fingers tap to the beat.

'*Death did come a knockin, a knockin it did*,' she sung. '*All the bad in my life, I swear I got rid.*'

She wasn't the only one singing along in the bar, but she was the only one Corvossier was listening to.

'*But Death didn't listen, Death didn't care. It pulled back the hood, revealing maiden's fair hair.*'

Her voice was somehow soft and husky at the same time, but striking none the less.

'*A beautiful woman, she stood in my door. Said "I'm sorry to say, sir, there's much to live for."*'

It was like everyone else in the room faded, it was just Corvossier and Opal.

'*Tears sprung from eyes, as I stood there and howled: "What a fool I have been, so much has gone foul."*'

The band and the other punters in the bar continued singing the rest of the verses without her and Opal smiled, taking a sip of her beer.

'You had time to learn the Cornish folk songs?' Corvossier asked. 'You've really taken this blending in thing seriously.'

'I like that one.' She laughed. 'It's called "Lady Death".'

'I lost the plotline about halfway through there.'

'It's a sad story about a man who's visited by Death in the form of a stunning woman. After admitting his shortcomings, she decides to give him a second chance at life so he can right his wrongs.'

'Women.' Corvossier sighed. 'Always having to do the emotional labour for dudes who fucked up.'

Opal nodded in agreement, the pair falling back into silence as they listened along to the rest of the song before the band played the final chords and were greeted with a rousing round of applause from everyone inside The Wellington.

'What are you doing here?' Corvossier asked, watching the witch's reaction carefully for any clue as to what she was thinking.

'Is singing songs in a pub with you not enough?'

She smiled, ducking her head as she glanced down at her hand wrapped around the nearly empty glass of cider. *That is more than enough*, she thought.

'I meant—'

'I know what you meant,' the witch said. 'I wanted to see how you were. I wanted to see you.'

'I'm exhausted,' she admitted. 'I honestly feel more tired than I've ever been.'

'What happened? Can you—'

'Not here,' Corvossier muttered, her voice low. She threw a pointed glance at the people around them, all of them jolly and drinking.

'The cottage, then. Or should I let you rest?'

She smiled, almost laughing at the word 'rest'. 'Let's go.'

Getting to their feet, they manoeuvred their way through The Wellington until they were outside, Corvossier breathing in the fresh, Cornish air. They were quiet as they walked back, the silence pleasant as Barastin followed behind them at a purposeful distance. She wondered if she would see Willa and Alistair back at the house soon, or if they would remain with the rest of the twins. Bunyip sprung from the garden as Opal pushed the gate open, the fat cat attempting to appear spry as it chased an unseen foe. They had barely entered the cottage before the witch was pouring them both significant glasses of wine, Corvossier needing a large sip before she was able to make the distance to the living room.

'This feels nice,' she said, curling up on the couch and tucking her feet beneath her. 'This feels . . .'

She was about to say 'like being home', but she stopped herself.

'Like what?' Opal asked, shrugging out of her jacket and sitting next to her.

'Like I need to take a well-timed walk around the house,' Barastin told his sister. 'To, you know, inspect the perimeter . . . or something.'

'You got there okay?' Opal continued. 'I know you got there okay, obviously, because you're back but—'

The witch was babbling and Corvossier couldn't help but find it adorable.

'—which was only two days all up, less than, and I worried the visibility spelled would have faded to nothing.'

'It worked great,' she said, reaching between them and touching her hand. 'It worked on Praetorian Guard soldiers, Askari, regular people, everyone . . . except a ghoul.'

'Huh. I never thought of that. I could make some adjustments to the charm, factoring in their natural biology.'

'I missed you,' she said, the words flying out of her mouth like they had their own agency.

The witch blinked, taking a second to reply. 'I . . . I missed you too. A lot.'

Corvossier couldn't stand it, she couldn't stand the feeling of relief she felt seeing Opal in person again – in that house – and not let her know what she was feeling. She leaned forward, watching as the witch's eyes tracked her movement. Slowly taking the wine glass from her hand, she placed it down on the ground along with hers. For as long as she could remember, the only true comfort she had found in another person was with her twin. Of all the times for her to find it with another living, human being, it just so happened to be while danger was swirling around them. Everything else in her life was manic, but when Corvossier was with Opal somehow everything . . . just . . . calmed.

She slid her fingertips around the witch's neck, pressing her lips to Opal's with tenderness. There was the smallest of sighs in response, the delicate gesture driving her crazy as Opal pulled her closer by the sleeves of her dress. Her hands were all over her, slipping around her waist and refusing to let her go. Gasping for breath, Corvossier inhaled sharply only for Opal to take the air out of her lungs as she kissed her way down her neck. The medium's skin felt *alive* as they connected, Opal's hands finding the hem of her dress and sliding up the smooth skin of Corvossier's thigh. She let out a small cry of pleasure as the witch found her weakness, with Opal silencing her with a kiss from her own wet lips. She felt her knees go weak as the witch explored further, her fingers tapping and teasing Corvossier towards a release.

'No,' she moaned. 'Not here.'

She felt Opal hesitate, before grabbing her hand and pulling her down the hall, up the stairs and into the sanctuary of her bedroom. The whole trip felt like it had taken less than a flash and Corvossier smiled at the thought of the privacy they now had. Nothing was guaranteed, not the next minute or the next second, and for once she was going to let herself get caught up in the moment. Shutting the door behind her, she yanked her dress over her head so that she was just standing there in her underwear and bra. She bent down to take off her boots when Opal's shaking hand stopped her, lifting her chin back up so that she was staring at her. Corvossier's hand slid under the witch's top as she pushed them both back towards the bed, items of their clothing falling like petals in the process. The witch shuddered under her touch, Corvossier letting herself be pulled towards the woman like a magnet.

Opal's fingers clutched on to the back of her head for dear life as she kissed her breasts, feeling deep satisfaction at the way the witch's body arched beneath her. It seemed as if there was more than sheer desire driving them together as their figures entangled, lips and mouths and hands moving to elicit the most pleasurable response from the other. Corvossier felt a longing so sharp it could have been a knife wound as she and the witch made love, their soft skin brushing against each other as if it was made for that one, specific purpose. All of the pain and all of the heartache and all of the fear that had defined her life for the past year melted as they came in unison, collapsing on the damp bed beneath them. Breathless, Corvossier let her eyelids flutter shut and sleep pull her away before anything could ruin the feeling of fingers interlinked in her hand and a witch nestled at her side.

She woke in a bed that wasn't her own, the darkness pressing down all around her. She felt the beginnings of panic forming at the base of her throat. Then Corvossier adjusted her weight, sensing the body that was tucked against her and realising who was wrapped tightly inside the protection of her arms: Opal. The witch was cupped within the larger shape of Corvossier's figure and dozing contently, completely unaware of the world that existed around her. There was almost a smile hovering on her lips and the medium reached down, sweeping one of her braids off her face so she could view it better. She liked it this way, with the witch sleeping and vulnerable: it was one of the few times she felt safe enough to look at her how she really wanted to, rather than through stolen glances. She was so beautiful, with her thick eyebrows framing the almond shape of her eyes and even tiny freckles that stood out on her dark skin, dancing down her nose and on to her cheeks in clusters. In just a pair of underpants, she was topless and Corvossier marvelled at the shapes of her body. She admired the juxtaposition of the alabaster shade of her fingers as they traced the lines of the witch's tattoos, unable to help themselves. Opal stirred beneath her and she stopped, worried she had woken her.

'Keep going,' the witch purred, her voice husky with sleep. 'It's nice to be tickled awake.'

Corvossier obliged, following the vine down her arm like the curve of a river. 'Whatever you say.'

'Hmmm. I like that, obedient. What time is . . . ugh, it's five a.m.? I have to open the museum at nine.'

'You should go back to sleep.'

The medium made to get out of the bed, wiggling free of the sheets as she sat up but Opal grabbed her shoulder, pulling her back down.

'Where do you think you're going?' she said, locking Corvossier's arms above her head. Shifting her body weight so that she was straddling her, Opal's strong thighs gripped each side of her hips and held her in place.

'T . . . to shower,' she stammered, excitement building in her stomach as she recognised the glint in the witch's eyes. Corvossier watched with anticipation as Opal kissed her collarbone, moving her way down her chest as her hands ran over the small mounds of her breasts. She couldn't help but wiggle beneath her, which seemed to encourage the witch even further as she kissed her, gently biting her lip before she hovered back over her frame. She craned her neck to watch as the witch made her way downwards, throwing Corvossier a deadly look.

'We've got plenty of time,' she said, before the medium heard her own moan through the room and Opal demonstrated exactly just how much power she held over her.

Only the faintest grey was sneaking through the gap in Opal's curtains and she was careful to roll herself out of the bed as gently as she could so as not to wake her. She padded to the upstairs bathroom, taking a long shower before slipping into her clothes from the night before. She was brushing out the knots in her hair when Barastin joined her. He threaded through the steam like he belonged there, the clouds of condensed heat rolling away from his form and reacting to something that nobody else could see.

'You're up early,' he noted.

'Is Opal still asleep?'

'Your lover? As if I hung anywhere near that bedroom overnight.'

'*Lover*,' she repeated. 'You make it sound so salacious.'

'She might be my favourite person you've dated.'

'What about Rebecca? You liked her.'

'I did *not* like her. She tried to tell me Patti LuPone was overrated: I will never forget it. Or forgive it.'

'Uh, that's right. And you told her to burn in hell, if I recall.'

'She deserved it. And hey, I liked … what was his name, brief fling with a Custodian who thought he was a Beat poet?'

'Christian.'

'Men from the forties,' her brother said whimsically. 'I wish I had tapped that well before …'

'Boys with manners were never really your thing. You always liked the rude, snooty ones.'

'Forceful,' he agreed, dropping his voice low. She laughed, reaching out to hug him and freezing as she realised the error of her ways. It didn't happen often, not anymore, but in the first few weeks after the accident she had found herself going to punch him playfully in the arm or tug his shirt out of place – both things that he hated in life – only to find her hands sliping through thin air. He tilted his head, giving her a sad smile. She cursed her mistake, standing there awkwardly for a moment before she squeezed out of the bathroom.

Tiptoeing downstairs, she inspected the fridge and assessed the options. She carefully began pulling out the ingredients she would need to make breakfast, smiling as Barastin began chanting for Bloody Marys. Sensing she had company, she spun around to see a bleary-eyed Sprinkle watching her from the doorway. Her hair was nearly vertical it was sticking up so much and her body was swallowed in a *Lilo & Stitch* nightie one size too big for her. She treaded over to where Corvossier was at the counter, her feet hardly making a sound through the thick padding of her bed socks.

'You're here early,' she said, looking at the items in the medium's hand. 'What are you doing?'

'I was going to make breakfast.'

'What kind of breakfast?'

'Pancakes, bacon, eggs, black pudding, hash browns, fried tomatoes, omelettes – the works.'

'Choc chip pancakes?'

'Well, I can make those just special for you if you like? You want to help me?'

She nodded, taking the bowl that Corvossier handed her full of dry ingredients for the pancakes. Sprinkle followed the instructions that she gave her, sitting up at the dinner table and mixing while Corvossier worked on some of the trickier stuff. The kid set the table for the three of them and arranged a selection of juices, while the medium started stacking plates with hot food as she finished it. She saved Sprinkle's special pancake for last, flipping the light-brown batter over just as it went golden and serving it to her with a small side of ice cream.

'Eat it quick before your aunt sees,' she whispered, Sprinkle giving her a cheeky smile as she dug in.

As if she had sensed them talking about her, the witch appeared not long afterwards and just as her niece bit into the last mouthful of pancake.

'Morning,' she purred, looking surprised as she walked around the dining table. 'This all your doing?'

'It is,' Corvossier chirped, shifting four perfectly cooked rashers of bacon on to an ever-growing pile and setting the plate down on the table. 'I thought I would pop by *earlier* than usual.'

While Sprinkle cut into a runny egg, the medium jerked her head at the child and Opal hid a smirk. She threw up an okay symbol with her hand, grabbing her own plate as she joined them. Being the smallest person with the smallest belly, it was the kid who finished up first, with Opal excusing her from the table so she could clean her teeth and wash her face. The witch added that when she was done, she could play a quick game on her Nintendo Switch. Sprinkle was clearly surprised, but didn't question it any further as she practically sprinted from the kitchen.

'I usually never let her play video games in the morning,' she explained. 'She's way too excited to wonder why.'

It wasn't until the game's theme music could be heard down the hall that Opal got up, shutting the kitchen door to give them added privacy. She pottered around for a few minutes longer, sitting back down at the table with a steaming mug of coffee and sliding one that she had made across to Corvossier.

'Two sugars, right?'

She nodded, not quite able to explain how much a little thing like the witch noticing how she took her coffee meant to her. Somehow she felt like Opal knew, as she could have sworn she saw a twinkle in her eye as she took the first sip.

'So I have to work today.'

'You mentioned that. In bed.'

'It's only a half day so I have the rest of the afternoon off if you want to keep working through the Oct files. I think I got another one while you were in Uzbekistan.'

'You did? That's great, that's five!'

'It was easier than the other two, their network simpler to identify once you have a few names.'

'I bet.'

'I've gotta get some groceries as well at some point and the kid will be around . . .'

She trailed off, as if both those things might be an issue. Corvossier reached across the space between them.

'I like Sprinkle. She's awesome. And if you want, give me the list of stuff you need: I can get it this morning so when you finish work, you've *finished* work.'

'Casper,' the witch breathed, 'you're really the best, you know?'

'I know.' She laughed, getting to her feet as she began to clear the dishes. Opal grabbed the rest, the two of them quiet and content as they worked away at the sink, their shoulders brushing against each other. As she handed the last plate to the witch, she leaned against the bench and watched her as she placed it on the rack to dry. Opal looked up from under her thick, dark eyelashes: the intent behind the stare warming

Corvossier's core. She remained perfectly still as the witch reached out, her fingers running down the medium's cheek softly. The kitchen door was thrown open, both of the women jumping apart as Sprinkle burst in.

'I made it to the next level!'

'That's great,' Opal said, smile plastered big as she picked her niece up into her arms. 'You got all your stuff for the museum?'

'Sure do.'

'Let's get going then.'

'Casper, are you coming?'

'Casper's gonna come back in the afternoon.'

'Cooooool!'

Sprinkle sprinted from the room, dashing down the hall to grab her things and wiggle into a backpack.

'I'll see you in a few hours,' Corvossier whispered, linking her fingers in Opal's. She looked down as something was pressed into the palm of her hand, her eyebrows shooting up as she realised it was a key.

'This is the spare,' the witch said, before pulling a list off the fridge. 'And you know where we are if you need us.'

'That I do,' she mumbled, unable to pull herself free from the woman's stare as easily as she would have liked. Eventually she managed to, feeling some kind of triumph in the small thing of it as she called goodbye to Sprinkle and strode from the cottage.

Treading down the path, she felt the strangest tingle down her spine and paused, casting a look behind her. Opal was watching from her bedroom window above and chuckled as Corvossier raised her eyebrows in surprise. She couldn't help but smile back, not even questioning how the witch had managed to reach her using her powers but just assuming that she could.

Boscastle was still waking up around her, some local villagers already returning from the school run while others were just stepping out for the first time that day. Letting herself into her room, she changed into fresh clothing and packed an overnight bag.

'Bit presumptuous, isn't it?' Barastin noted.

'Better to be prepared,' she told him. After a quick conversation with Mary downstairs about the best place to find a supermarket, she crossed the distance to where she had left her car after driving back from the haunted house at Hatherleigh less than twenty-four hours earlier. *God, that can't have been a day ago*, she thought.

Duo – as promised – had been more than capable at skirting international airspace and getting Corvossier back on the ground in Cornwall. She'd even asked her if there was anywhere in particular she wanted to be 'dropped off', as if flying a plane was the most casual form of transport in the world. She'd got her pretty close to Hatherleigh, not wanting to leave her too near the Treize outpost. Landing in a field only a few kilometres away, Barastin had guided her through the darkness and back to the country lane she recognised and her vehicle, undisturbed. One of the other perks of Heath's acquaintance was no airport security – no customs – and after paying adequately for it, Corvossier had walked away with her weapon of choice: a Glock 19.

It felt strange to move through Boscastle knowing she had a gun in her bag, but after everything she had learnt so far she also felt slightly safer for it. She could tell the weather was about to take a turn for the worse as she watched the dark grey and blue clouds swirl ominously overhead. The drive to Tintagel was brief and the traffic even briefer, with not even half an hour passing before she was wheeling a trolley through Tesco and working her way through the items on the list.

'Whiskey!' Barastin exclaimed, pointing as she passed the alcohol aisle. She gave him a look that said 'no' quite firmly. 'It helps with research.'

She raised a single eyebrow and he cocked his in response. *Fine*, she thought, reaching for the first bottle of Southern Comfort she saw.

'Stop it, choose wisely,' her brother scoffed. '3Souls is made by a Scottish alchemist in Australia. Trust me.'

She opened her mouth with surprise, about to ask him how he managed to know which international paranormal beings were running a distillery from his place in the realm of the dead. Corvossier thought better of it, shaking her head with amazement as she added the bottle to her cart. She took a moment to admire the alchemist symbols subtly worked into the logo of the 3Souls brand, which would act as a neon sign to anyone in the know. *Clever*, she thought, before grabbing a few wine selections she guessed Opal might like.

'What's the date?' she whispered, so it wouldn't be too obvious she was speaking to herself.

'The twenty-third,' Barastin replied.

'Toiletries next.'

'What does that have to do with the date?'

'My period,' Corvossier answered, rolling her eyes as they turned the corner. She also added two packets of Mr Kipling's

Angel Slice to the cart, knowing they were Sprinkle's favourite, then adding another packet to satisfy her own cravings. She'd eaten one of the leftover packets after the kid had insisted and she wasn't sure she was willing to admit it just yet, but she kind of liked the mouthfuls of moist sponge and icing. When she made it back to the cottage, it took her three trips from the car to get everything inside. As she began unpacking, The Mountain Goats started playing from Opal's stereo speakers.

'What?' Barastin said, as he salsa stepped backwards and forwards in moves completely wrong for the music. 'You like these guys! It was either them or a lot of Nick Cave.'

'I like Nick Cave too.'

'No one likes Nick Cave that much.'

'Witches do.'

Making herself a cup of tea, she settled down at the dining table and began perusing what Opal had left out for her.

'So this is who we have,' Barastin mused, as he looked at the Post-it notes stuck to the images of the Oct they had identified so far.

'Gerald Simpson, Harrison Taper, Carthy Diego, Siegfried McKenzie and now Danesha Bellay,' she replied, peering at the most recent name the witch had added.

'It seems weird, knowing their names, doesn't it?'

'You think that defangs them?'

'No, I think it makes them worse. The people who killed me have *names*. The people who did that to you have middle names, even. They're not monsters anymore, they're human beings who made a choice to do those things to us and the rest of the twins up there. That makes it worse.'

She nodded, knowing exactly what he meant. 'So much worse.'

They were silent for a long while as Corvossier's fingers gently touched the files, reading and rereading the information she had digested a thousand times at that point.

'I'll stay with you,' her brother said quietly, sitting down across from her. 'While you do this.'

She moved her hand towards him, the two siblings sitting side by side in a warm cottage, performing a task that made them entirely cold.

Chapter 16

The sea was choppy, with white foam appearing and disappearing at sporadic intervals. Barastin hadn't left her since she left the cottage, sitting and walking beside her silently. He hadn't said a word in a long while and she knew that he was familiar enough with her moods to understand that she needed the quiet to think. The sea salt smelled tangy on the air and she could taste it on her lips as she licked them, deciding to head back to the centre of town when her privacy was interrupted by New Zealand tourists coming to see the view. The Museum Of Witchcraft And Magic had the 'open' sign displayed back out the front and naturally she let herself be drawn to it.

One of the clusters of foxgloves had been knocked over and she bent down to fix it in the garden bed, propping the plant up against the tiny chalk sign that said it was used to keep evil out of the house.

Content with her work, she strolled through the doorway to find it packed with people. There were couples buying souvenirs, others exchanging money for tickets, and Sprinkle dancing around them all happily and leading them into the heart of the museum. The girl waved at Corvossier soon as she caught sight of her, but could only spare a second: there were customers to attend to. Opal was swamped behind the counter, yet she was remaining cool and collected despite the throng of people. Heck, she was much more patient than Corvossier would have been in the same situation. There was a line forming as tourists queued up to buy their items and she ducked behind the counter, sliding off her jacket and throwing her bag under the desk.

'Can I help you there?' she asked a woman clutching several mugs protectively.

'Oh yes, I wanted to grab these?'

Corvossier glanced at the price sign over the woman's shoulder. 'That will be thirty pounds, please. Will you be paying in cash or card?'

'Cash,' she said, handing over entirely too much money.

She sorted through the notes, passing back the change to the lady and grabbing a plastic bag from the hanger where they dangled. The witch looked up at her with a grateful expression and gently touched her hand, before returning to her customer. Corvossier gave her a small smile, turning back to the lady and bagging her items. They worked side by side as quickly as they could and soon the line was just one person, who the witch took care of, as they wanted to book a school trip to the museum in the coming weeks. The Goth girl who had worked the weekend shift appeared through the door once the man left, looking annoyed as she lingered near the stand of postcards.

'Charli, finally,' Opal sighed. 'What took you so long?'

'I walked.'

'You live thirty seconds away. I can literally see your house out that window.'

'I walked slowly.'

'Of course you did. Can you watch the counter for half an hour?'

'Where are you going?'

'To make sure no one is pillaging the exhibition while my eight-year-old daughter gives guided tours because you showed up an hour later than you were supposed to when I specifically asked for you to be on duty from two p.m.'

'Geez, you've already got help. There's that lady.'

'She's a friend, Charli. She doesn't work here. Now can you take the register or not?'

'*Fine*,' she huffed, casting Corvossier a disgruntled look as she stepped around the counter and put down her things.

'Come on,' Opal said, jerking her head at Corvossier. She followed the witch into the heart of the exhibit, finding the guests milling about as Sprinkle explained the history of local Cornwall witch Granny Boswell, who made a Tory campaigner's car break down by putting a curse on it.

'And when she died, her death was attended by hundreds of people,' the kid was saying with a flourish.

'She seems to be doing just fine,' Corvossier whispered.

'I know,' Opal replied, throwing her a devilish grin.

'Then why did you need—'

'Ssssh,' she said, grabbing her by the hand and ducking under a rope that separated part of the exhibit that was supposed to be a healing woman's home. The wall to it was actually a door and when Opal pushed against it, it swung back on a hinge to reveal a storage room. It was entirely dark and when the witch closed the door behind them, she moved around the space with ease despite the only glow coming from Barastin's body – something that she couldn't see.

He met Corvossier's gaze and she jerked her head at him, telling him to leave without vocalising it. He glanced between her and Opal, an understanding sweeping over his expression before he backed out of the room and through the door. There was a flicking sound and she turned to see a flame burst to life, a match protected behind the shelter of Opal's hand. The area was illuminated with a dancing light and Corvossier smiled, stepping up behind the witch and wrapping her hand around her waist. She felt her relax into her touch, her head rolling back so that it rested on her shoulder.

'I thought we could sneak away,' she said. 'Just for a moment.'

'You thought right.'

She wanted to kiss her gently, softly, and she did at first. But soon she found her passion almost uncontrollable, wanting to touch and taste every inch of the witch. She knew her quirks now, her weaknesses, and as they moved around in the near dark Corvossier soon had her begging for release. She gave it to her with her tongue, Opal tasting sweeter than anything she could possibly imagine as the witch collapsed into her. They had tried to be quiet, with stolen gasps and hands clasped over mouths so that no one would know where they were or what they were doing. She knew they couldn't stay tucked in a storeroom all day, but as Corvossier leaned back and watched Opal do up the clasp of her bra, she wanted to more than anything.

'Can you see spirits as well?' the witch whispered, out of the blue.

Corvossier thought about the best way to phrase it. 'Spirits are different to ghosts.'

'I know. But you can still see them?'

'Yes. Ghosts haven't moved through the lobby and are stuck there like smoke under glass. Spirits have moved through all of the stages. But they're tied to their people and the journey of their ancestors who have come before and after them. They have, like, a private car driving them through whatever plane they want.'

'Can you make them do stuff? Like ghosts?'

She smiled. 'Spirits will never do anything they don't want to do. They're stubborn and fickle. They won't even visit this plane unless there's something that really interests them, like werewolf coming-of-age ceremonies or certain times of the year.'

'Samhain,' Opal supplied.

'Exactly, which is coming up soon. But spirits can be reasoned with: you can ask them to do something, explain why, and if they feel like it's in their interests they might say yes.'

'Huh.'

'Here, you've got a strap tangled,' she said, stepping in and helping her wiggle into a backless sweater which had an elaborate spider web pattern on the back made from thread.

'Thanks, it took me ten damn minutes to get this thing on this morning. I only wore it to impress you.'

'Consider me impressed.' She smiled, her fingers running over the witch's exposed shoulder blades.

Opal straightened her clothing and whipped her thick plait of braids back behind her head. 'Suppose we should get back out there, before Charli glares everyone away.'

Blowing out the candle, Corvossier followed her as she pushed open the door and they sidestepped their way around the closed display. She was too tall to stand upright in the space, so had to duck as she threw a leg over the rope and bumped into Opal. She giggled, her hand running down the witch's back playfully as she scooped down to give her a quick kiss. Grabbing Sprinkle on the way out, the three of them burst from the museum like kids who had just been let out after the school bell.

'I wanna know how it works,' Sprinkle said, skipping along the road between. 'How do you see the dead?'

'Uh . . .'

'Sprinkle!'

'What? Why can't I ask? How come she can see ghosts?'

The kid had a point and she looked over at Opal for permission, receiving an obliging nod in return.

'Well, I guess the honest answer is I don't know how exactly. I just do: I have always been able to and so has my brother. There's a theory that mediums like me are born somewhere between the two worlds, so they're able to navigate them both and see when things cross over.'

'What do you mean *two* worlds? There's another earth like our one? Do you mean, like, another planet?'

'Not another planet, more like other realms: living people might experience them briefly, with near-death experiences. I can do that without having to nearly die, but I'm only allowed to go so far, just in the lobby.'

'The lobby?'

'You know when you to go stay somewhere and you have to check in?'

Sprinkle nodded enthusiastically. 'Oh yeah, we've stayed at *a lot* of places. Haven't we, Opal?'

'We have.'

'Right, well, this is that place. It's where people wait to find out where they're going and sometimes you can get lost there and end up waiting forever, endlessly, just drifting.'

'What does it look like?'

Corvossier tried to think of the best way to explain it: saying 'despair' would perhaps be too overwhelming for a kid, even one as smart as Sprinkle.

'It kind of looks like . . .' she started. 'Nothing that you can see or make out, just endless blackness: except it's not really dark. The only time you can properly see something is when you find another ghost and it can shift around their memories, things being built that are plucked straight out of their lives. Sometimes you might try to speak to them and they can't speak back because they've been there too long. When you dream at night or when you pass out, that's where you go except you're not aware of it. When you die and you're a ghost, you're aware of it.'

'What about ghosts then?' Opal asked, jumping in before her niece. 'Where do they come from?'

'Nowhere yet: they're supposed to have gone somewhere, but something in the way they died has messed that up and they haven't made the journey. Sort of like when you're play- ing Zelda and the game freezes.'

Sprinkle's eyes lit up. 'Argh, that's the worst!'

'Right? Most head in one direction and never come back.'

'And you can see the ones that are here? The ones that visit?'

'Yes, it used to be the job of my brother and I to see the ones that were troublesome and help move them in a direction. I guess it's just my job now.'

'No one else can see them?' Opal asked, pushing the gate open to the cottage.

'It depends.'

'On what?' the witch pushed.

'How strong the ghost is. For instance, the most common kind are invisible to people but can be felt in certain ways. Usually they're stuck within a specific perimeter where they died. Sometimes they can't see other people, they're trapped in a loop reliving events over and over. Those are the weaker kind of ghosts and the more powerful they are, the more likely it is they can affect things around them: doors that slam on their own, lights flicking on and off, sounds that can't be explained.'

'What if the ghost is, like, really strong?' Sprinkle asked, flexing her tiny muscles above her head to emphasise the point.

'Those kind of ghosts can choose whether they want to be seen or not,' Corvossier replied, careful about what she said. Her mind was thinking about what the girl's parents had told her: 'what matters is what comes next'. 'They can impact the world around them by choice rather than accident, and they can go wherever they want. Although they stick to a person, mostly: anything that ties them to this plane.'

The kid looked thoughtful, scooping up Bunyip from her position laying stretched out in the sun. The cat purred in her arms, seemingly enjoying the attention as Sprinkle scratched behind her ear.

'I'm gonna make you dinner,' she said, looking up at Corvossier.

'Okay,' the medium blinked, adjusting to the sudden shift in conversation.

'A Vegemite and cheese toastie, that's my specialty.'

'Uh, sure,' Corvossier murmured, not wanting to be rude but having a) no idea what Vegemite was and b) feeling reluctant about the notion of vegetables in mite form.

Opal smiled at her, as if sensing the medium's concern, and pushed open the front door to the cottage.

It was a surreal afternoon that turned into evening, the witch and Corvossier working on the Oct intermittently between visits from Sprinkle, as she updated them every few hours on her progress with whatever video game she was playing in her room. The weirdness of it was how non-weird it felt, Corvossier shocked at how seamlessly she fitted into the lives of the two witches and their Boscastle home. They had built a tiny family from the remnants of one that had been destroyed and she realised, with a start, that she hadn't built anything since Barastin died. She'd built a plan, they'd began executing it together, but she had run away from people and interpersonal relationships. Hell, she'd run way from the living. Her eyes flicked from the figure of the kid, who had just sat herself up at the table to rip into a packet of Angel Slice while her auntie did a rushed job of trying to sweep away all of the paperwork not fit for her eyes.

Opal had been right: with the names they'd put together, it seemed like the rest of the Oct were popping up easier as she trawled the database: Lewis Vinkle and Rhiannon Willersdorf were additional names sourced from her work with Barastin that day. And as the sun had set over the coastal, Cornish town, she and the witch had progressed with the last three: Samantha Franklin, Selly Rolon and Bleddyin Christophe.

325

'French Fancies are the superior cake.' Opal shrugged. 'That's all I'm saying.'

'You're wrong.'

'*You're* wrong. Your taste buds are too juvenile to appreciate what you're tasting.'

'What are you arguing over?' Corvossier asked, snapping back into the conversation.

'Mr Kipling,' the witch answered. 'Which is all your fault, by the way.'

'How is it—'

Suddenly there was a rumble through the house, the shock of it so strong Corvossier gripped the counter to steady herself against the vibrations. She had never been in an earthquake, but she was quite certain it didn't feel like that: just one big shudder and then nothing. All of the glasses and cutlery clanked together with the movement, the three of them remaining still for a beat after the sensation passed.

'What was—'

'Ssssh,' Opal snapped, cutting her off. 'Sprinkle, you remember the drills?'

'But it's—'

'*Now*, okay? No hesitation.'

The girl looked like she wanted to cry, but the expression was gone just as quickly. She sprung up from the table and sprinted to a cupboard under the sink, grabbing a small, camouflage backpack that was stored there. Snatching up her coat on the way out, she ran from the kitchen and disappeared down the hall.

'It's one of the protection charms,' the witch said. 'That one gives us a warning.'

'What does the next one do?' Corvossier asked as she watched Opal stand up on a chair and grab a shotgun from behind a series of potted plants that sat on the top of the shelf. Opening a cutlery drawer, she pulled out ammunition and loaded it as quickly as she could. Cocking it, she went to hand it to Corvossier. She shook her head, reaching into her bag to grab her own weapon.

'BYO.' The witch smiled. 'I like it.'

'I'm more comfortable with this.'

'Good, because I need my hands.'

The witch snatched an ornament off the fridge, which was shaped like a cartoon sun figurine. She snapped it in half, the entire house plunging into darkness with the gesture. There was a loud yell from the front yard, followed by a string of curses.

'The second charm does that,' Opal said, the two of them moving towards the door. 'Casper, can you handle the back of the house? You know the laundry entrance?'

'Definitely,' she replied.

She peeled off from her, moving down the hall and feeling her energy grow with each step as she prepared to call upon it. Opal headed in the opposite direction, her footsteps faint as the shouting grew louder. *Brother*, she thought, drawing him towards her with urgency from wherever he had disappeared to late that afternoon. He was there in an instant, lighting the way through the house, illuminating the open doorways with his unearthly glow. It was only when she stepped into the laundry room, the cat door flapping as Bunyip darted inside, that she realised something was wrong. She recognised that voice: she recognised the screams.

'HEATH!' she shouted. 'IT'S HEATH!'

'He's going to wake up all of Cornwall,' Barastin frowned.

'Come on,' she hissed, running urgently towards Opal before she did something irreversible. 'Don't hurt him, it's Heath!'

Opal was looking at her like she was mad. 'Who the hell is Heath? And is that *a ghost* behind you?!'

'Trust me,' she panted, yanking the door open so that they were bombarded with a string of Scottish curse words.

'ARGH YA FOOKIN BAMPOT, GET THE FUCK OFF ME!'

'Shit,' Barastin exclaimed.

'Are those ... bees?' Corvossier asked, lowering the handgun.

'It's a seasonal charm, I work with what I've got.'

'Which is what?'

'Badgers in winter, bees in summer.'

'Can you call them off?' she asked, watching as Heath tried to bat away the swarm.

'I mean, I can . . .'

She sensed the hesitation. 'But you won't?'

'He triggered two charms.' She shrugged. 'You can't pass the threshold if you intend to do malice or harm to the occupants of this home.'

'He's a friend. If he's here, it's to help us.'

'Which is why this should be a concern,' Opal said, the suspicion evident in her tone. 'And why haven't I ever heard of this *friend* before?'

'Whatever you're going to do,' Barastin muttered, 'do it soon, because your neighbours are starting to notice.'

He wasn't wrong, with one of the elderly residents in the street having stepped outside of their house to see what the commotion was all about. Others were peering out their windows.

'Train the gun on him and you two stay inside, out of sight,' the witch huffed, storming down the path.

'You alright there, Opal?' called the old woman.

'Just fine, Gertrude; it's an angry swarm of bees – better stay back now.'

'Oh dear, looks like they're honey crazed. That poor man a friend of yours?'

'Sure is, this is my cousin,' she said, her voice dropping low so that only Corvossier and Barastin could hear. 'My big, blond, white, Scottish *giant* of a cousin.'

She grabbed Heath by the hand, yanking him to the cottage as the bees followed. Pulling him inside and shutting the door, the angry insects seemed to disperse at the threshold to the home. Barastin looked fascinated, inching closer to Heath and where the bees had been just seconds earlier.

'Incredible,' he whispered. 'Where did they go?'

'GET 'EM OFF M . . . oh. Oh. Where are they? Are they in me hair?'

Heath ripped the tie out of his bun, his locks falling down around his face as he frantically ran his fingers through them. He shook off his coat, broad hands patting down every inch of his body for the flying insects. Corvossier shouldn't have found it amusing, but she did: she had never seen him panic before. Even his anger was usually quite well concealed, just simmering under the surface.

'They're gone,' Opal said. 'They can't pass into the cottage if the person is expressly guided inside by me.'

There was a thick trickle of blood dripping from Heath's nose to his lip and he wiped it along his sleeve, a side effect, Corvossier guessed, of the first protective charm.

'What did you do to me?' he panted. 'Was that in my mind?'

'No, they're real bees designed to sting and hurt.'

She wasn't wrong about that: several welts were already swelling up on his cheek and forehead.

'NO SHITE!' he bellowed. 'Why were they attacking me?'

'Anyone with bad will or malicious intent.'

'Well, what the fuck? You have Casper in here with a gun . . . that looks pretty bloody bad willy to me.'

'It has to be someone outside of the house,' she growled. 'They wouldn't have gotten in otherwise.'

'Gah, you're reminding me why witches drive me completely mental. You got beer?'

'And who *the hell* do you think you are? Barging into my house?'

'You didn't tell her about me?' Heath said, staring at Corvossier.

'You told me not to!'

'Aye, but I didn't think you'd listen. And hey, Creeper, you're looking good.'

'Tease,' Barastin said with a wink.

'Creeper?' Opal frowned. 'As in Barastin . . . your *dead* twin brother Barastin?'

The witch was scowling at her, taking a break only momentarily to glare between the ghost and Heath.

'About that . . .'

'Is there whiskey?' Heath asked, pushing his way through to the kitchen, the lights and music and electrical appliances turning themselves back on as they followed after him. He grabbed the bottle of 3Souls, skipping a glass altogether and downing a huge sip instead.

'I'm going to get blootered,' he muttered happily.

Corvossier frowned, turning to her brother who looked sheepish. 'You knew he was coming. That's why you made me buy the whiskey.'

'I have no idea what you're talking about,' he replied, eyes wide and innocent.

'Why didn't you say anything? Opal could have killed him!'

'I wanted to see her powers in action,' Barastin muttered. 'You can't say it's not fascinating.'

'My bee stings are bloody fascinating!' Heath shouted from the kitchen.

'You should probably put something on those,' the ghost remarked, gesturing to the swelling wounds.

'What are you, my fucking nurse?'

'Heath,' Corvossier snapped. 'Don't be such an asshole.'

'It's not my fault I'd rather let my face swell than take advice from a bloody dead man who was just curious to see what would happen.'

'Here,' Opal said, handing him a damp tea towel with ice wrapped inside it. He looked at it suspiciously, as if the very fabric itself was made with bees. He took another swig of spirits before accepting the witch's white flag.

Corvossier had inched around the kitchen to stand next to Opal, watching as she instructed Heath on where he should place the ice and how often to move it.

'You got here quick,' the medium noted.

'Had to,' he said. 'Needed to get this out of the country.'

331

Reaching into his bag, he slapped a book on to the dining table. It was black and bound with what looked like rotted leather, gold writing on the front in a language she couldn't read. The edges of the pages were a deep brown, almost red, and the whole tome smelled as if it was rotting from the inside out. They all stared down at it, unable to pull their eyes away.

'Get that out of my house,' Opal said, in a voice so lethal it barely sounded human to Corvossier's ears. She glanced up to see a mix of fear and rage sharing centre stage on the witch's face, but her laser-like stare didn't move away from the book.

'I truly didn't think it was real,' Barastin breathed.

'What is it?' she asked, tasting the tension in the room.

'Something that should *not* be in my house,' Opal repeated, whirling on Heath. 'No wonder the charms went haywire – that book brings nothing but death and danger!'

'Only if you know how to use it,' he replied, peering out from under a swollen eye that he had ice pressed to. 'Besides, Casper said you both wanted to know what the Oct were doing, what their end goal was.'

'What they were murdering supernatural twins for,' her brother murmured.

'There's your answer,' Heath said, pointing at it. '*The Book Of Species.*'

'Get. It. Out. Of. My. House.'

'Please, you probably rent this place,' he snapped at Opal.

'What *is* it?!' Corvossier begged, exasperated.

'There was a guy in the late sixteen hundreds,' Heath started. 'He believed that supernaturals were all branches of the same tree, that species could be fluid: you could shift from one to the other and back again.'

'What?' she scoffed. 'A demon can't suddenly switch its horns for a selkie tail. That's not only scientifically impossible but it's illogical.'

'People believed him.' Heath shrugged. 'He was a fanatic and he would travel throughout Europe, stopping in supernatural communities and building a following.'

'Tansel Kieger,' Corvossier whispered.

'Yeah, yeah, he was a real paranormal David Koresh,' Heath said. 'Point is, he worked with some witches—'

'Hey!' Opal objected.

'He did, what, you want me to rewrite history or tell the damn story? It was around the time when public persecution was beginning to step up a notch and there were more than enough desperate witches willing to be anything but what they were.'

'So they could survive,' Opal snapped. 'Because there sure as hell wasn't any support from you lot.'

'Stay on topic,' Corvossier urged. 'Both of you!'

'He had the methodology, the witches had the magic,' Heath pressed. 'They fused the two things and came up with the first blood rituals in existence.'

'They invented death magic,' Barastin said, as she glanced at him and felt his fearful expression mirror on her own face.

'It's all in here,' Heath continued. 'The specifics of what one needs to do to change into any sub-species of supernatural.'

'And it works?' she asked.

He shrugged. 'To a degree. You lose more than you gain and what you become is not . . . Say you want to be a werewolf, the book might tell you to sacrifice a virgin named Wendy on every blue moon for six years and then you'll achieve the transformation. But as you slowly begin to retain those abilities, you lose others.'

'Like what?' she wondered.

'Exactly what you would think,' Opal said. 'Any deal made in blood comes at a cost: you're not a werewolf like other werewolves, you're not a banshee or a goblin like other banshees or goblins. You're an abomination against nature and that requires your soul.'

She thought back to the night when her life had changed, the night when her brother was murdered and she looked into the faces of his killers as they tried to do the same to her. There was something different about them, she knew it from looking in their eyes. Hell, she knew it from looking at their Askari files: they were not the same people they once were.

'You felt it,' Barastin said to her. 'You felt it that night, like you were being watched and followed. It was because you were, but it was also because we're in tune with it. What is the nature of what we do, sister? We view souls when others can't: we interact and command them when no one else has the ability to. You recognised them without knowing it because of what they lack.'

'There were thirteen copies of *The Book Of Species* altogether,' Heath continued. 'Once Tansel Kieger was captured and executed, the Treize ordered all other copies to be destroyed. The witches were decapitated and the Praetorian Guard were sent on a mission to locate the remaining books.'

'That's what the Praetorian Guard soldiers were referring to,' Corvossier said. 'They knew this story; they knew the Kokand crime scene was familiar.'

'Iggy did.'

'How many copies did you get?' Barastin asked.

'Eleven. His believers carried them to every corner of the earth they could and we hunted them, one by one. The thirteenth was said to have been lost at sea when the ship transporting it went down over the English Channel. This is the first, the original: I found it buried in a tomb along the banks of the Angren not far from where Tansel was killed.'

'And you know this how?' Opal wondered out loud.

Heath met her stare. 'Because I was there, I watched it happen. And you want to know the clincher? He was Askari.'

'I need to sit down,' Corvossier said, her feet unsteady as she pulled out a chair.

'No,' the witch warned, dashing out and stopping her. 'Not here, not near the book: in the lounge.'

She nodded, taking the witch's outstretched hand and letting her lead her to the couch. She collapsed on to it, closing her eyes and letting her fingertips work away at the headache she could feel building at the side of her skull. In the kitchen, Opal was ordering Heath to put the book back in his bag while Barastin was arguing that they needed to look through it first to determine what blood ritual involved twins so they knew what they were dealing with.

'Do it at the museum then!' Opal snapped. 'I'll give you spare keys, there's enough old magic there to prevent any serious harm befalling you. Just take the damn thing out of my house.'

There were footsteps followed by the slamming of the front door as Heath and Barastin did as she said. Opal didn't sound relieved though, storming down the hall and pulling open a small door that was tucked under the stairs. It's where Sprinkle had been hiding, but that wasn't part of the plan apparently. She was supposed to have used an underground tunnel that would have taken her out into their neighbour's backyard, Corvossier overheard. But the little girl was scared and hadn't wanted to leave, especially when she didn't hear 'anything bad' for some time.

'I know.' Opal sighed, her voice muffled by the hug she had pulled Sprinkle into. 'But even if it sounds safe, that's not what we practised. You run and you get away from here as quickly as you can, remember?'

The girl said that she did and Corvossier listened to the muted sounds of her crying, the three of them stuck inside a house that suddenly didn't feel too safe anymore.

Chapter 17

Corvossier woke with a start, instantly mad at herself for having fallen asleep in the first place. She didn't know how long she had been out, but she guessed it wasn't long as the flames were still burning in the fireplace. She heard a door shutting down the hall and footsteps, only for Opal to stick her head around the corner and into the lounge. Her eyes zeroed in on Corvossier and she was across the room and next to her in a heartbeat. She pulled her into her arms, Corvossier gripping the witch as desperately as she gripped her back. She burrowed her face into the curve of the woman's neck, as if trying to inhale every part of her. They didn't move for a long time, the two just frozen in their consoling of each other. Eventually it was the medium who pulled back, stroking the witch's face as she did so.

'Is Sprinkle okay?'

She nodded. 'She's in her room watching a movie.'

'What movie?'

Opal's mouth twitched into a smile. '*Hocus Pocus.*'

Corvossier laughed at the absurdity of the situation.

'What? She likes it. When we first started running, we played a game that was supposed to keep her mind on fun stuff, positive things, which was coming up with the ultimate witch movie marathon.'

'Are the guys not back?' she asked, looking around.

'No, I think we should meet them but . . .'

'Sprinkle.'

'Yeah. I'm not leaving her unattended, especially right now.'

'So don't.'

'Huh?'

'I can organise someone to watch her, someone better than a human babysitter.'

'A . . . a ghost?'

'Ghosts.'

'I don't know how I feel about that. I know she seems cool with your whole "communicating with the dead" thing, but she hasn't seen a real ghost yet. She hasn't seen your brother. That freaked me out and I'm not an eight-year-old whose parent figure just told them to run for her life a few hours ago.'

'I get it,' she replied, gripping the witch's hand. 'I can make sure she doesn't even know they're there.'

Opal looked thoughtful, her mind ticking over the idea, before she let out a deep sigh. 'I'll tell her we'll be at the museum.'

Corvossier used the silence, letting herself slip away until she was greeted by some familiar faces. She didn't even have to open her mouth to speak: Willa and Alistair North were already moving towards her.

The words 'Are you ready?' echoed through the lobby, her vision blurring slightly. She pulled back, her senses re-forming so that she was looking up at Opal from her position on the couch.

'Are you ready?' the witch repeated. 'Or do you need more time?'

Corvossier's eyes darted to the figures that formed behind Opal's back: that of a sister and brother-in-law. They met the medium's gaze, before turning away and heading down the hall towards their daughter's room.

'I'm ready.'

The quietness of the night felt heavy as they hustled through it, their arms interlinked and their pace quick. The building was completely dark as they stepped inside, with Opal locking the door behind them and trying to discern what direction to move in. Reaching into her pocket, she pulled out something that Corvossier couldn't quite see at first. Suddenly a beam of light illuminated the front of the museum, where the souvenirs were stacked on shelves and dangling from the rafters at the ceiling.

'Magic?' Corvossier whispered.

'Torchlight,' the witch replied, holding it up for emphasis.

She snorted, laughing at her own foolishness. They didn't have to walk far to find them, heading up the stairs into the exhibit and seeing the pair sitting at a table that usually presented different types of homemade remedies. The display had been placed in a neat pile on the ground, with *The Book Of Species* open and spread out across most of the table's surface. They were working by candle-light and Barastin's natural glow, but Opal dashed around the space, switching on an overhead beam that gave them enough to see better but would have still disguised their presence in case anyone was looking into the museum from the outside.

'What have you got?' Corvossier asked, stepping around behind her brother even though she could read through his shoulder. She felt Opal's eyes on her, but when she looked up the witch glanced away.

'Something to do with babies if you ever find a bunch you want to get rid of,' Barastin mumbled.

'This is what I thought grimoires looked like,' she admitted as Heath continued to flick the pages. 'Before I met a witch, that is.'

'Gross,' Opal scoffed. 'Witches have better stationery.'

'You said the other one of these went missing en route between France and England, is that right?' she asked.

'It is,' Heath replied. 'In eighteen ninety-five.'

'The two Askari that started all this, the ones we think created the Oct . . . it's no coincidence they were based in the UK, is it?'

Opal looked up at her, thoughtful. Heath sucked his teeth with annoyance and pulled the book closer to him, whipping through the pages with haste.

'They were stationed on the Isle of Wight,' the witch said.

'You think that's how they found the book?' Barastin questioned. 'That could have been what started off the whole thing: they got their hands on the last reproduction.'

'Immediately they would have seen the potential,' Heath agreed. 'And they have better resources, better technology than Tansel Kieger. They would believe they could get it done.'

Something sparked in Corvossier's mind; something she had read. 'They had both been rejected.'

Opal glanced at her. 'Huh?'

'Harrison Taper and Carthy Diego – the two Askari – they both had applications to join the Custodians rejected. It was Harrison's second rejection, her third. Even to apply is bold: usually you work hard enough and a recruiter approaches you.'

'Same with the Praetorian Guard,' Heath said. 'I recruited for a few decades; we kept our eyes on human warriors that impressed us and then approached with an opportunity.'

'They must have known they were never going to be Custodians by this point,' Barastin muttered. 'Never have the offer of immortality on the table.'

She nodded. 'They were both human, trapped to live mortal lives serving beings they perceived as better than them. Superior, even.'

'Isle of Wight isn't a plum posting either,' Heath said. 'They must have been barely above competent.'

'Then *The Book Of Species* falls into their laps,' she continued, 'and suddenly they have the chance to create their own opportunity.'

They were all silent as the conclusion bore down on them, before Opal interrupted their individual trains of thought.

'But at what cost?' she asked.

Heath dropped the book from his arms on to the table, it landing with such a loud thud that they all jumped.

'There,' he said, pushing the pages flat with his hand. 'The Ritual Of Arachnia.'

They all leaned forward, heads crowding around the page. The illustrations were grim, to say the least, and Corvossier was certain droplets that obscured some of the words were from real blood spilled on the page.

'You were right,' she said to Opal. 'It's not just our deaths that give them power; they need the flesh too.'

'They have your hand but no death,' the witch replied. 'You're as much at risk as I am.'

'You're two women who are particularly important targets for this enemy,' Barastin whispered.

'Look,' Heath muttered, turning the stiff page. Opal seemed reluctant to touch it altogether and Corvossier didn't blame her. 'They don't need every species, they need nine.'

'Nine is a good number for any magical ritual,' Opal noted. 'It's three times three, which makes it triply as powerful, and can symbolise growth and change.'

'So they have seven,' she reasoned. 'That we know of. They probably need two more, maybe?'

Opal clicked her tongue. 'And us.'

'And us,' she conceded.

'How sure are we on the nine?' Barastin asked. 'It says nine here in the instructions, but what's to say they don't want more? Maybe they'll settle with the seven they've got or maybe they'll decide to go one more, really boost the juice?'

'In Tarot the number nine can also represent a process or at least the *going through* of a process,' Opal said. 'And they are *going through* a process.'

Corvossier's eyes pored over the pages, feeling the bad intent seep into her very bones. The instructions and illustrations were all in black and white save for the occasional splash of colour from the splatters or smears. They were written in multiple languages, which is why every ritual took pages and pages of space. Tansel Kieger had wanted to make sure his dark magic could be as readily accessible as possible: if the reprints were the same, then she had to assume the instructions and translations were as well. And the end goal for all this murder and chaos? Arachnia, a creature that was traditionally thought to be a nightmarish vision from Japanese folklore called Jorogumo.

The supernatural community learned much later that not only did they exist, they were everywhere: in Africa and the Caribbean they were known as Anansi, the Native Americans called them Ikotomi and Arachne in Greek culture. It was them, always present and always relatively private compared to the gaudier members of the community like demons or elementals. Corvossier sent a prayer of thanks to Collette, wherever she was, for making sure she had a basic grasp of the paranormal histories. It was only because of her dedicated tuition that she knew arachnia had officially come out of the shadows in the early thirteenth century, which was considered late compared to the other sub-species. Within a century they were formally part of the Treize and in the millenniums since, they had worked their way well into the organisation. In human form they were almost otherworldly in their beauty, but that also created problems for them as they struggled to fit in to the regular world or pass as ordinary people the way others could.

'What would arachnia transformed from a blood ritual look like?' Barastin asked, his voice raspy.

'Horrific,' Heath answered.

'Giant fucking spider people,' Corvossier said, repeating the words her brother had said earlier and throwing him a look.

'No.' Heath shrugged. 'When arachnia – *real* arachnia – change it's stunning, truly something to behold.'

'Like watching a witch use her magic for the first time,' Opal said.

'Or a werewolf under the full moon,' he added. 'There's no denying the power of what you're watching, but there's also no denying the danger. Arachnia under a blood ritual, I couldn't fathom to think. I saw only an attempt at a transformation into a shifter and we had to put that thing in the ground. It was a mutation.'

'How do we even stop them?' Corvossier asked. 'Is there nothing in the book?'

'They weren't designed to be stopped, kiddo,' Heath scoffed. 'Tansel's not going to put their Achilles' heel in his instruction manual. They can be killed like anything else, you just have to be quick. And inventive.'

Inventive, she thought, walking away from the table so she could pace properly in the open space. An army of ghosts was inventive, but this wouldn't be one arachnia: this was potentially ten. Yet for them to successfully complete the transformation, both she and Opal would have to be dead and their flesh used in the ritual. By that point, it wouldn't much matter whether the arachnia could be overwhelmed by the sheer number of their victims or not. It was likely she and the witch would be among them, fighting from beyond the grave.

'I don't know about you,' Barastin said, 'but I find it hard to concentrate when there's a mannequin dressed like a medieval Hannibal Lecter looking at me.'

Corvossier followed his gaze to the display on torture methods for suspected witches, which was directly opposite where they were clustered.

'It's called a Scold's Bridle,' Opal corrected. 'And strategy aside, there's not much point working out how we're going to fight them until we can find them.'

'You're right,' Heath agreed.

'If they need one or two more sets of twins.' Barastin nodded, gesturing to the page for emphasis. 'We need to get to them *before* that happens. You twins are already part of the ritual, so they can't complete it without you both, but we shouldn't rely on that when we have the opportunity to save the lives of others if we can.'

'If it's just the four of us,' Opal huffed. 'We can't worry about finding others to protect when we can't even find the creatures we should be protecting them from.'

'She's right,' Heath said, folding his arms as he leaned against the wall.

'I'm sorry.' The witch blinked. 'That's twice within the last five minutes you've said I was right. Did I have a stroke and not realise?'

'Think about it,' he said, smirking, an excited gleam shining in his eyes, 'we don't know where they are and we don't know which set of twins they could be hunting right now in order to complete the blood ritual.'

'True,' she conceded.

'But we do know what else they want,' he said, pointing a finger at Corvossier before moving it to Opal. 'You *and* you.'

She felt a sinking feeling deep within her gut. It was similar to that sensation when you rode an elevator and just as you arrived at your floor, there was a brief moment of suspension, just a split second where you felt unsafe before the ground steadied again beneath your feet and the doors slid open.

That's how it was for her in the moment as she exchanged looks with everyone there in the museum.

'A trap,' Corvossier breathed. 'And we're the bait.'

'We'd need to make sure we have home ground benefit, of course. Choose somewhere that puts us at the biggest advantage and them at the biggest disadvantage.'

'Here,' Opal said. 'I choose to hide here because of the magic that enriches Boscastle.'

'Where is it strongest?' Heath questioned.

'Up on the cliff top.'

'Too exposed,' he said, shaking his head. 'Although it would decrease the chance of civilian casualties.'

'Then here, in this building. The foundations are old and the power imbued in this place is more than just some tourist attraction.'

Heath nodded. 'That could work. Limited space means they'd struggle to physically manifest, if they even can at this point.'

'I know every nook and cranny of this structure,' the witch continued. 'If I had a few days to prep some spells and charms, I could make it a weapon.'

'Make it a tomb instead.' He grinned.

Barastin frowned. 'What about the kid?'

'We'd have to get her out of here,' Opal agreed. 'As far away from danger as we possibly could and with someone we can trust.'

'We could embed her in with the Rogues,' Heath said. 'They're a pack of rogue werewolves in Berlin, run a nightclub called Phases. There's five of them, plus a soldier, so there'd be safety in numbers.'

'I am not sending my niece into a den of werewolves, you must be fucking mad.'

'My place,' Corvossier said. 'The Bierpinsel, it's a fortress. Between a whole floor of Praetorian Guard soldiers and all the Askari and Custodians, it's the safest spot she could be.'

'This isn't a small task,' Barastin noted. 'We can't entrust it to anyone.'

'Who are you thinking?' Heath asked, watching her.

'Yu.'

'Yu?'

'*Yu.*'

'Who's Yu?' Opal questioned, while Heath snorted a laugh. 'What's so funny?'

'She's over eight hundred years old and not only can she fire every weapon under the sun, she can make them from scratch as well.'

'Sounds like the perfect bodyguard to me,' Barastin whispered.

'Yu is not to be trifled with,' Corvossier agreed.

'I need to think this through,' Opal said. 'I'm nervous about the two of us being separated as it is, let alone separated by an ocean.'

Heath nodded, getting to his feet and looking weary as he did it. 'I think we all need to sleep on this.' He went to pick up the book, but Opal put a hand down on top of it.

'That doesn't come back into my house.'

'Do we need anything else in it?' Barastin asked. 'If not, then we should destroy it.'

'I want to go through it again,' the medium replied. 'See if there's anything we can use, even the smallest morsel.'

'Then we leave it here.' Opal sighed, taking it from him. 'I know the place.'

She disappeared into the darkness of the museum, her footsteps fading away as Heath, Barastin and Corvossier stood there and waited. It was many minutes before she returned, with no clue of where she'd been or where *The Book Of Species* was resting. It was no longer near any of them and that was enough, with Corvossier already feeling like the load was somewhat lighter as they strolled back to the cottage through the Boscastle evening.

Heath hesitated at the edge of the perimeter, as if expecting bees to come swarming out of thin air like they had before. Nothing happened, however, and he took one cautious step after the other until he was through the door and over the threshold. Tiptoeing down the hallway, Corvossier peered into Sprinkle's room to see the little girl laid out in front of the TV and fast asleep. Her parents were casually laying on the bed and gave her a nod. The credits of the movie were playing and she sensed Opal behind her, turning to find the witch peering over her shoulder.

'She's out cold, huh?' she whispered.

'Should I move her?' Corvossier offered.

'Nah, she'll be fine. She's got a blanket and a pillow under her head. Best to leave her.'

The pair returned to the kitchen, where Heath was tidying up the remainder of a dinner he wasn't there for.

'Who the fuck is Sprinkle?' he asked, examining a spoon that had the girl's name spelled out along the handle in bright letters.

Corvossier let out a quick laugh despite herself, she couldn't help it.

'It's her niece,' she said. 'Sprinkle Thomas: eight-years-old and burgeoning witch.'

'That's the kid you want Yu to babysit? You should have opened with that.'

'You're staying here,' Opal said. 'If we're doing this, planning this, then I want a soldier at our house. I'll sleep easier. There's one bed in the spare room down the hall with the glass doorknob.'

'Good, I already put my weapons in there.'

'You . . . what?'

'Casper, you should stay here too.' Heath turned back in the direction of the whiskey and grabbed a glass. 'The less spread out we are, the smaller a target we'll be.'

He poured three glasses, handing one to each of them. Corvossier looked at the liquid suspiciously, before tossing it back and flinching as it burned her throat. Opal's face was neutral as she did the same.

'Check out of The Wellington,' Barastin said. 'Bring your stuff over here.'

'I can do it tonight.'

'Not alone. Heath, go with her. I'll stay with the witches.'

'So bossy, Creeper.' He grinned, downing his own whiskey. 'Let's go.'

He clicked his fingers and grabbed the shotgun Opal had slipped back behind the flowerpots, and Corvossier followed him out of the house. He threw a floor-length duster over his immense shoulders, disguising the weapon as he hitched it into a holster around his hips that she had thought served as a belt. They were silent as they marched, the only sound being the music that still poured from The

Wellington on one side of the river and the Cobweb Inn on the other.

'Do you want to talk about it?' she asked.

'Talk about what?'

'I dunno.' Corvossier shrugged. 'How you feel?'

He grimaced, throwing her a sideways look. 'How *I* feel?'

'The Treize are corrupt.'

'Watch your mouth.'

'Watch your bosses.'

'You work for them too.'

'Sporadically. And I haven't committed my immortal life to their cause only to find out—'

'Let's talk about how you feel then, huh? How do you feel about the witch?'

'Are you quitting the Guard?'

'Are you quitting men?'

'I'm bisexual, not the Rosetta Stone,' she scoffed. 'And if you stay with them—'

'I don't want to talk about my feelings.'

'Fine.'

'Fine.'

They maintained an annoyed hush the rest of the way, not a word exchanged between them as she packed up her stuff or as she made small talk with Mary during the checkout process.

The stroll back to the house was quiet and, when they entered the cottage, Heath disappeared into the spare room and slammed the door.

'What was that about?' Opal asked, appearing around the corner.

'Nothing,' Corvossier muttered, staring at the wood of the

door. Unwrapping the scarf around her neck, she followed the witch as she gestured for her, tugging her up the stairs and into her bedroom.

'What are you grinning about?' the medium asked, watching her smile.

'Nothing,' Opal replied. 'Just thinking about the fact there's only one bathroom downstairs so the bloke is going to have to share with Sprinkle.'

'Is that a bad thing?'

'For him. She's a tyrant when it comes to bathroom time. Meanwhile, we have one all to ourselves up here.'

'Ah.' She nodded, seeing the humour. 'Very wise you are, young witch.'

'Young.' Opal chuckled, watching as Corviossier strolled over to where she sat. 'I'm three years younger than you.'

'Exactly: I'm in my thirties, you're in your twenties. It's a whole different decade.'

'Oh, *okay*.'

Corvossier loved the sound of her laugh, looking down as she swept her hair back from her face. Opal craned her neck up, observing her observations, and wrapped her hands around the medium's waist. Pressing her face to Corvossier's stomach, they stayed there holding each other in the quietness of the room. There was little to say truthfully: they both felt the pressure of what was to come weighing down on them.

'I'm scared,' Opal whispered.

'Me too,' Corvossier replied, meaning it. The witch excused herself, muttering something about needing a long shower to 'cleanse her soul' as she closed the door behind her. Glancing up at the space Opal had just walked through, Corvossier saw the familiar glow of her brother as he entered the room. It took her a moment to decipher what the expression was that she was seeing on his face. At first she thought it was fear, but she had seen that on him and this wasn't that. He was relatively safe from harm, all things considered. No, she realised with a start: what she was seeing was *his* fear, but it was his fear for her. *Me too, brother*, she thought. *Me too.*

Breakfast the next morning was tense. Opal made a separate plate for the kid, letting her eat in her bedroom while watching episodes of *The Deep* back-to-back. It was a good call and it meant Sprinkle would be occupied for a while. That left Heath, Opal, Corvossier and the ghost of Barastin sitting around the table together, most of them not eating.

'Well, this is pointless,' Heath said, the first one to break the silence as he laid down his fork. 'We need to work out what we're going to do.'

'Calling the cavalry is out of the question,' Barastin suggested. 'We know they've infiltrated the Askari and have used not only their staff members but their systems against us. And we know the Treize has covered it up: none of us know who can be trusted.'

'Can *he* be trusted?' Opal asked, nodding at Heath.

'Witch, you need me.'

'We don't need—'

'Fuck this,' Corvossier groaned, pushing her chair back from the table. 'We're arguing over stupid crap and I don't want eggs for breakfast. If we're going to die, I'm eating Angel Slice.'

They were quiet as she got up, ferreted around in the

cupboard and ate one of the small cakes followed by another without taking a breath. Closing her eyes, she enjoyed the taste and the small pleasure.

'Heath, what's the penalty for treason within the Praetorian Guard?' she asked.

'Death.'

'You're on personal leave at the moment, are you not?'

'I am.'

'And if they found out, if anyone found out what you were doing and who you were with . . .?'

'Death. While I'm at it, if I resign from the Praetorian Guard, my reward is revoked.'

'What does that mean?' Opal questioned.

'Immortality,' Barastin answered. 'They'd strip his immortality.'

The witch blinked. 'So you'd die?'

'No, I'd revert back to mortality. I'd age at the rate any regular person would, from the age I was first officially made immortal.'

He spoke the last sentence while staring directly at Corvossier, making sure the meaning wasn't lost on her. He needed time, she realised, to plan his next move. So did she.

'He has as much to lose as we do,' she muttered. 'Which means we keep this small and we keep it contained.'

Opal did not look happy about that. 'Just us? We're a witch, a medium, a ghost and a guy with a sword – no offence.'

'It's a *big* sword.' Heath shrugged. 'But none taken.'

'Four of us face off against *ten*?'

'It's not exactly just four of us though, is it?' the Scotsman said, casting a pointed look at Corvossier and her brother. 'I said all cards on the table, so we know what our strengths and weakness are. Physically I know what I can do, not to mention a few booby traps here and there for shits 'n' giggles. And I've seen an inkling of what the witch can do. I can extrapolate from there. How about you, Death? Time to pull back the curtain?'

'What's he talking about?' Opal asked quietly, but Corvossier wasn't looking at her. She was staring at her brother, who uncrossed his arms and gave her a non-committal shrug.

'What have we got to lose?' Barastin muttered.

She sighed. 'Because my brother had spiritual power in life, he has it in death also.'

Barastin reached out, knocking over the empty glass of apple juice that was sitting in front of Heath, everyone in the room watching as it tipped over with a *clink*.

'I don't understand; how can this help us?' Opal questioned.

'Because I'm not the only one,' Barastin said, drawing the words out slowly for maximum impact. Heath straightened up in his chair, looking as if he had just smelled blood in the water. 'There are more like me waiting on the other side for you all to give us the opportunity we've been counting on.'

'How many others?' the witch questioned.

'Sixteen people all up,' Corvossier answered.

'Or seven or so sets of twins,' her brother added. 'Plus a few extras.'

'The dead that they killed,' Opal whispered. 'My sister?'

'And her husband,' she said. 'They're both there and both

are ready. They're all ready. But we're not sure how limited their time will be physically, so we don't want to risk tapping that resource until we absolutely have to.'

'They'll be able to physically fight with us?' Heath asked, directing his question and main concern to Barastin.

'Better,' he replied. 'We can physically drag the Oct to hell.'

Heath smirked, looking around at the other faces within the room. 'Now those are odds a little more on my level.'

Chapter 18

The plan was simple in theory, but there were enough varia-
bles to make Corvossier and Opal jumpy over the following
days. Heath, on the other hand, seemed entirely relaxed
about the whole thing. She guessed that would change signif-
icantly when it was all set in motion, but she wasn't sure.
Corvossier had spoken to Yu about Berlin and Sprinkle, with
Heath taking the phone from her when she was done. They'd
worked together in Vietnam, he said, as if that would help
somewhat. Opal was growing increasingly nervous, but she
wasn't holding back when it came to telling her the niece the
truth.

'There are bad people coming,' she had said. 'The ones that
killed Willa and your dad. Casper and I have a chance to make
sure they don't do that to anymore families, but I need you to
be far away from here with a friend of ours.'

'Why?' she whinged. 'You know my magic is getting
stronger.'

'I know, gumdrop, but I'm not going to be able to focus on
what I need to do if I know you're in danger. As soon as this
whole thing is done, I'll come and get you. Then we go home,
we can go wherever we want, we can use our *real* names.'

'I like Sprinkle.'

'Then you can keep it.'

'Where will I be going?'

'Remember that tower Casper told you about? The big colourful one where she lives?'

'In Germany?'

'That's it. A lady named Yu will be going with you, so you'll have a mate by your side the whole time. It just won't be me.'

Sprinkle had lit up at the mention of a new name. 'It will be an adventure.'

'Yeah, kid.' The witch smiled, the expression not reaching all the way to her eyes. 'It will.'

Yu was expected any day and when she arrived, she and the child would be travelling to Berlin. Once there, Corvossier would jump into the Askari database to make one tiny, almost insignificant addition to her file. To most, it would go unnoticed: but the Oct weren't most. They were looking for her, they were waiting for an opening, and they were paying attention. The annotation would say that Corvossier von Klitzing was visiting the town of Boscastle, Cornwall, to stay with a friend named Opal Thomas. They wouldn't use Kala Tully's real name or mention she was a witch, as they feared that may be too obvious, but they would provide enough information in the description of her that the Oct would be able to deduce who it was. They didn't know when they'd come, but they estimated it would be anywhere between a few days to a week before they showed up in town, with Barastin monitoring Boscastle to see who came in and who came out. The second they arrived, he would report to Corvossier, Opal and Heath and the note would be removed from the medium's file. In the meantime they had to get everything in place: Heath with his stash of weapons and the Museum Of Witchcraft And Magic rigged to his liking; Opal with all of the offensive and defensive charms and spells she could prepare; and Corvossier tapped in to the ghosts and ready to call them when the moment arose.

Corvossier and Opal would keep up a routine each day, where they would leave for the museum early in the morning and stay until late that evening – every evening – until their enemies made a move. The aim was to make sure the building was seen as the place most suitable to attack. Heath was not to be present at all: he was too old, too known. The Oct had seen him in Berlin that night when he had dragged Corvossier bleeding from the alley. No doubt they knew what he represented and who he was by now: someone they needed to avoid if they were going to successfully complete their transformation. He had supplies, a place to sleep, and a functioning bathroom at the museum, which is where he would remain day and night until they showed. The thought of just the witch and her alone in the cottage as they waited for the Oct to nab the lure unnerved Corvossier, but Opal assured her the defensive charms would hold. She recharged them and added a few more, with a back-up plan even being developed in case they tried to attack them at home. Yet they all knew the museum was a better prospect and they were relying on that.

The medium became obsessed with *The Book Of Species* and everything she could learn from it. Her skin just connecting with the pages made her feel dirty and impure somehow, with Corvossier falling into a weird ritual where she meticously washed her hands after every length of time she spent touching it. The instructions themselves seemed to pierce her, the illustrations accompanying them etched with fine lines and figures so haunting it looked like the work of Gustave Doré. If she closed her eyes, the images would sometimes remain burned in her skull long after she had put the tome away. She interviewed Heath about all he knew and the day Yu arrived, she sat down with them all and handed over three meticulously written reports – one for each of them – on the strengths, weaknesses and backgrounds on humans in the process of transforming to arachnia from a blood ritual.

'It says here they can change in part,' Barastin read, glancing up from his copy. 'Which part?'

'It's impossible to tell until you've encountered them. It could be physical aspects of arachnia or just signature abilities. Maybe nothing.'

'If I see a woman with eight eyes, I'm gouging them all out,' Heath said.

'It more likely won't be as obvious as that,' she replied. 'One of their best defensive weapons is a poisonous spider bite, but something like that would be the last thing to develop according to the book.'

'So the good news is they can't deploy their most dangerous tool until Casper and I are dead?' Opal asked. 'Talk about silver lining.'

'On the plus side,' Heath said, 'if we release a bunch of flies in the room maybe they'll get distracted.'

Corviossier chuckled, the gesture acting like a balm as it released the tension she had felt bubbling under the surface. Peering at Heath, who gave her a sideways smirk, she realised that may have been his intention.

'The con is their skin is likely to be thicker,' she said. 'Literally, and harder to penetrate. Their communication at this point may also be limited as they're in the final stages. They could be stronger too, given that your average arachnia can carry up to fifty times their own bodyweight.'

And suddenly the tension is back, she thought.

'Talk to me about these weapons,' Heath grunted. 'Silver doesn't work on any supernatural creature, why are you advising it here?'

'They're not a supernatural creature though, are they? They were something human who – through a ritual of ultimate evil – are turning themselves into an impure abomination.'

'Silver is a pure metal,' Opal noted. 'It's a great conduit for magic because there's nothing in its chemistry that would muddy the spells.'

Heath looked thoughtful. 'I could use anything? Silver daggers, silver bullets, silver sword?'

'Silver surfer,' Barastin muttered.

'Any of it, all of it. Whatever you can get your hands on.'

'Just remember,' Corvossier said, 'we only need to get them near death, not kill them outright. The ghosts can do the rest, so long as we weaken them enough.'

It was at that moment Sprinkle darted into the kitchen, a purple suitcase with yellow flowers dragging behind her. She sprinted right up to Opal, standing at attention next to her chair.

She smiled. 'You look ready.'

'I'm all packed! Ready to go.'

'Let's walk you out,' Opal said, the rest of the group disassembling as they followed the witch and one excited traveller to the front of the cottage. Barastin stayed in the house, where he could remain unseen. Yu was sitting on the stone fence that bordered the property, looking out over the town as the river flowed quietly by. She jerked her head in recognition at Corvossier before Heath wandered over to her and straddled the fence. Their heads moved closer together as they began talking in a flurry of whispers, it being obvious the Scotsman was passing on some last-minute instructions to their escort.

'You've got your phone?' Opal asked.

'Yes.'

'Good, you call me anytime, about anything, okay? Even if you just wanna talk, it doesn't have to be something important.'

'Like if I set something on fire?'

Yu, who had her back to them in an attempt at privacy, glanced around with curiosity.

'It's fine,' Opal assured her. 'It's just a little bit of fire magic.'

'Look.' Sprinkle beamed, clicking her fingers so that a small flame danced between her digits. Opal rushed to cover the girl's hand with her own.

'What did I say, huh? I know it's exciting when you can first start using your powers, but you need to be discreet. Not everyone will understand what you can do and those that can, they might be just as dangerous. No magic until we're back together, alright?'

'None?'

'None. Don't frighten Yu now, she's your new friend.'

'I won't,' she grumbled.

'And you've got your Nintendo?'

'Uh huh.'

'And your charger?'

'*Opal, yes.*'

'Come here,' the witch said, pulling Sprinkle to her. She held the hug way longer than was necessary, with Bunyip even emerging from the garden and brushing her fat cat body up against them.

'Opal,' Sprinkle choked.

'I know, I know. Off you go.'

Corvossier watched the woman pull back, gently patting the girl on the shoulder as she jogged forward to Heath's side. He was performing the introduction, which must have gone well as Sprinkle gestured wildly to Yu. The warrior smiled, pulling back her jacket so the tiny witch could view the daggers sheathed at her hip. She wasn't a great lip reader usually, but she was pretty sure Opal's niece exclaimed 'Rad!'

Subtly, she cast Opal a sideways glance: she thought the witch was fighting to hold it together. Sprinkle and Yu headed off down the path, while Heath remained where he was, watching the pair pile into a car before driving off and out of town. Opal sniffed and the medium glanced down just in time to see the witch wiping away a tear.

'Hey,' she said, rubbing her shoulder. 'She'll be fine.'

'I know,' Opal half sobbed. 'That's the problem. She didn't even look that sad about going.'

Corvossier chuckled, pulling the witch into a bone-crushing hug. 'Of course she is, she's just excited right now because it's fun: it's the adrenaline of going on a trip after being stuck in the same place and on her best behaviour for so long. Now she gets to go somewhere with new people and see new things and take new risks. Once all the excitement has died down, I'm sure you'll get a giddy phone call.'

'You think so?'

'A text at the very least. With emojis.'

'Come on,' Heath said, moving back into the house. 'We have a lot to do and a limited window to do it. Save the salt.'

He was right, of course. They worked and they prepped and they didn't stop moving even once she added the note to her file. Corvossier's whereabouts – her largely vulnerable, unprotected whereabouts – were now in the system they knew the Oct were monitoring, along with an enticing titbit about a woman named Opal Thomas. She didn't doubt that it would be enough to draw them in from wherever they were: two birds, one stone and all that. The scary part was not knowing when. So they started their routine, with Heath taking up residence in the museum and Barastin watching Boscastle twenty-four hours a day in anticipation of their arrival. Corvossier and Opal would walk from the cottage to the building at 8 a.m. and stay there until at least 10 p.m. each night, long after it had closed, making sure that the Museum Of Witchcraft And Magic was the one location they would be for the largest period. It was an anxiety-ridden, nervous time for all of them as they tried to keep up a façade while knowing all the while that danger was creeping closer at every moment. There was a reason so many creatures had the fight or flight instinct, and Corvossier found it incredibly hard to quell her desire to bolt at the first sign of trouble.

It felt like the only protected place was Opal's bed each night. The witch was like a safe harbour amid the chaos of the passing days, her touch and her kiss and her body giving

Corvoissier a comfort she found hard to believe was real among the knowledge of who and what was coming. But that was falling for someone, she guessed: it made you feel like everything was okay when the reality was far from it. It blinded you to the harshness of life, at least for a while. She was more than happy to let herself stay giddy and coast along on the fumes of that feeling, clinging to what she gave Opal as much as what the witch gave to her.

The Goth with an attitude problem, Charli, had been given two weeks' break, so just she and Opal were covering shifts at the museum. They couldn't risk Charli being in the building if and when an attack happened, so they were trying to take her out of the picture altogether to keep her safe. They couldn't do much about the customers, however, with an increased number of bodies through the doors as it crept closer and closer to Halloween. By October, apparently it would be madness. As it was, she struggled to keep up with the sale of souvenirs and handing out tickets to visitors, with Opal stepping away at intervals to keep people moving through the exhibit. After two days at the counter, Corvossier had taken to wearing her cosmetic prosthesis just so she could avoid dumb questions or – even worse – the sincere well wishes from people who wanted to tell her 'what a go-getter' she was at the same time as prying into what happened. Things were a little smoother after that, with a full five days passing in total without so much as a spider web from the Oct. Politely waving the last set of visitors out the door, Corvossier sighed with relief and locked it behind them. Opal was balancing the register and looked up in the middle of counting a wad of ten pound notes.

'That it?' the witch asked.

'That's it.' Corvossier sighed with relief. 'Do you feel like a salad for dinner tonight? I'm craving something light.'

'That couldn't be because of the ocean load of mussels you ate for lunch again, could it?'

'It could.' She smirked, looking in the direction of the heavy footsteps pounding their way towards them from the back of the museum. Heath tossed himself down the steps that led from the exhibit to the main floor, landing with such force the snow globes wobbled dangerously on the shelf.

'Fee fi fo fum,' the witch said, in a sing-song voice. 'Here comes the sound of the big blond one.'

'You're always full of so much energy at this time,' Corvossier noted. 'How is that possible? All I want is a cup of tea and a nap.'

'You try being cooped up in that manhole all day and you'd be doing somersaults off the ceiling.'

'Please,' the witch scoffed. 'You only sleep in there: you're in the staff room the rest of the time.'

'Tracking my movements, are we, witchy? And we're not having *salad* for dinner, Jesus fucking Christ. I'd rather eat my own bawbag.'

Corvossier made a retching sound at the thought, earning an appreciative laugh from Opal.

'Steaks?' He grinned. 'I can pick them up from The Wellington? My treat?'

She glanced at the clock. It was nearly 6 p.m. and Barastin was due to check in at any minute.

'Soon as he's back then – ah, speak of the ghost.'

Her brother appeared right in the middle of her sentence and she smiled at him, always grateful to see his face. She was still feeling the effects of having him out of her life for a few weeks, making every appearance a welcome one. Her grin faltered when she caught a look at his expression.

'They're here,' he said, the words coming out in a rush of letters.

'The Oct,' she whispered, her heart feeling as if it had stopped pounding in her chest.

Opal shoved the notes back in the register, pulling out a box she had stored under the counter. Opening it, she began looping necklace after necklace around herself and clipping a bum bag around her hips. She cracked her knuckles first, then her fingers twitched and moved through the air as she warmed herself up in a way that made Corvossier practically feel the magic pricking the air.

Heath simply pivoted on the spot, reaching up to a height few people could, and retrieving a silver sword from the rafters where he had stored it. He was already wearing a gun holster over his shoulders and he pulled the weapon out, double-checking the magazine, before putting it back and sliding daggers into sheaths at his wrist. Grabbing a small bag from behind a shelf, he handed it to Corvossier: inside it was her gun, now fully loaded with silver bullets that Heath had meticulously cast himself. She preferred a holster at her hip and slid the gun in there, making sure she could reach it a moment's notice. Removing her cosmetic arm, she passed it to Opal who dived under the counter with it. She returned a second later with something else Heath had made based off a comment from Sprinkle about the Terminator.

'Do you need—'

'No,' she said, turning down Opal's offer of help as she screwed the arm into place. The majority of it was carbon fibre, which was solid but light enough that she could throw it around comfortably. However, the final third was pure medieval shit: a serrated, silver blade that came to a head with a terrifyingly sharp point. Heath had spent the past few evenings running her through drills just so she would be extra comfortable with it. There was a chunk of foam on the end as a safety measure and holding it down, she used her foot to prise it off. She felt something slip over her head and saw a small charm dangling to her midsection around a piece of leather cord. Opal ran her hands down it, making sure it was affixed to her properly.

'What's this?' she asked.

'Small safety charm,' the witch replied, gripping both sides of Corvossier's face with her hands as she leaned in and kissed her. She was almost too afraid to move, too afraid to break away and find out exactly how long they had. She had to let the sweet taste of Opal's lips freeze time – even for a few seconds – as she kissed the woman back, her fingertips sliding round to the back of her neck. Eventually they did have to separate, their foreheads remaining pressed together for a moment as they recalibrated to the situation at hand. Heath had mercifully said nothing, wandering out of the room to give them their privacy. Or prepare booby traps to kill, maim and execute: they were all sides of the same coin to him.

With Opal's hand linked in her own, she twisted around to look at her brother.

'Where are they?'

'On the cliffs either side of here.'

'How many?'

'Ten. Still ten.'

'The upstairs windows,' Opal said. 'That's our best view.'

The witch peeled off in the direction of the right side of the building, taking Heath with her as Corvossier heard them dash away. She and Barastin headed to the left, going against the route visitors usually took to leave the museum. She ran up the stairs two at a time, puffing slightly as she reached the landing. She knew the windows up there were tinted, so she could view out but nobody could view in and she was grateful for that as she looked towards the cliff tops. It was dusk, the sun having almost set completely behind the horizon as a purplish, blue glow faded into night. And sure enough, exactly where he'd said they would be, five silhouettes stood out against the skyline. Spaced a few metres apart, they were perfectly still and indistinguishable from each other as they wore the same robes Corvossier and Barastin had seen them in so long ago.

'It's their killing uniform,' he whispered, as she watched the hem of one whip around in the breeze. 'I remember it well.'

'How long have they been like that?'

'Twenty minutes or so, in exactly the same pose.'

'What are they waiting for?' she wondered.

'Some privacy, I dare say.'

'Like hell,' she scolded.

'Why not? They waited until they could get us somewhere discreet. They don't like an audience if they can avoid it.'

She threw him a look before glancing back at their enemy. 'How are they going to get down from there?'

'Same way an arachnia would, I imagine.'

'I think I'm going to be sick.'

'No, you're not. Keep it together.'

There was a knock at the front door and she leaped about a foot in the air. Barastin disappeared for an instant before reappearing in front of her.

'It's not them,' he said.

'Who the hell could it possibly be?' she snapped, jogging down the stairs.

'I think it's tourists.'

'Tonight? Didn't they see the closed sign? God, what luck. How sure are you?'

'They're both wearing shirts with Union Jacks on them,' he said. 'So yeah . . . definitely tourists.'

Opal and Heath were at the counter, neither looking sure about what to do.

'We need to get them out of the way,' Corvossier said. 'The Oct could attack at any moment and they're right in the line of fire.'

'I don't like the timing,' Opal said, flinching as the knocks rang through the museum again.

'We gotta get rid of them,' the medium hissed.

Opal nodded, but Heath held out his hand in a halting gesture.

'No, it could tip off the Oct that we know they're coming.'

'So, what?' Opal scoffed. 'We risk the casualities instead? We risk their lives?'

'They're not *our* lives,' the Scot countered. 'But if we're overzealous about moving on some tourists from a popular tourist destination then . . .'

'He's right,' Corvossier sighed, understanding his logic.

'Creeper, status check on the Oct,' Heath barked.

Her brother nodded, dissolving for a beat before bouncing back into view.

'They're all still there. All still watching.'

'None of them have moved?' he asked.

'No.'

'Aye, Casper go and answer the door. Step outside if you can, let our spectators get a good view of you. Chat to the tourists. After a few moments, go and join them, Opal. Invite everyone inside, but linger long enough that anyone watching will get a glimpse of the both of you, here together.'

Taking a steadying breath, she marched towards the door without hesitation. She was just about to reach for it when she realised what she was wearing: the gun holster. Her arm! She was mouthing the word shit as she spun back around, but Opal had seen the same problem. She was already at her side and helping her shrug into one of Heath's enormous coats. It was fine in length, but far too big in size and it swallowed her whole. It was perfect, hiding everything that needed to be hidden. The witch fussed around her just to double-check, before stepping away so she could answer the door. Sliding back the locks, she caught one of the tourists right in the middle of lifting his hand to knock again.

'Evening,' she said, stepping out into the night. 'I'm sorry to say but the museum actually closed half an hour ago. We open again at nine a.m. tomorrow if you care to come back?'

'Oh, we missed it? We wanted to see the witches.'

'We love Harry Potter!'

'Yes, well—'

'Who is it, hun?' Opal asked, practically skipping outside to join them.

'Guests,' she replied. 'They wanted to see the museum.'

'Well, then, you two should come in.' The witch smiled. 'We're just closing up everything for the day, so you can take a look around for a quick twenty minutes.'

'That would be nice.' The man smiled, casting a sideways glance at his friend.

'After you.' Corvossier gestured, letting the men go first. She slipped her hand into Opal's as they watched them walk inside, following shortly afterwards before locking the door behind them.

'Good God, that man is huge!' one of them exclaimed.

'Aye, aye,' Heath replied, not bothering to look up from the long dagger that he was sharpening with a stone as he sat on top of the counter. 'I ate my greens.'

'Are you a practising warlock?'

Heath paused, glancing up from his task with an amused smile. Corvossier pushed past them, sprinting upstairs to the window as the conversation continued on down below.

'Did you call me a warlock?'

She made it to the vantage point just in time, letting out a puff of air as she saw the same five figures standing there. She counted them in her head twice, just to be sure, before hearing Opal call out that they were all there on her side as well. They had seen the show, now what would they do? Mentally she kicked herself for asking that question as the Oct moved so slowly she thought she might be imagining it at first. But no, she wasn't going crazy with fear: they prowled right to the edge of the cliff where the drop off would prove fatal. They crouched down and, for a second, she thought they had jumped. She gasped, hearing a reaction from Opal as well which meant she was watching something equally as astounding.

'What, did you think they were committing seppuku or something?' Barastin asked, his form appearing in the reflection of the window behind her.

'It would never be that easy, would it?' she replied, hating the fear she heard in her voice.

Because they hadn't plunged to the ground at all: instead she could see darker spots moving down the cliff face at a rapid rate, scuttling along the vertical surface the way nothing in nature ever should. They were coming and there was no more time to prepare. She could hear the tourists firing questions at Heath downstairs, while the Pict suggested they place the end of a broomstick somewhere very uncomfortable. She was almost relieved to learn they were innocent and not affiliated with the Oct in any form. That thought was chased away quickly as she was met with another: they were in the way now, casual bystanders that would be lucky to make it through the next few hours. Craning her neck up further, she tried to see where the Oct were but she had lost sight of them near the base of the cliff as it sloped towards the township.

'PLACES!' Opal called, Corvossier spinning on her heels and moving back down to ground level.

'Get under the counter,' the witch was saying, urging the guys to hide. 'Stay quiet and you might live through this.'

Heath had vanished, moving to his station and standing by.

'Survive through what?' one of them asked, just as the lights cut out. 'Is this a recreation?'

The only source of illumination came from Barastin, who floated down the stairs. She met his gaze in the darkness and gave him one stiff, quick nod. He returned it before fading away completely, leaving them all alone in the dimness of a museum surrounded by arachnia.

Chapter 19

There was a clatter of smashing tiles as they slid off the roof and landed on the ground outside, the ceiling straining under the weight of several arachnia. The sound of the pitter patter above them sent chills down Corvossier's spine and she swivelled her head this way and that, tracking the movement. Barastin remained in his preferred state, meaning only she could see him. He would be completely invisible to everyone else: the arachnia included.

'They're on the roof,' Corvossier whispered.

One of the tourists popped his head above the counter. 'Who are?'

'Your recreation,' Opal snapped, dashing to the front door. Corvossier switched places with her, pausing on the fourth and final step up into the exhibition. A floorboard above her head creaked as Heath moved around on the second floor. Her eyes darted back to the two men, the tips of their heads just visble on the other side of the cash register. She hesitated, knowing that every second she wasted could prove fatal. But still, Corvossier was aware of what was coming and if those bystanders remained where they were, they weren't going to make it.

'Get up!' she shouted, dragging the smaller of the tourists by his shirt and urging the other to follow her. 'Hurry!'

'Oh, she's good,' one whispered.

'Very convincing,' the other agreed.

She threw open the door to a tiny crawl space built into the wall, practically kicking the knees out from both of them and ordering them inside.

'Cool, an escape room!' The man beamed, scrambling forward with a huge smile plastered on his face.

'I'm writing the best Yelp review for this,' his friend responded as Corvossier slammed the door shut behind them and dragged a table in front of the entry.

Please stay quiet, she thought. *Please stay quiet.*

Spinning around, she watched Opal begin to whisper to herself, backing up slowly until she was wedged tightly between two of the souvenir displays in the corner. It was the safest spot to be. It was deathly silent for a moment, not a sound except her own breathing. There was a spray of glass as the window to the museum was shattered, something bursting through it so quickly Corvossier couldn't get a good look at it first. She held her ground, noting the sound of smashing coming from upstairs as well as the arachnia attacked on two fronts at once. Finally the figure stopped moving, coming to a halt right in the spot where you'd usually find dozens of tourists lining up for a ticket. It was a person, standing there in a robe that was shredded and torn in places. Somehow the hood was still covering their face, but they pulled it back slowly to reveal Siegfried McKenzie. *Oh, I know you*, she thought, resisting the urge to curl her lips in disgust: she needed all of them inside first.

Corvossier had thought her eyes looked dead when she looked into them back in Berlin, but staring into the hollows of what was left now she realised there had been something remaining, even just a shred of soul. That was now gone, her sockets housing no more than a swirling black hole with only a glimmer of human intelligence conveyed.

Three more figures dived in after her, two scuttling low to the ground as they moved across the floor. They refused to stand up, remaining hunched and their limbs quivering as if ready to attack at any moment. The only other one to stand up alongside Siegfried was Harrison Taper.

'Good,' Barastin said to her. 'I was hoping he'd be among this lot.'

It was likely they could see perfectly in the dark, she had learned, so she remained still as she gave them a moment to view her, digest her properly. They hadn't yet noticed Opal, who had made a conscious effort to make herself as small as possible as her hands moved in the dimness. One of them must have *sensed* where the tourists had been, crab shuffling over to the counter and springing up on to it in a way no earthly thing should.

'Go on then,' Corvossier said. 'What are you waiting for?'

Siegfried frowned, thinking that she was talking to them. She wasn't.

'SEAL IT!' yelled Heath, his booming voice travelling from upstairs. There was a flare of light as what looked like a sparkler shot forward from Opal's hands, flying around the room before disappearing out of sight. There was a loud crack and the whole building shuddered, the ground beneath Corvossier feeling like jelly. The window they had crashed through disappeared and the door to the museum melted into the walls, with every view of Boscastle outside disappearing as Opal's magic sealed the building shut. For better or worse, no one was getting in but, more importantly, *no one* was getting out.

Corvossier shrugged out of Heath's coat, letting it fall to the floor. Opal snapped an ornament hanging from one of her necklaces, the sound feeling tiny and pathetic compared to what had just come before it. The Museum Of Witchcraft And Magic slowly swam into view, every inch and corner and crevice of the building becoming illuminated as a warm yellow light grew and grew.

Corvossier let her fear show, let it sink through her limbs and power the surge of energy she felt building. It drew them to her and she pivoted on her heels, sprinting through the exhibit as she heard the Oct in pursuit. There was a woman's high-pitched scream above her followed by what sounded like a chainsaw starting up and she knew that Heath was doing just fine on his own. She hoped Opal would be as well.

'HOW MANY?!' she called out to her brother as he danced ahead of her.

'Three.'

Good. That left the witch with one. When they had gotten close enough that she could feel their breath on her neck, she extended her left hand, Barastin gripping it as he threw his weight behind it and helped her spin in a full circle. She swept her right arm out in a wide arc with the movement of her body, the gesture working perfectly as the sharp blade sliced diagonally down the person at the front of the pack. It was a man, maybe Gerald Simpson, with the weapon destroying any of his recognisable features. He clutched at his face, watching as a blackish blood poured from the gash that extended down his neck and to his chest.

'Ramona and Raymond!' she called, relishing the surge of power as her vision shifted between the two worlds for a second. The elementals disappeared from one realm and appeared in another, hers, grinning as they landed either side of the unfortunate gent. They didn't waste any time, with Raymond shoving the member of the Oct towards his sister who pulled him to the ground. Both siblings dived on top of him, his startled cries ringing out as they began tearing him apart with their bare hands.

'D-dead!' he shrieked. 'Deeead!'

Harrison had frozen on the spot, something in his face shifting to human as he watched the ghosts of two people he had killed enacting revenge on one of his own.

'Impossible,' he whispered, not bothering to help the man even as he reached out a bloodied hand towards him. '*Impossible.*'

'There are a lot of others waiting for you, Harrison,' Corvossier growled, hoping he could understand her properly. 'You'll get your turn.'

He looked surprised that she knew his name, his white eyebrows shooting up in shock. She knew all their names, as did Opal and Heath, because she had studied their files meticulously in order to recognise them on sight. She could tell by looking at his face that it was finally beginning to dawn on him what they had walked into. Siegfried let out an annoyed grunt, pushing Harrison out of the way and marching towards Corvossier with something that technically was a smile but lacked any of the human warmth behind it.

'I hope we didn't cut off your good hand,' she spat.

Corvossier tilted her head with interest. 'I'm ambidextrous, bitch.'

She lunged forward in the position Heath had taught her, thrusting the sword attached to her arm outwards and directly into her opponent. Siegfried dodged at the last second, scuttling to the side so that she missed what would have been a fatal blow. The blade – still slick with the blood of Gerald – sliced through her left side and she let out a cry.

Unwilling to give the woman her rear, Corvossier backed up as Siegfried continued to stride towards her, fluid now dripping from her side and down her leg so a trail was left in her wake. Her body seemed to be twitching as she moved, first a neck spasm and then her arms, but she either didn't notice or didn't care.

'That won't be enough to save you,' she whispered, her words barely sounding human.

'Nor you,' Corvossier replied, tossing a glass bottle at her from the healing woman's table as they passed it. The glass didn't penetrate her skin, she noted, but her blade had. The twitching continued until there was a sickening crack, followed by another and another as Siegfried tossed back her head and screamed. Fabric tore away from her body and fell to the ground in shreds as white limbs shot outwards: not one, but eight, each after the other ripping through her skin and landing on the wooden floor with a thump.

Corvossier felt her mouth drop open in horror as she stared at the thing – *the abomination* – in front of her. She tried to keep moving backwards but her legs ceased to work, stumbling and falling over each other as she landed on her arse.

Looking up, she met the terrifying grin of Siegfried as she advanced. Four limbs had burst from her body, her arms and legs morphing as well so she was left with eight: just like a spider. Except unlike a spider, these were made out of bone: human bone. Blood and flesh clung to the joints, her torso stretching unnaturally as it held everything together. It not only looked painful, but it seemed incredibly horrible for the subject as well with the woman coughing like she had a horrendous flu, only for blood to bubble out of the corner of her mouth. Corvossier pulled her gun from the holster, letting off three shots in quick succession.

Her target dropped low to duck them, scurrying up the side of the wall on all eight limbs like it wasn't a feat at all. Corvossier kept firing, feeling the panic rising as she counted in her head and knew that she was down to her last two bullets in the magazine as Siegfried sprinted across the ceiling and dived towards her. She rolled once to dodge her, twice, and then a third time until her back was against a hard surface. The creature has still charging and she steadied the gun, propping up her right elbow on the floor to give her left arm stability. She aimed not where the monster was, but where she was *going* to be, and landed her first two successful hits. The disgusting black blood that Corvossier had seen earlier sprayed over her, soaking through every inch of her clothing. The sound of the bullets entering the wet flesh of Siegfried's torso was a relief in that moment, the limbs made of bone closing in on themself like a spider as it twitched towards death. Her body skidded to a stop right in front of Corvossier and she let out a panicked yelp, trying to get away from her but being trapped against the wall. A groan escaped Siegfried's lips and she watched nervously as the woman's eyes looked desperately around the room. Her brother smiled, letting himself be seen by her as he planted his feet on the joints of two of her limbs. She didn't scream in pain, although it must have hurt, but her lips moved in a flurry as if trying to speak words that just couldn't be heard.

'You killed me,' he said, voice quiet but impactful all the same. 'You took my sister's hand. Now I have somewhere to take you.'

He threw Corvossier a sideways glance and she nodded, watching as her brother plunged his hand through the woman's chest. There was little more than a choked breath before the life left her eyes and Barastin disappeared with her, making sure she was taken somewhere there would be no return from. A small scream escaped her own lips as the body moved, but the medium's shoulders relaxed as she saw human hands wrap around one of the outstretched legs. Opal ripped Siegfried's corpse away, giving Corvossier enough room to crawl to her feet. They embraced for just a moment, with her looking over the witch's shoulder in the direction she had come from. She could see smoke pouring from the front of the museum, red and orange flames licking at the ceiling as a mangled figured burned at the centre of it.

'Who was it?' she asked, knowing that Opal had taken out a member of the Oct.

'Rhiannon Willersdorf.'

She closed her eyes for a beat, appearing in the lobby. 'Matias and Vincente?'

'Present.' One of them nodded.

'Rhiannon's down.'

'We'll chase.' Matias grabbed his brother by the hand and they both disappeared, sinking into the floor as if they were ice cream under hot sun.

She blinked, returning to the museum and where Opal was still holding her.

'The tourists?' Corvossier questioned, her voice hardly a whisper.

'They're still in there, still fine . . . I think.'

'What about Harrison? He was just behind me?' she asked, pulling back to examine the witch's face.

'There was no one there,' she said. 'I just sprinted right through. I thought she'd got you, crushed you underneath.'

'He's here somewhere.'

Her eyes ran over the room, wondering where he was or what exhibit he could be hiding behind. There was a clatter from above them and the sound of metal on metal. They were needed upstairs, with Corvossier handing her gun to Opal for her to reload it. Switching magazines and handing it back, she took point as the woman grabbed two witch bottles that she had planted in the shelf of herbal remedies behind her. They took the steps slowly, one at a time, flinching at the sounds of the fight happening above them as they moved closer towards it. Blood from one of the Oct was dripping down the top step and Corvossier was careful not to tread in it. The owner of those bodily fluids was still alive, but locked inside the Scold's Bridle. It had been repurposed into a trap there was no escaping from. She thought it looked like Lewis Vinkle, having that confirmed when he began wriggling desperately as he caught sight of Opal and her. This was also the creature Heath had taken a chainsaw to, she noted.

'Elodie,' she said. 'Adam.'

The two demons from Jerusalem appeared on either side of her, causing Opal to cry out in surprise.

'Look at him wriggling,' Adam said to his sister. 'Think he's in pain?'

'Not enough,' Elodie replied.

They slowly advanced on the man, Corvossier and Opal not sticking around to watch but hearing enough as they moved towards Heath. He had rigged the Scold's Bridle to the ceiling with a cable, along with what looked like a spiked javelin that swung in from the side. It had clearly hit something, with the silver-tipped wood painted in the blood of its target.

'MOVE!' Opal screamed, shoving Corvossier out of the way as said target ran directly at them on all fours. The witch hurled the bottles in her hand, each one smashing on the ground in front of the creature and silver clouds billowing up into air. It was moving too fast to avoid them and dashed right through, a rumbling howl coming from its mouth almost immediately as whatever Opal had conjured in there took effect. She couldn't tell if this was a man or a woman, even less so as their skin started to bubble and boil. She stretched her mind out towards Keziah and John, not even needing to say their names out loud before the two shifters materialised in buffalo form, pounding on their prey. It was bizarre to her, as they still had the bluish grey pallor of ghosts but they were in their preferred supernatural bodies. She let herself get distracted and it came at a price, with Opal's feet swept out from under her and the witch dragged along the floor towards a member of the Oct neither of them had noticed. She landed with a crack, Corvossier wincing as she watched the witch's arm bend at an unnatural angle and she knew it was broken.

She dived forwards, slapping down her weaponised arm so it sliced right through the human hand that was stretched beyond regular portions like a demented member of the Fantastic Four. She had to repeat the movement twice before the limb completely severed, with Opal crawling backwards and away from the arachnia hybrid.

Corvossier screamed as she felt something cut along her shoulder, glancing up to see a different foe looming over her with an enormous hook. The woman was swinging it down towards her and at the last minute she threw her arm up, watching as her prosthetic weapon was completely dislodged. Opal made a series of slicing gestures with her hands, looking like a lethal form of sign language as Corvossier sensed magic charging through the air. The witch hurled one of her necklaces across the room, the attacker looking momentarily stunned. She realised that had been the purpose of the spell, giving her just enough time to get to her feet. Opal darted forward, palms extended upwards and words flying from her mouth in a ferocious buzz. Corvossier watched the necklace the witch had thrown seconds earlier, the charm rattling on the floorboards the closer Opal moved towards it and the frozen arachnia.

'YOUR LEFT!' the medium screamed, horrified as the creature who'd broken Opal's arm scuttled directly at the witch from behind. She panicked, realising Opal would be trapped between the two monsters. Yet the witch must have scoped the scenario seconds before Corvossier had as she threw up her hand, ordering her to stay back as she dropped to the ground in a crouched position and her words increased in volume. She shrieked, Opal's cries mixing with those of the two Oct as they pounced towards her simulatenously, Corvossier squinting her eyes shut as a blinding light erupted. A disgusting smell singed her nostrils and she gagged, coughing and struggling for air as she pushed forwards. Batting smoke out of her line of sight, she saw the two charred arachnia figures frozen in their final positions as if they were victims of Mt Vesuvius. She reached out to the ghosts, dragging them towards the bodies before they fell apart like ash. She was aware when they joined her, but she paid them little attention as her eyes focused on a crumpled figure laying on the floor.

'Opal!' she gasped, dropping to her knees and sliding towards her. Rolling the witch over, she slapped her face as gently as she could to try and rouse her.

'OpalOpalOpalOpalOpalOpal!' she begged, her breath in ragged sobs. 'Opal please!'

Her fingers were shaking as she tried to feel the witch's pulse, eyes scanning the woman's body simultaneously for any additional injuries. She couldn't see anything, but that didn't stop the bile she felt rising in her throat. A physical injury she could deal with, but something caused by magic ... she was lost.

Corvossier had to get her up, had to bring her along and protect her. She couldn't go on if she had to leave Opal behind. Half dragging, half carrying her, she knew she'd lost her gun in the tussle but couldn't afford to waste time searching for it. She limped towards the broad back of the man she recognised. Heath was covered in blood, both his own and the creatures' as he faced off against them. One – Carthy Diego – was on her last legs, literally, but the others were putting up a formidable fight as he tried to keep them at bay by wielding two swords at the same time.

'We're here!' Corvossier panted, with him not sparing a look in their direction but slowly angling himself towards a wall so he had protection at his back. Carefully, she slid Opal to the ground and turned back to flank him on his right. There were three of the Oct left and just two of them still standing.

'You're outnumbered,' Carthy chuckled, her laugh sounding sick.

'We were never outnumbered, you old bag,' Heath teased. 'Do it, Casper.'

With every bit of herself she had left, Corvossier reached out to the others standing by. They were waiting for her call, craving it in fact, and with the mental curl of her finger she felt them follow her. Gravity pulled down on her body, the weight returning her to the earthly realm alone . . . to begin with.

Willa and Alistair were the first to arrive, standing protectively in front of Opal's unconscious form and sheltering her from the path of the hungry arachnia. Sally and Jeanette, the selkies, were next, then the werewolf boys and the others in sets of two until the room was crowded. Zane and Taj – the Ghana arachnia – were the last to arrive and she felt some resistance as they struggled at first, but then a familiar power joined her own as goosebumps sprung up along her skin. Her brother loaned her added force, bringing the last two twins with him so that they assembled as a trio.

'Now I'm not a mathematician,' Heath snorted, 'but that looks more like three on twenty now, innit?'

He inched forward, the ghosts moving with and ahead of him. Two of the Oct scuttled back, their eyes full of disbelief at what they were looking at.

'They're just ghosts,' one of them scoffed. 'They can't hurt us. Destroy them!'

'Just ghosts,' Corvossier muttered. 'They would be, but as you *took* power you gave them power. You're about to be annihilated by your own creation.'

And they were, the dead rushing them in a wave that consumed the monsters entirely beneath it. The ghosts were fully aware their physical presence wouldn't last, it would be fleeting, and that this was likely their only opportunity to claim justice in the biblical sense.

She and Heath stood back from the carnage, neither looking away as the effects of the blood ritual were destroyed with the spilling of more blood. The Scotsman had no doubt seen worse, but she was watching a real-life massacre. There was something compelling her to keep watching, as if she had to. Only that way would this hell finally be over. Periodically the ghosts began disappearing and reappearing as they made sure each person was dragged beyond and into a final death. Soon, there was nothing left except the remains.

'I didn't even get to use a single Molotov cocktail,' Heath huffed.

A few of the ghosts looked at him with amusement, others shifted their gaze to Corvossier as they waited for the next set of orders.

'It's done?'

She froze, her back stiffening as she recognised the voice that croaked out from behind her. The medium spun around, blinking rapidly as her eyes adjusted to the sight of Opal stumbling to her feet. She crept forward, arm cradled to her chest and leaning slightly to the left as if she was unbalanced. Her sister Willa was walking next to her, brother-in-law Alistair on the other side, like otherworldly crutches. She opened her mouth to say something, emotion and relief swelling in her chest as they locked eyes.

'It ain't,' Heath said, taking the words from her as he lit a cigarette. 'Count the bodies.'

Corvossier did the sums, factoring in who was on the first floor.

'He's right,' she said. 'There's nine here: we need ten.'

'Harrison Taper,' Barastin said, turning to the other ghosts. 'Treasure hunt?'

Willa and Alistair joined him as they headed downstairs, the rest of the dead following after them in a steady trail as they looked for the man who had helped instigate the whole thing. He was hiding somewhere in the museum, she realised, having let his disciples suffer horrible fates once he realised there would be no victory. Opal leaned into Corvossier, the medium slipping her hand around the witch's shoulders as they took the descent one stair at a time. There was so much she wanted to verbalise, but in the moment she was merely grateful for the woman's physical contact against her body. The remains of the first arachnia to fall weren't on fire anymore, with the corpse simmering in a pile as they shuffled past the counter.

'We've found him,' Barastin chirped, appearing back in front of her.

'What are you waiting for then?' Heath replied, blowing out a puff of smoke.

'Well,' her brother started, 'I was thinking there might be a certain book you need to locate.'

Corvossier held his gaze, knowing he was right. 'Take him to the lobby. I'll meet you there soon as I get rid of the tourists.'

'What the hell are we gonna say?' Opal asked, nudging the dead arachnia with her foot.

'They all think it's a show, right?' her brother asked. 'That this was some kind of immersive, after-dark experience where we shove them in a cupboard and scary noises are heard outside.'

'Er, yeah,' Corvossier said, uncertain.

'Give Heath your phone, turn on the flashlight and hold it up. Sister, let the tourists out, will you? All other ghosts, we'll rendezvous in the lobby.'

The three living occupants of the room glanced at each other nervously, but everyone was so exahausted they followed Barastin's instructions obediently. Using her hip to push the table to the side, Corvossier opened the door and stood back as the two men crawled out of hiding, sweaty but ecstatic. The first looked as if he was about to speak, but his acquaintance shut him up completely with a stiff whack to the arm. Both were staring, gobsmacked, at the light from the phone as Heath held it upright. Barastin's ghostly figure blinked into view, Corvossier hiding a smirk as her brother made himself flicker like a television with bad reception as he appeared in front of them, hands clasped formally.

'Thank you so much for visiting Boscastle's Museum Of Witchcraft And Magic,' he said in a perfectly robotic tone. 'To make sure the live experience remains enjoyable for future guests, we ask that you refrain from posting detailed online reviews so the adventure remains unspoiled.'

'That is *sick*,' one of the men whispered. 'A proper hologram and everything.'

'We hope you come again,' Barastin finished, bowing before he disappeared completely. Heath switched off the flashlight at exactly the right time, the two tourists blinking as they struggled to adjust to the sudden change in exposure. Opal already had the front door open, ushering them towards it and the Boscastle evening outside.

'Blessed be,' she said sweetly as they moved past her, muttering about 'how fake' the synthetic blood on her clothing looked. The entire room decompressed the second the door was shut – and locked – once again, Heath's face breaking out into a delighted grin.

'Humans are fookin' eejits.' He laughed.

'I was screaming on the inside that entire time.' Opal sighed.

'We hope you come again,' Barastin repeated, offering an encore performance to their small party.

Corvossier wanted to join them, to laugh along, but she had one final task as she turned to address Heath.

'The ghosts are taking care of Harrison. You two need to watch my body, make sure it doesn't come to harm.'

'You're bleeding profusely out of a cut on your shoulder,' Heath noted, jerking his head at the gash.

'Any other harm,' she corrected.

'Where are you going?'

'To follow this through.'

She didn't have time for anymore explanation than that, letting her mind and her body slowly begin to shut out the scene around them. Heath faded away, as if being obscured by muddy water until eventually he was gone altogether.

Glancing over her shoulder, she realised with a start that she was alone in the lobby. There had been a lot of action there this evening and it made her uneasy. That feeling was short-lived as Harrison arrived screaming and thrashing in the clutches of Alistair and Barastin. The others followed, natu-rally forming a circle around her and blocking the flaying's man view of anything outside the perimeter of their bodies. The panic never left his face, but after an agonisingly long time he physically began to calm himself enough that Alistair and Barastin were able to step back.

'W-where . . . where I am? What happened to the pain?'

'You're dead,' Corvossier snapped, not pulling any punches. 'The people you murdered killed you and brought you here.'

'The afterlife?'

She laughed: she couldn't help herself. She could tell purely from the tone of his voice that he thought it was over, that he was in some form of *heaven*. He couldn't have been more wrong.

'This is more like Hell's loading dock,' Barastin snarled.

'After everything you've done,' Corvossier said. 'All the suffering and selfishness you have inflicted, all of the blood you have spilled in the name of your ritual . . . you're going somewhere else, Harrison.'

His eyes widened with horror, but there was also a realisa-tion there.

'But first,' she remarked, 'you have something I want.'

'What?'

'*The Book Of Species*. I know you have a copy. I want to know where it is.'

He hesitated and she could almost see the evil spiders that crawled through his very brain and soul trying to come up with a way to leverage what she wanted.

'The Oct are all dead. You never finished your full transformation into arachnia. There's no one left to complete your "work".'

'Then why do you need it?' he asked. 'What do I get from telling you where it is?'

The questions were barely out of his mouth before his body made a sharp jerking motion and he fell to the ground. On his arse, he looked around him as if startled by whatever had dragged him to the floor. He tried to get to his feet, but was yanked back down and let out a pained cry. Lips shaking, he looked up at Corvossier with an accusatory glare.

'WHAT ARE YOU DOING TO ME?'

'Me?' she said, in her most innocent voice. 'I'm just asking you questions. You're the one who's refusing to answer.'

He let out a glass-shattering scream as he sprawled out on his back, his eyes darting to the faces of the ghosts.

'Don't even think of asking us for help,' Willa said, leaning down so that she was at eye level with him. 'Only she can control this or let it drag out as long as necessary.'

'WHAT IS HAPPENING?'

'You're being pulled where you need to go,' Corvossier replied. 'But I'm holding you here until you answer my questions.'

'AAAH!' he shouted, his hand disappearing through the floor slowly, inch by inch. Corvossier felt her powers flex as the strength of something *else* increased: it was hungry for Harrison Taper. It wanted him and it wanted him *now*.

'Time doesn't exist for you here,' she growled. 'I can make this go as long as I want to, endlessly, forever.'

A leg disappeared through the floor, the top half of his thigh stretching unnaturally as she used her mind to hold him in the lobby.

'*Where is the book?*'

He was screaming non-stop now, the feeling of one's soul – or what was left of it – being pulled in different directions was almost incomprehensibly painful.

'LEWISHAM! FIFTY-TWO LEWISHAM CLOSE!'

'Where is that?'

'England! It's . . . *argh*, Ruislip – where the banshees lived. *Please.*'

They had already selected their next target, she realised, and they had been camped out waiting for the perfect moment to strike. These twins, whoever they were, had been going about their everyday lives completely unaware that death was watching them the entire time, the scythe swinging lower and lower to their necks. Just like Barastin and her, as they'd been expelling ghosts and going to Phases and hanging out with Collette, never knowing they were being watched by people who wanted more than what life had given them.

It was the same for all of the ghosts around them, who'd had families and lives and children ripped from them. Corvossier felt like a downed power line slapping on the pavement, rage and anger flying from her in lethal sparks. She held on to Harrison with everything she had, letting him stretch beyond as his screams echoed through the lobby. *Suffer*, she thought. *Suffer the way we have.* She felt a hand close around her wrist and she found herself staring into the eyes of Akmal, one of the werewolf boys.

'That's enough,' he said.

Her clenched fist didn't think it was enough, neither did her barbwire mind, but as she stared into the young man's face she didn't like what was reflected there. And it was as instant and simple as that. She released the hate and rage in her brain, feeling it move away from her as if it was slipping rapidly down a water slide. The pull took over and Harrison Taper sunk through the floor, his face and his screams disappearing forever. Then it was just silence: the dead and Corvossier standing among them.

'You're free now,' Barastin told their forms. 'You should feel your own tug soon, leading you where you need to go. There's nothing left holding you here if you're ready to leave.'

It was a private thing and she knew she shouldn't be there for it. It was time for her to go too and leave the dead to their final journey without some tourist watching on. She glanced around the group, holding the gaze of each ghost for a beat. Some gave her a small smile or nodded, others just touched her shoulder or gripped her hand with surprising strength. Willa was one of those, telling Corvossier so much without verbalising it. *Look after my sister*, her stare said. *Love my sister*, her handshake communicated. *Watch over my daughter*, her touch whispered. She would do all of those things.

Turning to her brother, she embraced him in a tight, crushing cuddle that she felt right down to her bones. It was too soon to the events to feel relief just yet, but it was done: the months they had given up in order to pursue vengeance were over. Seperating from him slowly, she traced the sharp line of his jaw with her fingers and peered into the ghostly grey of the eyes that matched her own.

'You've done well, sister,' he whispered. 'Now go back to where you belong.'

She held his face in her mind as she released herself, feeling the tips of her limbs solidify as she fell back to her physical body. The sharp metallic tang of blood was in the air, along with smoke, burning and death: that last one was unmistakable. Her eyelids fluttered open as she processed the scene she had left behind. Heath was watching her closely, his eyes focused on Corvossier intensely. As soon as he registered that she was back, *really* back, he leaned away.

'Where?' he asked.

'Fifty-two Lewisham Close in Ruislip, England.'

'And him?'

'I took care of it.'

He nodded, not doubting that she had, before turning around to yell over his shoulder. 'Oy witch, she's back!'

There was a clatter from within the exhibit and running feet as Opal slid around the corner. She had a broom in her undamaged hand, wasting no time on the clean-up within the museum. Corvossier guessed the sling that was holding her broken arm to her body had come from the first aid kit open on the counter. Heath was partially patched up too and she noticed the cut on her shoulder had been bandaged together while she had been elsewhere. Opal threw the broom at Heath who caught it and stared down at the wooden object like it was a snake.

'What am I supposed to do with this?' he asked.

'I've gotten rid of all the broken glass, you said you'd take care of the bodies.'

'Not with a broom. I was going to move them all into a pile with my bare hands, then you're gonna have to do some hocus pocus on them.'

Opal gave him a scolding look.

'It's either that or my old friend lye.'

'I have a charm to turn them into dust,' she mumbled. 'Just get them all in one place.'

'Aye, will do.'

Finally the two women were left alone, but their injuries prevented them from embracing properly. They awkwardly shuffled together, their noses and lips touching as they synchronised a sigh of relief. Opal leaned up, kissing Corvossier gently as she looked at her with those big, brown eyes.

'Willa and Alistair?'

'They're leaving,' she said. 'I didn't stay, but they were happy to go.'

'Did you make him suffer?'

'Of course,' Corvossier breathed. 'I promised you, I promised the both of us.'

Opal lowered her head and rested it in the space between Corvossier's breasts, as if listening to her heartbeat. She slid an arm around the witch's shoulders, holding her there. She knew what she was feeling: sadness about her sister and brother leaving her finally, but also elation because they would be able to find some peace. Maybe that meant she too could find her own among the world of the living, after so long spent running and plotting and avenging. Closing her eyes, Corvossier savoured the feeling of the witch pressed tight against her. It was a little a bit of sanctuary, but it was start.

Chapter 20

Corvossier's legs dangled over the edge of the windowsill, their length long enough that they brushed the tips of the tree that grew down below the apartment. She was swinging them gently, the leaves feeling nice as they tickled the bare soles of her feet. Her gaze was fixed on the footpath across the street, where two young girls were rapidly jumping up and down in the air in perfect unison as others spun skipping ropes quickly. Their game of double Dutch had drawn a small crowd of onlookers from the neighbourhood, with the kids cheering and chanting along as their feet rose and fell so fast it looked like a blur. This was Athena and Christmas Tinibu, British-Nigerian twins and banshees the Oct had marked for execution. The girls weren't even thirteen yet, but their short lives had had an expiration date unbeknownst to them. If they hadn't turned themselves into bait and drawn the former Askari to Boscastle, the siblings would have likely been dead by now.

'Do you think they'll ever know how close they came?' Opal asked, watching them over Corvossier's shoulder.

'Hopefully not.'

The girls hopped out of the game as two others hopped in,

each giving the other a high-five at how perfect their routine had been.

'If both of you are done commentating the Jump Rope Olympics of West London, I could use some help.'

'Alright,' Corvossier replied with a sigh, swinging her legs back into the apartment where several members of the Oct had camped out to watch the movements of the Tinibu girls. Truthfully, it was creepy being there: like the malevolence almost lingered as a physical presence. It didn't, but it sure felt that way. Heath had torn the small unit apart, with dry wall and plaster scattering the pieces of carpet that hadn't been demolished, as he searched for *The Book Of Species*.

'It's definitely here,' Opal commented. 'I can sense it.'

'Could you triangulate that sense, perhaps?' he puffed, sweat glistening on his forehead with the exertion of giving the place a destructive renovation.

'My magic is not a magnet,' she remarked. 'Although I did hear of a witch in Samoa once who was particularly agile with metals.'

'Aye, excellent, where's she? Can you call her up? Cos your charms are great for melting flesh or turning a room into a tomb, but right now I'm looking for a bloody book.'

Corvossier smiled, walking past the enormous man into the centre of the space.

'Brother,' she called, turning towards the form of Barastin as he appeared, sitting casually on the kitchen bench.

'Sister,' he replied, inspecting his nails.

'Help the Pict, will you? He's about to lose it.'

'I am *not* about to lose it,' Heath growled, accent thickening the angrier he got. 'Eejit.'

'Sorry, it's radge, isn't it? You're about to go radge?'

'I think it's fully radge,' the witch noted.

'You know, I like you two a lot better when your tongues are down each other's throats.'

And with that, Heath stormed from the room while the medium did her best to swallow the giggles she felt building in her chest.

'Leave the poor man alone,' her brother said, although the huge smile on his face told her he enjoyed it. Hopping off the kitchen bench, she watched him prowl through the apartment as he viewed things the living could not see.

When she had left him in the lobby that evening after finally releasing Harrison Taper from the torment he deserved, a part of her thought that might be the last time she saw him. She had assumed he would go with the others and finally submit to the pull and wherever that would take him. But the next day, after Heath had set Opal's arm in a cast and they had worked through the night and early morning to return the Museum Of Witchcraft And Magic to the best state they could, she'd had a surprise.

All Praetorian Guard soldiers were well versed in first aid procedures and triage techniques as part of their training, so Heath had also cleaned and sewn her shoulder wound shut with eighteen tidy stitches. Exhausted from the mental and physical exertion of the fight, she'd barely been able to keep her eyes open at the dining table in Opal's cottage. Thankfully, it had meant she hadn't felt as much of the pain as she should have. When he'd patted her hand, telling her he was done, she had been surprised. Collapsing face first on the couch, her eyelids heavy, she'd begun to let herself doze off.

This is what she attributed Barastin's appearance to at first: her fatigue. She'd whispered that she was glad to see him before she'd let dreams carry her away. When she'd woken hours later, it had been dark outside again as the morning had shifted to day and then night, all while she'd been deep in slumber. Yet Barastin had still been there when the throbbing in her shoulder had brought her back to consciousness. He'd remained in the same position he'd been in before: legs crossed and head resting on his knuckles. His long eyelashes had fluttered as he'd blinked at her with exaggeration, his token smile sliding seamlessly into place. She'd leapt up to a sitting position when she'd realised what she was seeing wasn't a figment of her imagination. The sudden movement after laying horizontal for so long had made her head spin and she'd flinched as her shoulder ached beneath the loose shirt she'd been wearing.

'She wakes,' he'd said.

'Barastin,' she'd whispered, noting how her voice broke. Her brother had registered the emotion in her tone as well, inching closer to where she was.

'Yes, Casper dearest, it's me. You're not going nuts.'

'Are you sure? I thought . . . with the others, that you would have—'

'I'm not tied to them and neither is my ghost form. I barely even felt a tug.'

'Then what—'

'I'm tied to you, silly. I'm here as long as you need me.'

'Barry,' she'd whispered, 'I can't ask that of you. You should—'

'I need to stay too,' he'd said, cutting her off. 'I'm not ready to leave you, just as you're not ready to be left. Turns out you're stuck with me for some time longer.'

She'd closed her eyes, feeling a warmth spread through her body with the knowledge that her brother was there, with her, for a while. Tears had trickled down her cheeks and she'd expected him to scoff at her, make fun of her emotional reaction, but when she'd opened her eyes back up she had seen a flittering white on his ghostly cheeks as well. Opal had walked in on her then, having grabbed a few hours of sleep before needing to cover the rest of the working day at the museum. Combined with the painkillers she was on for her broken arm, she'd looked exhausted. Yet that had soon given way to shock as Barastin had let himself be seen by her. Heath was the only other person who knew her brother was there, with the three of them vowing to keep the secret unless Corvossier decided to share it with others.

Now, as she watched him reach up and through a hatch in the ceiling looking for *The Book Of Species* in the apartment, she knew she wouldn't be telling anyone any time soon.

'Casper, you're taller, grab this will you.'

She followed his order, stretching towards where he instructed and ignoring the sting in her shoulder as the stitches strained. It was mostly healed anyway: she'd have them taken out in a few days. Her fingers tapped around in the dust and dirt until they brushed against the spine of something leathery.

'That's it,' he said. 'Grab it.'

Pulling the book from its hiding place in a cloud of grit, she coughed as she dropped it down on to the ground at her feet. Opal crouched over to inspect it, flipping through the pages and comparing the original she held in her hands with the re-creation. Corvossier sensed Heath returning from wherever he had stalked off to behind her, the discovery having drawn him out.

'It's all here,' Opal said, 'word for word, with a few extra pages at the back for additional translations.'

'What languages?' Heath asked.

'Uh, I don't know. Russian, I think?'

'That's Russian,' Corvossier agreed. 'And that's Hindi and the other one is Chinese.'

'Really covering all their bases,' Barastin noted.

'What now?' the witch asked.

'If the Treize knew this existed, they would want us to bring *both* back to Romania, where it would be secured and stored for preservation.'

'I don't like that,' Opal said, her tone dangerous.

'Me either,' Corvossier agreed. 'It was a cancer that started inside their very own *perfect* organisation, after all.'

'That's why I brought these,' Heath muttered, holding up a tin of accelerant and a packet of matches for all to see.

She stalled, taking in what he was implying for a second. 'Destroy them?'

'I don't trust people,' he said with a shrug. 'I trust our people even less now. These books are too dangerous to exist.'

'What will you tell the Treize?' Barastin asked.

'Nothing. Let the power-hungry keep searching for a second tome that doesn't exist and we can all sleep easy knowing the *Satanists' Cookbook* will never fall into the wrong hands again.'

He'd barely finished speaking before both books were in his hands and thrown in the kitchen sink. Propping the two windows open as wide as they would go, Heath poured the fluid on to the pages, making sure as much was coated with the accelerant as possible.

'Is that a packet of matches from Hue?' Corvossier asked, recognising the logo of the famed supernatural strip club in London.

'Sure is,' Heath replied, striking a match and watching as he dropped the small flame into the sink. The books went up instantly with a *whoosh* sound, an orange and yellow flame rising as he fed the fire. Opal reached into her pocket, pulling out a small satchel and grabbing a handful of powder held within it. She sprinkled it on top of the inferno, watching as the flames turned to an unnatural purplish colour and the smoke disappeared entirely.

'Thanks,' Heath murmured. The three of them and Barastin stood by as the last remnants of the Oct turned to ash. A week earlier they had dumped the dusty remains of the bodies into the river that ran through Boscastle, the current flowing them out into the ocean where they'd be lost forever. When the flames finally stopped burning and the books were nothing more, Corvossier reached out and turned on the tap. There was something cathartic about watching centuries worth of evil washed down the drain.

Nobody knew anything had happened at the Museum Of Witchcraft And Magic in Boscastle except for the four of them. They intended to keep it that way, the quartet bound by the stakes and the threat to their own safety. They laid low for another week in the cottage, healing, tying up loose ends and waiting to see whether the Oct had left any trail that led to

Cornwall. They hadn't. No one came, no file was updated, and everything seemed perfectly ordinary.

One day they woke up to find Heath gone, Barastin informing Corvossier and the witch that he'd observed him leaving during the night. Opal wondered if that was something they should worry about, yet the medium felt it was a quintessential move of the hulking Scotsman ... right up until there was a knock at the cottage door early that evening. The witch had been at the kitchen counter, preparing a charm when she stiffened.

'*Sprinkle?*' she said, instinctively knowing that her niece was waiting as she sprinted towards the door.

A streak of brown hair darted through it and into the witch's arms in an explosion of energy. Heath followed at a much calmer pace, leaning against the doorway with a lazy smile as he watched the reunion unfold.

Corvossier made a move to join him, leaving the two witches to the wave of hugs and kisses and whispered words they were both drowning in. But just as she got to her feet, the kid attached herself to Corvossier's leg and squeezed tight, like a very small, but very deadly anaconda. She looked down at the girl's head, really the only part of her that she could see from above, and peered over at Opal who wasn't bothering to wipe away tears.

'I missed you too, little one,' she said, bending down once Sprinkle released her. 'How was Germany?'

'I loved it! I got to sleep in a huge double bed and everything in your tower!'

'Yeah?'

'Yeah! And Yu helped me write postcards, but I don't know

if they arrived yet. And I met werewolves named Clay and Zillia and Sanjay and Dolly and I forgot the big one's name. And I got to see lots of sick graffiti.'

'Sick?' Corvossier frowned.

'Fully sick,' Sprinkle affirmed.

'It means cool.' Opal laughed, patting a seat at the table so her niece danced back over to her. 'What else did you see?'

'Well, Casper has books everywhere in her house. I mean, *everywhere*. I wasn't allowed to read most of them but—'

Corvossier jerked her head at Heath and the two of them stepped out into the hall, closing the door behind them. He followed her outside and she heard the *click* of his lighter. He blew out a huge cloud of cigarette smoke. He offered her one and she shook her head, noting how Bunyip backed away from Heath with an unsteady hiss.

'Fookin' cats,' he muttered.

'That was nice of you, bringing her here.'

'I'm a nice lad.' Heath smiled, throwing his hands wide. 'Isn't that what everyone says about me?'

'No,' she said, her mouth twitching with amusement. 'But I think you know that.'

'Wanted to save Yu the trip. I'd say she had done enough, but by the time I got there Dolly and her seemed about ready to adopt.'

'I owe her. Big time.'

'Don't bother. I tried paying for her troubles, but she said she wanted to do "this one for free", which led me to wonder what previous ones there were and what you had her help you do?'

'The less you know, the less you have to lie about when you go back. If you go back.'

'I'm going back. Officially I return to duty tomorrow.'

'Heath . . .' She did know what else to say, but concern and worry were fighting for dominance in her thoughts.

'You're a big wide receiver, aren't you?' he said, thoughtful. 'Like a sponge for empathy.'

'I don't know if th—'

'I know what I'm doing,' the Pict said, cutting her off. 'I didn't know before about . . . I saw things, Casper, I did things that I didn't truly understand. I trusted the intent and the mission, but now . . . I'm not so sure. I'm beginning to wonder if they keep the heart, the head and the hand separate for a reason, lassie.'

She blinked at him, not registering the meaning of his words or too tired to put it together.

'The heart, Custodians,' he said, listing off on his fingers. 'The head, Askari. And the hand, Praetorian Guard.'

'And the Treize are the body that make it all work,' she murmured. 'You think you're more valuable inside the organisation than outside of it. So you'll continue on, being their good little boy, the reckless soldier who doesn't care about anyone.'

'You think I don't care about anyone?'

'I think it has been a long time since you truly did.'

He looked sad at that comment, introspective almost.

'We can't rush this,' he said. 'And I'm not feeding information to anyone, this is just for myself. We have to be careful, we have to learn more—'

'Before what?' she asked.

He pressed his lips together, not saying anything for a moment as he took his final puff of the cigarette and stubbed the rest out with his toe.

'Just before,' he muttered. 'I've done good in my time; I know I have. I've done some not so good as well, but I know I can do more with them.'

Walking down the path to the cottage, hands tucked into the pockets of his jeans and a tight, blue sweater, Corvossier watched Heath as he began to wander away. Barastin had been floating silently by her side, observing the exchange.

'You called on him,' her brother said. 'You asked a favour of him to come and exterminate the Oct when you needed muscle.'

'And?' Corvossier whispered.

'Heath Darkiro is the kind of man that comes to collect. Whatever he's up to, you can guarantee it's going to include asking a very difficult favour of you at some point.'

Heath paused, spinning back to face her.

'I forgot to mention the fire thing.'

'Fire thing?'

'Yu said it's no big deal, there's just a small burn in the gues-troom where the kid slept. She had a nightmare and a little bit of the duvet caught on fire. She got there before it was out of control, but . . .'

'I loved that duvet,' Barastin huffed. She threw him a look, which she hoped communicated the fact they both knew he had picked up that bedding on sale from IKEA.

'Just because it was cheap doesn't mean I didn't love it,' he replied, noting her expression.

Heath flashed them a grin that Corvossier had seen first-hand turn women into human jelly, before waving in farewell.

'The giant's not coming back?' Sprinkle asked, sticking her head out the door as she and Opal joined them.

'Hopefully not,' the witch muttered. 'I worry that if we see him again, it won't be for anything good.'

Barely twenty minutes passed before the kid was conked out on the couch, clearly exhausted from the recent travel she had done and snoozing heavily. Corvossier figured it might also have something to do with all the action packed into the past few weeks finally taking its toll. But it gave her a chance to talk properly with Opal, which was something she desperately needed to do.

'What's your plan?' she asked, as the two women sat in the kitchen, sipping wine. 'Now that this is over?'

'Nice attempt at casual,' the witch said, smiling.

'Come on, I know you. You always have a plan and then a back-up one just in case the first doesn't work out. Will you stay in Boscastle?'

'Boscastle isn't home. It's beautiful and we made it our tiny refuge, but it will be hard for me to view it as anything but a means to an end. I expected us to have to hide here for as long as we could and now that we don't have to anymore ...'

'The world is your oyster.'

'Pretty much. But I miss home. Being away from my country, it's almost like a physical ache that penetrates right through me. Sprinkle's too young to feel it now, but she will. I miss accents that are familiar, slang we recognise, good Asian food, our soil, our land, our people.'

'Are you sure you don't want to give Berlin a try? After all, it gets a glowing endorsement from your niece.'

'Shit,' Opal breathed. 'We can go back to using our old names now. I just realised that. Wow, that's gonna be weird. And I was so strict about keeping that up.'

'I think you're going to have a hard time prising Sprinkle from her.'

'Bloody oath. And no, to your earlier question.'

Opal put down her wine glass, reaching across the space between them to take Corvossier's hand with her arm that wasn't restricted to a sling. She gripped the witch's fingers tightly, before their hands separated and Opal's returned to the stem of her glass.

'Australia is home for us,' she said. 'It's home for my coven. I miss the strength and support of my sisters. My niece should have the option to grow up around that, not hiding who she is or being stuck learning from only one witch who has a very different skillset. Now that her magic has developed, I want to give her the best of everything.'

She didn't know what she expected: of course Opal would resign from the museum and go back to try and pick up the pieces of her old life. She couldn't stay insulated in Cornwall forever. But as she looked out the kitchen window and at the town on the other side, she knew they both viewed this place very differently. It was somewhat of a prison to Opal: it's where she had been forced to hide and to wrap the town's magic around herself like a protective shield. As she looked at the woman across from her, the shapes and designs of her tattoos proudly visible and her long braids draped over one side of her body, Corvossier realised this was the place she had fallen in love. She had come to this tiny coastal community looking for answers and she had gotten them, in a way. But she had also gotten so much more.

When Opal had taken Sprinkle for a bath and then carried her to bed, she spent a few minutes wandering down the hall and through the kitchen and the lounge, taking it all in and listening as the witch's voice could be heard telling a bedtime story about rebel girls from her her niece's favourite book. She even silently farewelled Bunyip, who barely acknowledged her presence.

'The longer you leave this, the harder it's going to be,' Barastin said, as he trailed behind her.

'Believe me when I say I know,' she whispered.

'She has a kid to raise, sister. A life to rebuild. You need to give her the space to do that.'

She turned to face him, unable to hold his gaze for much longer than a beat because she knew the pain depicted there was a mirror of her own. Heading up the stairs, she took a shower and changed into a new set of clothes before packing up the things of hers that were scattered around Opal's room. The witch joined her just as she placed her cosmetic prosthesis and a wig in her bag, feeling slight relief at knowing she wouldn't have to disguise herself multiple times on her journey home.

'I was thinking about sausage p . . . oh.'

Corvossier hated the sight of her shoulders deflating, hated the realisation that spread across her face.

'You're leaving?'

'I have to,' she replied. 'I have to get out of your way.'

'Get out of my way? What does that mean?'

'It means that you have a trip back home to plan, a lease you need to tidy up, arrangements to make, a job to quit and that's just the start.'

'I . . . yeah, there's going to be a lot going on.'

'And you have to explain all that to Sprinkle, adjust to your old names and lives. Can you do that with some girlfriend hanging around?'

Opal sighed, her exhale coming out somewhat shaky. 'I was sort of hoping neither of us would think that far ahead.'

Corvossier chuckled, stepping towards the witch until they were intertwined in a way that seemed so natural and seamless to them now.

'I'm older than you, remember? I have to be the smart one.'

'But I'm deep into my Saturn return. And a mum, so that gives me extra life years.'

'How many?'

'However many it takes so we're equal.'

Corvossier laughed, then took a moment to kiss her beautiful, soft lips. Pulling back, she brushed a finger over the arch of one of Opal's eyebrows that she loved so much.

'We won,' the witch said. 'We fought off arachnia abominations. I thought that would be the end of the hard stuff.'

'Me too. I guess I got so caught up in trying to stay alive, I didn't think much about what would happen once we were both on the other side.'

'Do you have to leave tonight?'

'The sooner I leave, the sooner you can start doing everything you need to and the sooner we can see each other again.'

They shared another long, lingering kiss. It felt like it stretched on for hours but in reality was probably closer to minutes, with Corvossier drinking in every taste, every sensation, every touch and every way this woman made her feel. From the tingle in her toes to the ache in her chest that spread through her body, no one could drive her crazy like this. No one had this power over her, except Opal. It was Barastin's clearing of the throat that broke them apart, something only Corvossier could hear but it served as the splash of cold water she needed in the moment.

Opal followed her down the stairs, carrying her bag despite Corvossier insisting she could do it. It was still only early afternoon when they stepped out into the cottage's front garden, the witch reluctantly handing over the luggage.

'This isn't goodbye,' Corvossier said. 'You know that right?'

'I know. It's hello.'

She looked down strangely at the hand suddenly thrust towards her. The gesture reminded her so much of what Sprinkle had done on that very first day they'd met. Reluctantly, she took it, her fingers interlocking as she shook the witch's hand.

'Hello?'

'Hello, Corvossier von Klitzing. I'm Kala Tully. It's a pleasure to meet you.'

It was weird being back in Berlin after everything that had happened. It was the city that had been the scene for the most awful moment of her life and the end of Barastin's, yet she couldn't begrudge it. When she had first left the Treize hospital, she was worried what had happened would ruin her home forever, that she wouldn't be able to look at the streets she'd once walked and the parks she'd loved the same ever again.

But from the second she stepped off the plane from England, she knew she was back where she belonged.

Corvossier kept thinking about the way Kala spoke of Australia and her home, the connection she felt to the land and her country. They weren't comparable, but there was a tangible relationship with her and the geography of Berlin. Even the Bierpinsel, with its primary colours and weird aesthetic, sent a surge of excitement through her veins as it loomed ahead in the distance.

Her place was mostly how she left it, but she kept discovering small touches Sprinkle had left behind (including the burnt duvet). Barastin seemed happy to be back there, only hovering between his room and his favourite view from one of the enormous windows for the first few days. There was little difference in the attitude people had towards her inside the Bierpinsel: Askari, Praetorian Guard, and Custodians all treated her the same, mostly avoiding *Death* if they could. It was she who had changed: she rarely had cause to question the cosy supernatural structure built around her before. Now, she viewed it with scepticism and suspicion. Yet like Heath, she had to be smart: she had to keep up appearances. She did that with little stuff mostly, dispelling a territorial ghost here or interviewing the dead there. The rest of the time, she felt more comfortable spending her days at Oslo Kaffebar than in her fortress, which had once been such a comfort to her.

'I don't know why you're hiding out here,' Barastin said, as he sat next to where Corvossier had curled up with coffee and a book on wicca practices.

'I want to chill out,' she whispered, her lips barely moving.

'There are more jobs and you know they pay incredibly well.'

'I have enough money.'

'It's not about *you*: I'm bored.'

'Then check in on Heath, will you? Watch his back for a few hours.'

'Spy. You mean spy on him.'

'Sure. And tell me what he's up to.'

It turned out her brother would not stop chattering about why that job didn't appeal to him, insisting she needed to take the Treize's money while they were 'dumb enough' to be doling it out willy-nilly. His arguments followed her out of the café and down the Berlin back streets as she walked through the city, reminding him that she had left home for peace and quiet, *not this*.

'Corvossier?'

She paused, turning in the direction of where her name had been called.

'Mia.' She smiled, genuinely delighted to bump into the woman who ran the Cyborg Sisters. 'How are you?'

'I'm great,' the chirpy blonde replied, stepping to the side of the footpath so they could chat. 'How are you? I haven't seen you around in ages! You missed our last two meetings.'

'I've been travelling,' she replied, her eye catching on the grocery bags Mia was gripping with her bionic arm. 'Is that . . .'

'The TecTonic 82? You're damn right it is.' She set down her bags so she could hold the arm up for Corvossier to view properly, the mechanical fingers curling and releasing at her command.

'Wow,' she breathed, watching as the tiny pistons and gears

moved under the clear casing. 'It's beautiful. How are you finding it?'

'Like a dream. I mean, there was an adjustment period, obviously, as I worked out what muscles trigger what movements. But I can crack eggs and wrangle a key now: I can open my front door with this hand!'

'I repeat: wow.'

'And it can charge from any USB port, which is a dream. I'm only the second person to have it out in the real world, but you know if you ever want to make the jump I can suggest some folks you should chat with. Just a casual meeting at the university, see what they can offer?'

'I'll think about it,' Corvossier said and for the first time, she actually meant it.

'Hey, I know it has been a while, but if you're not doing anything tonight we're getting together for Valentina's thirtieth birthday. The other girls would love to see you.'

'Tonight? Where at?'

'That place you mentioned ages ago; we're breaking out of our nightclub rut and trying somewhere new.'

'Phases?'

'That's the one. Listen, we're gonna be there from nine onwards so swing by, at least just for one drink?'

'Okay.'

'Okay? Seriously?'

'Yeah, I'll be there. Do I need to get her a present?'

'What? No, you know Valentina: just buy her a shot and she'll be happy.'

Corvossier laughed. 'I'll buy her two, just to make her *really* happy.'

'I gotta get back to the school,' Mia said, stooping down to pick up her bags. 'But I'll see you tonight.'

'Sounds good, see you.'

She watched her leave, the woman's platinum blonde bob with electric pink tips weaving through the throng of Berlin pedestrians.

'You're going out,' Barastin remarked.

She cut him a look.

'Socially. In a group activity.'

Brushing through his form, she didn't bother to hide the smile as she heard him mutter 'stranger things'.

Winter hadn't fully clenched its grip over the city, but it was late October and you could feel the Christmas cold waiting patiently for autumn to take a vacation. All of that was good news for Corvossier, as it meant she could dip into her borderline pornographic love of quality outerwear. Stepping into Phases that night, she almost felt sad to slip the handsome, dark purple cape she was wearing off her shoulders and over her arm as she adjusted to the club's warmth. Her pale skin was covered in a grey lace that snaked over her body, before fanning out into a dress that ended just below the knees. She navigated her way around a drunk man who seemed intent on spilling beer all over her boots that matched the shade of her cape perfectly. Her brother pointed out a path through the crowd that was a safer option. She didn't feel the creeping discomfort along her spine like she used to when surrounded by people, her eyes always scanning for a corner or a seat she could take far away from the action. There were still bad things that used sheer numbers to hide their intentions, but as she glanced around and spotted the

Rogues stationed at various spots she didn't feel so threatened. Deep down she knew that had less to do with the friendly local werewolf posse and more to do with what she had overcome. Corvossier towered above most of the other people in Phases, so it wasn't long before she spotted Mia and the girls at a table they had to themselves. Stopping by the bar first, she got a drink and one for Valentina.

'What'll it be?' asked a voice she recognised immediately. She raised an eyebrow as Yu shuffled over to serve her.

'You're working the bar,' she commented.

'We fired our deadweight barman in the last hour.'

She laughed, not wanting to be the guy who pissed off Yu and the Rogues simultaneously.

'Goblins are unreliable,' Yu said. 'The best thing to keep this place running is a healthy dose of fear: werewolves guarantee that. But *nooo*, Zillia wanted to open up their options.'

'What happened?' she asked, feeling slightly guilty about having suggested him per the favour she owed Hogan.

'Found him hoarding stray cats in one of the storerooms.'

'Aw, so he was an animal lover at least.'

'To *eat*, Casper. Which is fine, whatever, but on your own time – you know? And it's so hard to get goblins to show up during the moon's third quarter.'

'I can't even imagine.'

'We've got a new werewolf coming. Anyway, it's good to have you back in the city.'

'It's good to be back. And *thank you*, for—'

'Yeah, yeah, I know. Want me to bring your order to your usual spot?'

'No, I'm meeting people here. Actually, what's the most over-the-top celebratory beverage you can make me?'

'For you?'

'For a friend, it's her birthday.'

Yu's expression darkened in a way that Corvossier thought was lethal at first. A few minutes later, as she negotiated her way to the table with a blue drink the size of a fishbowl complete with maraschino cherries, whipped cream, sprinkles and no less than five lit sparklers, she realised that Yu had been amused.

'Yay, Corvossier! You're here!' Mia shouted. 'And what in the name of Bob the Drag Queen is *that*?'

'Uh . . . happy birthday, Valentina?'

The woman laughed, slipping by Mia to accept the gift and bowing as a chorus of 'Happy Birthday' was sung messily.

'It's obnoxious and I love it.' Valentina beamed, giving Corvossier a kiss on the cheek. 'Come on, come on, take a seat and join the fun.'

And to her surprise, it was fun. She didn't want to find an excuse to slip out of there early, the girls were all hilarious and the conversation was great. Clay – one of the Rogues – even stopped by at one point with a glitter cannon, showering Valentina in a haze of gold and silver sparkles.

'Get it, birthday girl,' he laughed. 'You're in a Mariah video!'

He threw Corvossier a wink and she heard Barastin sigh beside her with longing.

'Just look at those forearms,' he muttered.

Yet despite the upbeat mood and her having every reason to celebrate, there was something missing. Corvossier couldn't quite place it and she frowned as her fingers traced the stem of her wine glass.

'I didn't know you were such a grown-up,' Mia said, flopping down, breathless, next to her after spending the last three songs on the dance floor.

'Grown-up?'

'Everyone's drinking candy drinks and here you are, with glass after glass of fancy wine.'

'Oh.' She smiled. 'I didn't used to be, it's just something a friend got me into.'

A friend, she thought as she took a sip and let the flavours of the red wine swirl around in her mouth. Kala would like this one.

'Are you okay?' Mia asked.

'Yeah, I'm . . . I'm just missing someone, I guess.'

'Where are they?'

'In another country.'

'Oh, so it's like a long distance thing?'

'Kind of,' she agreed. 'It's only been a month, but we had to take time apart to sort out life stuff.'

'That sucks. At least you can use the promise of seeing each other again as fuel. I swear, Kareem and I always have the best sex the night I come back from being on a work trip.'

'I don't know if I believe in all that "absence makes the heart grow fonder" stuff,' she admitted, her eyes drawn to Yu who was dancing intimately with her girlfriend to a remix of a Jen Cloher song. Their arms were draped around each other, neither of them speaking but at the same time saying everything as they swayed to the music.

'Corvossier?'

'Huh?' Mia's hand was on her shoulder, gently directing her attention back to the conversation. 'Oh, sorry I . . . I've gotta go.'

She said goodbye to everyone in such a flurry of haste that leaving Phases was somewhat of a blur. Throwing the cape over her shoulders as she marched out into the night, she called a brief farewell to Zillia as she passed her at the door.

The air had dropped another few degrees since she had been inside and it was sharp against her chest as she breathed it, hiking through the streets and past restaurants and cafés and bars that she loved.

Barastin was hot on her heels, keeping her company but otherwise remaining quiet. She didn't slow down until she reached the Bierpinsel, dashing into the elevator and out again just as quickly when it reached the floor full of Treize workers. Her footsteps echoed through the offices as her heels made contact with the hard, concrete floor. There was a sense of urgency to her movements, adrenaline coursing through her veins that made her want to sprint up the staircase despite knowing she would look ridiculous.

'Well, aren't you strutting with purpose,' Barastin noted as she gave in, jogging up the last few stairs to their living quarters.

'I am.' She beamed, walking directly over to the couch where she had left her laptop. Sitting down next to it, she flipped it open and began navigating her way towards the relevant websites.

'And what is the source of this jubilant mood, may I ask?'

'You may,' Corvossier replied, throwing her brother a wide smile. 'I'm booking a ticket to Australia.'

Acknowledgments

From the top, cheers to the Little, Brown London team of Anna 'Boaty' Boatman, *always* Anna, Nazia 'ragin' Cajun' Khatun, Tim Whiting, Eleanor Russell, and essentially everyone from reception right up to the café that sells rainbow cake. To my agent Ed Wilson, for a willingness to discuss whale appendages and book ideas simultaneously. And for making sure the llamas had breathing holes: very important, that is.

Sammy, for being the sounding board on this and every story. Thanks for helping me work through it while driving through the Cornish countryside. Triple thanks for being the highlight of each day, every day, and supporting my stupid dreams.

Thanks to legit superhero Angel Giuffria for the gift of her time, perspectives and fangirl geeking out along with all of the IRL Cyborg Sisters for telling me what you wanted to see (or read, as the case may be). Quentin Kenihan, for always picking up the phone and breaking shit down. Here's to going off-road, as Corpus would say.

My mother, Tania, who told me countless times to stop casting spells on people I didn't like as a child (spoilers: I didn't). And my grandparents, Tom and Teresa, for still believing in traditional post, and Jolly Jingo.

Big ups to the entire Spettigue clan for showing me a Cornwall I loved so much I had to try and work it into a story. Mandy, my Motherland mother, thanks for always putting me up when I'm London bound and for not judging my love of British department stores too much.

My medical expert from here to eternity, Dr Nick Cocks, for walking me through transradial amputations and other important technical stuff. My legal expert, Tuyen 'Iceberg' Tran, for keeping my shit on lock and not joining Ringling Bros.

The all-wāhine, all the time, whānau of Sonja Hammer, my favourite person to fight racists with on the street, and Anna Gough, the quickest proofer and mean te reo study partner. The gaggle of first readers in Ramona Sen Gupta (may your fear of being murdered by a mediocre white man never come true), Jean-Anne 'Howares and Assessories' Kidd (and her dad), Caitlin 'hypewoman' Jinks, Kate 'when's the next one' Czerny, Caris 'Black Widow' Bizzaca, Denise 'never misses a typo' Pirko, the Nerdy Bird herself Jill Pantozzi, Kylie and her hot sex writing advice, Koorie Youth Council comrades Cienan, Heidi, and Kim, and Hancocks Two Bonnie and Indi (Courtz as well, even though I know you'll never read this but you deserve it for the decade+ of *Buffy* marathons).

Bad-asses Jo 'no relation to Matt and Kevin' Dillon and Tracey Vieira at Screen Queensland, for sharing knowledge and believing in female stories. Cleverman himself, Ryan 'rom com' Griffen for constant insight, guidance, and idea-bouncing. Rae Johnston, for helping walk and talk through this book during many a dip at Coogee Women's Baths. The Supanova family: Daniel, Libby, Mama and Papa Nova, Ineke, Paige, Juanita, Skye, Mark, Claire, Quinny, Bec . . . the list is legit endless, but thank you for supporting genre writers in a way few places Down Under do.

The Supreme herself, Nicola Scott, for years of witchy wisdom, magical education and making sure I didn't accidentally invoke Satan with a misplaced pentagram that *one* time. Hau Latukefu and the *Hip Hop Show*, for providing the weekly soundtrack I wrote this novel to. Alison Goodman, Alan Baxter, Angela 'Themiscyra' Slatter and Keri Arthur for keeping me mentally regular despite the fact we all somehow choose this idiotic job of professional writing. Tom Taylor, for always having my back, Cath 'bloody' Webber, Keegan for lending me his recipes for inclusion in the book (and his husband James who is definitely *that bitch*), Patricia Briggs and Purple Anne for sharing their knowledge on silver bullets, Tracey Robertson from Hoodlum, Greg 'you don't fuck with the Greeks' Vekiarellis, Alex, for helping me this far, the Berlin squad and Meat Grinders, always, Rachel 'Jungle' and the brood, Netherworld Arcade and Cara and Ben specifically, Jeremy Neal from QBD for always handling shit, Bridie and The Sisters Jabour, the legends at Advanced Arm Dynamics, and 212 Blu, who kept me caffeinated and fed as I wrote and edited majority of this book on their premises.

Finally to the booksellers, book stockists, readers, bloggers, journos and people who have come along for the ride so far ... fucking thanks heaps for that, aye.

Glossary

Alchemist Those who have the ability to infuse and convert materials with magical properties through a combination of symbols, science and ceremony. Alchemists were instrumental in the founding of the Treize, particularly the Askari themselves. Obsessed with immortality, it's rumoured their formula is responsible for the prolonged lives of Praetorian Guard soldiers and Custodians.

Arachnia Traditionally considered a nightmarish vision from Japanese folklore, Arachnia emerged from the shadows relatively late compared to other supernatural species and were discovered to have existed worldwide. Their natural state is comparable to a large, spider-like creature, with traits similar to the arthropod.

Askari Foot soldiers. The first point of call in the supernatural community, they simultaneously liaise and gather information. Mortal, yet members often work their way up into the Custodian ranks. Identified by a wrist tattoo, which is the alchemist symbol for wood to signify a strong foundation.

Banshee Thought to be extinct before re-emerging in the early eighteenth century, a banshee is a supernatural being cursed with the ability to sense impending doom. Predominantly female, they have been known to elicit power over others through their speech.

Bierpinsel A large, colourful tower in the centre of Berlin: the Bierpinsel is the base of Treize operations for Germany and much of Europe.

Blood pack The family unit a werewolf is born into by direct descent, usually operating on a specific piece of geographical territory.

Coming of age A ritual all werewolves must complete before they're considered mature members of their blood pack. A wolf can only choose to go 'rogue' once they have survived the coming of age.

Coven A grouping of witches within an area, covens can include members of the same biological family as well as women of no relation. No two members of a coven have the same magical ability, with similar powers spread out over other covens as an evolutionary defence mechanism. Members of a coven can draw on each other's powers, giving them strength and safety in their sisterhood.

Custodians The emotional guardians of beings without other help, assistance or species grouping. Immortality is a choice made by individual Custodians, with those choosing it identified by a necklace holding an Egyptian ankh.

Demon One of the oldest forms of supernatural beings, pure-blood demons are known for being reclusive and rarely interact with those outside of the paranormal world. Certain species of demon have a fondness for the flesh, leading to half-blood demon hybrids usually identifiable via physical traits like horns or tusks; these are often filed down to aid with blending into society.

Elemental Originally thought to be those who could control the elements – earth, air, fire and water – elementals are paranormal beings descended directly from nature. Able to physically become the elements if they so desire, they share a strong allegiance with shifters, werewolves and selkies.

Ghost Translucent and bluish grey in colour, ghosts are the physical manifestation of one's soul after death. Their presence in the realm of the living can be for several reasons, ranging from an unjust demise to a connection with a person or place. The strength of any particular ghost varies case-to-case.

Ghoul Usually found in underground sewer systems and living in nest formations, ghouls are considered a lower class of paranormal creature due to their lack of intelligence or individual personality traits. With razor sharp claws and serrated fangs, they can be deadly in large numbers.

Goblin Highly intelligent and supernaturally agile, goblins are lethal if provoked. Although not immortal, they have exceedingly long lives and prefer living in urban environments such as cities or large towns. They are one of several paranormal species impacted by the lunar cycle.

Medium A being that can communicate with and control the dead, including spirits and ghosts. Extremely rare, the full range of their abilities is unknown and largely undocumented.

Paranormal Practitioner The healers and medical experts of the unnatural world. Usually gifted individuals themselves, they wield methods outside of conventional medicine.

Praetorian Guard A squadron of elite warriors that quell violence and evil within the supernatural community. They're gifted with immortality for their service. Founded by a member of the original Roman Praetorian Guard.

Rogue A werewolf who chooses to live and operate outside of their blood pack.

The Rogues Comprised of rogue werewolves who have decided to leave their blood packs, this group functions from within the nightclub Phases in Berlin and includes global members who have come of age.

Selkie The source of mermaid and merman folklore, selkies are aquatic humanoids that inhabit any large body of water. Despite some human features, tribes of selkie from certain parts of the world have been known to take the form of marine animals like seals, dolphins and sharks.

Shifter Found globally, shifters have the ability to transform into one specific creature depending on their lineage. Often confused with werewolves due to their capacity to take animal shape, shifters can transform outside of the full moon.

Spirit The more powerful counterparts of ghosts, spirits can travel between pre-existing planes and occasionally take some physical form. They usually preoccupy themselves with the business of their direct ancestors.

Sprite Said to be the result of a union between selkies and earth elementals, sprites are secretive and rarely identify themselves to other supernatural creatures. They struggle around their own kind and prefer to live close to nature.

The Three A trio of semi-psychic women who guide the Treize in regards to past, present and future events. The subject of the phrase 'hear no evil, see no evil, speak no evil'. Origin and age unknown.

Treize The governing body of the supernatural world. Comprises thirteen members of different ages, nationalities, ethnicities, abilities, species and genders. Given their namesake by four French founders, they oversee the Praetorian Guard, Custodians, Askari and Paranormal Practitioners.

Vampire Rodent-like creatures who live off whatever blood they can get: animal or human. Endangered in the supernatural community due to disease.

Vankila The Treize's supernatural prison, located in St Andrews, Scotland and built hundreds of metres below a Cold War bunker.

Werewolf One of the most volatile and ferocious paranormal species, werewolves are humans that shift into wolf-hybrids during the nights of the full moon. Outside of the lunar cycle they retain heightened abilities, such as strength and healing, with the most powerful of their kind able to transform at will and retain human consciousness. Often found living in blood packs, they are resistant towards most forms of paranormal government.

Witch A woman naturally gifted with paranormal abilities that can be heightened with study and practice. The witch gene is passed down through the female line, however the skills vary. Witches believe their power is loaned to them temporarily by a higher being, who redistributes it to another witch after their death. Highly suspicious and distrustful of the Treize due to centuries of persecution, they are closed off from the rest of the supernatural community.

9·11·18

Praise for Maria Lewis

'Journalist Maria Lewis grabs the paranormal fiction genre by the scruff of its neck to give it a shake' *The West Australian*

'Maria Lewis is definitely one to watch' *New York Times* bestselling author Darynda Jones

'If you love a strong female lead, then *Who's Afraid?* by Maria Lewis is a must-read' BuzzFeed

'If you want a fresh, funny, sexy & downright sassy take on the werewolf genre then this series is for you' Geek Bomb

'She writes kick-ass monsters and things that go bump in the night with a flair for the awesome' Reviewers Of Oz

'Truly one of the best in the genre I have ever read' Oscar-nominated filmmaker Lexi Alexander (*Green Street Hooligans, Punisher: War Zone*)

'It's about time we had another kick-arse werewolf heroine – can't wait to find out what happens next!' *New York Times* bestselling author Keri Arthur

'It's *Underworld* meets *Animal Kingdom*' ALPHA Reader

'The next *True Blood*' NW *Magazine*

'Lewis creates an intriguing world that's just begging to be fleshed out in further books' APN